In The Shadows

Lawrence Medici

ISBN 978-1-7321540-0-1

To my family—my wife Debi who never wavered in her support and her belief in me, my son Joey, and my daughter Kelli, whose reaction to a homeless man during a trip to New York City, when she was child, gave me the idea for this story.

PROLOGUE

Northumbria, Britain, 1055 AD

Uther knelt at the base of the ancient, towering oak. The other trees of the great forest stood like old and venerable sentinels to the scene before them. The morning mist ebbed and flowed almost imperceptibly around the massive trunks, the moisture clinging to his cloak.

Uther's head was bent, his hands clasped before him as he prayed to the Gods of the forest. He had been at this very spot a year before, praying for the health of his young wife.

She had wandered into the forest looking for wood for their fire. When darkness had fallen and she still had not returned Uther had gathered some of the other men of the village and they began to search the forest by torchlight.

It wasn't long before they found her huddled, nearly naked, in the brush within a small gulley. Obviously the victim of a wolf attack, her clothes had been torn and shredded, and savage bite marks covered her shoulders and the back of her neck.

Uther had wrapped his cloak around her, the same cloak he now wore, and carried her back to their home. He had summoned the village Druid, the one that was with her now.

He had then come to this very tree, the tree that watched over their people, and prayed for her recovery.

She finally did recover physically, however for a very long time she was not as she had been. She rarely spoke, and never of that night. She often had a far-off, distant look in her eyes and many nights she woke up silently shaking in terror, cold sweat running down her temples.

It wasn't until shortly after she found she was with child that he began to see glimpses of the sweet, lighthearted girl she had been before the attack. As the weeks and months went by, her mood improved, and Uther was happy to see the worst was behind them and their lives could return to normal.

As the time for the birth approached she began to feel a great deal of pain. Many days she was unable even to rise from bed. The Druid had tried various potions and poultices, however nothing seemed to help.

Today she had awoken and the bedclothes were soaked with blood. She was writhing in agony. Uther had run to fetch the Druid and the matriarch of their village. They were with her now. Uther had come here to pray for the health and safety of his wife and the health and safety of their child.

He heard the crunching of footsteps in the snow behind him. He turned, rising to his feet; the Druid was approaching, a blanket-wrapped bundle in his arms and a grim look on his face.

"My wife?" Uther asked.

The Druid shook his head. "I am sorry, brother. But maybe that is for the best."

"What do you mean for the best? My child?"

He held the bundle forward. There was movement within. "Be strong, my brother. Look upon this and be strong."

Uther reached out with a shaking hand and turned back a corner of the blanket. He stepped back, eyes wide. There was an infant beneath, but not like any infant Uther had ever seen. A demon spawn.

The bald, earless head was covered in leathery grey skin so tight that it appeared the pronounced brow and angular cheekbones must burst through. The eyes were squeezed tightly shut. As the cold air hit its face, the infant opened its thin lips and wailed, a most unnatural sound. Uther could see the points of fangs protruding through the grey gums.

"This is the most unholy, the most unnatural of things. You must take it out into the woods and destroy it. We will tell everyone that your wife and your child died in childbirth. If the others in the village were to see this, your wife's body would be desecrated and burned and you would be driven forth. I know you to be a good man, Uther. I know not how this evil found your door, but you must destroy it."

Uther reached out and covered that wretched face. Silently he took the bundle and trudged off deeper into the woods.

****

Uther came to a large snow bank. He lay the bundle down upon the snow. Tears were streaming down his face. He was not a hard man like some. He had loved his wife and treated her well, had anticipated having a child as much as she. To have it all come to this, in one brief moment, for all his dreams to be swept away...

He pulled out his dagger and held it aloft over the squirming bundle. Doubt entered his mind like a whisper at sunset. He had only looked upon the child for a moment. Was he sure?

Blade still held aloft, he reached out with his other hand and turned back the blanket. There was no mistake; the same horror greeted his eyes, his breath catching in his throat at the sight of it. He raised the blade higher. At that moment the infant thing opened its eyes.

Uther found himself staring into the most beautiful set of azure blue eyes. The same shade as his wife's eyes. It was like seeing her soul peering from behind a hideous mask.

His blade hand wavered in the air. He dropped the dagger next to the infant. He couldn't do it. He stood on shaky legs. Off in the distance he heard the howl of a wolf; it seemed to be drifting through the trees borne by the mist. Without looking back, Uther turned and strode back toward the village.

Let the forest pass judgment.

CHAPTER 1

New York City, Present Day

1

Danny Edwards was not happy as he strode after his two friends. Every third or fourth step was punctuated by a little skip as he tried to keep up. The wind was blowing down the cold November city streets, papers skittering and dancing along the curb. The streetlights cast a silver-gray light over the asphalt. That light could not quite penetrate the darkness that lurked in the alleyways between buildings.

Several steps in front of him Carter Stevens and Sean Hutchinson forged ahead, fists jammed in their pockets, collars turned up against the chill. Carter was spewing a constant stream of curses as he walked; they drifted back to Danny on the night breeze.

Carter was pissed and Danny, for one, didn't like seeing him this way. In his relatively short friendship with Carter, he had seen bad things happen when he got like this. Carter had a mean streak. Generally it manifested itself in the wisecrack, the sarcastic comment, the mocking tone. He had a real talent for finding someone's weak spot and probing at it, picking at it, exploiting it, making you feel small and worthless. Yet despite this, maybe because of it, he was very popular. Like every petty dictator, demagogue or high school tyrant he had created an environment of "us and them" and set himself up as the sole arbiter of who got to be "us" and who was relegated to being one of "them".

Of course his looks certainly didn't hurt his popularity. He was tall, blonde haired, blue eyed and athletic. He also came from a wealthy family; his father was a big-time real estate developer in the city. So he had looks, he had money and at times he also had personality. He could be very charming when he felt like it; he was especially good at turning up the wattage on that charm when he was speaking to teachers or parents. Danny's father said Carter was a real Eddie Haskell, whatever the hell that meant.

But underneath the surface that meanness smoldered. When he lost his temper, and that happened pretty frequently, it was like throwing gasoline on those glowing coals of mean, causing them to flare up.

Carter was the alpha dog of their little pack. Danny was too new and a little too shy and withdrawn to exert much influence over the other two. Sean was more like Carter's yes man than friend. At first it was unclear why they even were friends; they didn't seem to have much in common. Carter was intelligent, articulate, polished. Sean was more of a brooder, tall and husky with dark hair and dark eyes. He was not particularly bright and no one would ever refer to him as chatty. However, on closer examination, it became clear that it was a typical symbiotic relationship; Sean was awed and charmed by Carter's looks, intelligence, charisma and Carter needed someone to be awed and charmed. His ego needed the continuous affirmation and validation. That was why Carter was friends with Sean and that was also why he continuously belittled others, to feed his need to feel superior.

Carter and Sean had known each other pretty much their whole lives. Danny had just met them this year. Before his junior year of high school his father, a commodities broker, had finally relented to his mother's desire to take him out of the public school system and enroll him in a prestigious private school on the Upper East Side. She was hoping the move would increase his chances of getting into a good college.

Though Sean and Carter had been in his grade, he hadn't really started to hang out with them until his senior year. They were part of a clique that Carter led. The clique contained the beautiful people, not necessarily the most popular, but the wealthiest and best looking. They were the high school royalty. They ran the school government, chaired the most important clubs and captained the sports teams. They also partied the hardest.

Normally Danny wouldn't have stood a chance of breaking into that group, but in September he and Carter had been assigned as lab partners in chemistry class. They had gotten along pretty well and Carter had invited him to a few parties. Then they had started to hang out together once in a while. Danny knew he was not in yet; he was basically up for membership. To be honest he wasn't sure how he felt about Carter Stevens.

It was the mean-spirited side that was gaining control now and picking up steam.

It had all started at the party they had just left. The party was in an apartment in Tribeca. Amy Peterson's parents were on a cruise so naturally Amy threw a party. Danny was usually reserved in social situations but he had managed to consume enough alcohol to get a pretty good buzz going, and that buzz had enabled him to strike up a conversation with a really cute brunette with a great rack. The conversation was going well, if Danny had to say so himself. She was laughing at his jokes and kept tossing her hair and running her fingers up and down his forearm.

Danny took a sip of his drink and happened to look toward the front door. He saw the doorknob turn, and with that turn of the doorknob Danny's evening would turn from good to unbelievably bad.

The door opened and in walked Samantha Evans, every blonde, blue-eyed, long-legged mini-skirted inch of her, and right behind her was her new muscular jock boyfriend. Until last week Sam had been Carter's girlfriend, but she had broken up with him. He hadn't taken it well and Danny thought it was probably lucky for her that she had chosen a public place to tell him things were over.

Samantha and her new boyfriend had headed for the kitchen where the alcohol had been set up. It didn't take long before the sound of raised voices could be heard from that direction, quickly followed by the sound of a scuffle and then multiple voices yelling. Carter came storming out of the kitchen, followed closely by Sean.

"Come on, Danny, we're outta here. I can't stand to be around that bitch!"

The bosomy brunette clutched Danny's arm.

"You don't have to go, do you?" she said, hitting Danny with her full arsenal: eyes lowering slightly, lips pouting, squeezing his upper arm while leaning in closer to him. But Danny knew he had no choice.

"Sorry, I gotta go," he said, pulling away probably harder than he should have, but when Carter talked Danny had, in a very short time, gotten into the habit of jumping.

"Now, Edwards!" Carter looked back, blue eyes flashing, mouth in a snarl.

Now, as they walked down the street, Danny sensed Carter's anger building. He started to get really nervous. This night was not going to end well.

Danny took a couple of running steps to catch up. Trying to capture just the right tone, casual and conciliatory, Danny took a shot at trying to calm Carter down.

"Carter, don't let that chick get to you, man, you can do better than her."

The words were out of his mouth, and he just had time to regret them before he noticed the "boy you are a dumb shit" look Sean gave him. Then Carter spun around and grabbed the shoulders of Danny's coat, bringing his nose within an inch of Danny's.

"What do you know about it, you dumb fuck! Have you ever even gotten laid? I half think you're some kind of fag the way you've been hanging around!" He turned to look over his shoulder at Sean. "Whadya think Sean, do we have some kinda fag here?" He didn't wait for an answer, turning back to Danny. "I don't need a fag like you giving me advice or feeling sorry for me! You piece of shit. You're lucky I even let you hang around. Don't think you know enough to give me advice."

He shoved Danny against a parked car and started to turn away, then suddenly turned back, his fist cocking back like a cobra ready to strike. Danny instinctively flinched, arms coming up to protect his face.

Carter laughed, dropping his fist. "I ain't gonna hit you, you pussy." He turned to Sean and they continued walking. "Come on, I gotta blow of some steam, let's do somethin'."

They came up to Sean's BMW. As Sean was fishing for his keys Carter stepped in front of him. "I know, let's take out the trash, whaddya say?"

Sean, more muscle than brains, was a go-along kind of guy. He never examined things too closely; if it was Carter's idea it was probably a good one. "Sure, I'm in."

Danny was still leaning against the parked car, feeling humiliated. He thought about walking away; he could always get a cab. Not for the first time in his life, Danny was ashamed of himself. Why didn't he stand up to Carter? Why did he put up with his shit? Unfortunately Danny wasn't exactly the poster child for self-esteem, he had generally lost these internal arguments in the past and this time was no different. When the car was unlocked he climbed into the backseat, head hanging, not saying a word.

Carter turned around and looked between the front bucket seats into the back where Danny silently moped. One side of Carter's face was bathed in silver from the streetlight, the other side was in darkness; he looked like some eerie jester's mask. "Come on, Danny, we're gonna have some fun," he said in a conciliatory tone.

Man this guy was a piece of work, Danny thought. Raving mad one moment, nasty and aggressive another, and now calm and contrite. All of this in the space of fifteen minutes. This dude had serious issues. But Danny knew it wouldn't do him any good to ignore him. "What did you have in mind?"

"Oh you'll see. Hey Hutch, I think it's about time to let Dan here in on the fun. You see Dan, my man Hutch and I have an obligation to this city. My dad owns a good portion of it and Hutch's dad is the police commissioner. So we have to do our part to clean this city up. Make it attractive for visitors; help promote tourism, all that shit. And I think it's about time you did your part as well."

Danny looked up at Carter. Where was he going with this? Was he making some kind of joke? But even though Carter had a smirk on his face, his blue eyes were like chips of ice.

"Wha— What are you getting at?"

"You see, when someone comes into the city they come for the shows and the restaurants, maybe the museums and art galleries. What they don't come to see is crime, and garbage in the streets and riff raff." He paused and turned to Hutch. "Make a left here, then let's take the West Side Highway up to Midtown; there are more of them up there."

They turned a corner. "What's that got to do with us?" Danny asked, all the while avoiding Carter's cold stare and looking out the window into that cold silver-grey night.

The street they were on was deserted and dark; on one side was a construction site, the bare steel girders rising into the night sky like the skeleton of some ancient prehistoric creature. The other side of the street was occupied by empty office buildings, the employees long gone. Probably sitting in front of their television sets in living rooms all throughout New Jersey and Long Island.

The street was almost deserted. There, moving slowly, was one homeless guy, at least Danny thought he was a guy. It was hard to tell. He had a knit cap pulled down over his ears and was wearing an old beat-up trench coat that had probably once been beige but was now a dingy brown color with huge sweat stains under the arms. He was shuffling along, kind of hunched over, and he was pushing a shopping cart loaded down with blankets and bags. His whole world loaded into a banged-up shopping cart with a back wheel that fluttered like a wounded bird.

"Lookit here," Carter yelled. "This is our lucky night after all. Pull over, Hutch, and pop the trunk!"

Sean pulled to the curb and hit the trunk release. "What's lucky?" Danny asked. "What are you talkin' about?"

"We got what we need right here," Sean said as he and Carter jumped out of the car. Danny looked out the back window; they were digging around in the open trunk. "Come on, get outta the car."

Danny got slowly out and walked to the rear of the car. Carter and Sean each had an aluminum baseball bat in their right hand and Carter was holding another bat out to Danny with his left. "Come on, it's time to do our duty to clean up the city, it's time for—" he and Hutch looked at each other and said simultaneously, "BUM BASEBALL."

Danny looked at the offered bat, then up at their two grinning jack-o'-lantern faces. At first it didn't sink in, then he glanced slowly over at the homeless guy. Comprehension and disgust were born in his mind like fraternal twins. "You guys aren't thinking of...." His voice just trailed of in disbelief.

"Come on, man, it's a rush, it's not like it's someone who matters. Shit! Let's move, Sean, before he gets too close to the highway where someone can spot us." With that he dropped the bat he was holding out for Danny, and it hit the pavement with a loud hollow pinging sound that reverberated through the night air. Carter was running toward the homeless guy and Sean was two steps behind him.

At first Danny couldn't move; everything had happened so fast and what was happening now was so bizarre that he stood there frozen. Then he saw Carter close in on the homeless man and cock his bat back like he was getting ready to hit one out of the park. The spell was broken. "No! Don't! Run!" he screamed as he started running after them.

With the yelling the homeless man started to turn around, but it was too little too late. Carter swung and connected with the small of his back. The bat made a dull thud when it hit and in the street light you could see the dust puff up from the guy's coat. The man let out a startled croaking sound and fell to all fours. Just then Sean laid a solid shot across the back of the man's shoulders, causing his arms to give way, and he sprawled flat on his face.

Danny caught up to them at that moment and grabbed Carter's right arm as he was preparing for another blow. "Stop it! What are you guys, crazy!?"

Carter turned, breaking Danny's grasp and raising the bat over his head. "Back off, or do you want some?" The look in Carter's eyes was like that of a drug addict who had just got hold of some really good stuff. He was mainlining. "Go get your bat and get in on the fun and get out of my way!"

Danny took a step back, shocked by what he saw, the wild look in Carter's eyes, the spittle speckling his chin. At that moment he was capable of anything.

Carter turned back toward the man who was crawling toward his shopping cart. "What do you have in there, old man? What is it, moving day?" said Carter, cackling. "Let's see what it is." He walked over, placed a foot on the top of the cart and with a grunt kicked it over; the blankets and bags tumbled onto the sidewalk in a huge heap.

Letting out a sound halfway between a growl and a scream, the old man sprang to his feet and grabbed Carter around the throat. Danny stood there in shock, shocked by the surprising speed with which the man moved and the apparent strength of the large gloved hands that now grasped Carter's throat.

Hutch, who was the best athlete of the group, was quickest to react; he brought his bat down hard on the guy's right arm. There was a muffled thud of the bat hitting the man's heavily clothed forearm, and beneath the thud you could hear a dull snapping sound like old wormy wood breaking. His right arm falling useless to his side, the guy continued to hold Carter by the throat with his left and amazingly began to shake him like a ragdoll. Hutch swung again, this time at the left arm, there was no snapping sound this time but the blow was strong enough to break the grip on Carter's throat.

Carter stumbled back, panting, clutching his throat with one hand and his bat with the other. His eyes were filled with fear and confusion; drool hung in a long ropey strand from his open mouth as he gasped for air. Then he seemed to regain some of his composure. He wiped his mouth with the back of his sleeve and took in several deep, racking breaths.

His eyes cleared further, his lip curled in anger. "You fuck! You fuckin' piece of shit!" he screamed, still laboring for breath. He grasped his bat with both hands and before Danny

16

could move, he swung. The head of the bat was near the ground and it came up in a long looping motion; at the same time Carter turned his hips, putting his whole body into the swing. The bat connected with the man's left temple, you could hear a dull crunch and the man collapsed like a bag of dirt onto the sidewalk. He lay there in a heap, not moving.

"Holy shit! I think you killed him!" Hutch said.

"He attacked me!" said Carter and, as if that was not a ridiculous enough statement, followed it up with, "It was self defense!"

It was at that point that Danny lost it. "Oh my God! Oh my God! We gotta do something! I'm calling 911! We gotta get some help!"

Carter wheeled toward him, his eyes filled with a mixture of fear and disbelief. "Call 911, are you stupid or what? They'll think this was murder. We'd all get nailed for this, don't think for a minute you're not involved, because you are. You're up to your ass in it! They'd lock all of us up!"

"But he may still be alive, we have to get help."

"I don't give a rat's ass if he's still alive. I'm not going to jail for some lowlife piece of garbage that attacked me. What are we talkin' about here? We did him a favor, who the hell wants to live on the street! Not only are we not going to get help, we have to figure some way to cover this up, make it look like an accident. Yeah, that's it; these guys are always getting offed. Let me think…"

"Maybe we can say he jumped out in front of our car," offered Hutch.

"No, dumbass, if that was the case your car would be damaged, besides we would have to hang around and answer questions and I don't think Mary here can handle it," Carter said, jerking a thumb in Danny's direction.

17

"We gotta turn ourselves in, try to get some help." Danny was whining now, practically in tears. He saw no easy way out of this.

"Shut up, let me think!" Carter's eyes were wild now, darting around like a rat looking for a hole to scurry down.

"Why don't we just leave him, get out of here?" asked Sean.

"Can't do that," said Carter, "not with him all busted up. The cops would conduct a full investigation. We all have cell phones, I hear they can track them now. They could find out we were in the area, then they'd bring us in for questioning." He glanced again at Danny. "We can't take a chance on being grilled about this. You know, maybe that 'hit by a car' idea isn't so bad after all. Just not your car, Hutch, we have to find a way to make it… I know, we'll throw him out into traffic on the West Side Highway. If we time it right, in the dark, the driver won't even realize what happened. They aren't going to waste too much time investigating a simple traffic accident."

"How we gonna do that?" asked Hutch. "I mean, he ain't that big but I don't think we can heave him that far."

"Do you guys hear yourselves? You are responsible for killing another human being and all you can talk about is covering it up." Danny had been able to suppress his tears, mainly because he was being overtaken by the shock of what he was hearing.

Being in shock, he was slow to see and even slower to react to Carter's fist arching toward his jaw. It caught him flush and laid him out. Carter was on his chest in a moment, pinning his arms with his knees and bending down so his nose was within an inch of Danny's for the second time tonight.

"You get something straight and you get it straight right now, it's not 'you guys', it's all three of us. You were here, you are an accomplice. If we go to jail for this, so will you, and I'm sure the guys in jail would love a little fag like you. As a matter

18

of fact…" Carter looked back over his shoulder from his perch on Dann's chest. "Hey Hutch."

"Yeah?"

"Who took the shot that killed the old dude?"

Hutch looked confused for a moment, as if someone had just asked him to explain nuclear physics. Then his eyes brightened, like someone opening the shades in an empty deserted house. "Why, that would be Danny. We just wanted to have some fun but Danny wanted to off someone. Said he wanted to 'see what it felt like'."

"Hear that, Dan my man? That's the story we'll tell, and you'll do harder time than both of us. So get your head right. Either we all fix this or we all swing with you leading the way."

With that Carter got off of him, slowly. As he stood he brushed off the knees on his pants, straightened his jacket. He looked around. It seemed by attacking Danny he had regained his composure—he was calmer, all business now.

"Hutch, stand up that shopping cart, bring it over here."

Sean stood up the cart. There was still an old battered and stained backpack inside; he grabbed that and threw it on the ground, where something inside clanked dully. He wheeled the cart over near where the man still lay motionless, the broken wheel on the cart fluttering and squealing.

"We'll load him in the cart and roll it out into traffic, it will look like he got clipped crossing the highway."

"Is that gonna work? We would have to time it pretty good, and what if the cart doesn't roll far enough? Won't the driver who hits it see that he's not pushing it?"

"We'll have to time it just right, and find a spot where the driver won't see it until just before he hits it. It's dark, he won't get that good a look at it, and with the shock of running someone down he won't be sure what he saw anyway."

"I hope you're right."

"It's the only thing that makes sense. Who's gonna question a cracked skull on someone that was hit by a car? These old winos are always wandering into traffic. The cops probably won't even question it."

Carter walked over to the body and bent down.

"Whew! Man, this guy reeks. Get over here and help me. That means you too, Dan-o, we are all in this together."

Danny got reluctantly to his feet and walked slowly to where Carter and Sean were now both stooped over the body.

Carter continued to direct the action. "All right, I want to lift him up and drape him over the handlebar on the cart, but we have to hang enough of him into the basket or else when we push it out into the street it will tip backwards and not go far enough. So basically bend him at the waist, upper body in the basket and legs dangling behind. Hopefully that will give enough of an illusion that he is pushing the cart, not in the cart. Sean and I will grab him under each arm, Danny you grab his feet." They took up their positions and stooped in unison to lift the body. Together they lifted, each letting out a little grunt. The guy was heavier than he looked. They shuffled over to the cart looking like some strange six-legged spider.

The first attempt to lift him in, his head bumped the handle of the cart and the cart started to roll away. Sean tried to hook it with his foot and almost lost his hold on the body. The cart came to a stop and they tried again; this time they got him over the handle bar and into the basket, however as Carter had foreseen, they did not get enough of the weight forward and the cart started to tip back. Carter and Sean pushed down on the front of the cart with one hand while holding the body steady with the other.

Danny dropped the legs and went to the front of the cart; he held it steady while they hunched the body forward to better distribute the weight.

They all looked around. They had been so engrossed in what they were doing they hadn't given a thought to the possibility of another car coming down the street until that moment.

"Come on," Carter said, "let's wheel him into the shadows until we lay out the next steps."

They were on the side of the street with the construction site; they pushed the cart up against the fence that surrounded the site and into the shadow of a wooden booth that stood near the gate in the fence.

Carter said, "You guys wait here. I'm gonna walk up to the highway and scout out a good spot to do this."

Carter headed up the street, hands jammed in his pockets, head down. As he disappeared around the corner Danny thought about making an appeal to Sean about calling the police, but he stopped himself for several reasons. First, Sean would never go against Carter; he really didn't have the brainpower to think for himself. Also, Danny felt the guy in the basket probably was beyond help. He hadn't shown any sign of life since he went down, even with all the jostling around he had just been through. Finally, and he hated to admit it to himself, he was scared. He was worried about what Carter had said. He didn't want to go to jail and he couldn't see how it could be avoided if they got caught. And really, when you thought about it, it was only a homeless guy. Some bum on the street with no home or family. Was it really worth him ruining his life over this? The deed was done, the guy was dead. Danny ruining his life wasn't going to bring him back. So if they could cover it up, what was the harm?

It seemed like an eternity but Carter finally reappeared, jogging, hands still stuffed in his pockets. "Come on," he said as he got near them. "I found the perfect spot."

2

They were crouched in the shadows next to a wall. The wall was mostly brick, interspersed with wrought iron inserts. The spot was perfect for Carter's plan: they could hide behind the wall unseen by oncoming traffic, and yet there were only a few feet of sidewalk separating them from the roadway. There was a crosswalk at that spot with a handicap ramp instead of curbing.

They had only had to travel a short distance from the side street where their crime had occurred to this spot. They kept to the shadows of the buildings but Danny had been panicked the whole way. He kept expecting to hear the whoop of a police siren and see the flashing lights as it pulled to the curb, catching them in the act. But it hadn't happened. Once they got behind the wall, Carter, still maintaining his cool, started giving orders.

"Danny, you look over the wall and let us know when to go. Remember to wait for a truck, and I want it to have a good head of steam, so it has to make it through the light without slowing down. If it has to stop for a red and then start up it will be moving too slow. And Hutch, when Danny gives us the go we push the cart along the wall, get it going as fast as we can but let go before we get past the end of the wall. I don't want to take a chance of the driver seeing us, got it?"

"I got it, I got it, you said it ten times already," said Hutch, sweat standing out on his forehead despite the cold.

"I just don't want any screw ups. We've got one shot at this!"

They had been there about fifteen minutes and things hadn't lined up right yet. There were a couple of times Danny saw a truck coming but the light about two blocks up would turn red and the truck would stop. Once it started up it wasn't moving fast enough for their purpose. Then one would make it through that light and would stop at the light in front of their position.

Finally he saw a truck barreling down the lane closest to the curb; it was going to make both lights. This was their chance.

"Now!" Danny yelled. "Now!"

Carter and Hutch started pushing the cart, getting up to a full run, the broken rear wheel fluttering and wobbling. Just before they got to the end of the wall they let go and sprawled flat on the ground.

The cart shot across the sidewalk. It rattled down the handicapped ramp and jumped the low curb into the street. It began to list sideways. All three boys held their breath as one rear wheel came off the ground and the body's legs swayed to that side like a ship's rudder, threatening to off balance the cart and send it over. Then they swayed back as the cart righted itself and continued into the street.

Like the beam from a lighthouse the headlights of the oncoming truck bathed the cart in light, casting an obscenely elongated shadow down the street. It was at that moment that Danny, from his perch behind the wall, saw something that made his mouth go dry. One of the corpse's arms reached up, the large gloved hand grasping the rim of the cart's basket. Then, unbelievably, the head began to lift from the bottom of the cart. He was alive! The guy was still alive!

The driver never had time to hit the brakes. The truck hit the cart full speed, flinging it forward and up in the air. As it flipped over, the body flew out in a graceful arch and smacked headfirst into the asphalt, bounced several times and came to rest in a heap in front of the onrushing semi. The truck came like a tidal wave sweeping over it. The body could be seen tumbling under the wheels like seaweed caught in rough surf. Meanwhile the cart, which had hit the street again, bounced into the air, where it was again struck by the grill of the truck and flung into the next lane. They could not see where it landed as the speeding truck blocked their view but they could hear squealing brakes, breaking glass and crumpling metal.

The truck roared past, completing its desecration of the body, which now looked more like a flattened pile of dirty laundry than a human corpse. The passing of the truck revealed two cars stopped in the far lane. One had a shopping cart lodged firmly in its shattered windshield, the other had its crumpled nose planted firmly into the rear bumper of the shopping cart car.

Sean and Carter both scrambled crablike from where they had lain prone on the pavement back to where Danny was still crouching. Sean looked slightly stunned by what he had witnessed. Miraculously, Carter was laughing. "Whoo man that was something, holy shit! Did you see that fucker fly?"

He looked up at Danny, still laughing. Danny was white as a sheet and mumbling something over and over. Carter's laughter slowly died away. "What's your problem? What are you mumbling?" Then slowly he made it out.

"He was still alive. He was still alive."

"Well he isn't alive anymore," said Carter, and this brought on another bout of laughter. "Pull yourself together. We gotta get outta here before the cops show up." As if conjured by these very words, sirens could be heard, far off but approaching fast. "Hutch, let's go. Grab this dumb fuck and let's get out of here."

They each grabbed Danny under an arm and dragged him stumbling down the sidewalk, keeping as best they could to the shadows. They made the corner and all three sprinted for Sean's car, Danny still looking pale and stunned, but at least he had gotten his legs moving.

They scrambled into the car and Sean lost no time getting it started, pulling a U-turn and heading away from the scene of the crime.

Carter turned in his seat to face Danny, who was still pale and now sobbing quietly. "Listen and listen good," Carter said, facing Danny but making sure he spoke loud enough so that Sean got the message as well. "We are all in this together. If one of us goes down we all go down. So if anyone is thinking of discussing tonight with anyone forget it right now. If you do, the best that will happen to you is you will end up in jail—that's if I don't get to you first. If I get to you first you're gonna consider that bum lucky by the time I'm done with you. You hear me?" There was no response. "You hear me?"

"Yeah, I hear you," mumbled Sean.

"How about you, Danny boy? You hear me?"

"He was still alive," was all Danny could muster.

"Get your head right! I'm not goin' down because you ain't got the sack to handle this shit, you hear me? You breathe a word of this before I take care of you, I'll take care of your whole family, even that little sister of yours, so you think about that. I want you to tell me you understand."

"I understand."

"I didn't hear that. What did you say?"

"I understand. I won't say anything."

"Good boy. Step on it, Sean, let's ride around for a while. I'm too wound up to go home yet."

CHAPTER 2

1

Al Russo woke suddenly; it was so dark in the room that at first he wasn't sure his eyes were open. He lay there for a moment feeling disconnected. Lost? Scared? No, that wasn't it, not scared, but apprehensive. What was it about the middle of the night that stripped you down, left you defenseless?

This happened to Al more frequently lately, waking in the middle of the night feeling anxious. He couldn't find the source of the feeling. Something he should have done but had forgotten? Somewhere he was supposed to be? Something bad about to happen? It felt like all of these and none of these, indefinable but undeniable at the same time. The feeling would pass, but it was strange nonetheless. Al wasn't the worrying kind. Maybe that was why he woke up feeling this way; maybe he did all his worrying in his sleep.

Now that he was awake he knew he wasn't going to get back to sleep without taking a leak. If you slept through the night there wasn't an issue. But just wake up and give your bladder that window of opportunity and it could not be denied, another middle of the night mystery to go along with the anxiety.

He pulled back the covers and swung his legs over the side of the bed, trying to be careful not to wake Carrie. He stood and shuffled a couple of steps, hands out in front of him like a blind man, knees complaining, muscles slowly loosening as blood began to flow through them. Al stretched, his back cracked. "God," he thought, "you'd think I was ninety." But he was only thirty-four.

As he got to the bathroom he felt on the wall and flipped the light switch. He paused and looked back at the bed. A thirty-four-year-old who happened to be dating a girl who was twenty-four. She lay there, dark hair spread out over the pillow, full lips slightly parted, sleep softening her features. One of her legs was sticking over the side of the bed from beneath the covers, displaying the long graceful curve of her calf, the delicate arch of her foot. Al felt a familiar ache and it wasn't in his heart. He debated whether it was worth waking her up after he was done in the bathroom and decided, regretfully, that he should probably let her sleep.

They had been dating about five months and Al wondered how much longer it was going to last. One reason he didn't have confidence in the longevity of this relationship was the age difference—not that the difference was that great, but it was enough to raise compatibility issues. Not sexually, that area was fine, God bless her youthful enthusiasm, but in other ways. And it wasn't, as you may guess, about her wanting to go out all the time and Al, being older, content to hang around the apartment. It was more subtle than that.

However, speaking about going out, that was an area that highlighted their differences. Carrie was into the latest, trendiest clubs: all chrome, glass, mirrors and loud music. The place was trendy, the clothes were trendy, the music was trendy, even the signature cocktail was trendy. Al liked quieter places: dark wood, slow jazz playing quietly in the background, the warm glow of a glass of single malt scotch, good conversation.

It was just a matter of time before the maturity that she currently admired shriveled under the harsh light of familiarity and became stuffiness. Before the world-weary outlook and dry sense of humor that now seemed so brooding and sexy withered in comparison to her youthful enthusiasm, until all she saw was a pessimist, a cynic. When that happened she would become restless. She would long for the company of youthful "glass half full" types like herself and she would move on.

Al was prepared for that inevitable day and to be honest wasn't really dreading it. He knew the day was coming; he was enjoying the ride while it lasted, but he was realistic. The effect of the inevitable break-up would be blunted by one insurmountable fact. You see, as much as Al found her attractive, and as much as he enjoyed the sex, Al was not in love with her. Al was still in love with his ex-wife.

He had been married to Anne for almost five years. They had been happy in the beginning, but things hadn't been the same the last few years of their marriage. Al knew it was mostly his fault that things had gone bad.

When they got married Al was a patrolman and Anne was an elementary school teacher. Looking back, those first few years seemed so light and easy; they loved each other and were comfortable together in a way that Al had not experienced with any other relationship. They didn't have a lot of money, but they had few responsibilities. Those first few years seemed impossibly carefree.

Then, as Al spent more time on the job, stress began to pile up like miles on a car—and not the easygoing highway miles either, but hard bumper-to-bumper traffic, stop-and-go kind of miles.

The job hardened a person; it had to or you couldn't survive. First, as a patrolman going out on calls, the abused children, the battered wives, the bar fights and muggings; dealing with humanity's lowest life forms on a daily basis. Then he had made detective and visited his share of grisly murder scenes, talked to his share of grieving family members and interrogated his share of cold-blooded criminals. You had to pull back, you had to become callous, you just couldn't afford to get emotionally involved.

The problem was once you built up that emotional scar tissue, once you deadened your feelings, it was hard to turn them back on again when you walked in your front door. Al found himself less able to relate to Anne, found it harder to find interest in her stories of schoolchildren and school budgets and parent-teacher meetings. It all seemed so boring, so trivial. He was more comfortable around other cops. He began to stop for drinks after work more and more often. This, of course made matters worse. Anne, already hurting from his emotional abandonment of the relationship, fought with him over the late nights and the drinking.

The strange thing was, and he really hated to admit this to himself, but on some level, he enjoyed the fights. They seemed real, they seemed visceral, they broke through the emotional scar tissue, got his juices flowing, got him to feel something. Sadly, the normal happy relationship had gotten too boring for him; only through the fighting, the shouting, the insults and the tears did he feel something. He was an adrenalin junkie, you had to be to be a good cop, and the domestic fights fed the habit.

Finally, the emotional distance became too much, the drinking, the fighting all became too much and she left him. Al realized he had become a walking cliché: the hardboiled, hard-drinking cop who couldn't maintain a normal relationship; the star of many a TV cop drama or Hollywood movie. And just like those cops on all those TV shows and movies, Al was still in love with his ex-wife. He didn't know what to do about it, didn't know how to change or if he could change. But that didn't change the fact that he still loved her.

So here he was working the job, dating a woman he cared for but could never love, and still in love with a woman he could no longer have.

These thoughts were interrupted by the buzzing of his cell phone on the nightstand.

2

The call had been from his partner, Mike Straten. Mike had just gotten the call about some homeless person being pancaked by an 18-wheeler on the West Side Highway. He gave Al the location and told him to meet him there.

Al walked up the street toward the flashing lights, hands jammed into the pockets of his black trench coat. The coat was too thin for this cold windy November night, but Al leaned into the wind, the bottom of the coat flapping and whipping against his legs.

As he got closer to the accident scene he saw two patrol cars sitting nose to nose, lights flashing, blocking the southbound lane of the West Side Highway. Uniforms were directing the traffic down a side street and around the accident site. He glanced back over his shoulder and could see, despite the late hour, that the traffic was backed up for blocks. You could hear the occasional car horn, but it wasn't too bad yet. It would get worse as time went on and patience wore thin.

Past the roadblock, in sharp contrast to the snarl of traffic before it, the street was relatively empty except for several police cruisers, the vehicles involved in the accident and the police going about their business. Everything was illuminated by the streetlights and accented by the flashing red and blue lights of the squad cars. It was as if someone had created a life-size diorama and set it in the middle of the street.

Pulled to the curb about fifty yards away was what he assumed was the offending truck. There was a police car parked behind it; lights flashing. Closer to where he stood and across the street near the median were two cars, one's nose planted firmly in the trunk of the other. The front car—it looked like a Honda from here but who could tell, all cars looked alike these days—had a shopping cart protruding from its windshield. The cars were bracketed by two more police cars whose lights were also flashing. The glass from the shattered windshield was spread across the hood of the Honda and fanned out on the street around it. The granules of broken glass reflected the pulsing lights like precious stones spread on black velvet.

The uniformed officers on the scene were going about their duties. One was taking measurements and another was talking to two people by the median, presumably the drivers of the two cars, though Al thought, looking at the shopping cart, the driver of the Honda may be on his way to the hospital.

In the glare of the headlights from the cruiser positioned behind the truck Al could see a group of cops talking to a man who was sitting on the curb, head in his hands, rocking slightly. In the group he saw his partner. Mike was hard to miss; he was over six feet tall, with blonde hair and a broad, slightly overweight football lineman-type build. He had actually played high school and some college ball. They made an odd pair. Al was thin, dark haired, and on a good day he may appear to be five-nine.

For the most part they got along okay. Mike was good to work with; it was only when they got around the higher-ups that Al had any issues with him. Mike was shamelessly ambitious and when it came to the brass, he never met an ass he wouldn't kiss. Sometimes his blatant pandering to their superiors was embarrassing. It was not like the brass seemed to notice though. It was either their own arrogance that made them blind to what was going on or they were well aware but never met an ass-kissing they didn't like; Al hadn't quite figured out which it was.

Al kept these feelings to himself and all in all they got along fairly well.

Mike looked up, waved, turned back to the patrolman he had been talking to, said something else, then started walking over to Al.

"Hey partner, what've we got?" asked Al.

"Not that big a mystery. Homeless person pushing a shopping cart walks out into the highway and gets creamed by a truck. Guy died from a bad case of Peterbilt."

"Funny."

"Yeah, it cracked up the fellas."

"Why are we out here if it's a simple traffic accident?"

"With the recent increase in attacks on the homeless in the area, the captain wants us to look into anything involving a homeless person."

"That the driver of the truck?" asked Al, motioning to the guy sitting on the curb.

"Yeah. He said he thought someone had rolled a cart full of garbage in front of his truck. Didn't even realize it was a person. Said the only reason he stopped is because he saw the cart hit the other car in his side view."

"I'm surprised he even stopped when he saw that."

"Probably wouldn't have except he figured the camera on the traffic light probably got a shot of him and he would have been tracked down and charged with leaving the scene."

"Where's the body?"

"The meat wagon already picked it up, I didn't have them wait around. The guy was road pizza. Staring at that mess wasn't going to tell you anything."

"So it was a guy?"

"I really don't know. Like I said, he was pulverized, I wasn't about to go searching around in the soup for his junk."

"You're on a roll tonight; flattened bums put you in a good mood?"

"They don't bring out the tears and violins. I figure the medical examiner can give us all the details. They get paid for digging around in dead bodies."

Al started to walk toward the two smashed cars.

"So the cart smashes into this guy's windshield, he hits the brakes and gets rear ended."

"That's about the size of it, The guy's lucky his airbag deployed and prevented him from getting a face full of broken glass and shopping cart."

Al looked around the accident scene; a puzzled look came over his face.

"What's up?" asked Mike.

"The cart's empty and I don't see any garbage in the street."

"So?"

"So did you ever know of a homeless guy who pushed around an empty cart? They carry their whole lives in there."

"Maybe it was a new one and he hadn't had a chance to move in yet," said Mike, grinning.

"That's all the driver saw was the cart and the guy? He didn't see anything else?"

"Nope. And he didn't really even see the guy, like I said, he thought someone had rolled a cart full of garbage in front of his truck."

"Which direction did he say the cart came from?"

"Came from his right, just past the traffic light. He said the light was green, he didn't even slow down, just barreled through it and the cart rolled out in front of him. He didn't even have time to hit the brakes."

Al looked over to the right by the traffic light. There was a brick wall with wrought iron inserts that separated a schoolyard from the street. On the wall in spray paint were the words "T5 LIONS".

"Mike, I'm gonna check out the area by the wall over there. See if you can get some of these uniforms together and have them canvas the area. See if they find anything—you know, blankets, clothing, empty bottles and cans. You know, bum stuff."

"Why? What's up?"

"I just want to make sure that's all. Like the captain said, there have been some cases of bums getting roughed up pretty bad the last few months. I want to make sure this isn't more than it seems."

3

Al searched along the wall looking for anything: a dropped article of clothing, a footprint in the dust, dirt and debris that had collected at the base of the wall, anything. The paint on the wall was dry but looked fairly fresh; other than that, nothing.

He looked up and saw Mike and a patrolman walking toward him. The patrolman was carrying something that looked like a sports bag or backpack.

"Detective, I found a pile of stuff around the corner—blankets, bags full of all kinds of shit and this."

He held up what turned out to be a canvas backpack, the material faded and worn. Dark, oily-looking stains covered the bottom.

"Look what's inside!" He reached in and pulled out a short sword. It was about two feet long and in remarkably good condition. The blade had a long triangular point, the edges of the blade bowed inward slightly. The guard and pommel were rounded and were made of wood worn from years of use. The design looked familiar, Al thought. Then he had it, it looked like the swords you saw in Roman gladiator movies. What the hell was something like this doing in a grimy backpack lying in the street?

"If this belongs to our friend, I wonder where he stole it from," said Mike.

"Show me where the rest of the stuff is," said Al.

They walked around the corner; there in the middle of the sidewalk was a pile of blankets and several brown paper bags.

Al started to reach out, thought better of it and used his foot to probe the blankets. Didn't seem to be anything wrapped up in them. Both of the paper bags were laying on their side; the tops of them had been rolled tightly closed but one had come partially open. Al reached down, grabbed it by the bottom and upended the bag. All three of them gasped and took a step back. A plastic milk jug full of water rolled out, rocking for a few seconds as the water—at least it looked like water—inside sloshed back and forth. Right behind it, three large dead rats flopped out onto the cement, stiff tails sticking straight out, dead little marble rat eyes glinting in the streetlight.

"Why do you think he was carrying those?" Mike had a puzzled, almost comical look on his face. Then he looked up at Al staring at him and realization mixed with disbelief spread over his features. "Nooo, couldn't be."

"Looks like lunch to me," said Al. "I think we're looking at this guy's provisions." Al grinned at the disgusted looks that spread over Mike and the young patrolman's faces.

"Seriously, does it make any sense for this guy to dump out his possessions here and wheel an empty cart around the corner and into the street?"

"I don't know," said Mike. "Maybe he was drunk, dumped the cart by accident and was too out of it to load everything back in. Or maybe this stuff isn't even his."

Al looked around, taking in the towering steel of the construction site and the office buildings across the street. "Those buildings have security cameras on them; we'll have to get a look at those tapes. They might have caught something. Let's get some photos and then bag and tag this stuff. Then let's talk to building security, see about those tapes and see if they saw anything." He stuffed his hands in the pockets of his trench coat and pulled it tighter. "Damn it's cold. I'm freezing my ass off."

4

He stood in a narrow alley between two buildings, watching the scene spread out before him. He was back in the darkness, the flashing lights from the police cars alternately painting the walls at the mouth of the alley red, then blue, then red. Neither the lights from the police cars nor the streetlights reached him. However, he could see the entire accident scene. He took it all in: the vehicles that had been involved, the various people either talking to police officers or standing with dazed vacant stares, the police themselves questioning witnesses and taking measurements.

He had watched them load the body into a vehicle and take it away. That would have to be addressed. But for now he had another purpose. He scanned the scene and finally found what he was looking for. There were two men—they were not in police uniforms but were obviously part of the police. They talked to the ones that were in uniform, they talked to witnesses, they walked around the accident scene. They would be the ones in charge of finding out what happened.

He had observed many similar situations in the past. The police in uniforms always showed up in the beginning, but it was these men, the ones in regular clothes that came back day after day and talked to witnesses and anyone in the area. They would hunt for those who had done this.

He watched them, one large with light hair, the other smaller, dark hair, wearing a black coat. They may not have the information he needed yet but they would have it eventually

.

CHAPTER 3

1

It had been several days since the night of the accident and Al hadn't really had time to even think about the case, let alone work on it. He had been in court the last two days. After court each day he had gone back to the station to catch up on his reports. That was one thing they never showed you on the cop shows—the time wasted in court or the mountains of paperwork that came with the job.

The other night, they hadn't been able to get the video from the security cameras Al had noticed. Neither security guard on duty had access to the computer equipment that recorded the video. Mike had had to follow up the next day with the security supervisor from each of the buildings. Mike also did the follow-up with the medical examiner.

Now they sat in a booth at O'Tooles's to compare notes and catch up. The bar was only a couple of blocks from the station house and a lot of the guys from the precinct hung out here when they were off duty. The place was your typical New York Irish pub, long and narrow; a battered and scarred dark wooden bar ran along one wall and some booths ran along the other. There was a step up to a back section that contained tables. The beer was cold, they made a mean Sheppard's pie and the waitresses had authentic Irish accents. What more could you ask for?

"I was able to get the videos," Mike said, "But the video from 101 doesn't show squat, just an empty street. The one from 103, now that's a different story. I think we may have something there. I will run it for you when you come in tomorrow, but basically it shows a car, a BMW, pull to a stop, some kids jump out, and get this: they pull bats from the trunk and take off up the street. Now, they go off camera and you can't see the section of the street where we found the pile of junk, but that was the direction they were heading."

"And the time they were there?"

"Right before the accident was reported. Later in the video they return to the car, throw the bats back in the trunk, pull a u-turn and take off. The timing is perfect, the accident happened between the time they ran off and when they returned."

"Pretty big coincidence. Now we just have to figure out who these guys are."

"That might not be so hard. The camera shot the tail end of the car; I have IT working on enhancing the video so we can get a plate number." Mike continued, "The only problem is if they did attack this guy, it's not on camera."

"Given the condition of the body, I'm hoping the medical examiner can determine if the guy received blunt trauma injuries before the truck did its thing. I'll contact them in the morning, give them a little push," Al said.

Mike took a sip of his beer, shaking his head. "No need, I gave you the good news, now here comes the bad."

Al looked up. "What do you mean?"

"I mean I heard from the medical examiner and you're not going to believe this."

"Believe what?"

Mike put his beer on the table and looked at Al. "They had a break-in."

"A break-in at the medical examiner's?"

"Yep, and that's not the strangest part. The strangest part is the only thing that was taken was the body of our very own dead bum."

"Wait, what? Someone broke into the medical examiner's and stole a dead body? And not just any dead body but our dead body? If you're joking, where's the punch line?"

"No joke. Whoever it was broke through a door in the back of the building. Actually it must have been several guys with a battering ram or something; they broke through one of those heavy steel fire doors. Just pushed it in until the hinges snapped. Took the body and didn't touch anything else. They hadn't even had a chance to take it out of the body bag and it was gone."

"No one saw anything, or heard anything?" Al asked, shaking his head. "Well that's not good. Without that body we've got nothing."

"Unless we can come up with a witness, all we have are some guys running down the street with baseball bats. Last time I checked there was no law against that."

"Hey, what about that graffiti on the wall? What was it? 'T5 Lions' I think?"

"Yeah, that was it, that's a gang. They started out in low income housing in Brooklyn, originated in section T building 5. They have been spreading though, getting new members. I think they got into peddling drugs for someone with a pretty big operation so they have some cash flow. I can start to do some checking, see if any of them got picked up in the area that night. Slim chance but it's something."

2

It was close to midnight by the time Al left the bar. Mike had hung around for a couple more beers but then he decided to head home. Mike had a family, Mike had a life; he couldn't spend the night in a bar. Al, on the other hand, had no such obligations. He didn't have a family to go home to and he didn't have any plans with Carrie for the night. He was looking at an empty apartment, takeout and TV.

He'd gotten up to leave when he noticed some guys from the precinct down at the end of the bar, so he headed over. Maybe one more drink, just one more to hold off the boredom of an evening at home alone. But the "one more" led to several more, and the beers had been supplemented with shots. The conversation had been about what else: the job. Sure, there was some talk in the beginning about other things—sports, politics, a few dirty jokes—but eventually, predictably, it always came back to the job. War stories: the tough case, the sicko case, the funny case. A continuous litany of what could be found when you spent your days dealing with the underbelly of society. Occasionally there was the human interest story or a situation that highlighted the best of human nature, but those were few and far between. More often it was about man's baser instincts. But they managed to find humor in all of it. Really there was no choice, there were no options, it was the only way to cope.

The liquor continued to flow and the conversation became less coherent. The group began to thin as guys began checking their watches and one by one heading home. Finally it was just Al and Eddie Finnerty. Eddie was the type of guy Al would normally avoid like the plague. Eddie was one of those guys who never let the truth stand in the way of a good story. The more Eddie drank the more the facts would be twisted and embellished, and the more earnest he became that what he was saying was the absolute truth. Al found his mind wandering as Eddie droned on and on, found himself thinking about Anne.

He knew this was a mistake. His mind had taken this path before when he had been in this state and that path never led to anywhere good. If you were lucky it only led to you hanging on some equally drunk friend and making embarrassing admissions of your pain and heartache. If you weren't so lucky it led to the even more embarrassing drunk dial where you made those admissions to the cause of your pain and heartache. Al knew this and he was determined not to take that path. He never wavered in his determination; all the while he was excusing himself, stumbling to the men's room, locking himself in the one and only stall and pulling out his cell phone.

The numbers on the screen were dancing around, if he had to punch in the number he wouldn't have been able to make the call, he would have been saved. But of course he had her number programmed into his phone. By squinting just so, he could make out her name in his contact list. He heard the phone begin to ring, once, twice, three times. He was about to hang up when she answered.

"Hello."

He froze. He knew immediately this was a bad idea.

"Hello."

There was no way out now. Damn modern technology, he couldn't just hang up, his name was being displayed on her phone right now.

As if in response to that thought she said, "Al, why are you calling me at this hour of the night? You're not in some bar, are you?"

Al took a deep breath, concentrating so as not to slur his words. "Uh no, I, I mean I'm at the precinct." This statement took way too long to come out of his mouth.

Just then someone opened the door to the men's room and the noise of the bar drifted in.

There was a sigh at the other end of the phone. "Al, go home." Her voice was soft, feminine. "If you want to talk to me call me tomorrow when you're sober." There was the slightest touch of disdain, or was it just exasperation, in the last statement.

Whatever it was, it made Al defensive. "I'm fine. I just wanted to check on you, see how you're doing."

"I'm doing okay, Al, considering."

"I do miss you Anne. I miss what we had together."

Another sigh from the other end. "Al, we've been through this. You don't miss me, you miss some fantasy that happens to include me. You miss the, I don't know, the idea of a happy marriage. But you weren't able or willing to personally invest in that idea to make it a reality. Normal married life didn't hold enough excitement for you, you were never completely engaged in making it work. But you expected it to be waiting there for you whenever you felt like dropping in."

"Yeah, yeah, I know. But that was then. I could change, I really could."

"I wish I could believe that. We've been down this path before, there is nothing new. I'm sorry that you're hurting, I am too. But you are hurting over the absence of something I don't believe you really want; you just feel you should want it. If you still feel like talking in the morning, call me then."

Al was about to protest, then the one sober brain cell he had left got control. "You're right, I shouldn't have called this late, never mind, I'll call you tomorrow."

"That would be best."

"Okay, bye."

"Bye, and Al, be careful, get home safe." The line went dead.

He hung up and stood there looking dumbly at the phone, not really sure what to do next. Then he heaved himself upright and stumbled out of the stall, brushing past a guy standing at the urinal. He didn't go back to the bar where Eddie was waiting to finish the tale of his latest adventure; he just walked across the room and out into the street, swaying like a sailing ship being buffeted by crosswinds.

It wasn't as cold as the other night but there was still a pretty brisk breeze. As soon as he hit the fresh air Al went from bad to worse. Now the ship wasn't only being hit by stiff winds but it was rudderless.

The street was fairly empty as Al weaved along. A couple coming the other way avoided him; the man grabbed the woman's arm and steered her expertly around him. There was a homeless guy in a doorway. He looked like he was in worse shape than Al, sprawled out on the pavement the way he was. His oversized coat was open and spread under him, the shiny material of the lining giving the appearance that he was sitting in a pool of oil. Al held onto a signpost, trying to get his head to clear a little, then, giving the post a push to launch himself, he got moving again. He shuffled a couple of steps and then stopped again, bent over, hands on his knees. He looked around. Something wasn't right. He realized he was heading in the wrong direction; the subway station was the other way.

Al made a slow, not so graceful turn, looking down at his feet so as not to stumble. He took two steps and walked right into someone. Al swayed back from the contact. *Man this guy is solid*, he thought. Just then a smell like rotting vegetation penetrated Al's alcohol haze.

"Sorry pal," Al managed, bringing his hands up in a "no harm done" gesture.

He couldn't see the guy's face; the man's head was bent forward and all that was visible was the top of a battered fedora pulled low over his brow. He was dressed in a long black overcoat. The collar was turned up and the coat reached almost to the sidewalk, covering the guy from head to toe.

It dawned on Al that this was the guy from the doorway; he had been sprawled out seemingly unconscious a moment ago. Drunk as he was, Al's instincts were not completely dulled; something was not right. He took a step back, keeping his hands up, palms forward, not wanting to alarm the guy but wanting to be ready in case he made a move.

The guy began to raise his head slowly and then suddenly his hands shot up and out, giving Al a quick shove. Al found himself tumbling backwards. He sprawled on his back on the sidewalk. His head snapped back but he managed to keep it from striking the cement.

The guy in the coat was coming toward him. From his position on the ground Al kicked out, trying to fend the guy off till he could regain his feet. His attacker grabbed his foot, gave it a twist and threw Al's legs to the side. He then stepped forward and planted a hard kick in Al's exposed ribs.

Al felt a sharp pain as the air rushed out of his lungs. He was lying curled up on his side; his vision was blurred but he made out the figure of his assailant running down the sidewalk.

Al rolled over, managed to pull himself up on his hands and knees. He stayed there gasping for air, a stream of spittle falling from his mouth to the pavement.

He heard a voice, Eddie Finnerty's voice.

"Jesus, Al, what are you doing in the middle of the sidewalk?" Al felt a hand at his elbow and an arm slipping around his waist, helping him to his feet. "Let me get you a cab, buddy, you're a mess."

A few minutes later Al was sliding into the back of a cab, where he closed his eyes and promptly passed out.

CHAPTER 4

1

Al heard a faint buzzing noise, very far away. He felt like he was floating slowly toward it, as if it had a gravitational pull. He drifted up through a dense fog, and the sound got slightly louder, then louder still. Al tried to open his eyes in the fog but his lids were leaden, much too heavy to move. The buzzing got louder. Finally, through sheer force of will, Al managed to drag one eyelid over the surface of one bleary eyeball. He could make out a blurry image of the nightstand next to his bed and the alarm clock on top of it. He reached out to shut it off, wincing with pain and stiffness. He felt a knife-like pain between his ribs.

He hit the button and lay there for a few moments, gathering his strength for the massive effort he knew it was going to take to lift his head off the pillow. He must have really tied one on last night. How had he even gotten home?

There was something else. It was coming back to him; he had been jumped outside the bar. Either that or he had dreamed being jumped outside the bar.

He rolled over and sat up slowly. Looking down, he realized he was still in his clothes from the night before, coat and all. He must have just collapsed into bed once he got home. His head pounded. He cupped his head in his hands and winced. Cradling his head more gingerly, he attempted to piece together the events of the night before. This proved more difficult than he could have imagined. His memories of the evening were floating just beneath the surface of his consciousness. Every time he reached for one it would sink deeper or drift away, like trying to pluck specks of dust from the surface of a pond.

"Just start at the beginning, from what you know," Al told himself. He had been talking to Mike at the bar, Mike had gone home. Then Al had been hanging out with a bunch of the guys, and that's when the drinking had kicked into another gear. Eventually it had been just him and Eddie. Things got really fuzzy at this point. Had he called Anne? Damn! He was pretty sure he had. That was one fact he could verify—the call would be logged in his phone. He didn't remember leaving the bar.

He swung his legs over the side of the bed. When his feet touched the floor he realized he was missing a shoe. He looked around the bed and on the floor but saw nothing. "Damn, that was a three-hundred-dollar pair of shoes," he muttered to himself.

Al wondered, and not for the first time, what the hell was he doing with his life? It just seemed like an endless, empty, meaningless progression of events. Like he was going through the motions, clocking time, but barely making an impact. When he was gone, what would he leave behind? His spot on the force, which would be filled by the next guy up, and a few empty bar stools around town.

"Introspection is a lousy way to start the day," he said to himself. "You're no good at it anyway. It never takes."

2

At this time of year he always sat in the same place. The tallest buildings in front of him formed a row that aligned perfectly with the rising sun. He could feel the power this alignment generated; he was bathed in it.

He sat there in a doorway, the fedora cocked forward, sitting low on his brow, a scarf wrapped tightly across the lower part of his face. His one remaining eye peered out through the slit they created. The eye scanned the flow of humanity before him. They rushed past, ignoring him; if they should happen to glance in his direction they quickly looked away and hastened their pace.

Only the occasional small child, clinging to the hand of a grown-up, would look more intently in his direction. Invariably their eyes would widen with fear and they would hold tighter to the hand of the adult, in most cases grabbing it in both hands, as they were whisked away down the street.

How he hated all of them, the thousands that walked past him every day in an endless procession, rushing off to their daily chores. As they passed he could smell them, the desperation of the men and, more maddeningly, the musk of the women.

Each one of them considered themselves special, unique, important. They did not realize their sheer numbers rendered them inconsequential.

Many times he thought about drawing the blade he had hidden under his coat. Even now his hand was reflexively opening and closing on the pummel of the short sword. He thought about drawing the weapon and leaping into the crowd before him, slashing and cutting. How many would he kill before the police came and brought him down? Ten, twenty, thirty?

Would it have any impact? Some would come and place flowers at this spot and light candles. But soon the candles would go out, the flowers would wither and be discarded and all the while the flow of humanity would continue the same as any other day, unabated.

Like a school of minnows in a stream when several are gobbled up by a hop frog. Do the other minnows even notice or care? The next generation of minnows certainly has no recollection of those that have passed. The dead here would also fade into obscurity, no one ever remembering who they were, what they liked and disliked, who they wed or bed.

Yet this inconsequential mass of humanity chose to ignore him. Worse, they felt they were superior to him, that he was something to look down upon, when he was their better by every measure.

He was determined to change that. He would be remembered and his accomplishments spoken of in hushed and fearful tones long after those before him now had turned to dust.

3

Carter Stevens had only one problem right now and that problem's name was Danny Edwards. Everything had gone exactly as planned. The days following the bumacide, Carter had watched the news and read the papers. It was mentioned as a minor story about a traffic accident that was under investigation but no mention of expected foul play. Some of the articles had contained a quote from the truck driver and he did not mention seeing anyone on the scene. There was no mention of other witnesses so the whole thing had gone down as planned.

Sean had been cool, holding it together, acting normal. Danny, however, was a different story. Ever since that night he had been dragging around school like he had lost his best friend. People were starting to wonder about him and that was not good, not good by a whole lot.

Carter waited around the corner from Danny's third period class. The bell rang signaling the class change and students began filing out of the room. Carter searched the ragged procession of kids spilling into the hallway. Why was it that the more money kids had, the more they wanted to dress as if they came from the street? All up and down the hall the rooms were emptying; the hall was becoming a bustling river of humanity. Finally, last one out of the room, came Danny, head hanging, feet shuffling, backpack draped over one shoulder.

Carter came around the corner, put his arm around Danny's shoulders and steered him toward the nearest exit.

"What are you doing? I've got chem, I've got to get to the other end of the building," Danny protested.

"You're gonna be late for chem," said Carter as he steered Danny through the doors to the outside and around, into the isolated corner formed by the vestibule for the doors they'd just exited and the wall of the building.

"You're starting to worry me, Danny. The way you're moping around, people are starting to ask questions. Eventually instead of just whispering behind your back someone, a teacher, a principle, a guidance counselor is going to ask those questions directly to you. How are you going to respond?"

Danny looked horrible. He was pale and had dark circles under his eyes. He looked like some kind of weird albino raccoon. He spoke in a strange listless monotone, barely more than a whisper. "Carter, I can't get it out of my head, we killed a person. There was someone, living, breathing, minding their own business, and we came along and ended his life. He's gone, we can't take it back, it's final, it's so fucking final. It can't ever be fixed." A single tear rolled down Danny's cheek. This was probably the last tear he had left; it looked like he had shed a lot of them recently.

Carter spoke, the exasperation evident in his tone, as if he was explaining the simplest concept for the hundredth time to a particularly dimwitted child. "We are talking about some bum on the street, it's not like he had a real life. We saved him from more suffering. And you are right, it is final, it can't be fixed, we can't take it back, so what do you expect us to do? Ruin all our lives for one dead lowlife? That's what is going to happen if you keep this up. Pull yourself together, it is over, it is done. You have to put it behind you or you are going to get us all screwed. There is nothing in the papers, there are no questions being asked, we are in the clear unless you crack. So forget it ever happened, put it behind you and get on with your life. If you don't, things could get really ugly. I will not have my life ruined by you. Maybe you ought to call in sick for a few days until you can pull it together. Now get out of here."

Through the whole lecture Danny didn't say anything; he just didn't seem to have the energy to argue. When Carter dismissed him, he silently turned and slowly walked around and through the doors with the same depressed, weight of the world on his shoulders, shuffle he had been doing for days.

Carter watched him leave and snorted disgustedly; this was a problem. He turned and walked to the street where Sean was waiting parked at the curb in his BMW. Carter opened the door and slipped into the passenger seat.

"How'd it go?" Sean asked.

"Not good, not good at all. We are going to have to think of another way to get through to that kid and fast. If he doesn't snap out of it soon, we are going to have to explore other options."

CHAPTER 5

1

Al had spent the morning in court. It was late afternoon by the time he got to the station. He felt it immediately as he walked to his desk: the sound in the squad room died out as all eyes glanced his way. When it came to gossiping, cops were worse than high school girls. Some version of what had happened to him the night before had gotten back to the station.

As if he had any doubt that was indeed the case, Mike was standing next to his desk, arms folded, a stern look on his face like a parent who just caught his kid breaking curfew. It was amazing. No matter how old you were, how strong those childhood memories and the feelings that went with them persisted.

"Interrogation room," Mike said in the clipped tone of someone in charge. He spun around and marched into the nearest room without looking back to see if Al was following.

Mike held the door as Al entered. Al didn't handle authority well, especially when the person trying to exercise the authority really had no right to do so. With an intentional air of nonchalance, Al didn't take a chair, he just hung an ass cheek on one corner of the scarred wooden table that was in the center of the room. He could tell by the slight contraction of the muscles along Mike's jaw and the even slighter tick at the corner of his left eye that Al's attitude was having the desired effect.

Mike closed the door, then stood staring at Al, arms folded again, that look still on his face.

"What is your problem?" he began.

"I don't have a problem, but from the look on your face I suppose you do?"

"Ever since your divorce you've been trying to live like you're twenty. Going out all the time, drinking too much, dating young chicks. None of my business, I know, I know, none of my business, and I haven't said a word."

"I assume that is all about to change."

"You're damn right it's going to change. When this bullshit starts to affect my career, that's where I draw the line."

Al could sense Mike's anger rising and realized this wasn't something he was going to joke his way out of.

"First of all, I don't know what you're pissed about or, for that matter, what my personal life has to do with you."

"Are you kidding me? Eddie Finnerty finds you drunk, sprawled out on the sidewalk. He loads you into a cab and sends you home. How do you think that plays with the captain? With the guys? You're a goddamn laughingstock. And if you don't think that reflects on me, as your partner, then you're an idiot. "

So Eddie had put him in a cab. That was good, one mystery solved; it was always a plus when you could figure out how you got home. Of course, Eddie was the last person you would want to find you in a less-than-complimentary position. Not only would he tell anyone who would care to listen, he would be sure to embellish the story to increase its entertainment value.

Still, Al wasn't about to answer to anyone. "First of all, be careful," Al warned. "Maybe that wasn't my finest hour, and I really appreciate you being concerned there, big brother, but when I'm on the job I deliver. That's all you, or anyone else, needs to worry about. What I do on my time is my business." Al saw the muscles in Mike's jaw flex again and knew that that wasn't going to be the end of it.

"Listen, unlike you I don't plan on picking over dead bodies like some friggin' vulture for the rest of my career. I want to move up, get off the street. And it isn't about how you do your job; it's about who you know and whether they see you as part of the club. Drunken fuck-ups, even partners of drunken fuck-ups, aren't seen as part of the club!"

"I don't want to join any club. I'll leave the ass kissing to you." Al regretted the statement as soon as it came out of his mouth. He knew it would only escalate things and he just wanted this conversation to be over with. His head was starting to pound more than it had this morning. "I just want to do my job and be left alone."

"Typical comment from a guy who wants to be a grunt his whole life. Anybody that wants to get ahead, wants to better themselves, is kissing ass. This way you can wear the fact that you're a loser like some kind of badge of honor. 'Look at me, I didn't get ahead, not because I'm a fuck-up but because I have too much integrity. I never sold out.' What a joke."

If Al had been in a more introspective frame of mind he may have admitted that there was at least some truth to what Mike said. But Al had had enough introspection for one morning. "You're crossing a line, Mike, and you need to stand down. Bottom line: what I do on my time is my business. Now we can stand here and debate the point all day or we can get back to work."

Mike's face turned red. He obviously was not happy with the way this little conversation had gone. He started to open his mouth to respond.

Al cut him off, realizing if he ever wanted this conversation to end he had to bend a little. "Listen, I got your point.

I've taken things a little too far lately. I'll rein it in. Let's just move on, okay? We've too much work to do to stand here arguing."

The redness began to drain from Mike's face. "Yeah, okay. It's just, you know, Al, this is important to me. The last thing I want to do is become your nursemaid, but I have to think about my career."

"Yeah I know; I was out of line with the ass-kissing comment. If it makes you feel any better, I lost a shoe last night. The pair cost me over three hundred dollars."

"Actually it does make me feel a little better," Mike said, smiling now.

2

With nothing else to be accomplished at the station while they waited for the tech guys to get done with the security video, they headed up First Avenue to the medical examiner's office. They didn't learn much more there than they already knew. The very night of the accident someone had broken into the building and stolen the remains of the accident victim. They asked about security footage but unfortunately the cameras at the back of the building where the break-in had occurred were not in operation at the time. It seemed that about a month ago, video from those same cameras had been leaked onto the internet. The film had captured the body of a young starlet who had OD'ed in a Midtown hotel room being brought in. The temporary fix in response to the shock and outrage expressed by the media had been to shut the cameras down altogether to avoid future incidents.

The young admin who was showing them around brought them to the garage under the building where the dumpsters were. Leaning against the farthest dumpster was the door that had been damaged in the break in.

It was obvious this was not a finessed job: the lock of the door had not been jimmied; the door was bent and twisted, the hinges broken. The curious thing was the door showed none of the scarring you would have expected had it been battered in. The metal was bent and bowed as if some great pressure had been steadily applied to the door until the metal gave way and the hinges snapped.

Other than the damaged door, there wasn't much else. No one in the building that night had seen or heard anything and, as reported, the only thing taken had been the mangled body of the accident victim.

3

Later that day, Mike and Al found themselves in a small office deep in the bowels of the Metropolitan Museum of Art. Behind the desk was Dr. Spencer Rhodes, the director of the Department of Arms and Armor. The sword that had been found in the stained backpack in the street was lying on the doctor's desktop.

The office was not at all what Al had expected. He had envisioned shelves full of old musty tomes and manuscripts, antique furniture from around the world, ancient artifacts. Instead the office was virtually pristine; the credenza behind the desk was barren except for a few family photos and a bonsai tree. The desk itself held a computer screen, a keyboard and a computer mouse perched on a mouse pad. At least the mouse pad was printed with a picture of a gargoyle.

The doctor himself, however, did not disappoint. His grey hair formed a slightly unkempt halo around his bald head. His clothes didn't fit quit right and were built more for comfort than fashion: soft plaid shirt, corduroy jacket and loose-fitting corduroy pants. Everything was in various shades of beige and brown. The guy looked like he was about to give a lecture on his latest archeological dig to a bunch of bored college kids.

Doctor Rhodes lifted the sword, hefting it thoughtfully in his pudgy right hand. "What you have here, my good detectives, is a very well-done replica of a Roman gladius, the short sword favored by the Roman legions. Notice the long point, how the blade is waisted—that is, it comes in slightly at the sides. Now the waisting is not as pronounced as a Mainz gladius, this would be a replica of a Fulham gladius. We know this sword was used by the Romans in Britain during the first century AD. As a matter of fact, the sword gets its name because this was the type of sword dredged from the Thames near Fulham."

"Doctor, if this is a replica, do you know where someone can acquire one of these? Is there a way to trace the owner?" Mike asked.

"There is no doubt it is a replica. Any authentic specimen would have lain over a thousand years in the silt at the bottom of a river or buried underground. It would be very badly corroded at this time. Now as for who manufactured and sold this particular gladius…that is a little tricky." He pushed back his chair and stood behind the desk, lifting the sword in his right hand. He began to rotate his wrist, the tip of the sword making graceful figures-eights in the air. "The balance is superb. There are several sources for good quality replicas, however I don't know of any that achieve this level of authentic look and feel. That being said, whoever owned this didn't take very good care of it, or care about maintaining its authenticity."

"What makes you say that, Doctor? The blade looks like it's in good shape, no rust or corrosion."

"Well, for one thing, the handle is wrapped in leather that looks like it was composed of strips cut from a normal belt. The pummel is worn and weathered. Also, the blade shows wear." He stopped twirling the blade and brought it forward, picking at a nick in the edge of the blade with the nail of his left forefinger. "See the notches in the edge? The edge has been sharpened, however this blade hasn't been just on display somewhere. It looks like someone has been using it to hack at things, maybe as a garden tool." He chuckled slightly. "And look at this," he added, squinting at the blade. "A symbol of some type has been etched into the blade." He tilted the blade toward them and Al could make out what appeared to be three or four concentric circles bisected by several lines that ended in another smaller circle. The pattern looked vaguely familiar.

"In its original state I would venture that this was quite an expensive replica," the doctor continued. "Based on where you say you found it, I would also venture it was stolen from some collector and then was lost or discarded and happened into the possession of your street urchin."

Al collected the sword. They both thanked Dr. Rhodes and headed for the door.

When they were in the hallway, Al turned to Mike. "We are grasping at straws here. Hopefully they can pull a plate number from that tape otherwise we've got nothing."

"Unless that body turns up, we don't have a hell of a lot either way."

CHAPTER 6

1

Al's alarm began its relentless buzzing. Yesterday had been a long day but Al had hit the sack relatively early and felt light years better than he had the previous morning. The blinds were up in his bedroom and the early morning light filtered through the window.

He reached out and slapped the top of the alarm and the buzzing stopped. Al lived on a very quiet street. It was rare when even a car would pass by, however instead of the silence he expected, once he had killed the alarm he heard laughter followed by a tinny clattering noise. Al stood and stumbled to the window, boxers clinging to his bony hips, hair spiked like a rooster's comb. He leaned on the sill and peered through the dingy glass.

He undid the latch, raised the window and leaned out for a better look. Down below in the middle of the street were hundreds of aluminum cans. They were carefully aligned in three concentric circles. Cans in two parallel lines bisected these circles, starting at their center and continuing for about ten feet past the outermost ring. These twin lines ended in a smaller circle of cans.

There were two kids, a boy and a girl, taking turns kicking cans from this smaller circle and laughing as they skittered along, knocking over others in the pattern.

"Hold on a minute," Al yelled down, trying to keep his voice calm so as not to scare the kids. They both looked up, puzzled. Al held out his hand in a "hold on" gesture. He went back into his room, grabbed his phone from on top of his dresser, unplugged it from the charger and went back to the window. Leaning out again he snapped several pictures of the design in the street. "Okay, carry on," Al said, closing his window again. There was a brief pause and then the laughter and clattering noises continued.

He wasn't sure what to make of it but the can pattern looked just like the symbol etched in the blade of the sword. And again he couldn't help but feel he had seen something similar somewhere before.

He went to the window again to get another look. The kids had done a pretty good job of scattering the cans at this point. Al was about to turn away when he caught a glimpse of a figure standing back in the shadows of the alley across the street. Al at first thought whoever it was might be staring at the kids, but as the figure stepped back deeper into the alley and disappeared, Al couldn't shake the feeling that he was the one being stared at.

2

Al got to the top of the stairs and immediately spotted Mike waving him over. He weaved through the other desks to Mike's. "What's up?" Al paused. "You don't look too good."

"I think we really stepped in it, partner."

"What are you talking about?"

Mike lifted the laptop off of his desk and gestured toward the interrogation room that they had had their little disagreement in the day before.

Mike put the laptop down on the table, dropped into a chair and pulled another over, indicating that Al should join him. As Al sat, Mike was mousing over a list of files. "I got the security video back from tech. They were able to blow it up and get the plate number." As Mike spoke, a window opened on his computer and the grainy security video began to play; there was the BMW and the kids opening the doors and heading for the popped trunk.

Mike paused the video and made the mouse arrow perform little circles around the head of a dark-haired kid, frozen as he rounded the rear fender of the car. "You're never going to guess who this is. I ran the plates; the car is registered to the police commissioner."

"Hutchinson?" Al asked, eyes widening.

"The one and only, and I think this is his son. We gotta take this to the captain."

"Wait a minute," Al said. "We have to make sure you're right and we have to see if we can identify the other kids. I want to know everything we can before we go in front of the captain. He is going to have a lot of questions and I want to have as many answers as possible."

"What are you thinking?"

"There isn't a kid out there that doesn't have a Facebook account or is posting shit online. Let's see if we can track these guys down."

They ran through the video several times, freezing it at certain moments to highlight one kid or another's features. Al thought one of them should be easy to identify: he had light blonde hair that appeared white on the black and white video.

They spent the next half hour scouring the internet. It had only taken a little poking around to verify that the youth

Mike had indicated was indeed the commissioner's son. A quick search on the commissioner revealed he had a teenage son named Sean. The search on Sean had provided articles and photographs. It seemed that Sean Hutchinson was quite the talented high school athlete.

There were articles on track meets and basketball games where, win or lose, Sean was mentioned as one of the leading scorers for his team. Sean's strongest sport was football. He played tight end and had been voted to the All City team.

It was because of football that they got their next break. There had been a photograph of Sean's entire team in a small neighborhood publication. Standing next to Sean in the photo was a player with blonde hair that appeared white in the black and white picture. A quick check of the caption identified the player as Carter Stevens.

Mike and Al stared at the computer screen in amazement. Two of the three teenage perpetrators they were looking for happened to be the sons of the police commissioner and the richest real estate developer in the city.

Carter Stevens had an extensive online presence as well. He was a linebacker on the football team and was involved in other sports as well. In addition, he had won several city-sponsored academic awards. This kid had really won the genetic lottery: smart, athletic and good looking.

They kept digging but didn't find anything definitive on the third kid. There was nothing distinctive about him that could be seen on the tape—he could have been one of any number of kids they saw in photos with Sean and Carter, or none of them.

Al sat back in his chair, running his hand through his hair. "Well, we've got two of them. It shouldn't be too hard to get them to flip on the third. But we still have one problem."

"What's that?"

"The homeless guy isn't in the video and we have no body, no way to show these guys did anything to him. All we have is some teenagers getting bats out of a trunk and running up the street. No law against that, especially with the juice behind these two. I don't think we can even bring this to the captain yet. We go public with this at this point and all we are going to accomplish is losing our jobs. These kids will lawyer up and we won't even get to talk to them."

"So what do you want to do?"

"Wait a minute." Al pushed his chair back, turning toward Mike. "The other homeless guys that were attacked over the past several months, what were their injuries?"

"The usual, bumps and bruises. Could be caused by a bat," Mike said, realizing what Al was getting at.

"Do we know where the attacks took place? If so, we could subpoena the phone records of these two, see if they were in the vicinity of the other attacks."

"We may have something, but these are homeless guys. The chances of getting reliable information from them is slim. Besides, most of the injuries were detected at shelters after the fact. Some of these guys didn't even remember being beaten until their own bruises were pointed out to them."

"It's worth a shot. *Now* I think it's time to take this to the captain. Considering who we are dealing with, he is going to want to tread lightly on this one."

3

Al and Mike sat across the desk from Captain Barry Sheffield. The captain was a tall, wiry black man with a perpetual pissed off look on his face and the demeanor of a Marine drill sergeant.

Their relationship had always been strictly business, but Al had a lot of respect for the captain. He was a good, hard-nosed cop who had come up through the ranks. When it came to police work, he knew his stuff, and he also had the political savvy to survive and thrive in a department that had become increasingly hard to navigate. Since the current commissioner had been in place, the department had been run more like a cult of personality: your loyalty to the commissioner, either real or perceived, was just as important as your job performance in determining career advancement.

The captain was staring at the computer terminal on his desk, brow furrowed. He glanced up from the screen. "So you're saying it's Commissioner Hutchinson's son and the son of Charles Stevens in this video."

Al and Mike both nodded. "We ran the plate. The car is registered to the commissioner and we found pictures of the two online. They match," Al offered.

"And you think this has something to do with the accident the other night?"

"We think they caused it. We checked into the reports on the other homeless that had been attacked. All showed signs of being attacked by a blunt instrument. This video was shot just around the corner from the accident. We think they were going after the homeless guy that ended up in front of the truck."

"But you have no body, no evidence that they attacked the victim. The victim doesn't show up on this video and you haven't found any witnesses."

"As far as the body, I don't think that will tell us anything. I think he probably ran out into the street to escape these guys and that is how he got hit," Al said.

"That may be, but the legal system likes bodies. Keeps things neat and orderly. You guys aren't stupid. You know the kind of money and political clout behind these two. They will have the best lawyers, and without an airtight case we are going to get laughed out of court. Provided we can even get it to trial."

"That's why we came to you, Cap," said Al. "Of the five other attacks, three of the victims could tell where the attack happened. If we can get the cell phone records from these two and put them near those locations at the time of those attacks as well, that should give us enough to at least bring them in for questioning."

The captain looked more pissed than normal, if that were possible. "And what will that get you? They aren't going to come in without a lawyer, and you will be lucky to get more than name, rank and serial number."

"Captain, isn't it also a little coincidental that someone steals a body from the morgue and it is the one body that these two rich kids may have something to do with?" asked Mike.

The captain snorted. "Don't start with the conspiracy theories. I read your report on that little incident. If the police commissioner wanted to make a body disappear from the morgue, don't you think he could have it done without demolishing a steel door? Not to disparage anyone down there, but he could arrange an internal job and then just scratch up a lock to make it look like it had been picked. No, I think you're just dealing with some sickos and an unfortunate coincidence."

The captain sat back in his chair and began to rub his temples as if he was just struck with the mother of all migraines. "Okay," he finally said, dropping his hands and looking at the two detectives. "Here's what I am going to do. I am going to call in a few favors and see if I can get a subpoena issued, but we are going to keep it quiet. See if we can place these guys at the other attacks. If we can, then we will see where we go from there. And for God's sake, try to find an actual witness. Oh yeah, and figure out who the third kid is. For all we know he may be someone we *can* lean on."

CHAPTER 7

1

Carrie sat alone at the long glass bar, surrounded by the press of the after-work crowd. The air was filled with a confluence of voices, laughter and clinking glasses. She glanced at the watch that encircled her graceful wrist, manicured French nails clicking distractedly on the bars surface. Al was late again. She had gotten used to this: Al would often get involved at work and lose track of time. That and the phone calls at all hours was just something you had to get used to when you were dating a cop.

"Waiting for someone?"

Carrie looked up. The guy standing there was handsome enough—clean-cut, expensive suit, incredibly straight white teeth. Veneers or teenage braces followed by Crest white strips? She couldn't quite decide.

"Yes, I am waiting for someone, actually."

"Well, I'm someone. So why don't you forget about a loser who would leave a beautiful woman like you waiting and let me buy you a drink."

"I am quite capable of buying my own drink, thank you. But just for fun, let me get this straight. Your take on this situation is that I have such low self-esteem that I would date losers, and you are going to rescue me from myself."

"Relax, beautiful, I'm just saying I would never leave you alone in a bar staring at your watch, and any guy that would probably doesn't appreciate what he has."

Carrie was tempted to go into a fake feminist bitch routine—"What he has! What he has! Nobody *owns* me!"—just to keep herself entertained, but she decided to go easy on the guy. He was like dozens of other guys she met every day. Coming out of college, she had gotten an entry-level position at an investment house downtown, and every day she met this type of guy: young, successful, conceited, extremely intelligent but, unfortunately, crushingly boring. The kind of guy they invented the term "stuffed shirt" for. The kind of guy who thought a big bank account and a nice car could take the place of actually developing a personality.

"Listen, you seem like a really nice guy," she lied, "but I really am meeting someone and I don't want to waste your time."

"See, that's the point. I'm the one that's trying to keep you from wasting your time, wasting your time on some other guy when we could have such a good time together." He leaned against the bar and put his hand on the back of her barstool, penning her in.

Just then, over his shoulder, she saw Al enter the bar.

Al stood out from the crowd. Not because of the way he was dressed; for a cop Al dressed really well. His suit may not have cost as much as the guy's standing next to her but it was stylish and well tailored. Nor was it strictly his physical appearance, though that was part of it; he had dark Italian good looks, large brown eyes and dark wavy hair probably a week past due for a haircut. She was happy he hadn't gone the way of many cops who shaved their heads; it seemed they all wanted to look like UFC fighters. So that was part of it. Next to the perfectly coifed, manicured and stiff corporate types, Al appeared more down to earth, more comfortable in his own skin. In addition to that, there was something else, something in the look in his eyes. He looked worldly, capable of handling himself. In this crowd of well-tailored suits and carefully polished personas, Al stood out like a wolf at the Westminster Dog show.

He stood there looking around, a vague, slightly annoyed look on his face. Carrie smiled. Yeah, this place certainly wasn't up Al's alley. She enjoyed her relationship with Al a great deal. Did she love him? No, she wasn't there yet. For one thing, Al was still carrying a torch for his ex-wife. He would probably be surprised to know she thought that, however it didn't take a genius to figure it out.

One time he had gone off to work early in the morning, when she woke she had opened his dresser drawer looking for a t-shirt to put on and there on top of his boxers was a framed picture of him and his ex. He had obviously dumped the picture in the drawer when he knew she was coming over.

It hadn't bothered her too much. First, as previously stated, she wasn't in love with him. Second, they had been married. Carrie was mature enough to realize those type of feelings don't disappear overnight. Third, Carrie knew something that Al probably didn't realize yet himself: it never was going to work out between Al and his ex-wife. She represented what Al thought he was supposed to want: the stable home, the white picket fence, a couple of kids, maybe a dog. However Al would never be truly happy in that type of environment. Oh, he could fake it for a while, but eventually the normalcy of it would drive him crazy. Eventually he may realize that for himself—or not—and eventually Carrie may fall in love with him—or not. But for now she was having a good time and taking things as they came.

He spotted her and began to weave his way through the crowd. Carrie turned to the guy who was still hovering over her. "It was nice meeting you, but my date's here."

The guy looked like he was going to protest, but then he looked over and saw Al. "All right, honey, but I come around here quite a bit if you ever change your mind." With that he went through the crowd in the opposite direction of Al's approach.

Al glanced at the guy as he came up but didn't say anything about him. That was one thing that aggravated Carrie just a little; he didn't have a jealous bone in his body.

"Hello, Alphonse, nice of you to show up."

He smiled. "I never should have told you my full name." Al's father had been a big fan of old black and white gangster movies and had named him after Al Capone. "Wanna get out of here, grab something to eat? I've had nothing but coffee all day and I'm starving."

This exchange seemed natural enough but Carrie couldn't help but sense something. He seemed distracted, something was on his mind.

"Sure, baby, let's go."

2

At dinner Al seemed preoccupied. He was pushing his food around his plate and only providing the occasional "Uh huh" in response to her discourse about her day.

"Al, am I going to have to do all the heavy lifting in this conversation?"

"What?" he asked, seeming to rise, if slowly, from the depths of thought.

"I feel like I'm doing a monologue here. Is something bothering you?"

"Oh, yeah, sorry. I've got this case I'm working on, can't really say much about it, everything is just conjecture right now and a little too sensitive to discuss."

"Doesn't bode well for interesting dinner conversation if you can't discuss it."

"Yeah I know, sorry," Al said with a grin. "You know, here's something, not that big a deal, just curious. The other morning I woke up and somebody—kids, I guess—had arranged hundreds of soda and beer cans in a pattern in the middle of the street in front of my building. Here, I took a picture of it." He fished his phone out of his pocket and began thumbing the screen. Finally he found the picture and turned the phone toward Carrie.

"Wow. Somebody sure put a lot of time into that." Carrie studied the picture for a moment. "You know what it looks like? Crop circles. Not the new ones that are geometric designs or pictures of presidents or something; you know, the old ones that started it all. They were in fields in England, random circles and lines laid out like they had a purpose, but no purpose that the people that found them could figure out. Used to think spaceships did it."

"Oh yeah, like the cover of the Led Zeppelin boxed set."

"Before my time, Al."

"Good music is timeless, Carrie." Al grinned.

Carrie laughed, glad to see his mood had lightened. "So why are people building can crop circles on your street?"

"I don't know. Like I said, probably just kids fooling around." He made no mention of the sword found near the accident the other night or the fact that it had a similar pattern on it.

"But that's all I've got. So I guess we're back to the exciting world of investment banking."

"You're a jerk." Carrie smiled. "You would think it would interest you more. If you listen to the Democrats you would think we are just as bad as the murderers you deal with."

3

The following morning, even though the sun was up and Carrie protested that the subway was only a couple of blocks away, Al had insisted on calling her a cab to take her to work.

She gave him a peck on the cheek and climbed into the back of the cab. As he closed the door, Al scanned the opposite side of the street. Was that movement he saw in the shadows of the alley across the way? He couldn't be sure, but he was glad he hadn't allowed her to walk those couple of blocks.

4

Al and Mike sat in their car and watched the two teenagers getting out of the white BMW across the street. Al had a strong feeling of déjà vu. He had witnessed this little scene before, played out in grainy black and white on the security video he had watched over and over. These were the boys he had seen on the tape: same stature, same coats, one with dark curly hair and the other with light blonde hair.

While they waited to see if the captain could secure the subpoena they needed, they had dredged the internet, scanning pictures of teenagers that had any association with these two, looking for their third kid. Going face by face through dozens of pictures of teenage parties full of glassy-eyed kids holding red solo cups. Guys with mouths wide open, cup held in the air and girls sticking their tongues out or puckering their lips into exaggerated pouts. Like a weird game of teenage *Where's Waldo?*, they searched for anyone who might be their guy.

Finally they had given up and opted for an old-fashioned stake out. So far they had spent two days in front of Sean and

Carter's school, watching them come and go. The pair seemed very popular; they interacted with a lot of students but no one who appeared to be their man.

Al knew they needed a break. Without more to go on, he didn't see a way they could move on these two. It would have been difficult with anyone, but with these two and their connections it was virtually impossible.

As if reading his mind, Mike said, "This is getting us nowhere, partner. If the captain can't get us that subpoena, we've got nothing; these guys are gonna walk."

"I was thinking the same thing myself. I think it is going to be out of our hands. You saw the look on the captain's face—even if we get the subpoena, we need to get something rock solid or he is gonna drop the whole thing, and can you blame him? If we don't get some ironclad evidence linking these two to the dead guy, the only thing we will accomplish is ruining all our careers."

They sat and watched the two teens leaning against the car joking and laughing with a couple of very attractive girls. They looked every bit the part of the anointed youth they were.

CHAPTER 8

1

Al approached the front of his building; it had been a very long and very unproductive day. He was looking forward to turning in early and getting a good night's sleep. As he got closer he saw the silhouette of a figure get up from where it had been sitting on his building's stoop, take several steps into the middle of the sidewalk and turn to face him.

At the initial sight of this figure Al thought of the barely glimpsed shadowy forms he had spotted, or thought he had spotted, lurking in the alley across the street. His apprehension just as quickly disappeared. Even in silhouette he could tell by the slight angle of the head, the way the hair draped to the side, the way the knee of the left leg was turned slightly inward in that familiar girlish way…it was Anne.

He felt a lump rise in his throat as he strolled closer.

"Hey, Al," she said as he got close enough to make out her achingly familiar features: the large eyes, the small slightly upturned nose, the mouth, a little on the wide side, that would be slightly crooked when she smiled. That crooked smile just added to her attractiveness, made her warm, approachable, desirable.

Al swallowed, hard. "Hey, Anne. What brings you out here at this time of day? Is everything all right?"

"Yeah, fine." She hesitated. "I don't know, ever since your call the other night I guess I've been worried about you." She paused again. "Thinking about you."

"Ah, yeah," he started. "Sorry about that. I was out with some of the boys and had a little too much to drink. You know how it is, started feeling sentimental. But I'm fine, really." Then, trying to change the subject, "You look great. How have you been? Good?"

"I've been fine."

Before he could stop himself he said, "You wanna come up? I could make some coffee. We could talk."

"No, I better not. It's not too cold out. Why don't we take a walk up to the park?" she said, nodding up the street. "We can talk out here."

"Okay." Al had mixed feelings about her response. On the one hand, he was disappointed she didn't want to come up to the apartment, but on the other, he was pleased that she was reluctant to do so. She knew she could trust him; he was not the type to make unwanted advances. So maybe she didn't trust herself, and if she no longer had any feelings for him would that be the case?

She turned and they started up the street side by side, each with their hands jammed in their coat pockets, either to ward off the cold or maybe the awkwardness should their hands accidentally touch.

Al shifted nervously. He suddenly had the feeling they were being watched. He casually scanned the line of buildings on the opposite side of the street, trying not to alarm Anne. He didn't see anything peculiar. It was not like him to be jumpy and he didn't like the fact that he was.

"So how's the young girlfriend?"

"Right to it, huh? It's not really fair, Anne. You know I never cheated on you and it was you who asked for the divorce, I never did."

"You didn't ask for it in words, Al, but your actions were pleading for it."

"Is this why you stopped by? To rehash this whole discussion?"

"You're right, I'm sorry. I don't know what made me say that. Truth is, Al, I miss you. I would be lying if I said I didn't occasionally have second thoughts about whether we did the right thing, whether we tried hard enough. But then I remember the arguments. After each argument you would try to change, and I loved you for trying, but then you would get restless, and I could tell you weren't happy. Knowing you were unhappy made me unhappy."

They had come to the small playground at the end of Al's block. They each sat in a swing on the swing set like they had done on evenings in the past, slowly swaying together, discussing their plans for the future.

Al felt his guard drop a little. The fact that she admitted she missed him weakened his usual reluctance to open up. Al was very good at not tipping his hand. *Never let them see you sweat.* It was great for police work, not so great for relationships.

"I can't deny what you're saying, Anne. At the time I was too wrapped up in the job. But I have begun to reevaluate things. At least in the past I had some balance. Yeah, I was caught up in the job, but my life outside, my life with you, provided some balance. I didn't realize it at the time. But now that it's gone, when I'm not at work everything seems so pointless. Dinners out, hanging out in bars, even the young girlfriend, it's like travelling endlessly with no destination. After a while it just seems so arbitrary, just a way to clock the hours and days with nothing to show for it."

"I wish I could believe what you're saying. Not that I think you're lying; I believe you believe what you're saying. But it is hard for someone to change their nature. If we went back to the way we were, the old issues would soon resurface. You just weren't built for domestic life, Al."

"I think I can find balance, I really do. Listen, I'm not gonna promise you anything, not because I don't think I can change but because I have made promises in the past and you have no reason to believe this time will be any different. How about we take it slow? Just go to dinner with me; just one night out and we will take it from there."

He could see Anne was thinking this over, staring at her shoes, chewing on her lower lip. He felt that an awful lot was riding on this decision; he was surprised at how anxious he felt waiting for her response.

"Okay, Al. One dinner."

He tried to keep his face impassive, play it cool. "How about Saturday night?"

"No, we go slowly, not a weekend night. How about next Thursday night?"

"Okay, Thursday it is. I'll pick you up around seven." He was grinning now, unable to suppress it, and he was happy to see her smile back. There it was: that crooked smile, the smile that made him feel warm and weak at the same time.

She stood up, still smiling, "I will meet you at seven, but now I really have to get going. Walk me to the subway?"

"Let me walk you up to the corner and flag you a cab."

"Why, Al? The subway's only a couple of blocks and I'm only a couple of stops away."

"There have been some incidents on the trains around here lately," he lied. "I would just feel better if you took a cab."

"Really? I hadn't heard anything. But I guess you're the cop; you should know."

As they headed toward the corner, Al had that being-watched feeling again.

2

He sat across the street in the shadow of the right angle formed by a building and the brick stairs leading to the front door. He was wrapped in a worn, threadbare overcoat, the battered fedora pulled low, the scarf in place covering the lower part of his face. Passersby averted their eyes from the pitiful wretch huddled on the sidewalk. He sat and watched the couple across the street. Watched and planned, planned and watched.

CHAPTER 9

1

Any detective that is being honest will tell you most cases are not solved by some Sherlock Holmes-ian deduction or a hair follicle found under the spare tire in the trunk of a car. They are solved by one of the criminals having a big mouth, just having to brag about the crime to someone, or by some witness coming forward. That, and a great deal of luck.

Al and Mike looked like they were running on empty in the luck department. They had come up short in their search for any witnesses and their efforts to identify the third person in the video.

They were sitting at Mike's desk discussing their next steps. The slow progress on the case could not dampen the good mood Al was in due to his conversation with Anne.

Mike couldn't help but notice. "You're sure in a good mood this morning. Not your usual hungover, surly self."

"Yeah, I'm feeling pretty good. I talked to Anne last night and…"

Another detective, Hector Ramirez, walked over, interrupting Al. "Here you guys are. Listen, you had that bum the other night, right? The one that got run down? Well, I got a guy down the hall that says he knows somethin' about it."

Mike spun his chair around. "You're kidding me. What've you got?"

"We picked him up on a drug bust last night. He is looking to make a deal. He says that he was in the area and it was no accident. Says he can give us information on who did it."

They followed Hector down the hall. "Who is this guy?" Mike asked.

"Name's Darnel 'Coochie; Barnes. He's a member of the T5 Lions."

"We saw some of their artwork near the scene," Al offered. "We had checked the arrests in the area from the night of the accident and got nothing."

"Like I said, we just picked him up last night. According to him, some guys threw that bum into traffic, but he isn't giving too many details. Obviously he wants to talk deal first."

They had arrived at the room. Hector opened the door and led the way.

In the center of the room was a scarred metal table. Across the table, draped in a chair, was a young black man in his early twenties. This guy had refined nonchalant indifference to an art form. He had one arm slung over the back of the chair, knees spread, butt forward, head tilted back, backwards baseball cap pulled low over his eyes. He looked like he had been poured onto the seat, as if he didn't have a bone in his body.

"Oh man, not more cops. I told you, I want to talk to somebody from the DA's office about a deal. I ain't sayin' nothin' to nobody till I get some guarantees."

Mike took a seat across the table from the man. Hector and Al went to opposite corners of the small room. Both leaned against the wall, arms folded, looking down at the prisoner. If he felt surrounded, threatened, he didn't give any indication that it affected him.

"Listen, Coochie." Mike practically spat the words. "We're not gonna run somebody down here from the DA's office for every punk who claims to know something. You have to give us enough that we know this isn't a bunch of bull-shit."

Barnes looked at Hector. "Who's this dude, man? I don't like his attitude. I expect a little respect. What are you doin', playin' that game on me? "Good cop, big dumbass cop"?

Mike went red; the vein in his temple began a steady beat. "If I was you, I would watch my mouth, Coochie. It is amazing how many times people trip in this room. End up smashing their faces into this table. Give us the basics and we will decide if what you've got is deal worthy."

"Oh, it's deal worthy all right, goddamn right it's deal worthy. I'm doin' your job for ya."

Al looked bored. "Again, just give us what you got."

Barnes' eyes went from one cop to the next, surveying all three, and he must have decided it was in his best interest to get down to business. "The other night I was down on the West Side Highway with one of our new guys. You know, had him taggin'. It was too windy, damn paint blowing all over the place, so we was headin' to the subway when this white boy comes around the corner. We duck behind a wall and watch him."

"Sizin' him up for a mugging," volunteered Mike.

Al shot him a look. Mike was a little testy this morning. The frustration of the last several days must be getting to him.

Barnes ignored him. "The white boy stops, looks around and then trots back around the corner he came from. We started to head down that way when we heard some talkin' and a squeakin' noise. It was a little way's off and we couldn't hear it at all when the wind wasn't blowin' from that direction. We kept walkin', but slower, when we seen three white boys, the one we saw before and two others pushing a shoppin' cart. There was something in the cart, couldn't make it out at first. We ducked out of sight and kept watchin'. They rolled that cart up near the stop light. When they went past a streetlight was when we seen that there was a body in the cart. You could see the legs stickin' out." He paused. "Hey, can I get a drink?"

Mike let out an exasperated snort. "No, finish your little story."

"I'm thirsty, man, I been stuck here for hours."

"You're breakin' my heart, just keep going and quit wasting our time."

"I'll get you some water," volunteered Hector and left the room. From the look on his face, Al thought Mike was going to object, but he must have thought better of it and turned back to Barnes.

"Okay, he's getting you water, so keep goin'."

"Well anyway, the white dudes wait there at the light and the cars are going by. The light changes, they could cross, but they don't cross, they just wait there. Then all of a sudden this truck passes where we are and them white boys, they shove that cart right out in front of that truck. And it hit like BA-BAMN! And the cart goes flyin' up into the air and hits a car. We couldn't see the body anymore from where we was. And them white boys, they head back around the corner, but slinkin' kinda, keeping to the shadows. It was kind of funny though. Two of them was practically dragging the other dude."

"What do you mean dragging him?"

"I mean they had him by the arms and was pulling him along, like his legs wasn't workin'. I turn to Feebs, the little dude with me, and he's all like 'Shit they just killed some dude.' And I was like 'Yeah we gotta follow them, see if we can see who they are,' and he says 'Are you crazy, we gotta get out of here.' And I said 'We gotta find out who they are, if anybody saw us at all tonight the cops are sure as shit gonna be lookin'

81

for the black boys in the area. We got to find out who those white boys are so this don't get pinned on us."

Hector reentered the room and handed a cup of water to Barnes. He paused to drink, taking his time, making a show of it. Mike rolled his eyes.

"We ran up to the corner and we saw them around the corner and they jumped in a car, then they turned that car around and took off the other way, away from the accident they had caused."

Mike shot a look in Al's direction. "That's it? What kind of car? Did you get a plate number?"

"I said all I'm gonna say for now."

"If you can't identify who you saw, how do we know they even exist? How do we know you didn't do it and made up the fact that you saw three guys?"

"Is he the brightest you got?" said Barnes, looking from Al to Hector. "You cops didn't even pick me up for the dead dude. Why would I make up a story that puts me there if you didn't know I was there in the first place? You must think I'm the dumbest dude on the street."

"Well, you saw these guys at night, from pretty far away. If they do exist, how you gonna identify them?"

"'Cause maybe I know the kind of car they had and maybe when they were pulling that U-turn I got the license plate number."

"If you've got it, let's have it."

"We're back to where we started, back to square number one. Let's talk deal first, and not with you cops. I want somebody from the DA's office."

"What if we just add obstructing justice to your other charges?"

"Now I said 'maybe' I remember the car and 'maybe' I remember the plate number, but memory is a funny thing, it kinda comes and goes." Barnes leaned his chair back and looked around the room, obviously pleased with himself.

Hector gave a little head jerk toward the door and they all stepped out into the hallway, leaving Barnes in the room.

"I've got a call in to the DA's office, but it's late. They said they couldn't get someone down here till tomorrow morning," Hector said. He turned to Al. "What are you grinning about?"

"This is the break we were looking for. We already know the car and the plate number and the guys we suspect are involved; this Barnes ties it all together. He ties it all together and ties them to the dead guy."

"Your partner doesn't look too happy."

"I'm just a little more cautious. Al, we better go back to the captain with this before we offer this guy any deals."

"Yeah, you're right, but what he said lines up with everything we already know."

Al turned to Hector. "Set up the meeting with the DA, all right? We'll run this by the captain."

"Will do. I'll hold him downstairs till the morning. By the way, the captain is out, so you won't be able to catch up with him until tomorrow either."

"As long as we clear things with him before we meet with the DA's office, we should be good." Al was in a good mood. Finally things were coming together.

CHAPTER 10

1

Al walked the couple of blocks from the subway station to his apartment. He looked forward to this part of his day. By the time he usually walked these streets it was just past dinner time and, especially on chilly evenings like this one, the people that inhabited these buildings were safely behind closed doors. The street was empty and Al enjoyed the solitude: his footsteps crunching on the pavement, the brownstone apartments standing in a silent row on each side of the street, their dark brooding exteriors softened by the glow from their curtained windows.

But tonight Al was too preoccupied to enjoy the solitude. Between his conversation with Anne and the possibilities it offered and the realization that what had started out as a simple traffic accident could end up having far-reaching implications, his mind was racing.

Al continued down the street, deep in thought, hands jammed in the pockets of his raincoat, staring at the ground. The night was clear but dark, the moon a mere sliver in the sky. A slight breeze rustled the few leaves that remained on the trees that were spaced out on each side of the pitch-black asphalt.

Al's concentration was broken by a low chuffing sound, like a grunt or snort, off to his right. As he turned toward the sound, a low guttural voice, just above a whisper, came to him on the gentle breeze.

"Detective Russo."

There, standing in the mouth of an alley, was a dark and indistinct figure. The person—Al could not tell if it was male or female, but judging from the depth and rasp of the voice he assumed it was a man—stood slightly hunched over, giving the impression of advanced age or infirmity. A security light high on one of the buildings that formed one of the walls of the alley backlit the shape, casting it in silhouette. Steam venting from a grate back in the alley added a surreal backdrop as it reflected the light, the light breeze causing it to slowly roil behind the figure, light clouds tinged in silver.

"Who are you? What do you want?" Al asked, instinctively slipping his right hand inside the breast of his coat and feeling the butt of his gun.

"Might you be scared, Detective?" the low voice rasped. "There is no need for that now." Al picked up a distinct brogue, though he couldn't tell if it was Scottish or Irish.

He unconsciously calculated the distance between them to determine if he would have time to draw his weapon should the need arise. It was pure instinct; there was nothing about the figure in the ally that appeared threatening.

The figure took several shuffling steps forward, and as he drew further into the light from the streetlamps, details began to emerge. An old, battered fedora pulled down low on the brow, head tilted forward so that the face beneath was hidden in shadow. A long black overcoat that dragged on the ground, the collar turned up.

At the sight of the hat and coat, recognition dawned. This was the bum on the street who had scuffled with Al outside the bar the other night. "That's far enough," Al said. "The last time we met, you had me at a disadvantage. Not tonight."

"You remember our meeting; that is encouraging," the response came. "You were deep in your cups. I thought you may have forgotten."

"I also recall you assaulted a police officer."

"Is that how you recall it? There is some question in that matter, is there not? As I recall it, you accosted me first."

What puzzled Al was that the first time he had run into this character was outside of O'Tooles, near the station. How had this guy gotten all the way over here? Had he been following him, taking the subway with him?

He looked like, if he stood up straight, he would be no more than 5' 6", 5' 7" and weigh maybe 150, 160 tops. He did not project strength and except for the underlying menace in the tone of his voice did not appear to be a threat. However, Al remembered he had given him a pretty good shove the other night, followed by a kick in the ribs; he wasn't going to take any chances.

Looking left and right and seeing the street was empty, Al slipped his gun from its holster and, palming it, he casually dropped his hand to his side. "How did you find me here and what is this all about?"

The response caught Al completely by surprise. "Have you captured the ones who committed the murder yet, Detective?"

Keeping his voice level, Al replied, "What murder?"

"Let us not waste time with games. The murder you are investigating. The three men, the homeless person murdered."

"Were you there? You seem to know quite a bit."

"I know it was murder and I know you are tasked with finding the murderers. I have been watching you, Detective. I am disappointed to say you don't seem to be making much progress."

Al ignored the last comment. "You know it was murder? If you were a witness, you need to come in and give a statement."

"I don't think that would be wise. Besides, I am not a witness, I just know what I know."

If this guy did see anything, Al needed to bring him in. Drug-selling gang-bangers and homeless guys were not the strongest witnesses, but if they independently corroborated each other's stories, that would carry some weight. *Just keep him talking,* Al thought. He had to figure out a way to get him in. "If you are not a witness, what is your stake in this? Why do you care if I am making progress or not?"

"I want them. It is that simple. When you find who did this, you must deliver them to me."

"Deliver them to you?" The statement was so absurd Al couldn't stifle a laugh. "That's not the way it works. If you want to see justice done and you know anything about what went on, you need to come in."

Al toyed with the idea of slapping the cuffs on the guy. He could use their altercation the other night as an excuse to make an arrest. However, this guy wasn't going to just let himself be cuffed. If Al was going to bring him in, he had to draw him further out into the street. He didn't feel like chasing him down a dark alley. Though, to be honest, it didn't look like the guy could run very fast.

As Al was running through his options in his head an exasperated sigh came from the figure at the mouth of the alley. "You need to listen to me, Detective, will you be listening now?"

"I will listen to you down at the station. Let's go." Al took a step forward and the man took two quick shuffling steps backward, hands raised in front of him fingers spread, signaling Al to stay back. The man's hands were very large, the fingers long and thick. "You are close enough, Detective."

"Listen, pal, you need to come with me. I'll call a squad car and we'll take a little ride to the station and you can tell me everything you know," Al said, keeping his voice calm and conciliatory.

At this the guy seemed to become more agitated. His hands dropped to his sides, the fingers twitching like a gunfighter getting ready to draw.

He began a rocking shuffle, back and forth, in the narrow confines of the mouth of the alley. He began to make a strange chuffing sound. As he paced he drew up to his full height. The shoulders were still hunched, the head slung low, however his back straightened. His movements became more deliberate, more fluid, dispelling the initial impression of age and infirmity.

He appeared almost catlike in his pacing. He dropped into a squat, slamming his open palms on the pavement, and just as quickly was up pacing again.

"This will not do," he said, his voice a low rumble, more chuffing, the large hands clasping and unclasping. The fingers on those hands were thick, long and gnarled; in the light from the streetlights they looked like grey and twisted driftwood.

In that instant Al had a flashback to a distant childhood memory. When he was ten, his parents had taken him to the Bronx zoo. He had been amazed by the big cats. In particular he had been mesmerized by a large Bengal tiger. The other big cats were napping, but not this tiger. He paced back and forth in the enclosure, head low, those golden tiger eyes fixed on Al's, staring. Those eyes and the fluid movement conveyed power, strength, danger. The hate seemed to come off the animal in waves. Al didn't know animals could hate, but after that day he had no doubt. The intentions of that creature, if he could have broken through the glass partition, were very clear.

Al had that same feeling right now, the grace, the power, the hate. Only now there was no glass partition.

"You see before you someone you think you can disrespect, Detective. You perceive me to be powerless. You perceive me to be a solitary and weak creature."

In the space of several seconds things had changed dramatically. A few short minutes ago Al had been facing a hunched, shuffling, pathetic homeless man. The situation had turned from vaguely strange to dangerous. The tension in the air seemed to crackle and hiss.

Al slowly let his weapon slip down in his hand until he had a firm grip on the butt of the gun and his index finger slipped through the trigger guard. He kept the weapon at his side and raised his free hand, fingers splayed. "Stay calm, just relax, no one needs to get hurt."

"I am not powerless or alone. You will be made to understand this. You will understand and then you will do as I say."

The pacing continued, the fingers clenching and unclenching. Al had been in many tense situations, had faced off with all types of disturbed or drug-fueled crazies. He never wavered. He could feel the energy building, but to show any weakness now would invite an attack.

Then the pacing abruptly stopped. The man stood facing him, his arms still at his sides in that gunfighter stance. Al could hear heavy, coarse breathing punctuated by that chuffing sound.

They stood frozen like that for several tense seconds. Al's left hand outstretched in supplication, his right down at his side gripping his gun. The homeless man in his gunfighter stance, chest rising and falling as his breath came in ragged gasps.

Al waited, fingering the trigger, feeling a rivulet of sweat trickle down his temple despite the cold.

"You don't understand. But you will, oh, you will. You must be shown, then you will understand," the man said and darted into the darkness of the steam-filled alley.

It had happened so quickly that Al stood frozen for a second, the quick shuffle of running footsteps receding in the darkness. There was a thud and then the sound of more footsteps, muffled, fading.

"Damn!" Al rushed forward into the alley, knowing it would do little good. Just as he had expected, he came upon a metal grate that had been lifted out of the sidewalk and pushed to the side, revealing an opening to a utility tunnel below. Faint wisps of steam drifted up from the pitch blackness. The escape route had been planned all along.

CHAPTER 11

1

Sean was running late. Carter was waiting to get picked up and it was never a good idea to keep Carter waiting, even more so recently. He had been in a foul mood lately. Danny was still walking around in a funk and Carter was concerned he was going to crack.

Sean scooped his keys off the kitchen counter and headed up the hallway toward the front door. He noticed a light coming through the crack of the partially open double doors that led to his father's study. That was odd; his father was rarely home.

Ryan Hutchinson had always been a hard man with ambition that bordered on the psychotic. He was consumed with his career, had worked his way up through the department to police commissioner, making few friends along the way. Ambition like that did not leave much time for family trips to the ballpark or the zoo.

Always stern, humorless, Ryan Hutchinson had very little in common with his son. They were strangers under the same roof. Sean and his mother, however, were very close; both suffering from the same neglect, they had found solace and comfort in the relationship of mother and son. However,

the absence of a father figure had left Sean particularly suscep-
tible to Carter's influence.

Sean was in a hurry and certainly not in the mood for
one of their few strained attempts at conversation, so he tried
to slip noiselessly past the gap between the doors.

"Sean." Damn, no such luck. He tried for the quick escape. "I'm just on my way out, sir."

"Step in here a minute, we have something to discuss."

That didn't sound good. His father never indulged in
idle conversation so "something to discuss" meant a conversation of some significance.

Sean stepped through the doors into the study. Testos-
terone practically dripped from the walls in this room. Three
of those walls were covered from floor to ceiling with solid
cherry bookcases filled with expensive leather-bound volumes.
The fourth wall, the one that faced the outside of the house,
contained a large stone fireplace flanked by floor-to-ceiling
windows with heavy drapes. Above the fireplace was a large
flat-screen television. His father was a faux intellectual; the
television received a lot more use than any of the books on the
shelves.

On the opposite side of the room facing the fireplace
was his father's large mahogany desk. Between the desk and
the fireplace were arranged a burgundy leather sofa and two
club chairs. You could almost picture burly men in tweed jack-
ets sitting there smoking cigars, sipping brandy and discussing
their next safari to Africa.

His father was seated behind the desk in a high-backed
leather chair, his thin lipless mouth a hard line, jaw set. Ryan
Hutchinson was a square, blocky man. Broad, square shoulders, thick neck supporting a cinderblock of a head. His arms
were thick and his powerful hands ended in thick sausage like
fingers. His entire presence projected strength, power and sin-
gleness of purpose.

In his youth he had used his physical strength to get what he wanted. As he aged, the declining strength had been supplemented by a strengthening will and the accumulation of professional and political power and influence.

Sean entered the room cautiously, like a dog that had just been caught soiling the carpet. He was in full fight or flight mode, emphasis on the flight. Dragging his sneakered feet, he stumbled slightly as he transitioned from the hardwood floor to the oriental rug in the center of the room.

His father had turned his attention to the computer screen on the right side of the mirror-like surface of the desk, one large sausage finger pecking at the keyboard.

"Look at the television, Sean, there is a little video I want to share with you." There was no humor or warmth in that voice; this definitely wasn't a "Hey check out the cool video I found on Youtube!" moment.

The TV screen flickered for a moment and then a grainy black and white image came into focus. Sean swallowed hard as he recognized his car; the shot was angled from above and behind the vehicle. Sean had a brief feeling of disorientation. When? Where? How? Then he noticed the trunk lid on the car in the video pop open and, as if in response, both doors of the car flew open and out jumped a grainy image of himself and Carter, followed by a straggling Danny.

He felt warmth rise inside him. All of a sudden it felt like there was too much saliva in his mouth. His stomach did a slow roll. Dampness began to spread in dark patches under his arms. By the time the video Sean and Carter had pulled bats out of the trunk he could feel a rivulet of sweat snaking down between his shoulder blades. There was a buzzing in his head; he could barely hear his father's voice through the static.

"It seems a few days ago some bum got hit by a truck downtown. Near the scene of the accident a security camera shot this video." As his father was talking, the video Sean and

Carter were running gleefully off-screen brandishing their bats. A moment later Danny followed, leaving his bat lying in the street.

Sean swallowed again, tried to gain some level of composure. He was not the most mentally agile person under the best of circumstances and this certainly didn't qualify as the best of circumstances. *Think, think, what would Carter do?*

"Wha-what does some bum have to do with us?" he started. For a moment he was afraid the camera was going to pan right and follow them up the street, but it stayed pointed at the car. "We were just chasing some street punks that threw bottles at my car."

He tried to keep his face neutral as he turned to meet his father's gaze. Despite his best efforts to remain calm, he could feel the back of his shirt sticking to him. He expected his father to slam a big meaty hand on the desk and bellow at him like a wounded bull. But what happened was far worse, no yelling, no gesticulating. He just sat there, his cold blue eyes staring at Sean. The voice, when it came, came in a whisper.

"I am warning you; do not play me for a fool. Better men than you have tried and failed. There is a witness that saw the whole thing, so why don't you try telling me the truth before I really become angry."

Sean's mind was racing. Had there been a witness? Was his father bluffing? If there was a witness, how much did they see? Left to his own devices, Sean would have caved at this point, but you couldn't spend as much time with Carter as he had and not have picked up a little bit of cunning. They had not seen anyone that night; chances were if there was a witness they had to be pretty far away. He still may be able to allay some of the accountability for what happened.

"All right, Dad, I'm sorry, I was scared. But we didn't hurt the guy, we were just trying to scare him. You know, havin' a little fun, just goofin' around, and I guess he had a heart attack or something. But he was gone and we never actually touched him."

Did he notice the slightest bit of hesitation in his father's gaze? He couldn't be sure and now was not the time to get cocky. He was still standing in the middle of a minefield.

Again the deliberate, controlled whisper. "So how did he end up under a truck?"

Sean was already overdrawn on his cunning account. The words began to spill out faster than his brain could edit them. "I don't know, I guess we panicked. I mean, when he fell he hit his head and had this huge bruise, and at first we tried to revive him, you know, CPR. But he wouldn't come around and then we were worried maybe we left evidence, you know, that CSI stuff, hair and clothing threads and stuff like that, and no one would believe he just died. So, we made it look like a traffic accident."

"You are either lying to me or you and your friends are some of the dumbest people to walk the streets of this city. Do you know what will happen to my career if this hits the papers? And your friend Carter, all of his father's money will not help him if this gets out. That will play real well on the front pages. 'Son of New York billionaire hunts the homeless.' My god, you boys are idiots!" Ryan Hutchinson's face had become a deep and mottled red. Sean thought he may be off the hook; the old guy was going to have a stroke.

"I swear, Dad, we didn't hurt him, he just died." If Sean was younger, he would have tried tears at this point, but now his father would just see it as weakness, though honestly he never felt more like crying in his entire life.

His father leaned forward, meaty hands pressed onto the desktop. He took a deep breath and his face began to return to an almost human color.

"You are very lucky there are people out there who understand who runs this city and brought this to me first. I am taking steps to clean this mess up and you boys have to do your part. You will say nothing about this, stay out of trouble, go about your business as if nothing has happened. What about this other boy? Who is he?"

"That's Danny Edwards."

"I know Carter can handle himself; he's a sly little bastard." Was that a hint of admiration in his father's voice? "What about this other kid? Can he be trusted to keep it together?"

Sean was about to tell his father that Danny would be fine, but he wasn't sure if the expression on his face would cooperate. "He should be okay, but he has been acting weird lately. You know, depressed."

"You and Carter better keep him in line. If he says the wrong thing to the wrong person, this could all blow up. Talk to him, threaten him, buy him off, do whatever needs to be done to ensure he stays quiet. Do we understand each other?"

Sean wasn't quite sure what his father meant by "whatever needs to be done" but he managed to mumble a "Yes, sir."

"What did you say?"

"Yes, sir," Sean repeated louder but not with much more confidence.

"No loose ends, I hate loose ends. All right, get out of here."

Sean felt a surge of relief and headed for the door. At the doorway something else occurred to him. He turned. "Are you going to tell Carter's dad?"

"I haven't decided yet. He does have a right to know. Let's see if you boys can do your part first. Maybe we won't have to get him involved."

Sean slipped through the doorway and headed for the front door, thankful for the quick escape.

2

Ryan Hutchinson watched his son scurry from the room like a frightened rabbit. A veteran of numerous police interrogations, he did not believe that the boys had not done anything more serious than try to scare this bum. They probably roughed him up a little bit and then maybe he did have a heart attack or stroked out or something. One thing he was sure of, the life of some bum was not worth ruining his career or his kid's future over. The guy had been put out of his misery, hadn't he?

He wasn't too concerned about Carter. From what he had seen, that kid had a well-honed survival instinct. He didn't know this Danny kid. Hopefully the boys could handle that situation. If not, things could get a lot trickier. The other loose ends, they were nothing he couldn't handle.

As for letting Carter's father know what happened…he would wait until he had everything sewed up. They had a close working relationship and shared the same vision for the city; a favor like this would ensure that relationship stayed close. There was nothing like having a multi-millionaire with tremendous political clout in your corner when it came time to cut the pie. If he handled this cleanly, and he had no intention of doing it otherwise, the gratitude and goodwill it would garner would be invaluable in the future.

CHAPTER 12

1

It had not been a red letter morning for law enforcement. Mike had intercepted Al as soon as he came in, informing him that the captain wanted to see them.

When they entered his office, Al could tell by the look on the captain's face that he wasn't going to like what he was about to hear.

"There's no way to sugarcoat this. I looked into getting a subpoena for the phone records you guys wanted and it isn't going to happen. No one wants to touch it, not with what we have; it is just too politically sensitive."

Al glanced over at Mike. "Did you fill him in about Barnes?"

Mike nodded. The captain added, "I know all about Barnes, they came to pick him up this morning."

"What?" Al said, leaning forward in his chair. "Pick him up for what? He was looking to make a deal. He saw what those boys did."

"I know what he said he saw; this was a separate matter. They came to get him for a line-up in Midtown. He is a suspect in a rape case."

"What about our case, Captain? Barnes not only puts our boys at the scene, but he saw them push the guy into the street. We are talking murder here, Captain, money and politics shouldn't matter."

"Look at this objectively, Al. A good lawyer will be able to get them off without breaking a sweat. What do you have? A video of some boys pulling bats out of a trunk, no proof that they did anything with those bats, no victim on the video. You don't have a body, so you don't have any physical evidence that anyone struck this homeless man with a bat."

"We have Barnes."

"A gang-banging, drug-dealing rapist, is your star witness and you are going to put his word up against the word of some Midtown private school kids. You'll get laughed out of the courtroom. All of this is very flimsy; you've got nothing. Maybe if this was three regular Joes we could bring them in, question them, compare their stories, see if they contradict one another, get one to crack. But these aren't three regular Joes. Two of them are sons of two of the most influential men in this city, so unless one of these boys kills some bum in Macy's window, we aren't even going to be able to get charges filed, never mind a conviction."

And that had been it. Al didn't bring up his visitor from last night. Al was sure the guy had witnessed the crime itself or knew someone who did, and the guy had also indicated that it was three men who had committed the murder, backing up Barnes' story. But Al had no idea who the guy was or how to find him.

Now, as they sat at their desks, Al was still complaining about their meeting with the captain. "You know, Mike, when we were beat cops we'd end up arresting the same guys over and over again. As fast as we could bring them in the liberal judges would turn them loose. We'd end up arresting the same guy five, ten times. I thought when I made detective, when we were talking more serious crimes, things would be different.

We can't even question these guys. Justice for all means justice for everyone except the victims."

"Forget it, Jake, its Chinatown," Mike said.

"What the hell are you talking about?" Al responded.

"You know, from the movie *Chinatown*. Things are out of your control, even when you think you know what's going on you don't, the fix is in, powers behind the scenes are controlling everything, the average Joe doesn't stand a chance."

"You and your movies. Not everything can be explained by watching movies."

"You are wrong, my friend, there is a lot of wisdom in movies. But come on, you are taking this way too seriously. Are you still trying to 'make a difference'?" said Mike. "That is just a one-way ticket to frustration and disappointment. The whole point of being a cop is putting in your twenty years, getting as far up the ladder as you can to pump up the old pension and then retiring while you're still relatively young. None of this protect and serve shit. Get in, stay alive, cash in."

"That's your plan? And once you cash in, what are you going to do with yourself for the rest of your life?"

"That's easy, move to Jersey and buy a Dunkin Donuts."

"A what?" Al asked, sitting up in his chair, grinning slightly, his mood broken. "A cop with a donut shop. Isn't that just a little too ironic?"

"No way, man. A Dunkin Donuts is the way to go."

"Why Dunkin Donuts? At least upgrade to a Starbucks—though does Starbucks even do franchises? I'm not sure."

"Doesn't matter, not interested, not my type of people," Mike said. "Have you ever looked in a Starbucks? They are full of yuppies in suits, preppies, and hipsters dressed like Euro-trash in their scarves and skinny jeans, all staring at their cell phones and lap-tops. Now a Dunkin Donuts, you get your construction workers, your truck drivers, teachers stopping in to get a box of donuts for the faculty room, you know, normal people."

"Do you ever actually think about the stuff that comes out of your mouth before you say it?" Al said, laughing now.

"I try not to," Mike replied, smiling himself. "I find too much analysis stifles the flow of creativity."

"And this river of creativity led you to a Dunkin Donuts in Jersey?"

"That's right partner, some of the best ideas are the simplest. They're right there in front of you."

They were both laughing now but Al knew his frustration with how things had gone with the case was not going to go away.

To that end, before he left for the day, he made a call to the precinct that covered his neighborhood and gave them a description of his visitor from last night. It was a long shot but maybe if he could bring the guy in and get something out of him, he might be able to get the captain to reconsider his stance on moving forward.

2

Al lay on his back in bed, staring at the ceiling, the faint scent of sex in the air. He was naked except for the tangle of bed sheet wrapped around his right leg and Carrie's own leg draped over his left. She was on her side facing him, her long nails grazing his chest in lazy circles.

"You have a little pent-up hostility there, Alphonse?"

"What do you mean?"

"Well, you were a little rough there, cowboy."

"Yeah, I guess I do. Sorry."

"I didn't say I was complaining, just wondering. Anything you want to talk about?"

"Just this case I was working on. I can't go into too much detail, and whatever I tell you stays between us, but it involves a couple of our city's most privileged, and I am getting stonewalled." He then gave her the highlights of his futile attempts to move the investigation against Hutchinson and Stevens along, without getting into specifics on what he was investigating them for.

Carrie started to laugh.

"I am glad my frustration amuses you," Al said, raising one eyebrow as he turned in her direction.

"Sorry, baby, but you really have to get your nose out of your precious streets once in a while and look around. You want to investigate Charles Stevens and Ryan Hutchinson's sons and you went to the DA's office with it. The DA's office headed by DA Bill Branson."

"Yeah, that's right."

"Al, my firm does a lot of business with the city. We know what goes on behind closed doors in those smoky rooms where deals are made. My colleagues in that area refer to Stevens, Hutchinson and Branson as the Holy Trinity. Those three are thick as thieves. Rumor has it that Branson is looking to run for mayor, he has Hutchinson's and the cops' support and he is being bankrolled by Stevens. Those three have this city tied up in a bow."

"How is that kind of big money cronyism possible in this day and age with all the unions, watchdog organizations and advocacy groups?"

"Wow, baby, you are naïve. The heads of those organizations love it. Oh yeah, sure, they will rail against big money, make empty speeches, make a lot of noise without actually accomplishing anything. You can't justify your existence or convince poor people to give you millions of dollars in fives and tens to fight the boogieman if there is no boogieman to fight. So they protest, they make noise, but they don't want real change because the status quo allows them to line their pockets with other people's money."

"Wow. For a young girl you are very cynical."

"Just telling it like it is, Al. Anytime someone in this city tells you they are doing something to help you, hold on to your wallet."

CHAPTER 13

1

William Mitchell III sat enjoying the crisp air and feeling the warmth of the sun on his round cheeks. His au pair, Brigitte, had brought him to their usual spot in the park, a large area of grass that, except for paths leading in and out on either side, was almost completely encircled by a sidewalk and, just past the sidewalk, a thick hedge. William knew the rules; he was to stay on the grass, not cross the sidewalk. He was deep into his terrible threes so rules were sometimes things to be followed and other times challenges to be overcome.

But for now he was proud of himself; he was being very good. He surveyed the area through a pair of bright blue eyes that peered from beneath a great shock of red curls. He didn't understand how lucky he was or how his looks played into it; all he knew was that every adult he met smiled at him and treated him with kindness.

Brigitte was talking to her friend Simone. Natalie, the little girl who Simone watched, sat near their feet playing with her doll.

William did not like Natalie. She was mean. When she was mad about something she didn't use her words, she pinched. William always used his words, well at least most of the time, but sometimes words just weren't enough.

He had grown tired of playing with the trucks he had brought and he sure wasn't going to go near Natalie and her doll. He carefully stood. He had pretty good balance but you couldn't be too careful; every once in a while he would tip over. Standing there, back straight, belly out, deliberately brushing his hands together, he surveyed his surroundings.

Then he spotted it, stuck under one of the hedges: a blue ball. It looked kind of old and dirty, but William was a sucker for a ball. He found their attraction almost irresistible. One problem—the ball was stuck under the hedge on the other side of the sidewalk. He was not allowed to leave the grass or cross the sidewalk.

He looked carefully back at Brigitte. She was still sitting on the bench talking to Simone. William could hear their soothing female voices and musical laughter. Those sounds made him smile. They made him feel safe and warm. He almost went over to them; maybe he could join in the fun. But then he glanced back and saw the ball again and the fun it promised.

He walked deliberately across the grass to the edge of the sidewalk. There he stopped and looked back at Brigitte. She was still involved in her conversation and did not look his way. He continued to watch her as he slowly lifted one sneakered foot. The foot hesitated in the air for a moment and then he placed it firmly on the sidewalk. He expected Brigitte's head to snap around and her to change from happy, chatting Brigitte to mad, scolding, disappointed-in-him Brigitte.

But nothing happened. He took a step, then another step. He was no longer looking back at Brigitte; the magnetism of the ball had pulled his eyes to it. They were fixed on his prize. He walked carefully across the sidewalk, hands outstretched like some preschool zombie. He got to the grass on the other side and carefully squatted down, hands out, to grasp each side of the ball.

Suddenly there was a rustling sound. Two large, grey, gnarled hands shot through the branches of the hedge and grabbed William by the wrists. Before he could even register what was happening he was yanked through the hedge, branches scratching those perfect cheeks. His clothes snagged for a second and he was stuck in the hedge. Then there was another violent yank and he burst through to the other side.

A hand rough as tree bark and smelling like dirt clamped over his mouth. An arm was wrapped around him, pinning his arms to his side.

His eyes, wide now with terror, stared up into a face that was very different than the warm, loving faces that had occupied his world up to this point. This face was grey, the skin tight and rough. The mouth was not a warm smile but a sneer, and the eyes were filled with hate.

The arm around his body let go but his head was still held in a viselike grip. Then he saw the free hand come up. It was holding a role of that silver tape that his daddy used sometimes. The name always made him laugh—"duck tape". His captor grabbed the end of the tape with sharp strong teeth, pulled out a length, then quickly removing his hand slapped the tape over William's mouth. William could hear the ripping sound the tape made as it was wrapped around and around his head.

William was starting to fade now, his body's defenses kicking in. He became very still, his limbs getting rigid, eyes staring, almost catatonic. He barely noticed his assailant lifting old clothes and rags from a cart next to him, the kind of cart with a seat that William rode in when his mommy went food shopping.

He was lifted, placed in the bottom of the cart, and musty-smelling clothes were piled on top of him. It smelled but it felt warm, he felt hidden; he began to slip further away, deeper, safer.

Sounding muffled and very far away he could hear Brigitte's voice calling "William! Willie! Don't play games! Please!"

2

Brigitte was frantic, running back and forth wild-eyed, looking under benches, scanning the park. Simone clutched Natalie close to her breast, casting her eyes about, looking for any glimpse of red curls.

Other people began to run over, alarmed by the obvious panic in the young girl's voice.

No one paid attention to the bag lady in the large rumpled coat, wild grey hair sticking out from beneath a floppy wide-brimmed hat, wheeling a rickety cart with a squeaking, complaining wheel toward the exit to the park.

3

Fifteen-year-old Carmella Manfradi glanced furtively to the left and right before swinging open the board in the fence and slipping into the vacant lot beyond. The board was nailed at the top, but the nails had been removed from the bottom so that it could slide open and then be put easily back in place. Carmella and her friends used the empty lot as a hangout. The perimeter of the lot was overgrown with high weeds and strewn with trash, but they had cleared out a small space in the center and set up some beat-up metal chairs they had salvaged from one of the abandoned buildings that bordered three sides of the space. Their furniture had included a musty old couch, but that soon became bug- and mouse-infested and had been moved to languish amongst the weeds at the back of the lot.

She and her friends would hang out here sometimes on weekends, but usually they used the spot during the week for those times they cut class. They would sit around just talking, fooling around and occasionally, when someone got their hands on some pot, getting high. They also had broken into the boarded-up side door of one of the buildings and would occasionally go in there when it rained. But generally they avoided the buildings because there were times when addicts or homeless people were there.

Getting high was exactly what was on Carmella's mind today. Her friend Rosa had scored some pot and had said to meet her here at 3:15. Carmella looked at her phone—it was 3:30—and then looked around. No Rosa. She sat in one of the chairs, folding her arms in frustration. She was not the most patient person in the world and had purposely shown up a little late so she wouldn't have to wait.

Carmella sat uncomfortably on the cold metal chair. To make matters worse, a cold breeze found its way between the buildings to swirl around the lot, rustling the dry, dead weeds. Five minutes passed. Ten. She was just about to give up when she saw the board in the fence swing open. It was not Rosa who stepped through the opening. It was a stocky guy, average height, with dark, close-cropped hair. He wore a dark pea coat and jeans. He started to walk over, shoulders slightly hunched as if from the cold, hands crammed in his pockets.

"Hey there," he said, a slight smile playing across his face. "I've been noticing you and your friends sneaking in here."

Carmella was no fool. Alarm bells began to go off in her head. She slowly stood up, trying to appear calm. Since the guy was between her and the fence, she quickly calculated the distance to the side door of the building on the right. Unfortunately those calculations did not come out in her favor.

"What do you want?" she said, trying to keep her voice from wavering.

"Whoa, calm down there. I just wanted to talk to you for a little while. No harm in talking, is there?" He came closer, casually, almost too casually. It appeared more like stalking than walking.

Carmella backed up a step, bumping into the chair, knocking it over. "I'm not in the mood to talk. Besides, a friend of mine will be here any minute, then I have to go."

"Well, I'll keep you company till she gets here. It's not safe for a pretty girl like you to be here all by yourself."

The warning bells going off in her head turned into a four-alarmer. She had to get past this guy; she had to get out. Carmella widened her stance, ready to break in either direction and gave a little feint to the right. The guy stutter-stepped and stayed in front of her.

"What's your problem? Don't be unfriendly. It's not nice when girls are unfriendly."

He was no more than ten feet away now. If she was going to make a break for it, she couldn't wait any longer. If she got past him she wouldn't have time to find the loose board, open it and get out. Would she be able to get over the fence? She had a feeling that the adrenalin now pumping through her veins may just give her the boost she needed.

She juked right and cut left. His hands came out of his pockets, arms wide as he tried to coral her. It was at that moment she noticed the knife in his left hand. It was small, probably a penknife, but long enough to cut her up pretty good.

He overstepped to his left and she saw her chance, breaking to his right side. Despite her complete lack of interest in participating in any sports, Carmella was a natural athlete and dashed wide of her assailant.

"You little bitch!" he yelled and half stumbled, half dove after her.

She would have made it past him except for her long hair. She would never find out if she could have made it over the fence; his outstretched hand grabbed a fistful of her hair and twisted it, violently snapping her head back.

Her scalp screamed in protest, but held, and she stumbled backwards toward him. She whimpered in pain, then opened her mouth to scream but instantly felt the point of the knife against her left cheek. She was facing away from him. He had gathered her hair, twisting it around his hand, reeling her in until he got to the base of her skull. He was pressed up against her bottom, left hand reaching around to press the knife to her face, hot breath on the back of her neck.

"Make a sound and I will slice you up and you won't be pretty no more," he whispered. "Do as I say and you will walk out of here the same slut you walked in. Give me a hard time and, well, let's just put it this way: Ain't nobody gonna ask you to the school dance."

He dragged her down to the ground by her hair, moving to his left and twisting his hand in her hair so that he could move around in front of her, stepping over her, straddling her, as she lowered to the ground. The entire time he kept the knife within inches of her face.

He sat back on his haunches, his weight now pinning her legs to the ground. She was flat on her back in the dirt, gravel and broken glass that covered the ground. She stared up at him, trembling, her eyes wide with fear. Her arms were free and her mouth wasn't covered but she dared not make a sound or try to push him off; one quick flick from that blade and he would open her face up.

His right hand still knotted in her hair, his weight pinning her down, he leaned forward. His face was now inches from hers. She could smell pizza on his breath. He brought the knife up, the point of the blade hovering over her right eye, so close she could not focus on it; it was a silvery grey blur.

"You do exactly as I say or I am going to pop your eyeball like a grape."

She began to tremble violently, uncontrollably. Tears began to spill down her cheeks, her lips quivering. "Don't hurt me. Please. Don't hurt me."

"That all depends on if you behave yourself and do what you're told."

"I'll do whatever you say. Just don't cut me."

"We'll start with those jeans of yours. You need to get them off. Now I'm gonna give you some space to do that, but don't get any ideas, you yell or scream or try to buck me off and I'm gonna take your eyes, and that's just for starters. Then I'm gonna start cutting."

Carmella let out a small whimper but managed not to scream. The tears were now streaming, running down the sides of her face; she could feel drops collecting in her ears.

He let go of her hair and used that hand to grab her by the throat. He then lifted his hips, putting his weight on his knees. "All right now get them jeans off, panties too." His breath was more ragged; he was getting excited, working himself up.

Carmella sobbed quietly. Her hands, shaking nervously, scrabbled through the dirt and gravel at her sides like two pale crippled spiders. They scrambled over her hips and began to fumble with the metal button at the waist of her jeans. Her fingers were twitching uncontrollably and she could not get a good grasp on the button to work it through the buttonhole.

She heard a snort of frustration from her assailant. "Hurry up. Maybe you need some motivation."

Carmella squeezed her eyes shut, expecting any moment to feel the bite of the blade. "No, no, please. I'm trying."

She heard mocking laughter but that was all. She tried to concentrate, to calm herself. Maybe this would all be over soon. Her fingers finally worked the button through and began to fumble with the zipper. After a few moments she worked it down far enough and hooked her thumbs into the waistband of her jeans and the panties underneath. She lifted her hips slightly and began to slide the garments down.

His breathing was becoming more labored and he leaned forward, nuzzling his face in the nape of her neck. She cringed from the contact but dared not push him away; the knife still hovered menacingly over her right eye.

Her jeans and underwear were now below her hips, she could feel the gravel and broken glass biting into her naked buttocks. She felt so vulnerable, so exposed; a wave of shame and humiliation washed over her and she began to sob louder.

The sound of her fear and degradation seemed to excite him more. He rose higher on his knees, reached down and yanked her pants further down her thighs. He then sat back on his haunches, pinning her with his weight, unbuttoned his coat and began fumbling with his belt buckle with one hand while still holding the knife in the other.

"All right, baby! Get ready for some fun. You be a good girl now and treat me right." Again the mocking laughter.

She lay there, too scared to move, eyes squeezed shut, crying, praying.

Suddenly she heard a startled yelp and felt his weight lift, no longer pinning her down. She heard scuffling and muffled grunts.

She opened her eyes and tried to see what was going on. A first all she could see through her tears was a blurry image of her attacker standing above her, arms flailing. Carmella wiped her eyes with a dirty, trembling hand and tried to blink away the tears.

He was standing above her, his right arm swinging, his feet shuffling in the dust trying to gain traction. Someone had grabbed him from behind. One large hand completely obscured the lower portion of his face, trapping his head and bending his neck at a painful angle. Another large hand had control of the hand with the knife. The arm stretched out and twisted.

The scuffle didn't last long. Carmella heard a sickening snapping sound and saw the fear in her attacker's eyes replaced by sheer pain. A muffled howl emerged from beneath the large hand covering his mouth. The arm attached to the knife hand was bent at an unnatural angle and appeared to have gone limp. At that moment, the hand with the knife, still in the grasp of his attacker, drove repeatedly into his chest as if he was doing some type of Roman salute over and over again.

His coat was open, exposing a blue work shirt underneath. With each salute the knife punched a hole in that shirt. Soon red flowers of blood blossomed across his chest.

The knife blade was not that long; each wound, though painful, was not fatal. But the assault continued. Like some kind of macabre sewing machine, the pistoning arm stitched its way up the man's chest until finally the blade was plunged into his exposed throat.

A fountain of blood shot out, spattering Carmella where she sat, a wide-eyed witness to the deadly struggle before her. After the initial burst, the fountain subsided to a gurgling red flow that quickly soaked the front of his shirt, drowning the blood flowers that had bloomed there moments before.

Her savior loosened his grip and her would-be rapist slumped to the ground in a pool of his own blood. Carmella sat up, still trembling, still scared. She felt relieved; however, the violence of her deliverance left her stunned.

The man standing above her seemed to be a street person. His clothes were dirty and rumpled; on his feet were a worn-out pair of black sneakers. The baseball cap on his head was oily and soiled. He was standing there looking down at the body, the brim of his hat obscuring his features.

He carefully stepped over the corpse, stood over Carmella and offered her his hand, the one that was not soaked in blood. She looked at that hand as it hung in front of her. It was large, the skin dirty and grey. The fingers looked like knotted tree branches, rough and calloused.

She remembered her jeans and quickly pulled them up to cover herself, then accepted the offered hand.

He helped her to her feet. She found her legs to be unstable. Stumbling, she fell against the man, her face against his chest, and unable to help herself she burst into tears again.

Her hero's hands came up slowly. "Shhh, shhh, wee one, it's all right."

The hands moved slowly, cupping her face, gently stroking her cheek.

"Shhhhhh, it's all right."

She looked up at the face of her savior and froze. She was staring up into a pair of eyes. What should have been the whites of those eyes were a dull parchment yellow, the irises a darker mustard color. She opened her mouth to scream but one of those large hands slipped down and constricted her throat so all that came out was a strangled croak.

"Farewell my little one." The hands clamped on each side of her skull and suddenly twisted.

The last thing Carmella ever heard was the ratchet-like cracking of her own neck.

The last thing she ever saw, before her eyes went cold and dead, were the grimy bricks of the wall directly behind her.

4

Two boys were on basketball courts in the city. One was on a court in the Bronx, the other was on a court in Queens. One paced impatiently, bouncing a basketball every third or fourth step. One bounced his ball against the chain link fence that surrounded the court.

They were not much alike, these two boys. One was black, one was white, one did well in school, one was barely getting by, one was poor, and one was middle class.

But they had two things in common. Both were waiting for their best friend who promised to meet them on their respective courts after school. Both would not see their best friend that afternoon or ever again for that matter.

CHAPTER 14

1

Darnel Barnes was only slightly worried as he sat in the back of the squad car heading up to Midtown. The cops who had picked him up said they were bringing him for a lineup but he hadn't been involved in anything in Midtown for years.

He tried several times to engage them in conversation but they weren't in a conversational mood, had told him to shut up. They pulled into the garage under the station house. The cops got out of the car, and the tall black dude came and opened Darnel's door.

"Watch your head stepping out."

Darnel's hands were cuffed in front of him and the cop grabbed his right arm so he wouldn't lose his balance.

Once he was outside the car, the black cop let go of his arm and stepped back. "Mr. Barnes," said the other cop; he had come around the car behind Darnell.

As he turned toward him, Darnel heard the cop say, "I can't believe you went for my partner's gun."

"What?" Darnel asked. He now faced the cop and, looking down, saw the guy had his gun drawn. "What the fuck, is this some kind of joke?"

Echoing off the cement walls of the parking garage, the gunshot sounded more like a cannon. Darnel felt like he had been punched in the chest. He looked in disbelief; first at the smoking barrel of the policeman's gun and then down at the ragged hole in the middle of the spreading red stain on the front of his shirt.

Everything around him started to spin. He reached out a shaky hand, trying to grab hold of the police officer to steady himself. The cop stepped back just out of his reach. Everything went black as Darnel pitched face first onto the cement floor of the garage.

2

As Danny entered his family's apartment, he heard his mother call from the kitchen.

"Danny, is that you? You missed dinner again. Come in the kitchen, dear."

Danny wasn't in the mood for idle conversation about how his day had gone. His disposition had not changed since the night of the incident and he had been successfully avoiding contact with his family since then. He didn't feel completely confident that he wouldn't break down and spill the whole story if his mother or father pressed him regarding his depression.

As he entered the kitchen, his mind was scrambling for some kind of excuse so that he could make a quick exit. He rounded the corner and froze. There, seated at the kitchen table, having a bowl of ice cream, were his sister and Carter Stevens.

"Hey, buddy, how ya been?"

"Wha-What are you doing here?" was all Danny could muster.

"Carter drove your sister home from band practice. Saved me a trip, wasn't that nice, dear?"

"Yeah, I had stopped off at the school to visit one of my old teachers. Your sister was leaving when I was so we gave your mom a call and I ran her home." He was practically beaming handsome all-American wholesomeness.

"Wasn't that nice?" his mom repeated.

"Yeah…nice."

"Why don't you boys go in the den? Dan, honey, are you hungry? I could bring you a sandwich."

"No thanks, Mom; I grabbed something on the way home," Danny lied as he headed for the hallway and the double doors that led to the den with its comfortable furniture and big screen TV.

Carter followed, thanking Dan's mother for the ice cream. She thanked him again for driving Dan's sister and he proclaimed that it was "No problem, no problem at all."

Danny zombie-walked into the den. The shock of finding Carter sitting in his kitchen was slowly giving way to feelings of fear and apprehension, but mostly anger.

Carter had turned to close the doors behind them. As soon as Danny heard the snick of the latch, he wheeled around and hissed, "You stay away from my little sister."

"Ho, slow down there, buddy, I was just being nice. Though it is amazing that in this day and age your sister just jumped into my car. If I hadn't made her call your mom, no one would have known she was with me."

"Even you aren't that low, to threaten a child."

"Who you calling low? And who's threatening, I'm just making an observation, that's all."

"You have a problem with me, that's fine, but leave my sister out of it. I'm warning you."

Carter seemed calm, almost amused by Dan's outburst. "Did you ever see *The Godfather II*, Danny boy?"

"What?" Dan said, confused by this comment from left field.

"*The Godfather II*. Great movie, I liked it even better than *Godfather I*. Anyway there is a character in the movie, Frank Pentangeli. Well old Frank, he gets mad at Michael Corleone and he decides he is going to testify against Michael. Make a long story short, some things happen and he changes his mind about testifying, and then Tom Hagen, you know, Robert Duvall, meets with him and explains to him how he can keep his family safe and cared for even though he is a traitor."

"Wow, very subtle, Carter. I am no traitor and I already told you I'm not telling anyone anything. As for what Robert Duvall says, I never watched two, only the first one, so I don't know what you are talking about, trying to come off like some movie villain hardass."

The smile faded from Carter's face and morphed into a cold hard sneer. "You are making me nervous. You're still moping around; even your mother told me she was glad I stopped by as it may cheer you up. You don't snap out of it and people are going to start asking questions and you might get stupid."

"You don't stay away from my sister and it won't take people pressing me for me to get 'stupid'."

"See, comments like that aren't helpful. Comments like that are troubling, even dangerous. Rent the movie, watch it, you may learn something."

With that, Carter turned and left the room. Danny could hear him saying goodbye to his mother and sister on his way out.

Danny stood there, fists clenched, helpless. He was trapped. Even if he did tell someone, go to the police, he felt Carter would be able to get out of it some way with his money and connections. Danny would only be screwing himself over; somehow they would dump it all on him. Maybe that was okay. He had played a part in it. He hadn't stopped what was happening; maybe he deserved to take the rap. He may feel better if he got what he deserved. He couldn't bear the guilt gnawing at his insides any longer. Maybe confessing would bring some relief.

3

Officer Scott Brody eased the police cruiser down the service road between several warehouses. He and his partner, Jose Ruiz, came down to this area of the waterfront periodically. Occasionally you would come across individuals attempting to help themselves to a truckload of merchandise; either that or the occasional drug transaction.

Some cops hated street patrol. Officer Brody loved it. The low rumble of the cruiser's engine, slowly gliding through the streets, like a shark hunting for prey.

They turned a corner. At first the street appeared empty, just dusty, litter-strewn asphalt between warehouses, the warehouse loading docks jutting out like parched, cracked tongues in front of the steel-shuttered mouths of the loading bays.

Several blocks up he noticed a group of people standing near the corner of one of the older abandoned warehouses. The structure probably hadn't been used in years; most of the windows high up on its discolored, cracked walls were busted. A couple of the loading bay doors appeared to be off their tracks, hanging crookedly.

The group looked pretty ragtag, probably using the building for shelter. He pointed it out to Ruiz.

"What do you think?"

"Screw it, I ain't in the mood to roust a bunch of bums. What's the point? They ain't hurtin' anybody."

Brody started to pull a U-turn, glancing up once more at the group in the distance. Suddenly one of them trotted forward a couple of steps and reared back like a quarterback launching a desperate Hail Mary in the closing seconds of a big game. Brody looked on, amused. If the guy was throwing something at them, good luck, he was well over a hundred yards away. Brody was amused right up until the moment the brick smashed the windshield of the cruiser. The crash made him jump in his seat as the windshield went white in a million spider web-like cracks.

He recovered quickly from the shock of the sudden impact. He hit the button bringing down the driver side window and stuck his head out to see as he hit the gas and shot down the street. Ruiz was on the car's PA system. "Hold it right there, don't anybody move."

Of course they all scattered like roaches when the lights were turned on. All except the brick thrower; he stood there defiantly as they roared closer.

The man just stood there, frozen, until they got within fifty yards. Then he suddenly bolted toward the abandoned building. Brody brought the car to a screeching halt just as the guy slipped through a gap left by one of the canted loading bay doors.

Both cops were out, bolting for the loading dock, the instant the cruiser stopped. Scrambling up on the cement dock, Ruiz right behind him, Brody approached the damaged door. Not taking any chances, he drew his gun and stood just to the left of the opening between the door and the wall. He looked in to the right, then flipped to the other side of the gap and checked left. He wasn't going to chance this guy hiding around the corner and braining him with a two by four.

The coast was clear, so he ducked through the opening, scanning the interior for his prey. There was plenty of light inside the building and he spotted the guy just as he slipped out through a small doorway on the far side of the building. *Man, that guy can move*, thought Brody. He was about to give chase but pulled up short as the details of the scene in front of him completely registered. Behind him Ruiz had just come through the opening and he could hear him gasp "Hoollly Shittt."

The interior of the building was well lit because, in addition to the busted and broken windows encircling the structure's walls high up near the ceiling, the ceiling itself had a huge hole in the center.

Large iron beams supported the roof, however the ceiling in the center had collapsed around several of these beams and the sunlight streamed through the huge opening in curtains of light. It was like being in the belly of a whale whose flesh had fallen away due to decay and you could see up through the ribs. The rancid smell in the building did nothing to dispel the illusion.

The sunlight pouring through the opening in broad golden beams illuminated a large blackened area on the warehouse's cement floor. Someone had had a large bonfire in the middle of the floor. The heat from the fire had blackened the cement and caused it to crack and buckle. Ash interspersed with large charred pieces of lumber—from here they looked like railroad ties—as well as the burnt remains of various pieces of furniture covered the center of the floor.

There were strange structures bridging the area blackened by the fire. Each one consisted of two vertical X-shaped crosses of iron, possibly rebar, holding up a horizontal bar. There were four of these.

Brody, forgetting momentarily about the brick thrower, walked forward slowly to get a closer look. Ruiz followed, neither saying a word; there was no sound except the shuffling of their feet.

Brody inspected the constructs over the burnt area. As he had suspected, they were composed of rebar. His foot hit something that rattled dryly along the cement. He looked down and realized the area around where the fire had been was littered with bones.

Brody called Ruiz over and stooped to have a closer look. The bones were not blackened like the wood; whatever they belonged to had not been consumed by the fire. They were, however, charred, and some had pieces of cooked meat and gristle still clinging to them.

"What the fuck, somebody have a luau in here?" said Ruiz.

"Look over there," said Brody, pointing to a small pile of bones. "That looks…"

"Human," Ruiz finished, and indeed it did appear to be a human pelvis with the top half of a shattered femur clinging to it by a burnt, twisted piece of gristle.

"And those things?" Brody asked, pointing to the rebar structures.

"Roasting spits," Ruiz answered.

CHAPTER 15

1

Al sat behind his desk, his mouth hanging open in disbelief. "You aren't serious?"

"As a heart attack," Mike answered. "Barnes got capped the other day. The idiot went after the gun of one of the guys taking him for that lineup. They didn't have a choice, they had to pop him."

Al sat there in silence for a moment. "Well that is just too convenient, don't you think?"

"What do you mean?"

"We have one witness linking the children of two of the most powerful men in this city to a murder, and yes, let's start calling it what it was, a murder, and that witness gets shot."

"Come on, Al, you can't believe this was some type of hit. I mean, you heard the captain, Barnes or no Barnes we didn't have enough to go forward."

"Yeah, not enough to go to court, but guys like that don't like bad publicity and Barnes' story was a whole shitload of bad publicity. If he had gone to the papers…" Al never finished his statement. At that moment, the captain came out of his office and addressed the room.

"Listen up, fellas."

There was the scuffling of feet and creaking of furniture as guys either took chairs or parked a buttock on a desk corner.

"This just broke this morning but I'm already getting a lot of pressure from above on this and once you hear the details you'll understand why. Seems like we have some real sick individuals on the loose. Well, sicker than usual. This morning, down near the waterfront in an abandoned warehouse, a couple of our officers came across a pretty fucked-up scene. There were human remains. The medical examiner will be performing their investigation and we will be getting more information but for now, from the size of some of those skeletal remains we know at least several of the victims appear to be children."

Sounds of shock and anger came from the detectives.

"It also appears there may have been cannibalism involved."

Again, the shocked response.

"This looks to be the act of more than one person. Maybe some type of cult or devil worship ceremony. Whatever it is, we want to get a jump on this so the brass wants a full court press on all missing child cases. It may be a while before we get a positive ID on the victims. The heads were not found at the scene, possibly an attempt by the perpetrators to thwart identification through dental records."

"What about fingerprints, Cap?"

"There wasn't enough flesh left on the remains to draw a print from. So like I said, we are not waiting for an ID of the victims. We want to look at every recent missing child case. Now, we had a ten-year-old reported missing yesterday. He was supposed to meet a friend to play basketball and never showed; nor did he come home last night. Marcus and Beth have already interviewed the family and will be following up with them again today but I want the rest of you guys to canvas the neighborhoods both around the family residence and around the kid's school. Obviously ask if anyone was seen with the child, but also any indication of suspicious persons in the area. So far we have been able to keep a lid on most of the details to avoid panic but we need answers and we need them fast."

He looked around the room, making sure everyone understood the urgency. "Any questions? Okay, let's hit the streets."

2

Al unlocked his door, hearing the liquid metallic snick of the latch. He pushed the door open, reached inside and flipped the switch for the foyer light.

The light from the tiny foyer cast a soft glow over the living room to his right. Straight ahead he could see up the hallway that led to his bedroom. Off the hallway, past the living room, were the kitchen and a spare bedroom he used as an office and for storage. The light barely penetrated into the hall; he could make out the entrance to the kitchen and the near side of the doorway to the spare room and that was it. The end of the hallway was shrouded in darkness.

It was cold in the place; the heat was probably out again. He was going to have to call the super. When he stepped into the living room he caught movement out of the corner of his eye. Al turned quickly, immediately feeling a jolt of adrenalin. The hairs on the back of his neck stood up. Across the living room the curtains from the window were gently undulating in the breeze. The window was broken.

The top pane of glass had been broken to get to the latch and the bottom pane had been raised. The breeze picked up and the curtains rose, settled and rose again. He could not see any evidence of the security bars that had been over the window.

Al went into a crouch and pulled his gun, cradling it easily in his two hands. He scanned the living room, which honestly didn't take too long. The room wasn't very large and there wasn't much furniture. There was a couch against the wall the room shared with the kitchen. On the opposite wall was a stereo cabinet under a wall-mounted flat screen television. Next to the couch was a small end table with a lamp. In front of it was an oval coffee table. Against the far wall, the one with the window, was an overstuffed chair with another end table next to it. This table contained a reading lamp that arched toward the chair. Not really a whole lot of places to hide. Al could tell, despite having only the foyer light to see by, that the room was empty.

He stood there for a moment, trying to control his breathing. He could hear the blood pulsing in his ears; his heart was beating rapidly. He listened intently. The only other sounds he could hear were the ticking sounds of the metal fins in the baseboard heat register expanding as the heat tried to battle the cold created by the broken window and the buzz of the old refrigerator in the kitchen.

He started to edge farther into the living room, keeping his eyes and his gun pointed toward the hallway. If there was anyone in the apartment, they were either in one of the other three rooms or in the hallway back in the shadows. The breeze from outside died momentarily, the curtains gave one last flutter and then hung limply from their rod. At that moment Al noticed a strange smell in the apartment, a thick cloying smell.

He headed toward the hallway, leading with his gun in his outstretched hands. He came alongside the entrance to the kitchen, pivoting neatly into the entryway. Even in the dim light he could see the kitchen was empty. However, the refrigerator door was open and the interior had been ransacked, the shelves pulled out and food was strewn about the kitchen floor.

He turned back toward the hallway and flipped a switch on the wall. The hallway light came on, and he paused, listening for any movement. Nothing. He approached the door to the spare bedroom and grabbed the doorknob firmly. Taking a deep breath, he turned the knob and threw the door open. The light from the hallway spilled into the room. Again, nothing, just the revolving Windows logo on the screen of his computer that sat on the desk facing the doorway.

Again he turned up the hallway toward his bedroom at the end. Carefully he approached the door, his nerves now thrumming like over-tight piano wires. He reached for the doorknob and repeated the procedure: quick turn of the knob, fling the door open, lead with his gun. He could see the bed and the left side of the room, both empty. The far side appeared empty but the light from the hallway struggled to illuminate it fully. Al flipped on the bedroom light, dispelling the shadows in the far corners. Nothing.

That left just the closet. He approached the closed closet door, reached for the doorknob. This time as he threw the door open he quickly crouched so he could see under the clothes hanging from the rod. There was no pair of intruder legs beneath the clothes. The closet was empty.

Whoever had broken into his apartment was no longer here.

Al went back down the hallway, gave the mess in the kitchen a quick glance and continued to the living room. He wanted to examine the broken window. As he entered the living room, he flipped on the light. He immediately noticed something he hadn't before in the paltry light from the foyer. On the couch were several bundles. Four, to be exact.

Al felt a sinking feeling in his stomach as he took in the shape of the four objects, individually wrapped in dirty grease-stained cloth, on his couch. They were round, like four melons lined in a row, their cloth wrappers dirty and frayed. Under each, a dark, oily-looking stain spread out on the couch cushion beneath.

There was a puff of breeze from the broken window that wafted over the melon-shaped bundles. Well, that explained where the foul odor was coming from. Al took a breath, held it and stepped forward. He reached toward the nearest parcel, grabbing a corner of the dirty cloth and slowly pulling it toward him.

The cloth began to unwrap, the object inside turning as he pulled. It tumbled free of the cloth and onto the couch, rolling against the back cushion. Al saw a thick shock of red curls, the bloody stump of a neck; mercifully the face was pressed against the back cushion of the couch.

Al took a step back, dropping the stained, filthy cloth to the floor. Then he noticed his coffee table. Across the surface of the table, written in what appeared to be dried blood, were the words:

I Am Many

3

Al was beat; the long day had bled into a long night. Once he had made the gruesome discovery in his apartment, he had called it in. Then he had gone over to the window. There was shattered glass on the sill and the floor beneath. The security bars were gone. They had been pulled right out of the wall. Jagged, broken brick showed where the bars had once been anchored. Al had stuck his head out the window, expecting to see the thick iron grid lying on the fire escape, but it was not. He leaned out the window farther and could just make them out on the ground two stories below.

He had then gone back across the living room, giving the couch a wide berth, and headed for the kitchen. He had planned on taking a closer look at the mess in there, but he spied a footprint in tomatoes smashed on the floor and, not wanting to disturb any evidence, thought better of it. At that point he had heard sirens in the distance getting closer, so he went back into the living room, sat in a chair facing the couch and stared at his grisly presents until the cops arrived.

He had been questioned by the detectives and had stayed around when the medical examiner showed up to answer any questions they might have. Then he had gotten a call from the captain telling him to come down the station to follow up.

He was surprised to see Mike at the station when he got there. He had given the captain and Mike a rundown on what he had observed at his place leading to the discovery of the four heads. The captain said the initial investigation indicated that the heads probably belonged to the remains found at the abandoned warehouse and those remains had, at least tentatively, been matched to four child abductions that had happened about the same time in different boroughs.

Al decided it was time to tell them about the encounters he had had with the guy from the alley. Needless to say, the captain wasn't too pleased. What had seemed to be just another street crazy had, in hindsight, taken on more significance.

Still, they couldn't be sure that Al's street loon was connected to the child murders.

"Do you think it was a disguise? That this guy was pretending to be a homeless person?" asked the captain.

"That was the strange thing. It was obvious from the way he talked and moved as he got more agitated that he was not how he first appeared, bent over and frail. His initial demeanor must have been an act."

"Why didn't you bring this up before?"

"Because I wasn't sure there was anything to it. You run into crazies on the street all the time; you can't raise an alarm every time."

"Normally I'd agree with you, but a street person saying crazy things is one thing, a guy pretending to be a street person, expressing interest in an investigation and making threats is a whole other area," the captain admonished. "And what did he say about the accident?"

"Honestly, his story backed up Barnes. That it was no accident, that three men had deliberately thrown that guy in front of that truck."

"And you think this guy could be responsible for those dead children?"

"Well, Captain, he said he was going to teach me a lesson and prove that he was not alone and that he was not powerless. Then those four heads show up in my apartment. If they do match the remains at the warehouse, and those are the children that all went missing on the same day at about the same time in different parts of the city…"

The captain finished Al's train of thought. "Not only could this not have been done by one person, it was a planned and coordinated operation. It certainly would demonstrate what he intended it to. Listen, there are some details I found out about a little while ago that we have not shared. It seems that a good many of the bones found in the warehouse had been gnawed, chewed on. Some of the bones had been splintered as if to get at the marrow. Now the lab guys were floating theories that maybe a pack of wild dogs had gotten to the remains before we got there."

"So what are you saying, Captain?"

"I'm saying there are a lot of unanswered questions about this case but we are dealing with some severely deranged individuals. Also, next to where the bodies had been roasted they found some of the bones spread out on the floor in a pattern."

"In a pattern you say,", said Al, fumbling with his phone. "Did it look something like this?" He showed the captain the picture of the soda can crop circles he had taken a picture of.

"Yes, exactly like that."

CHAPTER 16

1

Al and Mike were back at their desks packing up. Al had decided to head over to Carrie's to crash since he wasn't allowed back in his place yet due to the investigation.

They were about to head for the door when the phone rang in the captain's office. They froze, exchanging glances, both feeling this call was going to mean their night was not over.

Sure enough, the captain hung out of his doorway, phone against his ear, giving them the "hold on a minute" sign. He talked into the receiver for another minute or so, nodding and providing the occasional "uh huh". He stepped back into his office, motioning them over. He was just hanging up as they entered the room.

"That was the commissioner himself on the phone; this case is really hot. He wants us to wait here. He is putting a special investigator on the case; the guy's coming down now."

"Now?" said Al, thinking that there went what little chance he had to grab some sleep.

"It seems the preliminary blood tests support what everyone already expected: the heads found in your apartment belonged to the children found butchered in the warehouse down by the docks. The commissioner is concerned that this will cause a panic across the city. He wants this case locked down at least until we have a better idea of what we are dealing with. No talking to anyone outside the immediate investigation and definitely no press."

2

Al was again sitting in the captain's office, staring into a Styrofoam cup half full of cold coffee. Mike sat to his right, the captain behind his desk. He looked more unhappy than usual, maybe because he had been up all night, maybe because this case looked nasty and would probably get nastier before it was over, or maybe because he was pissed that one of the commissioner's pets had invaded his turf. Maybe it was a combination of all three.

The only other person in the office was the special investigator. Karl Schrager. Schrager was short, thin with a balding head and wireframe glasses. The guy looked like Himmler without the little mustache, more like a librarian than a policeman.

Schrager was not seated. He was standing next to the captain's desk, arms folded, the lips on his pinched face pursed in a disapproving manner.

"Again, Detective, why did you not bring this encounter to the attention of your superiors?"

Al sighed. He was physically tired and he was also tired of the third degree from this paper cop. The guy had been grilling Mike and him for a while now and it appeared he was more interested in finding someone to feed to the press as a scapegoat than catching the perpetrators. "We hear threats and outrageous claims on the street every day. I'm not going to waste the captain's time with every crazy who makes a threat. Even now we don't know for sure this guy is responsible."

"Well considering, Detective, that he seems to be targeting you alone and the remains of those children were found in your apartment, I would say the chances are pretty good he is to blame."

That was obviously true and Al was sorry he had inadvertently played Schrager's straight man; he must be more tired than he thought.

"Listen, we've been through this. What's done is done; I didn't think I had enough to bring it to the captain. That was my call. If I was wrong then fine, write me up, reprimand me, do whatever makes you happy, but we can't change that. But isn't the point of this little get-together to figure out what we are going to do now?"

The captain turned to Schrager. "If this person is responsible for the murdered children, and it would appear he is, he is not acting alone. Each child was abducted on the same day at approximately the same time in different boroughs. So we are looking for more than one person and I think we can throw out the notion that this guy is simply a homeless person." He turned back to Al. "What about this accident that he seems so interested in? What do we know?"

Al gave a rundown on all that he knew regarding the accident, what his pretend homeless guy had said about the accident and how his version seemed to be backed up by the claims made by Darnel Barnes but there was no concrete evidence to back up their stories. Knowing where Schrager's loyalties lay, Al left out any mention of the security tape and what was on it.

The captain shot a quick look in Al's direction, one that Al could not quite read. "Then we have to move on two fronts. We have to dig deeper into this accident, find out what really happened, find out who this guy was that was killed and if someone is responsible find out who it is, and we have to follow up on the evidence gathered at the warehouse and at your apartment, Al."

Al couldn't believe his ears. Knowing that the captain knew it may be the commissioner's own son that may be involved, he was going on a risky fishing expedition.

Schrager, who had been listening silently with arms folded, finger tapping his lower lip, rose to the bait like a large mouth bass. "I don't agree." he said. "Our primary objective should be to bring those responsible for the deaths of these children to justice as soon as possible. Any allocation of manpower that detracts from that effort is not permissible. The commissioner is adamant that the murdered children are the only priority at this time. In addition, the entire investigation must be kept quiet, until we have a resolution. No press leaks! We must avoid alarming the citizens."

Al noticed the muscles in the captain's jaw clench as he pressed on. "We should follow up on the accident as well. Find out what we can about the victim. That may give us some lead to this person who has been in contact with Detective Russo. He must have some connection to the victim of the accident."

Schrager's face flushed. "We will get to that person through a thorough investigation of the crime scene at the warehouse and the apartment. Detective Russo stated that the body from the accident is missing; there is nothing to follow up on at that end. I am here to find the murderer or murderers of those children and bring them to justice as soon as possible, not clean up every traffic accident on your docket, Captain."

"Now," he continued, "the commissioner has given authorization to deploy a special tactical unit. Now that our suspect has made his point to Detective Russo clear, he will be contacting him again to see if the detective is ready to cooperate. The special unit will closely monitor Detective Russo's movements and will be in position to execute the capture when he is contacted."

"I don't think it is going to be that easy. The last time he contacted me he had an escape route all planned. As soon as I tried to move on him, he dropped into a utility tunnel and was gone. He will have a similar escape route planned the next time he makes contact. Besides, don't we want to get all of them? If we move on him, the others will get spooked and we may never find them."

"What do you suggest, Al?" the captain asked.

"He is hung up on this accident. He thinks three guys were involved and he wants me to turn them over to him once they're caught. Let's play along, wait for him to contact me and make believe I am going to cooperate. We may be able to set up a sting and grab the whole bunch."

"We know this guy is crazy and you are gonna be on your own for this next meeting."

"I should be okay. He is crazy, but he is crazy with a purpose. He thinks I am the key to getting what he wants; I think I am safe as long as he thinks I am cooperating."

"He needs to be able to get in touch with you; we need to get you back into your apartment as soon as possible so this guy can find you," Schrager offered. "Captain, we'll have to get the investigation at the detective's apartment wrapped up so he can return."

"We'll get it wrapped up."

"Good, well I think that is it for this evening. See you in the morning, gentlemen. And may I remind you, do not speak of this to anyone. We must avoid panic at all cost." With that, Schrager walked out of the office, leaving the three sitting there staring after him.

"Captain, can I trust this guy? Do you think they know anything about the commissioner's son and the other kids?"

"I think they know. He was very sensitive whenever the accident was mentioned, however, I don't know if they know the tape exists and we are going to keep it that way. Let's not forget the main goal here really is catching those child killers. Bringing up the tape now will just make things more difficult. And I will deny I ever said this, but if you are out there working with Schrager and his men, you will be a lot safer if we don't mention the tape."

"That's real reassuring, Captain."

CHAPTER 17

1

Al had heard from Anne and Carrie, both giving him an earful for not contacting them before they saw his apartment on the five o'clock news. The level of true concern and caring in Carrie's voice made Al feel guilty about his plan to see Anne. He had felt a little underhanded when he originally made the plans but quieted his conscience by reminding himself that his and Carrie's relationship was casual, just for fun. However, the concern he heard in her voice made him feel like a heel anyway.

He told each of them only what had been released to the media: that human remains had been found in his apartment and that it was under investigation. He was reluctant to meet either of them considering he was probably being stalked by a psychopath. However, in talking this over with the captain and their new best friend Schrager, it was determined that he should behave as naturally as possible and that the chances were slim that he would be contacted when he was with someone else.

They wanted to control the situation as much as possible, which meant limiting the times he may be contacted, so for the next several days he rode a desk. The only time he left the station was to travel to and from his apartment.

Al was wired for these trips. He looked like ninety-nine percent of the New Yorkers walking the streets with earpieces or headsets on. The only difference was, instead of talking to a girlfriend or listening to Coldplay, he was either in contact with guys tailing him on the subway or guys with automatic weapons and body armor in a van parked on his street.

Several nights had gone by without any luck. Al memorized every door and alleyway he passed on his walks to and from the subway station. He started to play a little game with himself, laying odds as to where the contact would take place.

Finally, on the third night, as Al approached a boarded-up storefront, he noticed red painted letters on the plywood covering one of the windows. He was almost positive the painted letters had not been there the previous night. The message was clear:

RUSSO

His name was followed by an arrow pointing to the door of the store.

Al stepped toward the doorway. Not wanting to draw the attention of passersby, he peered through a crack between two boards as if he was just checking out the inside of the place. He waited for several people to pass. Once there was a break in the foot traffic, he tried the door. No surprise, it was open.

Al contacted his backup, giving them the store's address. "I'm going in. Get close but don't make a move unless you hear from me."

He glanced around once more to ensure there was no one close by. He pulled a small flashlight from his pocket and drew his gun. One more glance around, then he opened the door and slipped inside. Holding the flashlight next to the barrel of his raised weapon, he swept the interior of the store.

There was no one there. The store appeared to have been a jewelry store or pawn shop in its past life. There were dusty, finger-streaked glass counters on either side of the store and along the back wall. In the middle of the store was a pedestal supporting another, smaller display case, purportedly where high-end items would have been displayed. The floor surrounding the pedestal was covered in dust. There were no footprints in the dust on the floor and Al thought for a moment he had only imagined that his name had been painted outside.

But then he picked up something. In addition to the expected musty smell of a place that had been abandoned and boarded up, he detected a strong musky animal scent. He stood where he was, listening intently. He thought he could make out the sound of low, ragged breathing.

He heard a slight shuffling noise coming from the back of the store. Al shined his light in that direction and noticed a doorway in the back wall that he had not spotted before. The opening was obscured by a tattered and dusty curtain. The curtain was swaying slightly, and Al could feel cold air from that direction.

There were no doors or windows in either of the side walls of the shop. The only entrances were the one at his back and the curtained doorway straight ahead. Al kept the light and the gun pointed at that curtain.

"Detective. So you've come."

The voice was unmistakable. At the sound of it, a picture of those four stained bundles on Al's couch flashed through his mind. He fought the urge to pump several shots through the dusty cloth hanging before him. He had to remind himself that there were others. They needed to get them all.

Still, he couldn't resist saying, "Why innocent children? How do you expect me to deal with animals who would harm innocent children?"

"It is exactly for that reason that you are dealing with me now, is it not? It is all about balance and leverage. When we first met, you saw before you someone unworthy, someone who could be discounted. I had to demonstrate to you that that was not the case. I had to achieve balance between us and I had to apply leverage to bend you to my will. The very fact that you are now aware of what we are capable of is why we are talking. As for the fact that we used children for our demonstration, I do not know why that concerns you so. Children die in this city all the time, from sickness, being rundown in the streets, murdered by strangers, even their own parents kill them. What do four more or less matter?"

"And what about what we found in that warehouse?"

"More leverage. But I am not here to discuss these matters. Are you prepared to deliver the men I seek?"

"It's not that simple. I can't just drag three men through the streets and hand them over to you."

"How you do it is none of my concern. Once you are prepared to bring them to me, light a candle in the window of your rooms. I do not care if you bring the men to me one at a time or all at once, just as long as I have them all. Light the candle at night. The next day you will return here and will be given an address. You will bring them there. If you can't deliver them all the first time, we will follow the same approach the next time. The location will change each time."

Al frowned at the curtain. "All right, but you have to give me some time after I know the location before we meet. I will need time to figure out a way to get them to you. Like I said, this is not going to be easy."

He heard that frustrated chuffing sound from behind the cloth. "Very well, once you have the location you will have one day to bring them there. But I warn you, if you try to betray us, or if you make this known to anyone else, we will know. You cannot possibly fathom the consequences of such a betrayal."

Al was about to ask "What consequences?" when he heard a door shut and a slight gust puffed out the curtain before it fell back straight and still. Al realized he was alone. He had all the information he was going to get.

2

Sean looked nervously at Carter. There was a storm brewing behind those cold blue eyes and Sean wished he could evacuate before it made landfall.

"Your father knew, or he suspected, and you rolled over like some little pussy?"

"No, he knew, honest, he knew the whole thing. He had a video; we were all in it, plus my car."

"Us and the car. Did it actually show what we did?"

"No, no, it didn't. It just showed us getting the bats out of the trunk. Everything else was off camera. I told him we just wanted to scare the guy and he had a heart attack or something. That was good, right? I did the right thing?"

"If he had a heart attack, how did he get out in the street, genius?"

Sean's still looked hopeful. "Well I said we panicked, thought we might get blamed, so we made it look like a traffic accident."

"If we hadn't touched the guy, why wouldn't we have just left?"

"Because we tried to revive him and we thought we might have left, you know, CSI stuff on him," Sean said, his voice fading along with his confidence.

"CSI stuff, CSI stuff, how stupid are you? And if we did try to revive him, why wouldn't we have just put the bats back in the car, dialed 911 and said we found him and tried to help him!"

"Well I, I didn't really think…"

"You're right, you didn't think, you dumb shit. Well think now. Do you think your father is stupid enough to believe that story? Or do you think he knows you're lying and he knows we caused that guy's death?"

"Well he didn't say he didn't believe me and he said he had people handling it. And he's worried about Danny," Sean added, trying to shift the attention from himself. "Said we should handle it, make sure he doesn't crack."

"I'm worried about him too. I tried to put a scare in him, but I don't know. We may have to get rough."

"What do you have in mind?"

Carter ignored the question. "What about my dad? Did your father say anything about telling him?"

"No, he didn't. He probably doesn't want to get him involved, wants to handle it on his own."

"I doubt it. Your father isn't as stupid as you and he's ambitious. He's gonna use this as leverage at some point."

Carter seemed to consider this for a moment; he cast a glance Sean's way.

Carter had to be careful here. He wasn't concerned with Sean; Sean was as dumb as a box of rocks. It was his father he was concerned about. What did he mean he was going to "handle" it? Was he going to clean things up behind the scenes, sweep all evidence under the rug? Then tell Carter's father what a great job he did and hope it led to favors down the road? Or was he going to spin things so most of the blame would fall on Carter, make him the scapegoat to get his son off? Maybe have his son and Danny turn state witness against

Carter? Carter's dad had money but Sean's dad had the entire police department at his disposal.

No, that didn't ring true. Someone as ambitious as Sean's father would want to avoid any hint of scandal. Even if he got his son off, having him associated in any way with such an incident would be very damaging to those ambitions. Still, Carter had to make sure; he had to show he was part of the solution, not part of the problem.

"Set up a meeting for me with your father."

Sean choked and sputtered in surprise. "You want to meet with my father? Are you sure?" Sean avoided contact with his old man at all cost; he couldn't imagine someone, especially just a kid, wanting to meet with him on purpose.

"Yes I'm sure. We have a mutual problem we need to discuss."

3

Al, Schrager, the captain and Sergeant Tasker, the CO of the tactical unit that was assigned to the case, had been debating how to proceed for over an hour. They listened to the tape of Al's encounter and then began to float plans for their next move.

"He doesn't appear to be too bright," Schrager said. "How would he seriously expect you, one man, to pull this off and keep it a secret? It's virtually impossible."

"Yeah, that is one thing that is bugging me. He is obviously crazy but he doesn't come off as delusional. He has to see that what he is asking is ridiculous. But he doesn't seem to care; he expects what he expects and the how is my problem."

"Well, we should play along. We give him what he wants. We set up a meeting and have undercovers pose as the perps. They will be armed, of course, and that will give us plenty of firepower onsite," said Schrager.

"Yeah, but we have to be careful we don't tip our hand."

"How do you mean?"

"Well, for example, we are obviously not apprehending anyone. We still have to make it look good. We should let a few days pass before we contact him to give the illusion I needed time to pull things together to be able to hand these guys over to him. If it all comes together too quickly he is going to expect it's a setup."

"I don't want any delays. As long as these people are on the loose we could have another situation."

"I don't think so, I agree with Al," the captain said. "As long as they think Al is cooperating, I think Al is right. We have to go through the motions to make this look legit. I am also concerned about turning over all three people they are expecting at once. Are they really going to believe that Al singlehandedly rounded up all three at once and delivered them without outside help? Won't that raise alarms?"

"We will have to take that chance," Schrager said. "I want to ensure we have enough firepower on site if it is needed. I'm standing firm on that. Wherever the transfer is supposed to take place, they will probably have the immediate area under surveillance. Any backup is going to have to come from blocks away so we don't tip our hand. That means Russo and the undercovers are going to have to be able to hold their own for five, ten minutes. Four have a better chance than two or three of doing that. The last thing I need is for these men to end up on roasting spits."

"I can appreciate that," Al said.

"We aren't going to have much time to plan this," Tasker chimed in. "We know they have used the tunnels to get around, so we are going to have to ensure we have those covered. Wherever the transfer is, we are going to have to have schematics of the underground in the area in addition to street maps so we can lay out our approach."

"Most of those records are electronic now; we'll reach out to the appropriate agencies to make sure we have access when we need it," said Schrager. "I think that's it for now. We will get things lined up on our end and then have Russo set things in motion."

Al was glad for the delay; he was going to be in the middle of this and he had no delusions regarding the danger he was going to be in. Though part of him fed off situations like this, he was happy for the time to touch base with those he cared about. He had a dinner planned with Carrie tonight and tomorrow was Thursday; his date with Anne.

The feeling of being a heel crept up again, but he did his best to suppress it. He owed it to both of them to sort things out, to be sure of how he felt, didn't he? It may make him feel like a creep now but it would be better in the long run.

CHAPTER 18

1

Carrie was running late. Dinner the previous night with Al had been strange to say the least. He seemed distant, preoccupied. She had pressed him about the gruesome discovery in his apartment. There hadn't been much in the papers, just that there were human remains and that it was being investigated.

Al swore her to secrecy and then revealed that the police thought it was a drug ring sending a message; they just had the wrong address. Carrie was not a stupid person. That didn't ring true. There was more to it than that, and the more to it was probably the reason Al seemed so distracted.

But since he assured her he had been off the streets working a desk all week and that they had his apartment under surveillance, she wasn't too worried. After dinner they had gone back to Carrie's apartment and had sex. Nothing seemed to distract Al when it came to that, she noticed.

He had stayed over. Al woke before her and had showered and dressed, letting her sleep. He was almost out the door when he came back, lifted the pillow she had pulled over her head to drown out the noise of him getting ready, and made her promise to take a cab.

"Why a cab?" she mumbled.

"There's been trouble in this neighborhood lately. Humor me and call a cab, have them pick you up at the door."

"Yeah, sure, okay."

But now, showered and dressed herself and looking out the window at the cold, crisp sunny morning, it just seemed silly. The subway was literally two blocks away. Even though she had woken in plenty of time to get to her own job she had lingered in bed. She didn't have time to call a cab and wait for it to show up.

She made up her mind; it was only two blocks. Carrie scooped up her bag and headed for the door.

2

Thursday evening had finally arrived. Anne had insisted they meet at the restaurant; no awkward doorstep goodnights tonight. Despite the cold, Al waited on the sidewalk in front of the Italian restaurant in Little Italy they had chosen for their date. Was it really a date? Al wasn't sure Anne saw it that way.

Al had been looking forward to this night all week and he actually found that he was nervous. He hoped he wouldn't blow it.

On top of everything else, it had been decided that tonight would be the night they would send the signal. Considering the chain of events that would set in motion, Al was going to have a hard time giving Anne his undivided attention.

Even as he stood here in nervous anticipation of her arrival, his mind kept going over the details of the operation that would start with the sending of that signal. Al had been involved in several raids and sting operations in the past and he always felt the same before each one. It brought him back to when he was a kid, the first time he rode the Cyclone at Coney Island. His feelings of anticipation and trepidation had grown with each clack of the chain hauling the coaster to the top of that first hill. Clack, clack, clack, higher and higher with no way to get off, no way to stop it, no turning back. His nerves were drawn taught, vibrating like piano wire as it reached the summit. Nothing could stop it; he was committed to plunge into the drop and all that followed. Then had come the release and the flood of adrenalin as the coaster screamed down that first hill, and Al was hooked. The signal tonight, the candle in the window, would bring the coaster to the summit; there would be no turning back.

Al had to try to put the operation out of his mind for tonight. His preoccupation with the job had been one of the things that had caused friction between him and Anne in the past; it wouldn't be good to have it interfere tonight. He had to try to let it go for a few hours.

He saw her then, coming down the street, and breathed a sigh of relief. It wasn't till that moment he realized he had been afraid she wouldn't show. But here she was, petite despite her long legs, an anxious look on her pretty face. Anne hated being late and she was weaving through the scattered pedestrians between her and the restaurant, like a slalom skier, trying to make up time.

She looked up as she got close, saw him and smiled that slightly crooked, sexy smile. "Sorry," she mouthed as she got closer.

When she was close enough, Al said, "Hi," and kissed her on the cheek. He slipped an arm around her slender waist, something he had done hundreds of times in his life, but this time it felt new, like it was the first time. He cursed himself under his breath. He was a world-weary, jaded cop and here he was feeling like a nervous teenager.

"Have you been waiting long?" Anne asked.

"Not long, but we better get inside. They're holding our reservation." He opened the door and with his hand in the small of her back ushered her through it. It felt natural, it felt right.

3

Al and Anne had a pleasant dinner together, each trying hard to keep the conversation light. There was a lot of history between them, many good times but also hurt feelings and things said not easily forgiven. This was not the time to dredge up the past but to carefully, patiently see if there was a way forward.

Al did a good job through dinner of keeping his focus on Anne. But as it got later he found thoughts of the pending operation competing for his attention. He heard the clack, clack, clack; he was getting closer to the summit.

Anne sat back in her seat, studying him closely. "Al, you have something on your mind, don't you? Something at work? It's dangerous, isn't it?"

"What? No, it's nothing really." She was always good at reading him and obviously hadn't lost the knack.

"Al, don't kid me, I've been around you long enough. When something big is about to go down, you get preoccupied. That's probably a good thing, keeps you prepared, keeps you safe, but it is noticeable."

"Okay, yeah, there is something we're running but it's pretty simple, not really dangerous."

She stared at him for a moment and he felt she probably didn't believe him about the danger.

"Don't take this the wrong way, I had a great time, but maybe we better call it a night."

"Why, because I have a little something on my mind?"

"No, and that's exactly what I meant about taking it the wrong way. I said I had a great time and I meant it. I've missed

151

you, Al, more than you can imagine. But I also know how you get before a dangerous assignment. You're an action junkie. Not all of our problems in the past were your fault, you know. Don't smirk." She laughed. "Most of them were, but not all. I've grown since then too. In the past I would get upset if you were preoccupied with work, but I want you to be safe and I realize now that that preoccupation is what helps keep you safe. If you've got something important going on, you need to focus, not sit here trying to pretend you don't just to make me happy. If something happened to you I wouldn't be able to forgive myself."

The concern on her face made Al feel good. "Can we do this again? Soon?"

"Sure, Al, I'd like that. But now I think I better head home and you better make sure you're prepared for whatever it is you're involved in. Please call me when it's over and let me know you're okay."

"I'll be fine, but I will call, I promise."

4

Al stood in the darkened window of his apartment, studying the street. It was late; the amount of foot traffic on the sidewalks below was minimal.

Al placed a candlestick holder he had picked up in the drugstore up the street on the window sill. He stuck the candle he had gotten at the same store into the holder. He fumbled with a book of matches, lit it, then backed away from the window and walked around the bed to the window on the other side.

The bedroom was dark except for the light from the candle. Al stood back in the darkness and watched the street below. At first he didn't see anything unusual—some couples strolling down the street, probably coming from a nice dinner at the restaurant up the block. A group of guys in their twenties, laughing and joking, emerged from the bar several doors down.

Then he noticed a stooped figure in a long grey coat shuffle and weave out from a doorway across the street. The one couple in his path gave him a wide berth. Even the guys grew silent and averted their eyes or gave furtive glances as their group split wide to pass on either side of the shambling figure.

The shadow man stopped under the streetlight and looked up in Al's direction. For a moment Al thought the man below must see him and he stepped farther back into the dark. But then he thought he was being silly, it was just the candle he was looking at.

By a weird trick of the lighting on the street, two eyes seemed to glow a dull amber below the hood covering the head of the man below. Then he turned and shambled away into the night.

Clack, clack, clack, there was no turning back.

CHAPTER 19

1

Danny lay in his bed staring up at the ceiling. On that ceiling, the scene that had haunted him day and night since his life had been changed forever was playing out. He could see the gloved hand reaching for the top of the cart. He could see the head slowly lifting. Then the truck hit and the image shredded like fog in a light wind.

Would he ever be able to get rid of those images? He couldn't eat, he couldn't sleep, he found he couldn't concentrate in school and his grades were suffering. The worst part of it was he couldn't talk to anyone about it.

He couldn't tell anyone in his family. He wouldn't be able to handle the consequences. His parents were the most decent, honorable people he knew. They would be disgusted by what he had done. They would never be able to speak to him again. How could they love someone who would do something so despicable? This was what he feared most of all: losing their respect and their love.

The scene started again on its endless loop. The cart, the hand, the head. This time the truck's air horn was blaring loudly as it approached. The blare became a buzz, buzzing, over and over, buzzing, buzzing, buzzing.

Danny, shaking himself out of his torpor, realized it was the doorbell. Whoever it was wasn't going away. Each buzz became longer, more insistent.

Danny hauled himself off the bed. He was barefoot, dressed in an old sweatshirt and baggy grey sweat pants. It was his usual outfit when he had a cold or the flu or was responsible for the death of another human being. He shuffled toward the front door, flipped the latch and opened it, not taking the precaution of using the chain. Who cared.

Carter was standing in the hallway. *How did he get in the building?* Danny wondered. That was quickly followed by the answer. *Oh yeah, his father owns it.*

Carter came in and threw an arm around Danny's shoulders. "How's it going, Danny boy? You're not still moping around, are you?"

"Carter, why don't you leave me alone?" Danny offered in the tired monotone that had become his normal speaking voice lately. "I told you I wasn't going to say anything."

Carter looked around nervously. "Will you watch what you say?"

"Relax, nobody's home but me. And I told you, I'm not saying anything to anybody. I just can't shake this feeling. Doesn't what we did bother you? Aren't you sickened by it?"

"No, and I'll tell you why," Carter said, his arm still draped across Danny's shoulders, as he guided him across the living room. "The way I see it, we did that guy a favor. He was leading a miserable existence. Living on the street, cold, dirty, hungry; suffering every day. We put an end to all that. Come on, let's get some fresh air. You'll feel better." He slid open the glass doors and they both stepped out onto the terrace, the cold air stinging their faces.

The wind in his face and the cold of the travertine terrace floor on his bare feet began to penetrate the fog in his head. Why was Carter bringing him out on the terrace? *Maybe*

155

he wants to throw you off, make sure you stay quiet for good. Danny felt Carter was capable of many things; that had been proven already, hadn't it? But could he really murder someone he knew, someone who had been a friend? Danny wasn't sure he knew the answer and, what's more, he wasn't sure he cared.

He let himself be led to the railing. "Look at all those people down there," Carter was saying. "We are up here above them for a reason, Dan. No matter what crap society fills your head with, there are some that are better, more deserving, than others. We are up here looking down at them because this is where we belong. We are modern-day royalty; they are the peasants. If this were ancient times we could have any one of them killed just because we wished it.

"Now beneath even them is the guy from the other night. He is lower than a peasant. Should we, royalty, ruin our lives for the passing of someone whose life is so meaningless, so worthless?"

Danny wasn't listening to Carter's drivel; he was staring over the railing at the people and the cars far below, flowing in steady streams up and down the street. All those people going about their lives, their decent, normal lives. They worked at their jobs. They loved their families. They worried about money, and their children and their relationships. But basically they were good and decent, just trying to get by, just living their lives.

That's all Danny wanted now: to have a normal life, to be at peace. That was forever impossible. He would forever be haunted by what he had done and there was no way to change that. It was permanent, it was final, there was no taking it back, no way to reverse it and make it right, no do-overs. Peace, he just wanted peace.

Standing there, Danny half wished that Carter had come to finish him off. How convenient that would be. One quick push and the pain that Danny felt would be gone forever, a moment of falling, weightless and then peace.

"Hey Dan." Danny blinked; he had been lost in his thoughts, fixated on the flow of the traffic below. For a second he had almost forgotten Carter was even there.

Danny turned. Standing behind Carter were two very large men. They looked like drill sergeants: close-cropped hair, thick necks as wide as their heads.

Carter stood in front of them, grinning. "I guess I forgot to close the front door behind me."

"So this is it," Danny said, his voice carrying that same monotone, showing no emotion.

"Yep, Danny boy, this is it, time to go."

The men stepped forward, grabbing Danny under each arm. "Come on, kid, it won't be that bad. It'll be over in a few seconds," one of them offered.

Danny didn't resist. They led him back to the railing. Each man had an arm in one hand and reached down and grabbed the inside of Danny's thigh with the other. They didn't even let out a grunt as they lifted him easily off the ground. Danny closed his eyes, thought to himself, *come on, do it, do it*.

He pitched headfirst over the railing, his legs flipping up in the air. In that first second of flight Danny felt release, he felt peace. The next second his mind screamed in protest; this was a mistake! He desperately wanted to live! His eyes flew open wide with fright, his body turned in midair, his hands frantically clutching, looking for something, anything to hold onto. "Nooooooo!" he screamed.

Danny found peace all right, but not until he hit the pavement thirty stories below.

2

Carter headed down the hall toward the service elevator followed by the two members of the NYPD loaned to him by Sean's father. *Well, one problem solved*, he thought, a self-satisfied smirk playing across his face. This was so clean. As depressed as Danny had been the past several weeks, everyone would believe this was a suicide. He had practically offered himself up as a sacrifice anyway. That was weird, but Carter wasn't going to over-analyze his luck. He was a big believer in carpe diem.

3

On his way into the station the morning after lighting the candle, Al again entered the abandoned store. He wasn't sure he would find anything there yet but decided to take a chance.

Under the light of his flashlight, the interior appeared much as it had the night before except it was obvious someone had been there. The floor, which the night before had been covered with an undisturbed layer of dust, now showed the signs of footprints. The footprints were peculiar in that the right foot had left a clean print, however the print of the left foot looked like a large scuff mark, as if someone had tried to wipe away the print or the foot had been dragged sideways.

From Al's position inside the front door, he followed the prints with the beam of his flashlight. They came from behind the counter on the left, crossed in front of where he stood and then up to the pedestal in the middle of the shop. Al moved the beam from the floor up the pedestal to the display case on top. There, sitting atop the display case, was Al's shoe.

The shoe he had lost the night he had gotten drunk and called Anne. The first night he had ever encountered the strange homeless man. Sticking out of the top of the shoe was a scroll of paper.

Al walked up and took the paper from the shoe. Unrolling it, he saw there was an address written on it in large, crude print. Al stood there puzzled. He wasn't sure why they had taken his shoe, or kept it until now.

The thought caused questions, questions that had been lurking just below the surface, to reveal themselves. It wasn't one thing, it was a lot of little things that when strung together had weight. And it wasn't the corruption he was witnessing regarding this case—on some level he always knew that was how the city worked. This was just the first time he had been slapped in the face with it.

No, it wasn't that, it was the people that they were after. He had been focused on the corruption and the injustice of it and had not focused on these people that they were going to attempt to apprehend. They really didn't know anything about their suspects or what actually drove them. They didn't know how many there were or what they were capable of. They were going into this operation blind, plunging ahead, assuming it would play out a certain way. Everyone was more concerned with a quick resolution to placate the brass than checking all the angles to ensure a smooth execution.

Al also knew it was too late to do anything about it now. This operation would proceed. The coaster had cleared the crest of the hill.

CHAPTER 20

1

Al entered the squad room. The chairs had all been pushed to the sides of the room like they were getting ready for a dance. In the middle of the room was a large conference table. Spread over the table, looking like a large schematic of an electrical system, were the engineering blueprints depicting the various utility, steam and sewer tunnels that ran under the streets in the neighborhood of the meeting place.

The captain and Tasker were on opposite sides of the table, bent over the diagrams. Schrager was pacing the room, brows knit in concentration, thin lips set in a firm line.

Three other guys who Al knew to be undercover cops had grabbed chairs and were sitting around the room. The undercover guys looked and dressed like street thugs—unshaven, hooded sweatshirts and baggy jeans. The three were to be Al's captured "killers".

As soon as Al had closed the door behind him, Schrager began to speak.

"All right, this is what we have: the building indicated for the handoff is an abandoned plant. They use to manufacture the material for hospital gowns and bed pads, that kind of stuff. The place is abandoned now the business was moved overseas, big surprise there. Anyway, we don't know what's in the building. Could be empty or they could have left equipment behind. We don't want to send someone down to check it out in case the place is being watched.

"If the place is loaded with equipment, I don't want our guys going in and searching through the place. Too dangerous, too many hiding places. We will surround the exterior and try to drive them out. The only ones that will enter will be Russo, Rogerio, Kennedy and Holmes. Once they determine that our suspects are present, they will make the arrest. If they can't make the arrest, they will withdraw and we will wait them out."

"What if we can't withdraw?" Al asked.

"If you find yourself in a compromised situation, Detective, contact us and we will move in."

"What is a greater concern is that they will escape. Now, we will have all exits at street level covered by snipers on nearby rooftops. One here," Schrager said, pointing to a spot on the map, "will have command of the north and west side of the building, and one here that will have command of the south and east side. In addition, there are two tunnels that pass under or near the building that are large enough for a man to pass through. There is a utility tunnel running electric cables and a steam tunnel. Tasker will have two-man teams at each of the access points to these tunnels that are closest to the building, or at least as close as we dare to get, here, here, here and here," he said, pointing out the four spots on the map. "I will be coordinating from a command post, and at my signal, each squad will enter their assigned tunnel and proceed in the direction of the building. If anyone enters a tunnel from the building and tries to escape, they will run into one of our teams."

"We are not positive of the number of individuals we will be up against. Are we sure two men per squad is enough?" asked the captain.

Tasker, clad in the black military-style fatigues of the tactical squad, straightened up. "Two is actually generous. Two of

161

my men with automatic weapons in the narrow confines of these tunnels will not have a problem holding their positions."

"Ballpark, how many perps do we think there are?" asked Rogerio.

Schrager jumped in. "Due to the timing and distance between the child abductions, we know there are at least four people involved, and we feel there could be as many as six."

The captain shot Schrager a skeptical look. "Based on the evidence found at the warehouse, I thought it indicated there were many more involved."

"After further analysis, we feel that the scene at the warehouse was an elaborate hoax intended to cause widespread panic. The amount of flesh removed from the victim's remains, the large area of disturbed dirt and dust on the floor would indicate there were a large number of people involved, maybe as many as thirty. Even the indications of cannibalism are suspect. It is illogical to think there is a group that large that would engage in this kind of depravity and be able to fly under the radar.

"We feel this is a small group, six at most, bent on causing terror and panic, who staged the whole thing. This should be a standard arrest. The only reason we are employing the special units is the elusiveness of these individuals and the brutality of their crime, not because we feel there are large numbers of individuals involved."

Holmes cut in. "Do we expect these guys to be armed? What type of firepower are you suspecting?"

Schrager seemed grateful for the chance to take the conversation in a new direction. "Nothing we have seen would lead us to believe that they possess any guns, however we are sensitive to the fact that this elaborate hoax may also be an elaborate setup to ambush police officers. Now, obviously those entering the building, due to the roles they will be playing, will only be equipped with handguns. However, all other teams will go in heavy. Each team will have M4s in addition to their side arms.

"As far as the decoy criminals, we are using three. This is what the person that contacted Detective Russo is expecting based on comments he made. This will allow us to have quite a bit of firepower in the building."

Al smirked but kept his comments to himself. They weren't sure about anything, but he noticed Kennedy had very light blonde hair and the other two had dark hair.

"Rogerio, Kennedy and Holmes will enter the building with their hands behind their backs as if handcuffed, guns behind them in their belts. Detective Russo will have his gun out as if he is bringing them in."

"What if they search us?" asked Kennedy.

"You only have to deceive them until they show themselves and we are sure they are there. If you are approached, draw your weapons and make the arrest. If they flee, we will have all avenues of escape covered. We don't know how many will be there, but we have to take at least one alive so that we can question them and make sure we've gotten everyone. If this is some kind of cult or terrorist cell, we need to capture them all. You are cleared to use deadly force, however, we must take at least one of them alive.

"If there are no further questions, let's move out. Good luck."

CHAPTER 21

1

Schrager was using the tactical squad's panel truck as his command center. The truck was parked several blocks from the abandoned factory. The equipment within the truck allowed him to have radio communication with all squads and to track their movements on an onboard computer via GPS. A schematic of the streets and the tunnels underneath had been loaded onto the computer and each squad appeared as a green dot, with its call designation above it, on the map.

The two techs he had with him working the equipment looked to be all of fifteen years old but seemed efficient enough. In addition to the techs, Tasker and two of his tactical squad members were in the truck. Schrager turned to Tasker, who was staring at the computer screen. "All teams in position?"

"Yes sir," came the response.

"All right." Into his microphone on his headset he said, "Russo, move in now." He watched as the green dot that represented Russo and the undercover cops began to move slowly across the screen. He didn't trust Russo in this situation; the man was not trained for this type of tactical encounter and was obviously a liability. Unfortunately he was the only one who had been contacted; his presence was key. Schrager had full confidence in Tasker's men. They had all been handpicked by the department for these types of special operations. They were more a para-military unit than cops.

2

It was a cold, crisp, sun-filled day as Al received his order from Schrager and began to cruise slowly up the street in an unmarked police car. Holmes, Kennedy and Rogerio sat in the backseat behind the screen, playing their part as captured thugs.

As the car rolled along, Al noticed small groups, twos and threes, of homeless people on several of the street corners. This was not uncommon. Most of the industry had moved out of this area of the city and there were no private residences. The empty streets and buildings provided refuge for the city's less privileged.

Still, given his recent experiences Al couldn't help but wonder if any of those who seemed to absentmindedly stare at the car as he passed were who they appeared to be. Or were they members of the group they were after? How often did anyone look, really look, at a homeless person? They were something to be avoided, something to avert your eyes from. You may see something unsavory or trigger an incoherent rant, a stream of profanities or worst of all appear sympathetic so that they followed you looking for a handout. They were generally avoided, not scrutinized.

3

Schrager watched the screen as Russo approached the building. "Okay, Alpha, Bravo, go go." Both squads were at manholes several blocks away and would need time to close the distance. The other squads were closer. Schrager would time their advance so that all squads would be in position when Russo entered the building.

4

Clarke of Bravo team was standing next the open manhole, looking into its depths, when the order came in. "All right, let's move." He turned to take one last look at the bright November sky before he went down into the dark.

Wasn't that strange? Across the street from their location he saw some guy hanging off the roof of a building by one hand. He looked like an oversized monkey, just hanging there, staring at them, large coat flapping in the breeze. Very strange. He gave the guy one more look, then went down the ladder.

As he descended it got warmer and warmer, till he finally dropped into the tunnel below. Goldberg was already down in the tunnel. "Damn, it's hot down here!" he complained.

"Yeah, steam tunnel. The steam in that pipe is over two hundred degrees," Clarke said, indicating a large, two-foot-wide pipe that ran along the top of one wall of the tunnel, disappearing into the dark in either direction. The pipe was supported by iron braces, jutting from the wall. The end of each brace was anchored to the ceiling by a heavy chain. "It's probably about one hundred in the tunnel. All right, tac lights on. Let's get moving."

They switched on the tactical lights attached to the barrels of the M4 carbines they carried and started down the tunnel in the direction of the abandoned factory. The light revealed the ancient red brick that made up the walls and arched ceiling of the tunnel. The heat down here baked everything; a dry grey dust coated the interior of the tunnel. As they walked, the dust kicked up in miniature clouds, like walking on the surface of the moon.

5

Alpha team was moving along a utility tunnel. The tunnel was dank and cramped; they had to stoop as they moved. There were lit sodium lights periodically along the tunnel's ceiling, however they were also using the barrel-mounted lights.

The tunnel was rectangular in shape and made of poured concrete. Moisture could be seen seeping through the walls and floor in several areas. You could hear the squeaking and scurrying of rats just ahead of the advancing beams of light.

"Nice place, all it needs is a coat of paint."

"Very funny. Keep moving." Just then, through their earpieces they heard the command, "Charlie go, Delta go."

"We must be getting close. Stay alert."

CHAPTER 22

1

Al pulled to the curb across from a grey metal door in the southwest corner of the building. Not knowing for sure if they were being watched or not, he went through the motions. He got out of the car, drew his gun and walked around to the rear door on the passenger side. He unlocked the door and motioned for his prisoners to get out.

They all played their part, stooping to get out, their hands cuffed behind their backs and black bags over their heads. Tasker had decided on the bags the night before. Considering the officers were not actors, he did not want their facial expressions to give anything away before the time was right. The bags were made of material that, while giving the appearance of being opaque, the officers could see through. The cuffs had links that had been cut so that they could be easily pulled apart. If they were being watched, they would appear to be blindfolded and cuffed prisoners, but they could spring into action in seconds.

Al grabbed each one by the arm as they climbed out of the car to keep them from pitching face-first onto the sidewalk. He lined them up on the sidewalk. Keeping his gun trained on them, he walked over and tried the steel door. It was open. He went back, pushed and prodded, and herded them through the door.

The four of them stepped into the building. Al tried the switch by the door but nothing happened. The electricity must have been shut off when the company moved out.

Al was hoping for an empty building with clear sight-lines, but that was not to be the case. The previous tenants had left machinery behind. There were two parallel production lines stretching into the darkness. Both lines looked identical: at the end of each and closest to them was a machine about six feet wide and ten feet long; a collection of large rollers driven by chains and belts. Beyond them in each line was a larger machine that contained two vertical columns of drums, each drum about five feet wide and three feet across. Each column went up about twenty feet; there were six of the drums in each column. Al could see ladders up the side of each column and catwalks between the ladders at different levels.

Sunlight entered into the building from the row of windows up near the ceiling and several large skylights up above. The light filtering through the grime-covered windows was ethereal, uncertain. Combined with the shadows caused by the irregular surface of the machinery, the interior of the building looked like some strange alien landscape at dusk.

Al stood there with his three prisoners lined up in front of him. He could tell by the way all three were gripping the butts of their side arms that they were feeling as apprehensive as he was.

He didn't want to walk between the two production lines. Between the uncertain light and the dark shadows in and around the machinery, it would be very easy to be jumped.

They waited.

Seconds ticked by and they saw and heard nothing.

Then, silently, three figures emerged from the shadows up ahead, walking silently up the wide aisle between the two production lines. They walked into the pool of light formed by one of the skylights and stopped. None of the three presented a very imposing figure. All were around 5' 6", 5' 7" and were completely covered by oversized, hooded coats. The hoods were up so that their features were hidden and the sleeves so long they covered their hands. The coats dragged on the ground as they walked, their arms folded in front of them. They looked like medieval monks who got their clothes at the Salvation Army.

Since they had made their approach in the car, Al had felt the flow of adrenalin steadily increase. By the time they found themselves standing there facing these three, Al's senses had tuned to a fever pitch. He could feel every muscle fiber twitching; he could hear the blood pulsing in his ears. He could see the three men in front of him, hands behind their backs, nervously grasping the butts of their weapons. The call for his team to make their move had been left up to him and every instinct told him to act now, but he held.

"They could have anything under those coats—suicide vests, assault rifles, anything. Let's move," Holmes whispered from under the cloth bag.

"Hold your water," Al replied in equally hushed tones. "They didn't go through all this trouble just to ice cops. Let's give our guys a chance to get into position."

The figure in the center spoke and Al knew immediately he was the one that Al had dealt with in the past.

"So, Detective, these are the ones responsible? These are the murderers?"

"Yes, they are," Al answered.

"How very brave of you to bring them here singlehandedly. You must be very good at what you do."

Al didn't like the sound of that. They were already suspicious. Al tried to keep the conversation going, give their backup a chance to get closer before they made their move.

Keeping his voice calm, Al said, "How do you want to do this, uh…you have me at a disadvantage, I don't even know your name."

"I am known as Einarr," came the reply. "You can have them walk forward and you can go. We will take them from here."

"You said you had a witness. Is he here? Aren't you going to ensure you are satisfied I've brought you the right individuals?"

"I did not bring our witness. What if it was a trap you were laying? I would not endanger her. Are you laying a trap, Detective?"

"No, I just want to make sure we are done. That you are satisfied and there will be no more incidents like what happened to those children." With that, Al prodded each of the undercovers in the back, urging them forward. They took several steps, spreading out slightly as they did so.

Now!" shouted Al, raising his weapon as he took a step back. Rogerio, Kennedy and Holmes broke their cuffs, drawing their weapons with one hand and pulling the hoods off their heads with the other. They spread out further as they did this so they could flank the three before them.

"NYPD, freeze where you are, get those hands up where we can see them!" shouted Holmes.

"Detective, you do disappoint," said Einarr.

All three opened their arms and gave a slight shrug. Their coats parted and slid to the floor, forming pools of material at their feet. At that instant the four cops saw the three before them weren't human.

They stood there naked, except each had cloth wrapped around his waist, covering him to just above the knee, forming a type of kilt. A broad leather belt crossed each of their chests diagonally from shoulder to waist.

There was little doubt they were not human—their proportions were off. The legs were longer in relation to the torso than a normal person. Those long legs had well-muscled thighs and bulging calves. The torso was extremely lean, every muscle, tendon and rib visible beneath drab grey skin. Those muscles looked like braided steel cable beneath rough leather. Despite their small stature, their entire structure implied great speed and strength.

Their skulls were misshapen, more oblong than a human's, with a low forehead and raised crests running from the temples to the back of their heads. There were no outer ears, just holes in the sides of their heads like a lizard. The face culminated it a set of powerful jaws.

The worst parts were the eyes. They were a sickly shade of mustard yellow. The one called Einarr was missing one; a gaping black hole was located where the left eye should be. The lower left side of his face was disfigured, the lips and skin on that side were gone, the fangs beneath exposed in a permanent snarl.

It only took a second for Al to take all this in. He heard Holmes, to his left whisper, "Holy shit." All three creatures reached over their shoulders and drew large swords from scabbards on their backs. The blades on these swords were three times the size of the short sword found in the backpack the night of the accident.

Al heard a whistling sound and felt a breeze across his face as something flashed through the air from his right. The whistling ended in a sickening thud, followed by a scream. Al turned and stared, amazed, as Holmes dropped his gun and fell to his knees, the blade of an axe lodged firmly in his shoulder. Blood from the wound was painting the floor with large gouts of red.

In response to the scream, both Kennedy and Rogerio also turned in Holmes' direction, momentarily stunned by what they saw. Al looked up in time to see the creatures on each side of Einarr charging forward, covering the space between them in long, leaping strides. As they came, they raised their swords over their heads, fanged mouths open, letting out screams that sounded like an unnatural cross between a howl and a roar. The other officers began to fire, the sound of gunshots echoing through the building.

The creature to the right, juking left and right as he came, closed on Kennedy with remarkable speed. Kennedy fell back, firing as he went. The creature covered the remaining six feet in a single leap, reared up and swung his sword as he descended, driving the blade at an angle through Kennedy's collarbone down to his waist. Kennedy, his body almost completely cut in two, toppled to the floor.

Al pumped three shots into the chest of the creature standing over Kennedy's bisected body. The slugs smacked home and Al noticed there were already several bullet wounds from Kennedy's own gun. Thick, tarlike liquid flowed from the holes, but the creature just looked down at them, seeming more puzzled than hurt.

Al felt something hit his foot; he glanced down into the cold dead eyes of Rogerio, his head lying at Al's feet. Al looked left: there was the other creature standing in front of Rogerio's headless body, which had sunk to its knees, blood gurgling from the severed neck.

"Officers down! I need backup *now*!" Al screamed, pumping shells into Rogerio's killer as he backed toward the door. The creature began to advance, lips pulled back in a snarl of rage, sword raised above its head.

2

Tasker looked toward Schrager, the sound of gunfire and calls for backup ringing in his headphones. "We have to move *now*!"

Schrager was ghostly pale, his thin lips drawn in a tight red line. "We have to, uh, maintain the perimeter. All squads hold your position. Snipers, maintain street surveillance."

"Screw that! Now hear this; this is Tasker. Charlie and Delta teams, get to street level and move in now; we have shots fired and officers down. Sniper squads, maintain position; if you get a bead on a bad guy take your shot. Alpha and Bravo, stay underground but advance. When you get to the next manhole, hold position and await further orders."

Schrager snapped, "I am in command here. You are opening up avenues of escape. We should hold the perimeter."

"We have men dying in there; we can't sit back and do nothing."

3

"You heard the man, let's move," Clarke said. "There's a manhole about twenty yards up." Goldberg took the lead as they headed down the tunnel.

"There's an opening in the wall up ahead on the left, that wasn't on the map," Goldberg called back. "Looks like another tunnel."

As he got even with the opening, Goldberg flashed his light down this side tunnel. The light reflected off of two glowing orbs off in the dark but advancing fast. "What the fu…"

Golberg started as the glowing orbs morphed into a snarling face with bright yellow eyes.

Goldberg never finished his sentence; he could see gnarled bony hands grasping the handle of a large axe raised over that snarling, spitting, hate-filled face. Flipping his M4 on full auto, Goldberg pulled the trigger, teeth gritted in satisfaction as the bullets stitched a neat seam across the oncoming creature's chest. It staggered, but kept coming. Goldberg jumped back just in time as the axe descended.

Goldberg landed flat on his back at Clarke's feet, a large clanging sound echoing through the air. From his position on the tunnel floor he saw the creature crumple to the ground on the spot he had just vacated. Looking up, he saw the axe was buried deep in the side of the large pipe. Steam was whistling around the edges of the blade.

"Holy shit," yelled Clarke, grabbing Goldberg under the arm and dragging him to his feet. "Get back now! Now! Get the fuck out of—"

His words were drowned out by what sounded like a crack of thunder followed by Goldberg's screams.

Clarke was shielded from the full force of the initial blast by the man in front of him; however the shockwave knocked him off his feet. As he lay on the floor of the tunnel trying to protect his face, he could hear the steam roaring overhead with the sound of a freight train. He could feel his uniform fusing to his skin like boiling hot tar.

4

The radio crackled with the screams of the dead and dying and then went silent. Schrager looked at Tasker, both men sharing the same shocked stare. Then the radio jumped to life again. "Command! Command! This is sniper team Tango. We felt a shock, and now there is a crack in the street here and a thirty-foot geyser of steam!"

"What the hell is going on?" exclaimed Tasker.

Schrager's eyes appeared glassy, darting about, not focusing on anything. "We need to pull out now!"

"We still may have men alive in there. Snipers, hold your position," Tasker commanded. He put his hand over the mic and spoke to those in the van. "Those tunnels may be booby trapped." Removing his hand, he continued, "Alpha, hold your position. Charlie, Delta, move in. Be careful; we do not know the situation in the building."

Tasker glanced at Schrager, waiting for the latter to protest. He was pale; beads of sweat lined his upper lip. His jaw was set and firm but he said nothing.

"Driver, let's move in. We may have to extract our boys."

The driver hit the gas and the van lurched forward and then slewed sideways. The driver fought the wheel to the flapping sound of flattened tires. As the van came to a stop, something slammed into the rear doors. The doors bent inward to the hollow banging of metal on metal.

Tasker grabbed an M4 from one of the officers and emptied the clip through the rear doors. Gun smoke filled the back of the van and swirled in the beams of light streaming through the bullet holes.

5

After the seventh or eighth slug hit home, the creature sank into a heap on the floor, that thick, tarlike goo spreading underneath it. The sword dropped from its hands and clanged to the cement floor. Al reloaded, glancing to his right just in time to see a second axe flying toward his head. He ducked and it passed harmlessly over his left shoulder. As he ducked, he squeezed off a couple of rounds at the axe thrower. The creature darted behind the machinery and Al saw his shots bury themselves in the cement wall, kicking up sprays of chips and dust.

"I want him alive!" roared Einarr.

Al spun back toward Einarr and the creature that had killed Kennedy. Too late. Kennedy's killer, obviously still unfazed by the five bullets in his chest, had already closed in. Al just had time to register the large fist wrapped around the hilt of the heavy sword speeding toward his temple.

The blow rocked him backwards. Head spinning, he fought to maintain consciousness. He raised his gun but his assailant was quicker, bringing the flat of the sword down on Al's gun hand. The gun absorbed most of the blow, preventing Al's hand from being broken, however he lost his grip and the weapon went skittering across the floor.

Al landed a left hook to the creature's ribs, turning his hip, putting all his weight behind it. He felt like he had just punched a leather-wrapped tree trunk. He was rewarded with an astonished grunt from his attacker. Then the hand holding the sword came down again, connecting with his jaw, and again on the side of his head.

The lights switched off, and Al crumpled to the floor.

CHAPTER 23

1

Einarr took the lead as they proceeded down the tunnel, his single eye having no trouble seeing in the darkness. Things had gone much as he had suspected. The humans had tried to spring a trap instead of turning over the killers, just as he knew they would. He could not let the others know that this was what he suspected all along if he was to accomplish his ultimate goal. He had to pretend he was dealing with the humans in good faith and that his only objective was getting justice for the killing of the Holy One.

Also, as he had suspected, the humans and their weapons were no match for his warriors. They might not believe in their strength themselves, but a few more encounters like this and their confidence would grow. Grow to the point that he could fulfill his plans.

They had left the fallen humans where they lay and had carried off the detective and the body of their own. Einarr was not ready to have the humans find out the truth about who they were dealing with. He couldn't risk them organizing against him until he was ready, until he had the full support of his own kind.

They were moving quickly down the tunnel; the others were jabbering excitedly, flushed with the excitement of their easy victory despite the one casualty.

Einarr held up his hand, signaling the group to stop. He saw faint wisps of vapor trailing along the ceiling of the tunnel; up ahead he heard a muffled rumbling sound. The good half of his mouth curled in a savage grin. Everything had indeed gone as he planned. Trygrr had done his duty.

"Cover the human," he commanded, taking his coat and passing it to the warrior behind him. "They are weak. He would not be able to survive what is ahead."

Al had been draped over the shoulder of the third in line. He was unceremoniously dumped to the cement floor. The coat was wrapped around him. One grabbed him by the shoulders, another took his ankles and he was lifted as they again began to move forward.

The rumbling sound got louder. There was light up ahead—a large crack had been blown in the pavement overhead. Piles of rubble covered the tunnel floor. The steam billowed about the tunnel before funneling up through the crack in the street and into the air above. The sunlight filtered through the steam gave it a silvery, ghostly appearance.

The party scrambled over the rubble. They faced away from the main force of the steam streaming from the blasted pipe, raising their arms and hunching their shoulders in an attempt to protect their faces from the intense heat. The two carrying Al held him near the floor and bent over him as they passed.

Einarr felt the skin on his back bubble and blister and ignored the pain, knowing it would heal quickly. Amongst the rubble they were stumbling over they saw the bodies of two humans. One was face up, countenance frozen in a scream of pain, obviously dead. Large blisters covered the exposed skin of his face; his eyes were swollen shut, his lips swollen and split like overripe fruit. The other was face down, his uniform stripped away in places, his exposed skin a moonscape of large swollen blisters and bloody red craters.

They made it past the ruptured steam pipe.

Einarr heard a low groaning sound and stopped. Up ahead there was a figure lying in a heap on the tunnel floor. It was Trygrr. Einarr went forward and knelt by his side.

His skin was covered with blisters that even now had begun to heal. However, a string of gaping, bloody wounds stitched a seam from his right hip to his left shoulder. A large piece of iron from the exploded steam pipe jutted from a large wound in his neck. The black blood of the Eaton stained the cement floor.

The cracked and blistered lips began to move. "I have fought well, Einarr? It is as you asked?"

"You have fought well," Einarr said as he drew the short sword from Trygrr's belt and placed the hilt in his outstretched hand. Drawing his own sword, he placed the tip flat on Trygrr's sunken and blistered stomach. "It is time for you to join those in the Great Hall," Einarr said. The blistered eyelids fluttered in response; a faint breath whispered over the cracked lips. "Safe journey," whispered Einarr as, with a quick thrust, he drove the blade up under Trygrr's ribcage. Trygrr shuddered once and lay still.

Einarr looked up at the sullen faces of the others that had gathered in a ring around him. He felt his anger begin to rise. How weak they had become over these many years.

"Do not pity him. He has died in battle, a sword in his hand. What greater honor is there? If you want to pity some-one, pity those of us who have died these past hundreds of years skulking in the shadows, hiding from those weaker than us! Pity them. Do not disgrace this brave warrior with your pity."

With that he stood. "Take his body. We must keep moving." He turned and strode off without looking back.

2

Al began the slow road to consciousness, clawing his way up through the levels of gauze that swaddled his brain. As the fog began to lift, the pain and stiffness set in. For a moment his mind rebelled, teetering on the edge of a return to the bliss of senselessness.

However, the messages of pain coming in from various points of his body prodded his mind toward consciousness. The hand that had been struck by the sword throbbed incessantly. His arms were drawn painfully behind his back, ties of some type cutting into his wrists. With each ragged breath pain stabbed his right side.

The worst was the pain in his jaw and the throbbing in his head. His skull felt like someone had used it for batting practice. He tried to carefully work his jaw and pain shot out in hot bands encircling his skull and down his neck. He fought to draw breath; his nose felt swollen, clogged. He opened his mouth, a slow and painful process, and drew in needed oxygen. The coppery taste of blood covered his tongue.

Al struggled to open his eyes. His right eye opened, his left was stuck shut. The lids of his left eye stretched in response to his efforts but refused to part. Vision blurry, he blinked rapidly, trying to focus. The room was dark, with two bright, unstable blurs hovering in front of him.

As his vision cleared, the blurs solidified into the flickering flames of two torches made from greasy rags wrapped around metal broom handles. The handles each had a cinder block as a base.

The torches were about five feet apart and six feet in front of Al. They cast a golden circle of light in the room. The light did not show any walls, only floor. Beyond the circle was only darkness.

As Al's head continued to clear, he heard heavy breathing in the darkness. That and something else, as if someone was whimpering, crying, softly in the dark.

"Ah, I believe he is awake. Detective Russo, are you back with us? For a moment I was afraid we were going to lose you," Einarr said, stepping into the golden glow of the torches, his one yellow eye glinting ominously. Al realized they had bound him to a wooden chair. He leaned his head back to get a better look at the creature standing before him. The movement was rewarded with more shooting pain across his neck and shoulders.

The pain eased and his vision cleared. He was able to get a better look at his captor than he had been able to in the warehouse the few seconds before all hell had broken loose.

He studied the unnatural countenance before him. The left eye socket was completely empty, grey, scarred and withered skin surrounding a dark hollow cave where an eye should be. The right eye, as if compensating for its missing counterpart, glowered with a hate-filled intensity that was hard to look upon. What should have been the white part of this single orb appeared a sickly parchment yellow; the iris was a deeper, mustardy color.

The face was narrower than a human's and the skull more oblong, like a cross between a great ape and a man. The thing was also completely hairless, no hair on its scalp, no eyebrows. The sickly looking grayish skin was stretched so tightly over the face and head that Al felt like he was looking at a living skull. Every muscle and tendon seemed to be visible.

The ravaged jaw Al had noticed earlier was the result of a horrendous wound. The right side of the face was intact, with stretched grey skin, thin cruel lips. On the left side the skin and lips had been torn away, exposing the wolf-like fangs, ivory colored and powerful looking. The canines had to be two inches long.

"You are admiring my old battle scars," Einarr said, raising his hand. The large fingers looked like gnarled grey driftwood. He traced his jaw. "This." And pointed to his empty eye socket. "And this. These wounds were caused by weapons like the ones you and your men carried today, and yet here I stand, and where are the wielders of those weapons? They are here." He pointed to his chest. Around his neck was a strip of leather forming a necklace. Einarr lifted the necklace away from his chest to give Al a closer look. From this leather strip hung four police badges. Between each badge and the next was something fleshy and brown, like dried apricots. The sight of them triggered a memory and Al knew them for what they were: human ears.

About a month ago, two officers had radioed for backup. Two other officers responded to the call but, after having reported they were arriving onsite, were not heard from again. When no further reports came in, a third team was dispatched and found the bodies of the other four cops. They had been butchered, hacked to pieces. Their badges were gone and each body had its left ear removed. The perpetrator was never found, until now.

As Einarr let the necklace fall back into place, Al's eyes followed and he found himself focusing on the chest beneath. The chest was bare and Al could see concentric circles and patterns of stippled scarring covering the creature's entire torso, his shoulders and his arms. The patterns by now were familiar; they resembled those formed by the empty cans on Al's street and the pattern he had discovered on the blade of the short sword.

Einarr held a similar sword in his right hand now. He came forward, his wrist rotating, the sword smoothly tracing patterns in the air, as if he were testing its balance. "I tried to deal with you, Detective. Tried to deal with you, how does your kind say it, 'man to man'. I told you to tell no one about us. You did not listen. I warned you of what we were capable of, even gave you a small demonstration. You did not listen. Now, by not listening and by your betrayal, you have caused the death of several of your kind and put yourself in a very dangerous situation." The sword tip flicked out and Al felt a burning sensation on his right cheek.

"What did you expect? You murdered children. After you killed and mutilated innocent children did you really expect cooperation?" Al managed through cracked and bloody lips.

"I thought that would inspire you, Detective. I had tried to talk to you. Tried to reason with you without bloodshed." He had turned now as if he were directing his comments to someone off in the darkness instead of Al. "I thought with that little demonstration you would see I was serious and you would do the honorable thing: turn over those who had wronged us. Instead you tried to trick us; to have us killed."

He turned back toward Al, the tip of the sword forming figure eights in the air. "I suspected such a thing may happen. The demonstration we provided lacked a personal nature. I thought it would work anyway but I prepared in case it didn't." He made a gesture toward the darkness and Al heard a shuffling sound and more sobbing.

Two figures, bound to chairs in the same way Al was, came floating out of the darkness. It was only a moment before Al realized they were suspended from behind. Each was being carried by a single creature, grasping the back of the chair and holding it out in front of him as easily as if the chair were empty. Each figure had a cloth bag over their head. Al could tell immediately they were female; muffled sobs were coming from under each sack.

The chairs were set down in the circle of light facing Al. The creatures that had carried them stood behind each chair. Einarr gave a slight nod and both creatures reached out, grabbed the top of their respective sacks and lifted them with a flourish, like a magician performing a magic trick.

Al groaned as he looked into the gagged and blindfolded faces of Anne and Carrie. Carrie was gently sobbing. Anne was silent, her jaw set and firm as if she were fighting not to give in, not to show fear. Al lunged against his binds, his chair tipped sideways and he toppled to the floor. Rasping laughter rang in his ears.

3

Lying on the floor of the steam tunnel, partly covered in rubble, Officer Clarke began to stir. The steam in the tunnel had dissipated except for slight tendrils drifting from the jagged end of the blasted pipe. Someone, somewhere down the line had closed a valve to cut off the flow of steam.

As he shifted, dirt, gravel and broken pieces of pavement tumbled and flowed in rivulets off his body. The concussion from the blast had caused him to black out. He had awakened several times, only to be overcome by the pain of his injuries and slip back into the safety of unconsciousness.

Now, as he slowly rose to all fours, his back screamed in pain and his head began to spin. Biting down on his lip in concentration, Clarke fought to maintain consciousness. His head cleared but the pain continued relentlessly, seeming to wash over his ravaged flesh in waves of intensity.

He found he was still clutching his M4. Using it as a crutch, he pushed himself to his knees and finally to his feet.

He could see daylight filtering through the ragged rift the explosion had made in the street above.

Bent over with pain, fighting against the urge to lie down, to give up, he pushed forward, stumbling over the rubble that covered the tunnel floor. He shuffled on, leaning heavily on the butt of the gun. He felt if he gave in to the urge to lie down, if he took the easy road, he would never rise again. Not sure where he was going but feeling instinctually that he had to keep moving, he gritted his teeth against the waves of pain and took one step, then another.

CHAPTER 24

1

His chair had been righted and Al was once again upright, staring at the pale and shocked faces of the two women in his life. Standing between them looking down at Al, the good half of his mouth curled in a maddening smile, the ruined half frozen in its perpetual snarl, was Einarr. The flickering light from the torches brought into sharp relief not only his hideous features but the corded muscle that covered his frame. He still held the short sword, the sword tip absently performing those maddening figure-eights in the air.

There was more shuffling in the darkness beyond the reach of the torchlight. Slowly they emerged into the light, forming a half circle behind Einarr and the women. There were about ten of them, all with the same sickly, mustard-colored eyes, misshapen skulls and powerful jaws. They all were clad only in kiltlike garments and, though the patterns varied, they were covered with the same circular scarring that covered Einarr's body.

One of the ten appeared deformed. He was hunched over, his spine twisted. His left leg was shaped like an S, the foot twisted inward at an unnatural angle. Al remembered the footprints in the dust of the abandoned store—clear print on the right, scuffed print on the left—and thought he must be looking at the one who had placed his shoe there.

"Females are very rare for my kind, Detective. Most newborns are male. They are so rare that they are guarded and protected by our Clerics, like the one that was killed by the murderers you protect. However, you…you have two females. You are a very fortunate man."

"Let them go. I get your point, there is no need to go any further," Al managed through cracked and swollen lips. "I'll do whatever you want."

"I wish I could believe you, Detective. Surely I do, but you have lied to me in the past." The blade tip continued to move gracefully. "I have explained to you before; it is all about leverage and balance. I believe that now it is I who have the leverage."

"Let them go and I will do what you want. If you don't let them go, if you harm them in any way, I will never do as you ask."

The other creatures became restless, shifting from foot to foot, hands on sword hilts flexing. Al heard a deep rumbling noise coming from their throats.

Einarr stepped from between the two chairs and began to pace between Al and the women. He continued, seeming not to have heard Al. "Now as to balance, that is a little trickier. I have to properly encourage you to do as I say, however, if I go too far you may lose sight of your best interests and act irrationally. I have to maintain proper balance."

He stood in front of the women, turned slightly to give Al a good view. He began to move the sword tip like a metronome from one woman's face to the other, back and forth, forth and back. "I know," he said, "one will die and one will live." As he said this, both women began to cry, their sobbing muffled by the gags in their mouths. "But who lives and who dies? What will maintain balance? If I choose the wrong one, you may lose all reason."

"Enough!" screamed Al. "You made your point, you sick fuck. I said I would do what you want."

"That's it," Einarr said as if he just had a revelation. "I will let you decide. Just give me a nod, Detective. Who dies?"

Al's eyes widened in disbelief. "I'm not playing this game. Let them go. I will do what you want, and after, you can kill me if you need more blood on your hands."

Einarr snickered, the grin on the right side of his face getting broader. "I know what troubles you, Detective, but you needn't worry. They are blindfolded. The one you condemn will never know and the one who lives will be grateful to you for the rest of her life." The sword tip continued moving as if keeping time to the final beats of one woman's heart.

"I won't. You can't ask me to do this. If you harm either of them you might as well kill me because I will not give you what you want."

"Oh, but you will," hissed Einarr, "because I am going to kill one and keep one. If you do not do as you're told the other will die as well." He turned toward Al. "Now choose," he said.

Al looked down at the ground, afraid to do anything, even blink, that may be interpreted as a signal. "I won't do this, you can't make me do this."

"As you wish," said Einarr. With that he spun away from Al, and in one fluid motion, grabbed the crown of Carrie's head in a large gnarled hand, tilted her head back and drove the sword blade into the bottom of her jaw and up into her skull. Large gouts of blood spouted from the wound, bathing the hilt of the sword and the hand that grasped it. Carrie's body twitched in its binds; blood soaked the front of her clothing. The twitching slowed, stopped. Just that quickly, she was gone forever.

Al stared, stunned. He could hear Anne screaming around the gag in her mouth. The assembled creatures exploded in a chorus of grunts, howls and snarls.

A wave of emotions flooded Al's mind—rage, shock, sorrow, anger, hate. And deep down, down in the depths, a fleeting whisper of another emotion. Way down, barely heard, but there, an emotion that he would feel guilty about for the rest of his life: relief. Relief that it had not been Anne.

Einarr withdrew the blade. Carrie's head slumped forward, blood continuing to pour from the wound. Einarr turned toward Al. Bringing the hand with the sword up to his lips, he slowly licked blood from the blade with a coarse black tongue. Bending close to Al's face, he grinned. Al could see Carrie's blood outlining the fangs in that ragged mouth.

"Now, Detective, let the hate you feel drive you. Embrace your sense of shame, your sense of helplessness. Know that you never want to feel that way again. For the same fate will befall this other one if you fail us."

As if to punctuate his statement, he turned and, with one sweep of his foot, knocked the legs from under Carrie's chair, toppling her corpse to the floor. Her head hit the cold cement with a sickening crunch.

He straightened and turned to the others. "Take her," he said, flicking the sword blade in Anne's direction, "and release him."

Al watched helplessly as Anne was lifted, chair and all, and carried out of the torchlight and into the darkness. One of the creatures came over and, lifting a foot, kicked Al's chair over. He landed hard on his side, wincing from the pain that flared in various locations on his bruised and battered body. The creature then stomped repeatedly on the spindles and legs of the chair, snapping them into so much kindling. From his position on the floor, Al found himself staring into Carrie's face. Her blindfold had slipped and he was looking directly into one cold, dead, accusing eye. The emotional paralysis caused by the shock of the sudden and brutal violence shattered and Al felt waves of sorrow and despair wash over him. Just like that, she was gone. Intelligent, fun, beautiful, full of life, gone. In one quick, violent moment, all she was and all she would have been, snuffed out forever.

Einarr walked over to where Al lay. Bending, he took a scrap of paper from the waistband of his garment. "When you have captured those we seek, bring them to the location written on this paper. There you will be given further instructions. Do not delay in the fulfillment of this task, Detective, if you don't want to be the cause of more bloodshed."

Einarr stuffed the paper in Al's pocket and stood. "Grab the body," he said, and one of the creatures bent toward Carrie's corpse.

"No!" croaked Al from his place on the floor. "Leave her. Don't you touch her."

Einarr turned, smirking. "You humans and your arrogance. You think you are special, that the gods smile on you. You even have the audacity to think you are made in God's image. Know this, you are no different than any other creature on this earth; when you are alive you exist, when you are dead you are just meat. Bring her." Then he followed the others off into the darkness, leaving Al lying on the floor, wired to the remains of the shattered chair and staring at Carrie's face.

The final creature bent, grabbed Carrie by the ankle and dragged her, chair and all, across the floor. Her hair swept through the pooling blood. Acting like a paintbrush, it painted a crimson swath along the floor and into the darkness.

CHAPTER 25

1

Al lay in the glow of the guttering torchlight, his cheek resting on the gritty, cold cement, the combined scents of blood and bile filling his nostrils. Slowly, painfully, he rolled onto his back and managed to bring his knees up and work the wire that bound his wrists past the soles of his shoes so his hands were in front of him. With the help of his teeth, he untwisted the wire that bound his wrists. Once his hands were free, he was able to free his elbows from the broken pieces of chair they were wired to. This was accomplished with frequent breaks to work through the pain and stiffness from the recent beating and bondage.

Finally he was free and able to slowly get to his feet. Of the many emotions that had swept over him during the whole ordeal, anger was winning out. That and a sense of urgency— he had to try to get help and fast if he had any chance of saving Anne.

He moved in a stiff-legged stagger across the room and grabbed one of the torches, wresting it from its cinderblock base. He held it aloft, moving it about, trying to see where he was. He had assumed that he was in some abandoned warehouse, but the flickering torchlight revealed a vaulted cement ceiling and, as he turned slowly around, several tunnels leading in different directions. He was in some type of underground vault or cistern. He could see clearly the path his captors had taken. There was a wide, reddish brown trail heading into the tunnel straight ahead.

He thought for a minute about following the trail, but quickly rejected the idea. Even if he found them, what could he do by himself in his current state? He had to get to the surface, get backup. Choosing randomly, he headed down the tunnel to the left of the one taken by the creatures.

2

Al limped down the tunnel. The flame of the torch had died down considerably. Either because it had burned through whatever flammable liquid it had been soaked in or due to the reduced oxygen in the fetid air, or both. As long as it lasted long enough for him to find a way out, a grate or a manhole. In a way Al was happy the light from the torch had dimmed. He didn't like broadcasting his location in case he was not alone down here.

As if in response to that concern, he heard a halting, shuffling sound from up ahead. He hesitated, not sure at first what to do. Al was normally pretty good at thinking on his feet, but the events of the day and the beating he had taken had had their effect. He stood in a daze as the seconds ticked by. The shuffling got closer. Al shook his head to clear it; pain tightened in an iron band around his temples but it did the trick. He carefully laid the torch on the tunnel floor slipped back down the way he had come, into the darkness. As he moved, he cast about, looking for something to use as a weapon or for a hiding place. The damp cement walls, electrical conduits running in both directions into the darkness, and the barren cement floor were all that met his gaze. He pressed himself against the wall in the shadows and waited. The shuffling noise came closer. Al tried to control his breathing.

Time seemed to slow down to an unbearable crawl as he waited, the sound getting closer and closer. Al stood there, barely breathing, his eyes staring into the dark, straining to see something, anything. The wait was becoming unbearable. He fought the urge to rush forward and confront whatever it was. Then a shadow broke off from the darkness up ahead. It continued toward the light, hunched over, feet dragging along the floor.

Al picked up the smell of steamed vegetables and wet moldy cloth mixed with something else, a burnt odor. The shadowy form was almost doubled over, as if under a great weight.

The figure stumbled, almost fell, but somehow retained its balance and continued forward. Al could hear strained, ragged breathing.

As it entered the circle of light made by the torch on the tunnel floor, it paused as if undecided how to continue. In that uncertain flickering light, Al got a better look at the hunched form. Its clothes were in tatters. Through the tears in the clothing, Al could see exposed skin that was covered with open and oozing blisters. Al recognized the black boots, black pants, the remnants of the shirt and the tattered, bulletproof vest that clung to the ravaged torso. It was one of the tactical squad. As if deciding the torch on the floor was something that deserved worship, the tac officer sunk to his knees, arms hanging limply at his side.

Forgetting caution, Al rushed forward and caught the man as he slumped to the floor.

Al sunk to his knees, cradling the man's head. Remarkably, he still had his M4 clutched in one blistered and burned hand. The man turned his face toward Al. That upturned face was a mass of blisters and bright red skin. The lips were swol-

len, cracked and oozing. The eyes were practically imperceptible slits between the swollen and blistered lids. He felt hot to
the touch.

Al looked over him to see if there were injuries other
than the severe burns. He noticed the nametag pinned to the
remains of the shirt. "Clarke." Al remembered him from the
briefing—young, good-looking kid. Clarke's lips parted and
drew in breath, making a reedy wheezing sound.

"Gone," he rasped. "Goldberg gone." His head sank
back. His body slumped and seemed to wither as air whistled
out between those ruined lips. The air was foul and rancid, the
body giving up its final secrets.

Al carefully laid Clarke's head on the concrete floor and
then looked over the body. The M4 seemed to have come out
of the ordeal in good shape. Feeling guilty, as if he were grave
robbing, Al pried the weapon from those hooked and blistered
dead fingers.

There was a light clamped to the barrel of the rifle. He
switched it on and a beam knifed up to the tunnel ceiling. He
turned the beam on the body. Several ammo clips were in
Clarke's belt. Al grabbed them.

He knelt there for a moment, staring at the gun and the
ammunition. His first instinct had been to escape. Get out of
the tunnels and get help. He had been battered, bruised and
weaponless, certainly not in any condition to make an attempt
to save Anne by himself. But now it was different. He was still
battered and bruised but no longer weaponless.

But was this enough? He had seen what those things
were capable of and how much punishment they could take
before they went down. But did he have a choice? What
chance did Anne have of surviving the time it would take him
to get help and return?

Al searched his own pockets and found his phone. The
battery was almost dead and he had no signal. He looked back

at Clarke. The guy's radio was shattered. He shut off his phone to save power. He decided to return to the spot of Carrie's murder and follow the blood trail. Once he had located where they had taken Anne he could get to street level and call in some backup.

3

Al had no idea how long he had been underground following the trail of blood, but the bulb in the under-barrel tactical light was beginning to dim. He had come across sections of tunnel with old dusty sodium lights flickering dully, bathing the cables, pipes and walls in a dull monochromatic wash. At these times he had switched off his light, attempting to preserve the battery.

When he would hit another dark section of tunnel, he would switch the light back on and the beam would knife through the darkness, accompanied by the rustling, skittering sounds of rats retreating into the black.

Al began to worry the battery or fading blood trail would die out before he had found Anne. All he could do was push on and hope he would find her before that happened. And then what? Was he going to take on those creatures by himself? They had taken out a squad of trained professionals, how could he hope to save her? The answer was simple, he had to try.

As if to mock his determination, the light flickered and went out. He stood in complete and utter darkness. Seconds ticked by as he waited for his eyes to adjust. But there just wasn't enough light. He felt for the wall of the tunnel, half expecting to grab something furry as the skittering and squeaking seemed to draw in around him. Like a blind man he began to feel his way along the wall, knowing that he had no way to follow the trail. Only blind luck—he smiled ruefully at the term—would allow him to find her.

At that moment he heard something out of place, something from the real world, the world above ground. Faintly, he heard music. He moved toward the sound. The guitar riff was familiar. As he got closer, he made out the lyrics. "Excuse me while I kiss the sky." Hendrix. "Purple Haze."

4

Al followed the sound of the music. He slapped the light's casing a couple of times and, miraculously, it flickered back to life. The tunnel he was walking down appeared older than those before. The concrete walls showed signs of their age. There were spider vein cracks running up the walls and rough patches on the walls and ceiling where the surface of the concrete had crumbled and fallen away.

Moving closer toward the source of the music, Al came to one of those electrical cabinets he had seen periodically during his underground trek. The others had been closed, the doors locked. The doors on this one were wide open, and when Al shined the light inside he could see it was a dummy. The electrical conduits that entered near the top of the cabinet passed right through it. The cabinet itself was empty. There were no transformers, or circuits or switches, just an empty metal cabinet.

The cabinet had no rear wall. There was a large hole in the cement wall of the tunnel behind it.

Al moved the light to the hole in the wall and, to his surprise, it did not shine on dirt and rock but into an open space. He stepped closer to peer through this opening. Through the hole he could see a second tunnel wall about six feet away. The two tunnels ran parallel to each other. The hole connected them.

Al leaned forward, ducking his head under the conduit and through the opening, looking down the adjacent tunnel. It was even older than the one he was in. The floor, walls and arched ceiling were made of ancient-looking brick. Al could hear the music even clearer now. It was coming from down this second tunnel.

Al stepped through the opening, having to almost double over to fit through the hole, and into the ancient brick tunnel. Jimi was now singing about manic depression. Al followed the sound.

5

Up ahead, Al saw a light. He turned off his own light, checked the M4, making sure it was ready to go, and walked toward the distant glow.

As he got closer he could make out a seated figure hunched over a desk. The person's back was to Al and he was deeply involved in working on something in front of him on the desktop. The desk was surrounded by precariously piled stacks of books, magazines and old, yellowed newspapers. The light came from several of the sodium lamps that Al had noticed in some of the other tunnels during his trip through the underground. The lamps were hanging from the arched ceiling by chains.

Between the stacks of books and papers were other artifacts from the civilization above: an old refrigerator, door ajar, shelves filled with more books; shopping carts full of broken clocks, radios and assorted electronics. There were bins and an old battered dresser, drawers hanging open, packed with vari-

198

ous electric and machine parts. The entire space looked like a hoarder's paradise.

In the middle of it all, the strange figure sat in one of those old wooden office chairs, the ones that rolled around on heavy brass casters, hunched over the old, beaten-up wooden desk.

On the desk to the left of the seated figure, Al spotted the source of the music. His older brother had one in his car when Al was a kid. It was an 8-track tape player. The unit sat on a couple of bricks that resembled the ones that comprised the tunnel walls. The player was wired to a circuit board and car battery. A tangle of wires ran from the back of the 8-track to car speakers propped up at various locations in the piles of books and magazines. The entire setup looked like an electrical fire waiting to happen.

Even from behind, Al could tell the seated figure was one of the creatures. It wore a long camel overcoat. The vent of the coat had split up the center seam to the creature's lower back. The two sections of the coat draped on either side of the office chair. The back of its head, however, was unmistakable: the grayish skin, the absence of outer ears.

There was one difference between this creature and the others he had seen. The others had been completely hairless, their misshapen skulls covered in nothing but leathery skin. This one had long black hair running in a crest down the center of its skull to the nape of its neck like a horse's mane.

Al raised the M4, taking careful aim at the back of the head in front of him. He had seen how quickly these things could move and he wasn't taking any chances. He knew he couldn't afford to kill it, however; he had to persuade it to show him where Anne had been taken. He opened his mouth to order the creature to freeze. Before he could say a word, it raised its head from what it had been working on, and without turning around spoke.

"Put down the weapon, Detective. I am of no use to you dead, so threatening me with a weapon will have little effect. Besides, as things are, I need you as much as you need me." With that, it swiveled the chair slowly around, and Al found himself staring into a very blue, very human-looking, set of eyes.

CHAPTER 26

1

The creature snorted a short rueful laugh at the sight of the look of astonishment on Al's face. He rose from the chair, turned and switched off the 8-track. His eyes locked on Al's like a snake charmer willing calm but watching for any sign of aggression. "My appearance is not what you expected," he said.

The general look of the creature matched the others, the same pronounced jaws, the broad flat nose with V-shaped nostrils, the thin-lipped mouth. However the skin, though still gray, had a slight pinkish hue to it and the deep-set eyes were a bright azure blue. The large hands came up and out in front of him, thick fingers splayed in a "nothing dangerous here" gesture. "My appearance is easily explained. You see, I am half human. My human mother was raped by my Eaton father. When I was born, the humans, forever a compassionate folk, left me in the woods to die. The Eaton found me and raised me. Not exactly as one of their own; they believe in keeping their bloodline pure. But I fared better, certainly, than I would have amongst man. They have treated me quite well in their own way." The voice was rough and smooth at the same time, like oiled sand. Al picked up the brogue in the speech similar to Einarr but not as pronounced.

It took a step toward Al, hands still spread before him, eyes locked and unblinking.

"That is close enough," Al said, pointing the barrel of his weapon at the creature's chest. It froze in place. "You know who I am?" asked Al. It nodded its head slowly. "Do you know why I am here?"

Again, the slow nod. "Yes, I know why you are here, Detective. I probably know more about why you are here than you do. You are attempting to rescue your woman."

"Where did they take her?"

"Right to the point. Aren't you curious about who and what we are? Don't you want to understand the truth about what is really going on?"

"After I find Anne and get her out of here, you and I can sit down and have a nice long chat. But right now all I care about is getting her to safety."

Al's statement was met with a sigh of exasperation. "There is no getting around it, then. I must show you. However, you may as well stop pointing your weapon at me. We both know you can't afford to use it."

Al lowered his gun. The thing was right, it was not intimidated by the gun and it was no value to him dead. "All right, show me. Let's go. Do you have a name?"

"Of course; I am called Tabon."

2

Tabon had retrieved a lantern from the desk. It was one of those battery-operated hurricane lanterns people often keep in case of blackouts. He turned the knob and the harsh metallic glow of the LED bulb formed an island of light around them. He then turned and squeezed past the desk between its scarred wooden top and the stack of books next to it.

As he followed, Al noticed the top of the desk was cluttered with various electrical components that gave no clue as to the appliance they had originated from. There were also tools—screw drivers, pliers, wire cutters. All the handles of the tools were wrapped with layers of tape.

"Makes them easier to hold," stated Tabon. He was looking in the direction of Al's gaze and holding up one of his hands with its thick, powerful fingers. "We don't have the manual dexterity of you humans."

Tabon made his way along a path that wound through towers of more boxes, newspapers, magazines and books. Here and there were shopping carts overloaded with other bits of machinery, automotive parts, and electrical components, wires sticking out of the latter like arteries in a robot heart.

Al followed, all the while thinking about the time when, as a patrolman, he had entered the house of a hoarder after the neighbors had reported a foul odor. The interior looked very similar to what he was walking through now. They had worked their way through the garbage in the living room and into a back bedroom, where there was a huge mound of refuse. Sticking out of the mass of debris was one clawed and wizened hand. They had dug through the mound, knowing by the hand and the smell that they were already days, if not weeks, too late. They finally uncovered a woman's corpse, or what was left of it. The rats had gotten there first. That's one thing they never tell you in the newspapers—the rats always get there first.

Tabon slipped effortlessly between the stacks. Al followed, keeping a wary eye on the columns of refuse that began to sway as he squeezed by. He had no desire to feed the rats.

Tabon held up his hand, signaling Al to stop. "We are getting close. I will have to extinguish the torch or the light may be seen." Al started to protest, but Tabon turned the knob and the light from the bulb dimmed to a low glow, then went out. Al had been concerned about being plunged into complete darkness in this confined place with his strange companion. However, the darkness was not complete. There was light coming from farther up the tunnel. It had not been visible when the lantern was lit. They moved farther along and Al could see the faint glow was coming from the tunnel mouth up ahead.

There were iron bars running vertically from floor to ceiling across the arched opening. Tabon turned and whispered, "You need to follow me. I would show you what is beyond those bars, but we must move with caution. Stay back in the shadows as you peer through or you may be seen from the other side."

They moved forward again, slowly. By the time they got near the opening they were shoulder to shoulder. Al's nostrils recoiled from the moldy smell of the tunnel and the strong animal scent of the creature next to him.

Tabon put his hand out against Al's chest in a "don't move any further" gesture. They both leaned forward to peer over the lip of the tunnel mouth.

Al found himself looking into a large, underground chamber. The grate he was looking through was about fifteen feet up the wall from the floor on the other side. At first he thought this may be an old abandoned subway station. The walls, however, were not covered with the tile you saw in the stations he was used to. They were built entirely of brick. The ceiling above was supported by pillars and arches composed of the same aged and weathered brick as the tunnel he was in. He did not see a train track or the channel to run the track in. This may have been an old city reservoir, long since built over and forgotten, or an old underground cistern.

The size and expanse of the space was not the most remarkable feature. The area was lit by torches sputtering in wall sconces spaced around the perimeter, as well as tall, freestanding torches. Al felt like he was looking down into some third world slum. The entire expanse was covered with ramshackle shacks made of various combinations of every material known to man. Plywood, plastic sheeting, sheet metal, wall board, cardboard and dozens of other materials had been incorporated into the structures.

At first it appeared to Al that there was no rhyme or reason to the structures below; then he realized they were laid out in concentric circles similar to the pattern he had become all too familiar with. Pathways through the dwellings formed the circles; these were dotted with the freestanding torches. These circles were connected by straight paths coming out from the center like spokes of a wagon wheel.

Amongst the dwellings, sitting at small cooking fires, walking along the paths or just standing around, Al could see hundreds of the Eaton. Most were almost naked, clothed only in material wrapped kilt-like around their waists. He noticed a few entering the area from a tunnel at floor level, dressed in human clothes, coats, pants, knit hats. As they entered, they discarded these garments, depositing them in large drums near the entrance to the tunnel. There were dozens of these drums by the entrance, overflowing with old tattered clothing, like the world's largest Salvation Army drop.

At first Al thought all the creatures below were grown males, but then he noticed a few that were obviously children and even fewer that were female. A small civilization was laid out before him, right under the streets of the country's largest city.

In the middle of the concentric circles formed by the shacks and pathways was a central area, dominated by a much larger structure. Al's vantage point was level with the rooftop of this building. The structure had neither windows nor any doors that Al could see. It was shaped like a loaf of bread and, like the smaller shacks around it, constructed of a patchwork of materials.

"You are looking upon the Long House of the Eaton," stated Tabon. "It is the center of our society."

Al barely heard the words. His attention was elsewhere. Next to the large building was a large cage. More accurately, it was one of those hotel elevators made of ornate iron bars that you sometimes saw in black and white films from the forties and fifties. Its days of carrying Humphrey Bogart and Lauren Bacall, however, were over. It was now sitting underground, doubling as a jail cell.

Anne was sitting on the floor of that elevator. Her arms were raised in a V, her wrists bound to the bars behind her. She sat with her legs folded to one side, her clothes in tatters, head hanging forward. Her whole body was slumped forward in either unconsciousness or despair, Al couldn't tell which. She was still blindfolded.

Al felt his fingers tighten on the stock of the M4, knuckles turning white. He fought the rising urge to jab the barrel of his weapon into the abdomen of the creature next to him and empty an entire clip. Could picture the barrel bucking, the flash, the tunnel filling with smoke, as slug after slug ripped through the tattered clothes and grayish pink flesh to shred the vital organs underneath.

The only thing that held him back was the realization of the selfishness of that act. Sure, it would vent his anger, make him feel like he was doing something, was taking action. But in the end it would bring him no closer to saving Anne from her predicament. He still didn't know how to get into the compound below or have any idea how to pull off a rescue if he did. In the end, he would only accomplish killing this one creature next to him, exposing himself to discovery and probably getting Anne killed in the process.

As if reading his mind, Tabon whispered, "Stay calm. Other than fear and discomfort, she is in no danger at the moment. But if you let your humanness get the better of you and react irrationally, you will ensure her death. "

"I can't leave her there," Al murmured almost to himself. He noticed two of the creatures, two of the Eaton, standing near the cage. Each of them held a spear and had a long sword in a scabbard strapped across their backs.

Al took a deep breath. He suddenly felt very tired. The events of the past twenty-four hours or so—the ambush where he watched the other officers get butchered, the beating he had taken, Carrie's heartbreaking murder and his long trek through the tunnels—seemed to descend on him all at once. It was as if bags of wet sand had been laid across his shoulders.

From his position crouched near the grating he leaned back against the tunnel wall and slid to the floor, his legs folded in front of him, the gun across his lap. Tabon also backed up from the opening and sat against the opposite wall, facing Al.

Al's only hope was to find out as much information as he could. He realized he had wasted valuable time reacting, with no knowledge and no plan. He had to get more information, had to know what he was up against. He fought the desperation he was feeling, knowing the situation Anne was in, how scared and alone she must feel. But without more to go on, he was powerless.

"Come, let's go back." And with that, Tabon stood and headed back through the stacks of refuse. Al rose with some difficulty. His muscles had stiffened and his joints creaked and complained. There was nothing his body wanted to do more than lie down and sleep, to start to repair itself.

3

"Why did you bring me there? It was not because I have a weapon. If you are as strong and as quick as your friend with the one eye, you could have overpowered me and taken it. You didn't bring me there to help me. You took care to show me were Anne is but without actually showing me the way in. So what exactly did you plan to accomplish?"

They were at the scarred wooden desk. Tabon was again seated in the desk chair, turned to face Al. Al was sunk into an old cushioned couch that was to the left of the desk and facing it, back pushed against the tunnel wall. The couch smelled of mold and mildew, the upholstery worn and threadbare. The springs had long since given out. Al's ass was almost dragging on the brick floor.

In spite of the weariness and the pain and the concern for Anne, as he looked at the being before him he still couldn't help but appreciate how surreal his situation was. Up until a few days ago, no one knew these creatures existed, and now he found himself sitting down in this post-apocalyptic man cave with an M4 lying across his knees, trying to engage one in conversation.

The sense of strangeness was enhanced by the contrast of those very human-like blue eyes and intelligent speech with the gaunt, taut-skinned face and strong, wolf-like fangs.

"I wanted you to understand the futility of your current course of action and the danger you would be putting the woman in," Tabon said, leaning forward, his hands on his knees. He fixed Al with a steel blue stare. "I knew only once you realized that your current course would doom you to failure that you would listen to me and not force me to have to kill you."

"All right, you have my attention. I'm listening," Al said.

"What you saw there was just a portion of our clan. There are over three thousand of us living in this city. Most of them are males of warrior age. Most are spread throughout the city, living in the shadows of your society. Dressed in discarded human clothing, we mingle with your homeless, sleep in your parks and abandoned buildings, walk your streets."

Al's eyes, at least his good eye, grew wide in disbelief. The eye that was swollen shut attempted this maneuver but could only manage a small slit. "You are saying that there are over three thousand of your kind living in the city without anyone knowing."

"It is quite an easy thing. Ask yourself, Detective, when was the last time you stopped and looked closely at the features of a homeless person? You humans go about your business and avert your eyes from any unpleasantness. You go out of your way to give homeless people a wide berth and are afraid to make eye contact. This behavior suits our purposes perfectly.

"We have been living in this city for decades without being discovered. We keep to ourselves, we generally sleep underground, and if we have to travel more than a short distance or there is a large group of us travelling together, we move beneath the city to avoid discovery."

This raised many more questions than it answered, however none of it was getting him closer to rescuing Anne. "All right, let's just assume that is all true. If you have been hiding this long, why the violence now? Why the murder and cannibalization of those children, and why Anne's abduction? It makes no sense to successfully hide for decades and then commit acts that will ensure you are eventually discovered."

"Things are more complicated than you realize. Similar to you humans, we are not always of one mind. There are those among us who do not wish to remain hidden. Who are not content to do so. Who would risk everything in a futile attempt to grab glory for themselves and return our species to its former place in the world.

"Our history or how we got here is not important right now. But to understand, you need to know this," Tabon continued. "We are a proud and warlike people. At one time we challenged humans on equal terms and often bested them on the battlefield. We are in many ways superior: we are stronger, faster, more agile. Our senses are keener. We can live hundreds of times longer than a man.

"However, in the end we could not compete. Not with man's ability to reproduce like the rats in the sewers and—" Tabon looked down at his large hands with their thick gnarled fingers, spreading them out, studying them as he spoke, "—mankind's ability to build intricate and powerful weapons. Eventually, through sheer numbers, better weaponry and through treachery and deceit, mankind drove us to the brink of extinction. Most of us realize that the only way for the remaining few to survive is to stay hidden. It is mankind's world now and we must accept that.

"There are those among us who long for the old days. Einarr is one of these. He is a brave and fearless warrior, has defeated men in battle many times. He would rather die tomorrow with a sword in his hand than live another thousand years hiding. There is a small group, about ten or so, who believe in him and follow him without question.

"He has tried for years to get all the Eaton to follow him, to start a war against man. He attacked several of your police officers to show how you could be defeated, even with your guns. He was wounded; the bullets tore away part of his face. One took out his eye and that bullet is still lodged inside his skull, but he survived and killed the four police officers involved. He wears their ears and badges around his neck as a symbol of his bravery and as a talisman to protect him from harm. After that, some of the younger, more impressionable among us took up his cause. However, most understand that to attack the humans would mean the end of our kind. With so few committed to his cause, Einarr has been powerless to move."

Al leaned back with a sigh, "Well, he is moving now. And if he has wanted a war all along, what is all this nonsense about a holy man?"

"That is the thing: left to his own methods, Einarr would never be able to sway enough Eaton to his cause. But those three humans that you are protecting provided him with the means to attract thousands. We hold very strong beliefs, and once man killed the Druid Kustaa, the Eaton are honor-bound to avenge that murder."

"How are you so sure it was a murder?"

"There was a witness to this crime. Kustaa was transporting a young female. Very few females are born to the Eaton, and those that are, are under the protection of our Druids. They even decide who they will mate with to ensure we preserve the best and bravest bloodlines. He was transporting her in a cart hidden under some blankets and old clothes when he was attacked. The cart was dumped over during the attack and she spilled out with everything else. She was still hidden by the blankets and managed to slip into nearby bushes as the men continued to beat Kustaa. We teach our females to hide. There are so few they must survive at all costs."

"So if Einarr is using the death of your druid to draw more to his cause, he wouldn't really want me to find them. If he is trying to start a war over this, the last thing he would want is for me to hand over the killers."

"Finally we are getting somewhere, Detective. That is right exactly. He is hoping you never provide them. Then the Eaton would be honor-bound to fight. They would be dishonored; they would not be able to enter the Great Hall when they died if they did not do so. He has played this very carefully. The acts he committed supposedly to get you to cooperate have been carefully measured. To our kind, the acts he and his group have committed, the killing of the young ones and the abduction of your women, are very reasonable ways to force you to cooperate. However, to a human with your false sense of outrage, it would cross a line that you could not accept. It would have the opposite effect. You would be less likely to cooperate."

'What do you mean 'false sense of outrage'? No civilized race would butcher children and then feed on them."

Tabon threw his head back in grating laughter. "Spare me, Detective. Humans butcher each other all the time. Oh, you lie to yourselves and say you fight by certain rules, but humans have killed each other—men, women and children— in horrific ways for centuries. We are the same, your species and mine; the only difference is we don't pretend we are something we are not. Civilization is a garment you humans wear when it suits you, a disguise, like our own discarded human clothing. And it slips off just as easily when it suits your needs."

Al had no desire to get into a philosophical discussion; he needed information, needed to find answers.

"Einarr has counted on that false human outrage," Tabon continued, "counted on the fact that though these acts would seem reasonable to the Eaton, they would cause you to refuse to cooperate. Then he could use your refusal to sway others to his cause."

"I am only interested in getting Anne out of there. What happens after that, happens. It's your problem. Even if this Einarr fires up all three thousand of you, you don't stand a chance. It is not really my concern."

"It is your concern," Tabon said, his large hands clenching into fists. "You are right, the final outcome would be that we would be wiped out, but what would happen until the last of us is killed, eh? If each of us goes into a building and sets it on fire, are you prepared for three thousand fires set all at once across this city? Then if each of those warriors goes onto the street and starts killing humans, how many could they kill before your police could stop them? Ten each, twenty each, thirty? Are you willing to accept three thousand buildings aflame and ten to thirty thousand dead? The streets of this city would be lined with fire and flowing with blood. We would be destroyed, but could man bear the cost?"

Tabon sat back in the chair again, his voice dropped, his clenched fists slackened. "This can all be prevented if you just find the murderers and turn them over to us. It would foil Einarr's plans and the Eaton would return to living peacefully, hidden away as they have for decades."

"We have laws that we live by. We have a legal process. They must be tried and, if convicted, we will punish them." In light of what had been going on with the investigation, Al knew this was a lie, but what was he supposed to do? Agree to hand over human beings to these creatures?

Tabon looked at Al in disbelief. "Your laws don't apply here. Think of who these men are that you are protecting. If Kustaa had been human, these three beat an old man and threw him into the street to die. Do you want to risk tens of thousands of lives to protect men such as these? Risk your woman's life to protect them? We will be able to determine if the ones you find are indeed the ones who did it. There is no chance a mistake will be made. Do all of my kind and thousands upon thousands of yours deserve to die for three such as these?"

"Even if I agreed, how am I supposed to round up the three and deliver them to you singlehandedly? It's impossible. And even if I could, I can't leave Anne in that situation the whole time."

"I am afraid you have no choice in that regard. I will promise you that I will keep her from being harmed while you search for the murderers. But you must act quickly. I will not be able to protect her forever."

"How do I know you will be able to protect her at all? It seems this Einarr is running the show and, as you said, he really doesn't want to deal."

"Yes, but to get the rest of the Eaton to support him he has to give the appearance that he is sincere in his desire to catch the killers. If he harms her before the exchange then his sincerity will be questioned and his plans will fail."

"There is another issue. He and his group murdered and cannibalized children and killed police officers. The police department is not going to stop digging until they find out who committed those crimes and bring them to justice."

"We will have to go deeper, stay off the streets for several months. This will pass."

"Don't fool yourself, he fixed you good. The police will keep looking until they have someone to blame for those murders. Eventually they will find your kind."

"What is done can't be undone. We will have to take the chance."

"You had your turn, you stated what you want, now hear me out. If I agree to this, you need to hand over Einarr and those that support him."

"You are in no position to dictate terms."

"It is the only thing that makes sense. Do you think for a minute that if this plan fails, he will just give up? No, he will find another way to provoke a conflict. You can't assure me that he won't kill others and he will constantly put your kind at risk. The only way this works is, I capture the ones you are looking for. You hand over Anne and then you set up Einarr and his followers."

"Impossible. Your people started this. That is what put these events in motion."

"You said yourself it was just an excuse. If this doesn't work the way he wants, he will find another excuse. This way, you get what you want, I get Anne back and the police get their murderers. Up until now, no one knew you guys existed. They will be more willing to believe there were only ten or fifteen of you than that there are thousands. It will work. I get the killers, you set up Einarr and his group for the cops, and this is done."

Tabon sank into thought. Al could not read the various emotions that played across those misshapen features.

"It is the only way to ensure he doesn't put your kind in danger in the future and to get the police to stop looking."

Tabon looked up and Al could read the sadness and resignation in his eyes. "I feel you were right the first time—they will never stop looking. But maybe if we give them something, they won't look as hard and will give up the search sooner. In any event, you are also correct in that Einarr will find another way to get what he wants." With a sigh, he stuck out a large, calloused hand. "We have an agreement then?"

CHAPTER 27

1

Al woke in his own bed. Even though his thoughts upon waking were foggy, there was no false illusion that what he had experienced had all been a dream. The pain signals were coming in from all sectors of his body, verifying every physical assault he had been under.

After he and Tabon had made their deal, bargaining with the lives of men and Eaton alike as easily as if they had been trading baseball cards, Tabon seemed to relax, as if the path forward was clear and not littered with a thousand possibilities for failure.

He had gotten up from his chair and began rummaging around in a large plastic bin filled with clothes.

"You are a mess," he said. "I will find you some clothes so you can travel without raising suspicion." He pulled out an old knit cap and overcoat that Al used to cover his blood-caked scalp and torn, filthy clothing.

"This reminds me," Al said, "Why my shoe?"

"What?" Tabon asked.

"Why did he take my shoe? When I first bumped into Einarr on the street, he stole one of my shoes and then it was returned, I think by the crippled one."

"Oh, you mean Hop Frog."

"Who?"

"Hop Frog. That is the nickname I gave him after the title character in the Edgar Allen Poe story. His real name is Knud. He used to like to ride on the outside of subway trains. He lost his grasp one day and got caught between the train and the tunnel wall. His leg and back were broken and mangled, but he survived. The accident twisted his mind as well; I started to call him Hop Frog and now they all do. Einarr uses him for much of his unsavory work."

Al paused. "You read Edgar Allen Poe?"

"Yes. Don't look so surprised, Detective. Look around you," Tabon said, gesturing toward the piles and piles of books and newspapers. "I taught myself how to read. I have gone through garbage dumps, abandoned homes, closed stores…I've even broken into a few libraries to gather all the literature I could, and I have read a great deal of it. I also read your newspapers, so I am very aware of what is going on in the human world. Not only does this satisfy my own desire for knowledge, but it makes me valuable to the Eaton, as I can learn of anything occurring with the humans that may affect them."

"They don't read, the Eaton?"

"To some extent. Simple things. They are cunning in their own way but they don't have the capacity for it. Since I am half human, I do have abilities that they do not."

"But again, why my shoe?"

Tabon smiled a disturbing, fang-filled smile. "To get your scent. How do you think we located where you live? Having your scent for an Eaton is as good as having your photograph. There was an Eaton stationed on every subway platform along the line you took from the police station. Once you got off the train, you were recognized by your scent and they followed you to your apartment. After that, they no longer needed the shoe."

"So they can track me by my scent?"

"Like a bloodhound."

Al had realized there was much about these creatures he didn't know, information that may be critical in knowing the safest way to eliminate them. Unfortunately he didn't have time for further discussion. He was anxious to get going, to start to work on getting Anne out of there.

Tabon led him to the surface through a very circuitous route. There was no way Al was going to be able to retrace their steps and find Tabon's hideout.

Once on the street, Al was able to hail a cab. He slouched in the shadows of the back seat so as not to alarm the driver with his beaten and battered countenance. He had been surprised to find his wallet and money still in his pants pocket, but then, why wouldn't they be there? What use did the Eaton have for such things? It was not like they could wander into a bar and buy themselves a beer.

He did not go to the police station, had no intention to, at least not yet. He would not be able to accomplish what he needed to do if he had. Once there, he would fall back into the world of rules and procedures and protocol. Well, there was no protocol for circumventing the law and dealing in human lives. He would have been forced to tell his story and, whether they believed it or not, the captain would have formulated a response. A review of old city maps to identify any past structures that would match the description of the chamber that contained the Eaton settlement. The deploying of personnel and the careful sweep of any possible locations identified. This activity would certainly result in getting Anne killed and little else. No, he had to go this alone.

At this point they probably assumed he was dead, and that was just fine with him. It would allow him the freedom to do what he needed to do to secure Anne's safety.

He had the cabbie take him to his apartment. He was banking on the fact no one would be looking for him there. The police had no reason to believe he would not return to the station if he was okay. He would be able to spend the night and get cleaned up before his next move. By the time he had climbed into the cab, he had a clear plan. He intended to honor his deal with Tabon. He would find the perpetrators and turn them over to the Eaton in exchange for Anne. Tabon would then betray the whereabouts of the rogue Eaton led by Einarr.

That is when Al would bring in the police to deal with them. This would ensure Anne's safety and remove the most dangerous and immediate threat to the city. At that point Al would break his word. He had promised Tabon that he would not expose the existence of the rest of the Eaton, but he had lied. He had seen what they were capable of. He believed they could, as Tabon himself had said, kill tens of thousands before they could be stopped. Tabon had also admitted their warlike nature. What was to prevent others from turning to violence in the future? Al could not leave that ticking time bomb living under the streets of New York. Once Anne was safe and the immediate threat had been removed, the rest of them needed to be hunted down and destroyed.

He entered the building, being careful to keep his head down so that the security camera in the entryway wouldn't get a good shot of his face. He entered his apartment and flipped on the lights. The cushions from his couch that had been sent for lab tests were still missing. There were still traces of fingerprint powder on the coffee and end tables as well as the windowsill.

Al had gone into his bedroom, taking off the hat and shrugging out of the old threadbare coat as he went. He had started to pull some clean clothes out of his dresser when he decided he needed to sit on the bed, just for a moment. He was exhausted both physically and mentally. His head was drumming and his body was beginning to stiffen. He lay back just for a moment.

2

Anne was seated cross legged, a dirty cloth bag over her head and her arms suspended above her in a V, wrists tied to iron bars. She did not know how long she had been here but her arms and shoulders had gone numb and her legs screamed their protest as she tried to shift positions.

Anne was shivering in fear, trying not to cry but losing the battle. Tears rolled down her face and she began to whimper softly. Her mind was racing; she couldn't focus, overwhelmed with the feelings of utter helplessness and fear.

Her ordeal had started the day after her dinner with Al. That night she had trouble sleeping. She could tell that Al was preoccupied and that was normal, but he also seemed stressed, and that was not like him. If anything he was the opposite—nothing got Al flustered, at least not that you could tell. He was always calm, cool and collected. It was one of the things that had been frustrating about their marriage. No matter what type of troubles they had, personal, financial, Al never thought it was a big deal. It was frustrating when you had to do all the worrying for two. The way he was probably served him very well in his chosen profession, but it made it awful tough to have a meaningful relationship.

So when she was able to pick up on Al's stress, it was very disconcerting. She could only conclude that something extremely dangerous must be going on for Al to let his calm facade slip. Not that she wouldn't have been concerned anyway, but she still had feelings for Al, had often wondered if they had given up too soon. It all made for a fitful night. It had seemed she had just fallen to sleep when her alarm went off.

She had the day off and spent the morning cleaning her apartment. When she had finished she showered, dressed and headed out the door. As she stepped out on the front step, she noticed a large dark patch on the sidewalk down by the street. She went down the walk and looked down at the sidewalk. Someone had spilled some type of brownish red stain or paint on the sidewalk. The liquid had dried but various symbols had been drawn in it before then. There were concentric circles with several lines crossing them. Probably just some kids fooling around.

She hurried down the street toward the subway.

It was early and the street was empty. The air was so still that Anne had felt like she was walking on a Hollywood sound stage depicting New York rather than a real city street. She was about a block from the subway when she thought she heard someone behind her. Glancing back, she noticed a hunched figure following her. The person moved with an awkward, limping gait. He was clad in a battered black trench coat that was too large for his form. The coat dragged on the cement, sweeping the sidewalk as he went.

That hunched, shambling gait made Anne apprehensive. She started to walk faster. She felt self-conscious, fought the urge to break into a run. She glanced back again. The figure was not moving any faster and she let out a sigh of relief. Some poor, crippled homeless man, she thought, and immediately felt sorry and a little ashamed for her initial reaction.

As she looked forward again, she caught movement out of the corner of her eye. A cloth bag was whisked over her head, strong arms wrapped around her waist and she was jerked violently sideways. She opened her mouth to scream and the cloth of the bag was stuffed into her mouth. Something was wrapped or tied around her head, holding the sack cloth between her open jaws.

"We can't have you screaming your head off, now can we?" said a voice in a gravelly brogue.

She lashed out with her fists, and the arms that had been around her waist moved, easily trapping her own arms to her sides in a bear hug. She was lifted and turned sideways as if she were a stack of books being carried under a school child's arm. She tried kicking as hard as she could but another pair of arms wrapped around her legs, pinning them together. She was carried between the two like a rolled-up section of carpet.

After several minutes, she heard the sound of metal grating on pavement and then she was being lowered down feet-first to other waiting hands. She struggled, banging her elbow against the side of the opening she was being lowered through, but again she was easily restrained. They carried her a little farther and then she was being forced onto a chair. She felt her arms and legs being bound to the legs and arms of the chair. The bag was removed—at least, she felt it being removed. She could not see anything because she was in complete darkness. She began to scream for help. A gag was forced between her teeth and tied behind her head, a blindfold was tied over her eyes, and the sack was replaced.

She sat there listening to the distant drip of water, smelling a damp basement smell through the cloth of the sack. She lost track of time she could have been there minutes or hours, she had no way of knowing.

Anne was lifted, chair and all, and transported again. She was finally set down and the bag lifted from her head. Light filtered in around the edges of her blindfold and she heard quiet sobbing next to her. The sound of sobbing was drowned out by cruel, rasping laughter. Then she heard something that surprised her to the point that for a moment she forgot her fear.

There was a gravelly voice, with the same brogue as the others she had heard, and it was saying Al's name. She was even more surprised when she heard Al's voice reply. It sounded hollow and tired, but there was no mistaking it was Al's voice. As ridiculous as it was considering her current situation and the desperation and weariness in Al's voice, the sound of it gave her hope.

The sobbing next to her got louder. Anne fought to maintain her composure, to not give in to the fear. Then she heard the harsh meat grinder of a voice saying things that at first didn't completely make sense. But then it became clear he was threatening the life of Anne and whoever was next to her, telling Al he had to choose between the two. Only then did it dawn on her that the other must be the woman Al had been dating.

At that point Anne lost her composure and began to weep. She heard Al saying he would not make such a choice and she knew him well enough to know it was true. Al could never consciously cause an innocent person's death, even if it meant saving someone else. Yes, even if it meant saving her. Nor would she want him to. How could you love someone who could be callous enough to do such a thing? She also knew that it meant there was a good chance she was going to die in the next few moments.

The tears came; she couldn't help it. She heard the anguish in Al's voice and the tears came, for him, for herself and for the other woman.

There was a split second of silence and then Anne heard a strange meaty sound, followed by a choked, liquid gurgling. Anne's nostrils were filled with the noxious, coppery smell of blood and feces. She heard a pitiful wail of anguish and realized that noise was coming from Al. The quiet sobbing next to her had suddenly stopped.

The fear and panic had risen within her until it started to trip circuits in her brain. A dark hole opened before her. She offered only token resistance as she slipped into that welcoming darkness.

She was vaguely aware of what had happened after that. Of being carried a long distance and the pain in her arms, legs and joints. When she slowly emerged from the safety of the black depths where her mind had taken shelter, fear and dread had been right there, like long-lost friends awaiting her return.

CHAPTER 28

1

He woke in a panic. Al didn't know how long he had been asleep. In that time, his body had tightened like wet leather left in the hot sun. As he tried to climb out of bed, his joints creaked and groaned. It felt like every joint, muscle and tendon had fused and would split and snap if he pushed too hard.

He rose and hobbled stiffly into the bathroom. He bent forward, grabbing the sides of the sink in each hand, and examined his face in the mirror. What stared back at him looked more like an old catcher's mitt than a face: filthy, crusted with grime and dried blood. The left side was a puffy, bluish-purple mass, the left eye a barely visible slit. The right side of his face was in a little better shape, still somewhat swollen but with just some minor cuts and bruises; his right eye, however, was glassy and distant.

He gingerly touched a large cut on his right temple and decided, though not pretty, it also was not too deep. "You've seen better days," Al said to his reflection. He then leaned into the shower, turned the water on and grabbed the sink again to steady himself as he waited for the shower to get hot.

As he showered, letting the hot water slowly loosen his constricted muscles, he began to think about his next steps.

His mind wandered to the sight of Anne in that cage, surrounded by those beasts. He fought to push those thoughts out of his mind. He couldn't afford to get stuck in the emotional quicksand that train of thought would create. If he gave in to his emotions, the hopelessness of the situation would drag him down into depression and inertia or worse. Acting out of desperation, he could do something impulsive and get Anne killed.

As desperate as the situation was, he had to think clearly, stay focused. He had to suppress his sorrow and concern for Anne. He had to coldly and logically work through what needed to be done.

The more he thought about the logistics of what he had to do, he didn't see how he could handle it alone. He had to capture three individuals. Hold them somewhere while he set up the meeting for the exchange with the Eaton. Transport them to the meeting place and make the exchange. And he had to fly under the radar the whole time.

He wrestled for a little while with the moral aspect of what he was going to attempt. Surprisingly, what Tabon had said made some sense. For all these three had known, they beat a helpless old man and threw him into traffic. Even so, Al was going to have sleepless nights thinking about what was going to happen to them once he handed them over. But if this did haunt him, it would be a small price to pay if he could get Anne out safely.

He was going to need help. There was only one person he could think of that might help him out and keep things quiet. The problem was that person was going to have to be convinced, was going to have to arrive at the moral destination that Al was still struggling to reach himself and be willing to go to jail or worse if they failed.

After his shower, Al dressed quickly. He dug his badge out of the pocket of the filthy and torn leather jacket he had worn into the tunnels. His handgun was long gone, dropped somewhere during the events of the other day. He had the M4, had kept it concealed under his borrowed coat during his cab ride home. He slid that under his bed; it may come in handy later.

He got his personal handgun and shoulder holster out of the lockbox in his closet and strapped it on. He was glad to see he had plugged his phone into the charger before he had fallen asleep. Didn't remember doing it, but there it was.

Al rummaged around in the top drawer of his dresser. He found an old pair of aviator sunglasses. He slipped them on and checked himself out in the bathroom mirror. The shower had done wonders for the way he looked. The dried blood and grime were gone and the cut on his right temple didn't look nearly as bad as it had previously. The sunglasses covered his swollen left eye. The side of his face was still a puffy kaleidoscope of yellows, purples and blues but at least he wouldn't scare anyone.

It would have to do. He went back to the dresser and pulled out some extra cash he had hidden in an old sock stuffed in the back of his sock and underwear drawer. He straightened up the apartment and wiped down the bathroom to cover his tracks, just on the off chance somebody came here looking for him. He wanted to remain missing as long as needed to do what had to be done.

2

Al stood across the street from Mike's home in Queens. It was one of those "All in the Family" type houses: small, with a tiny front porch. There didn't appear to be anyone home; the house looked completely dark.

He had been to Mike's house only once before, for dinner, when they had first become partners. Mike's wife, Joan, was quiet and reserved; the exact opposite of Mike's gregarious personality. Physically they were a mismatch as well—Mike large, blonde haired, Joan petite with mousy brown hair.

Al had just gone through his divorce from Anne and was not dating anyone at the time, so it had just been the three of them. Mike's two daughters had been at a sleepover. The dinner and Joan had been pleasant enough but he had not been back to the house since. He and Mike, though they developed a good partnership on the job, had never had enough in common for that to translate into a deep friendship outside of it.

Al had thought about calling Mike first to arrange to meet him, but decided against it. He wasn't sure how Mike was going to react. Al had been missing since the operation, and even if he told Mike, he wanted to keep the fact he was alive a secret. Mike may notify the captain, thinking he was doing it for Al's own good. He decided not to give Mike advanced notice.

Al crossed the street and climbed the four creaking wooden steps to the porch. There was a metal screen door over the front door, the screen not yet replaced by glass for the winter.

Al rang the bell and waited. The wind had kicked up and he couldn't hear if there was movement inside or not. He was about to ring the bell again when the door opened. Mike's face appeared in the space allowed by the chain on the door, peering through the screen.

"Yes? Can I help you?"

Al realized between the swelling and the sunglasses, he was barely recognizable. He took off the sunglasses. "Mike, it's me, Al."

Mike's eyes widened with recognition and surprise. "Holy shit, it is you. We all thought you were dead. What the hell happened to you? You look like you've been hit by a truck."

Al thought it was a pretty interesting choice of words, considering what had started this whole mess. "Why are you sitting here in the dark? Where are Joan and the kids?"

"They're visiting Joan's mother," Mike answered. "And yes, just a regular visit, we didn't have a fight or anything. But Jesus, Al, what happened to you? The whole department thinks you're dead. Have you called in yet?"

"No, I haven't checked in; don't think that would be a good idea just yet. But Mike, I really need to talk to you. Can I come in? It's kinda cold out here."

"What the hell's wrong with me, sure, sure, come on in," Mike said, closing the door to unlatch the chain and then stepping back, opening it just wide enough for Al to slip in.

Mike led the way into the living room just inside the door. He switched on a lamp on an end table next to a large easy chair that appeared worn and comfortable. The lamp barely lit the room in a dull glow. Al came in and sat on the couch that was at right angles to the easy chair. His body, still achy and tight like his joints had rusted, welcomed the homey comfort of the couch.

Al glanced around the room. The furniture was a little dated and worn, but exuded comfort and a feeling of home.

Al forced himself to remain calm. He was desperate to rescue Anne, felt an urgency to get moving, to just blurt everything out to Mike in a torrent of words and get his assistance. But he knew what he had to say was unbelievable, and if he was going to get Mike's help, if he was going to be able to convince Mike he wasn't crazy, he was going to have to approach this carefully.

"You want a drink or somethin'?" Mike asked.

Again the opposing forces within Al pushed and pulled. He decided he could use a drink desperately. It may help him get the words out and it may help Mike believe him.

"A scotch would be good," Al answered, shutting his eyes briefly as Mike went into the kitchen for glasses. Al could hear the ice from the ice maker clinking into each glass.

He felt a cool glass touch his fingertips. He hadn't heard Mike come back in the room. He had dozed, still so tired. He thanked Mike, who sat in the easy chair. Al stared into the amber liquid, thinking of where to start.

3

Mike was staring wide-eyed at Al. It had taken about an hour and a half, plus three scotches apiece, for Al to relate the details of the failed operation, the murder of Carrie and Al's subsequent trip through the New York underground, his conversation with Tabon and what Tabon had shown him. There had been many stops and starts to the story as Mike asked questions or looked for clarification.

"I'm tellin' you, Al," Mike said, shaking his head, "normally if you had come to me with a story like this, I would think you were high or nuts or both. But some of what you said matches rumors that have leaked out about that operation, especially around the nature of the injuries to the cops that were killed. It matches. Still, an entirely different species living under the city, like a whole village of mole people or somethin', that is hard to swallow."

"I know it is, but that doesn't make it any less true. I'm sorry, but I don't have the time to debate the issue. Every hour I waste is another hour Anne is alone, scared and in danger."

"Why didn't you go back to the station then? If what you describe is true, that old reservoir or whatever it is must be on some of the old city maps. The captain could send a SWAT team and raid the place."

"All that would do is get Anne killed, and maybe it would get me killed too. Besides, I'm not so sure the captain can be trusted."

"What do you mean?"

"Aren't you just a little suspicious of everything surrounding this case? As soon as we suspect the sons of two of the most powerful men in the city, one of them the police commissioner, the captain tries to squash the investigation. Tells us we don't have enough to bring them in, can't get us the subpoena we need. Then when we find a witness and tell the captain about it, that witness is conveniently killed while trying to escape. Be honest with yourself, Mike. You talked to Barnes. He was a wise ass, but did he really seem to you to be someone who would be stupid enough to go for a cop's gun?"

"What are you saying? The captain had him killed?"

"I'm saying the captain was covering his ass and let the commissioner know what was going on, and the commissioner had it taken care of."

"But Al, the captain was yanking Schrager's chain about the accident, remember? And the captain advised us to stay quiet about the tape."

"I don't know, maybe that was all a smoke screen, maybe he was playin' us. I mean, I always thought he was legit, but when I think about how he was so down on pursuing the case and then saying he couldn't get the subpoena… I mean, we don't even really know if he tried, and then Barnes gets killed. It all kinda adds up. But besides all that, even if the captain was clean, he would never be on board for what needs to be done."

"I'm almost afraid to ask. What do you think needs to be done?" Mike said.

Al hesitated for a moment. He had not said it out loud even to himself, and he wasn't sure how Mike would react—

hell, he wasn't even sure how he would react once it was out there in the open and not just a crazy thought bouncing around his head. Things had a way of being more real once they were said out loud.

"I have to do what they ask. I have to round up those three kids and turn them over and get Anne back."

"Are you out of your mind?" Mike said, sitting up so quickly scotch sloshed onto his pants leg. "Besides the fact you probably couldn't pull it off, you're gonna end up in prison for the rest of your life, or more likely, end up dead. And I'm not even getting into the morals of it."

"Think about that video, Mike, think about what Barnes said," Al countered. "Do you doubt for one second that they are guilty?"

"Well, no, I guess not."

"Does Anne deserve to die for people that are capable of doing what they did? Nothing deserves to happen to them for what they did? We know they will never be charged, they will never face one day in prison, they will just go on with their privileged lives while Anne dies. Anne dies and maybe thousands of others."

"I wish you hadn't come here, Al. I wish you hadn't told me all this. Why are you here? You're putting me in a bad spot."

"I'm here to put you in a worse spot. I'm here because I need your help," Al started. "I have run this through my head over and over and I can't figure out how to do this alone. I need at least one other person."

"Al, what you are thinking of doing is crazy. It will never work."

Al looked around the room, took in the comfortable, homey surroundings. He noticed a picture in a frame next to the lamp. It showed Mike's daughters in soccer uniforms, each holding a soccer ball, and Mike and his wife standing behind them, beaming with pride. At that moment Al realized he had no right to ask Mike to do this. Being partners had its limits, being partners only went so far. Mike had built a real life for himself. Al couldn't ask him to give that up for him, or even for Anne.

"You know, Mike you're right. I shouldn't have come here. This isn't your problem. But I have to do something. I can't leave Anne down there. I only ask that you don't tell anyone you saw me. Things will be easier if they aren't hunting for me." Al stood, his joints complaining as they were called back into action. He tossed down the last of the scotch, put the glass down, held his hand out to Mike. "Sorry. No hard feelings?"

Mike looked up at Al and shook the offered hand. "No hard feelings. Be careful, partner."

Al turned toward the door. He walked to the front door and had just put his hand on the doorknob when he heard Mike clear his throat behind him.

"Hold on, Al, I need to tell you something," Mike said. "I've got a confession of my own to make."

Al stood at the door. He had turned to face Mike, his hand still on the knob. Mike looked down at the floor and cleared his throat again. "It wasn't the captain that let the commissioner know what was going on. As far as I know, the cap is legit. I told the commissioner about the tape and Barnes and his kid."

"What!" Al said in disbelief. "Why? Why would you do that?"

"It was right after we had gone to the captain with Barnes's story and he shot us down. I figured the case wasn't going anywhere anyway, so maybe I could leverage what we knew to get in good with the commissioner. You know, with the girls getting older and college right around the corner I've been dying for a promotion. I figured if I did a favor for him, the commissioner may throw something my way."

"Barnes was killed, Mike."

"I know. I didn't expect that to happen. I figured the commissioner would just squash the investigation, you know? It wasn't going anywhere anyway. But obviously our commissioner does not like loose ends."

"What did he promise you, Mike?"

"Nothing, that's the kicker, not a thing. I gave him a copy of the tape and told him about Barnes, told him I would do what I could to keep things quiet. The whole time I'm thinking I'm not going to have to do anything because the cap already said to drop it. Well, he thanked me, said the force needed cops who remembered where their bread was buttered and that he would be getting in touch. Only he never did get in touch." Mike paused and took another slug of his drink.

"I caught a glimpse of the cops that came to transport Barnes. They were plainclothes, which surprised me. Why hadn't they sent uniforms for something as routine as a transport? Then I hear about Barnes being shot. Finally, a couple of days ago I get a feeling I'm being followed. It was right down the block here, so I duck into this bagel shop I go to on Sundays; I know the owner. So I go through and out the back door and come up the alley. Across the street I see two guys looking in a shop window, but I can tell one of them is one of the cops that picked up Barnes. So I cut through to the next block and came home."

"Jesus, Mike."

"Yeah, I know. I sent Joan and the girls to stay with Joan's parents and I called in sick the last couple of days. But buddy, I'm fucked. Our commissioner really does not like loose ends."

"That means…"

"Yep, you're fucked too. They know you saw the tape, so if they are after me, they will be after you too if they find out you're alive. If you do what you are planning, they will know you have a connection to those kids. You will be one of the first ones they suspect."

"What about the captain?"

"I don't know, maybe the captain too, maybe not. I never told him we showed the tape to the cap, so it looked like I had controlled the whole thing from the start, figuring that would give me more leverage. So the captain may be safe."

Leverage and balance. Al thought he had heard that before. "Well, if I do what I am planning, chances are I'm a dead man anyway, so I guess it doesn't matter," Al said. "So what is your plan? You can't hide out in your house forever."

"That's why I told you to hold up," Mike answered. "I'm going to help you. Just like you, I'm a dead man anyway. I really fucked up. If we're both fucked, the least we can do is save Anne."

CHAPTER 29

1

There came a voice. The tone was harsh, grating, like a file being dragged across rough wood. Like the other voices Anne had heard, there was an unmistakable but unidentifiable brogue in the speech.

"If you do as you are told, you will not be harmed. Nod your head if you understand me."

She had focused on that voice, nodding slowly.

"You will be held here until we get what we want. Then you will be freed. I am going to have your hands untied. You are not to remove the sack from your head until you are told to do so. And henceforth, if you are instructed to place the sack back over your head, you will do as you are told. Do you understand?"

Again Anne had nodded.

"This is very important. Do not obey and catch even a glimpse of any of us, you will be killed instantly. Try to escape and you will be killed instantly. Otherwise, you have nothing to fear. Do you understand?"

Anne nodded for a third time. Amazingly, instead of causing her greater fear, this exchange calmed her somewhat. Her mind began to focus. She locked onto that voice like a lifeline and began to think of one thing—survival.

She had heard some mumbling and shuffling and then her wrists were untied. Her arms fell uselessly to her sides. It was a few minutes before that prickly feeling began to enter her limbs, followed by pain and cramping. She heard the voice again, slightly muffled.

"When you are able, you may remove the sack."

After several minutes of working the pain and stiffness out of her arms and shoulders, she had reached up and pulled the cloth bag off her head. That was when she got the first look at her ornate, canvas-enshrouded prison.

The elevator must have once had a glorious existence in one of New York's finer hotels. The iron scrollwork that adorned the sides of the elevator car showed a high degree of craftsmanship. The paint on the ironwork was stripped from some sections and flaking on others, rusted bare metal showing through. There were tarps draped on the walls. These were oil, paint and dirt stained. In one corner of the cell was a rusted bucket. She didn't have to tax her imagination to know what that was for.

Through the grillwork on the top of her cell she could see the remnants of the pulley system that had once operated the elevator. Past that, high above, was a vaulted brick ceiling. Considering the dampness and foul, moldy smell, Anne guessed she was in an underground chamber. The dampness and chill penetrated the jeans, sweater and leather jacket she had been wearing at the time she was abducted.

A torch had been lashed to the frame of the elevator so that it protruded over the top at a forty-five-degree angle. The flickering torchlight caused shadows to dance on the tarps.

Anne was calmer now. Well, maybe calm wasn't the proper term—more like focused and watchful. You couldn't maintain the level of fear that she had been experiencing and survive. At some point, the body's defense mechanisms would kick in and you would slip into shock. Either that or you would fry the circuitry in your brain and there would be no coming back. Anne had teetered on the edge of that blissful abyss, consciousness slipping in and out, the sensory input of the physical world fading and sharpening and fading again like a radio signal on a long drive through the mountains.

She had spent the next few hours seated on the floor of her cell, shivering and hugging herself against the cold. Then she heard the voice from beyond the tarp again. "Place the sack over your head."

She did as she was told and heard the rustling of the tarp and the grating sound of iron on iron. After several minutes, the voice was back. "You may remove the sack."

She lifted her blindfold and saw that two deep bowls had been placed on the cell floor. One contained brackish-looking water and the other contained grayish chunks of meat. The sight of them made her realize just how hungry and thirsty she was.

Anne lifted the bowl of water. She could see oily islands of residue clouding the surface. She was too thirsty to care. She greedily gulped down the water, barely noting the sooty, oily taste. No sooner had she taken several large swallows then she felt her stomach convulse into a knot. She doubled over and her stomach clenched, pumping the rancid water from her gaping mouth. It splattered on the floor at her feet.

She stood there for several minutes, bent over, wiping the ropes of spittle from her mouth with the back of her hand and trying to gain control of her stomach. Once she had a semblance of control, she lifted the bowl of meat. She didn't think she had ever been this hungry before; her stomach ached with emptiness. She lifted the bowl and cautiously sniffed the non-descript meat within. Her stomach immediately started to convulse once more. She put the bowl down and pushed it away.

Anne felt a wave of despair wash over her. How long could she survive without drinkable water? Why was she even here? She took a deep breath, trying to screw up her courage.

"I can't drink this," she said. Her voice came out cracked, rasping, meek. She swallowed hard and tried again, louder. "Hello, whoever you are, I can't eat or drink this."

She listened but there was nothing but silence. She carefully lay on her side on the cold dank cement, pulling her knees up to her chest and hugging her legs, trying to stay warm. Her thoughts spiraled, getting darker and darker, her despair growing. She thought of the woman she never knew, Al's girlfriend, and what had happened to her. This was one time Anne thought that imagination was not worse than reality. And Al, what had become of Al? Was he nearby being held captive as well? She hoped that were true, because the alternative was too frightening to think of.

Without realizing it, she began to rock, gently humming to herself, trying to sooth her nerves, gain control. She was exhausted both physically and emotionally, but her mind was racing. As exhausted as she was, she thought she was too frightened to rest. She was wrong—the body and mind have their limits, and soon she began to doze.

2

Anne awoke to complete darkness. The torch above her cell had been extinguished. She was lying on her side in a fetal position. She heard a bare whisper of a sound like a dried leaf being pushed along a sidewalk by a gentle breeze. The sound became slightly louder; now it sounded like a skittering, scratching noise. Then she heard one of the bowls sliding on the floor, wobbling.

Something furry brushed past her hand, not six inches from her face. She let out a small moan, all that her dry desert of a throat could muster, and pushed herself backwards, scrambling until her back was against the cold bars of her cell.

She sat there, eyes wide, staring into the darkness. She kicked her foot out in the direction of the noise. It struck a bowl and sent it sliding across the floor. Anne heard angry squeaking and that dry, whispery sound again as her visitors scampered across the floor. A shiver of disgust went down her spine and she used the bars of her cell to pull herself to her feet. She stood there shivering, feeling tired and weak, but too disgusted to sit down. She felt her stomach cramp with hunger, but the thirst was worse. Her lips, despite the humidity of her subterranean prison, felt cracked and dried, her throat like it was coated with sand.

She felt the moisture of the bars of the elevator. Condensation had formed a film of fine droplets on the iron. She turned and pressed her dry, cracked lips to the cool wet metal. She ran her tongue over her lips, trying to collect just a little moisture. She ran a finger slowly up the bar and carefully touched the drop of water it had collected to the tip of her tongue. It was an agonizing tease, but it was something. A wild thought ran through her head: the elevator was so old, it was probably covered in lead-based paint. Trivial concerns from another world. She continued to collect drops of water and rub them onto her parched lips.

It was then she heard voices on the other side of the tarp. There were two distinct voices, and though she couldn't make out what was being said, they seemed to be arguing. The voices startled her furry visitors who must have returned while she was preoccupied trying to sooth her thirst. She could hear them scampering off beyond the tarp.

She lay back down, listening, her eyes straining to see in the darkness. Time ticked by. She heard nothing more. Then, so suddenly it made her jump, she heard a voice in the darkness. "Please place the bag back over your head." This was a different voice than the one that had spoken to her before. It had the same accent, the same brogue, but it was somehow smoother, less gravelly. She felt around on the floor, found the cloth sack and pulled it over her head. She then backed up again against the cell bars.

"Okay, it is on," she said. She heard the rustling of the tarp and the sound of metal on metal. There was movement in her cell and she could hear heavy breathing. Unbidden fear began to climb within her. She cringed, not sure what was next.

She again heard the sound of metal on metal and the movement of the tarp. "You may remove the bag," the voice said.

She reached up, grabbed the edge of the sack and slowly pulled it over her head. The torch was lit again, smoke from the guttering flame trailing up toward the vaulted ceiling above. Her vision, blurry at first, adjusted to the light. There were new items in her cell. Slowly they came into focus and at first she thought she must be hallucinating. But no, they were real. On the floor, like artifacts from another time, were a bottled water and a battered pizza box.

Anne let out a small whimper, slowly crouched down, and half crawled, half scrambled across the floor. She grabbed the bottled water first and brought it to her lips. As she raised the plastic bottle she could actually smell the water. She carefully took a little in her mouth, letting it trickle slowly down her throat. She wet her dry lips with her tongue. She sipped a little more water, careful not to drink too quickly, afraid she wouldn't be able to keep it down.

Once she had slackened her thirst somewhat, she turned to the pizza box. Inside were four slices of cheese pizza. The cheese had coagulated to the consistency of rubber but to

Anne it looked like a gourmet meal. She took several bites and immediately began to choke, her throat still dry and constricted. With the help of some more water, she managed to choke the pizza down. Her stomach began to rumble but held. She almost wept with relief.

After that, the bowls never appeared again. There would always be bottled water and some form of food from the world above: a half-eaten Whopper, a box of stale donuts, a Styrofoam container half full of lobster risotto. Anne never stopped to question where the food came from or who had sampled it before it got to her. As soon as she determined there was a good chance it hadn't gone bad yet, she ate it and was grateful.

CHAPTER 30

1

The fact that he had been the one who tipped the commissioner was not the only surprise Mike had for Al. He had also discovered who the third kid in the video was.

He showed Al a newspaper article about a teenager committing suicide, and who should be quoted in the article but Sean Hutchinson and Carter Stevens. It seemed they had been classmates and best friends of the deceased. They both spoke eloquently of being concerned about their friend recently as he had seemed depressed, and try as they might, they could not find out why. If that weren't enough, a picture accompanied the article, and Al found himself staring into the face of the kid they had spent so much time searching for.

This resolved one dilemma for Al but created another one. The kid's name was Daniel Edwards. In the video he had appeared a reluctant participant in what had gone on. He had not taken a bat, leaving his lying in the street where Carter had dropped it. Al had been conflicted about this kid, unsure how much responsibility he had for the murder. Al didn't have to be concerned about that any longer. Danny had seen to that.

This presented Al with another dilemma, however. How was he going to deliver a dead man to the Eaton?

He decided to pay Daniel Edwards' family a visit. Al hadn't felt good about disturbing the family at this time, but he found once you started on the road to hell, each step, even one that would have been unimaginable even a day before, became possible.

He easily got past the building security by flashing his badge. His job didn't take him to these high-end buildings too often, but he was not in the frame of mind to appreciate his surroundings. A quick elevator ride and he was standing outside the Edwards apartment.

Mrs. Edwards answered the door. The perfectly styled hair, flawless makeup and tailored clothes did nothing to hide the fact that this woman had spent a great deal of time crying recently.

Her eyes, red-rimmed and blurry, had a lost, faraway look. She held tissues in her hand that she kept wringing and twisting. Al flashed his badge again.

"Hello, Mrs. Edwards. Matt Johnson, Special Children's Unit," he lied. She barely glanced at the badge, not looking too closely; they never did. "I would like to ask you a few questions about Daniel."

"I've already spoken to the police. They have been all through Danny's stuff. Really, I would like to just be left alone," she offered in a tired, distracted voice.

"I understand, ma'am, but I am with a special unit looking into the causes of teen suicide. If we can get a better understanding of what leads a promising teenager to take their life, maybe we can save another family from experiencing your pain." Al hated himself for this charade. He thought about Anne in that cage and pushed ahead.

"If I could come in, ask a few questions, maybe get a look at Daniel's room…?"

"I guess so," Mrs. Edwards said. That faraway look never left her eyes as she stood to the side, letting him in the apartment.

Al sat in the Edwards' immaculate living room and asked Mrs. Edwards about her dead son. Watched as she fought to maintain composure. Finally had her take him to Danny's room, where he asked further questions regarding Danny's state of mind prior to his taking his own life. When he had what he wanted, he had thanked her and left. As he rode down in the elevator he felt dirty. He doubted the day would come when he would ever feel clean again.

That feeling came back now as he sat in his car and looked at the Yankees cap on the seat next to him. He had stolen it from Danny Edwards' room, had slipped it under his jacket when Mrs. Edwards had turned to lead him from the room. Between the scent on the hat and the newspaper article about the suicide that contained Danny's picture, he hoped it was enough to satisfy the Eaton.

Al hadn't just crossed an ethical line, he had obliterated it. He knew at this point there was no return. He was still wrestling with his decision but his mind kept coming back to the same point, circling round and round but always returning, like a moth to a flame. Did Anne deserve to die to protect the likes of these two people?

As for any concern he had that having given in to the Eaton's threats once would encourage more violence in the future...Al fully intended, once Anne was safe, to take steps to ensure the Eaton would never be a threat again.

2

Anne had lost all track of time. Down here, there was no sunrise, no sunset. The torch above would be lit for a period of time and would be extinguished for a period of time. Whether those times corresponded to day and night in the world above, she had no way of knowing. She had no way of knowing if she had been down here for two days, three days or a week.

She found herself sleeping a great deal. There was nothing to do to occupy her time. The boredom coupled with the stress of her situation and the fact that even when she did sleep, it was a fitful sleep, left her tired all the time.

The torch was currently lit, the light dancing on the tarps. Anne sat in her usual position, knees drawn up, her arms wrapped around them, trying to stay warm. The dankness of this place had long since permeated her clothing so that it provided her with little warmth. She heard a rustling as if someone or something was brushing against the tarp.

"Your name is Anne, correct?"

She recognized the voice as that of her benefactor, the one who had provided the food and water.

"Yes," she responded. "Why am I here? What is this all about?" It was the first time anyone had spoken to her except to give orders. She was hoping for some answers.

"I cannot explain to you what this is all about," said the voice after a brief pause. "You will not be harmed as long as Detective Russo does as he promised."

"Al? Al is alive? He's not hurt?" She practically wept. She had been sure, based on what she had heard, that he had been severely injured or worse.

"Detective Russo is very much alive and right now, hopefully is working to attain your freedom."

"If it is money you are looking for, Al doesn't have any. He's just a cop," Anne said.

Grinding laughter came from the other side of the tarp. "We have no use for money; it is not money we want. No, the detective is performing a task, and once that task is done you will be set free."

Anne wasn't sure she believed what she was being told but even the slightest spark of hope has a way of lifting spirits. Anne changed tactics. "Are you the one who has been bringing me the food and the bottled water?"

Again a pause, then "Yes."

"I want to thank you for that. It is very kind."

"Do not misjudge, it is not out of sympathy. I only did that because I cannot have you getting sick and dying. I gave my word to Detective Russo that I would make sure you were not harmed."

"Well, I thank you for the food and water anyway. I would like to ask another favor?" There was no response so Anne forged ahead. "If your intention is not to harm me, then I see no reason that my prison must be so barren."

"What is wrong with it?" said the voice. The puzzled tone of it might have been comical under other circumstances.

"I have nothing to sleep on; I have to lie on the cold hard floor. There is nothing to sit on. When the torch is out, the rats come. It's not safe."

She heard a snort of frustration. "Very well. I will see what I can do to make you more comfortable."

"I would greatly appreciate that."

"Your appreciation is not being sought," came the gruff reply. "As I said, I cannot have you getting sick. You are all so frail."

With that, Anne heard movement beyond the tarp and her visitor was gone.

He did not return, and the torch was extinguished once again. Anne spent another "night" curled up on the cold floor trying to sleep, all the while hearing the skittering of the rats in the dark.

3

It wasn't long after the torch had been lit once again that her visitor returned. "Move to one side and place the bag over your head," she was instructed.

Anne did as she was told. Once the bag was over her head, she heard the sound of the tarp on the cement floor and the metal-on-metal sound that meant her cell was being opened.

She heard something being dragged across the floor, the shuffling of feet and the rattling of the bars of her cage. This went on for several minutes. Then came the metal-on-metal sound again and the dragging of the tarp as it was put back into place.

"You may remove the bag."

Anne slowly lifted the bag off her head, not knowing what to expect. Her eyes widened with surprise. Some heavy rope netting had been tied cattycorner from the back wall of her cell to the side wall, forming a hammock. Heavy blankets had been draped over the netting. In the middle of the floor were a wooden chair and an old, scarred wooden desk. Both looked like the kind Anne had as a child in elementary school. Several books were stacked on the desk and, next to them, a candle in a holder.

Anne walked over to the desk and chair, running her fingertips lightly over the wood worn smooth by thousands of hands. She lifted the books one at a time. They were hardcover volumes, worn with age. She turned each in her hands, reading the titles on the spines. *Tarzan of the Apes*, *Tarzan and the Golden Lion* and *Tarzan and the Jewels of Opar*, all written by Edgar Rice Burroughs. They wouldn't have been Anne's first choice for reading material, but anything to relieve the boredom and help distract her from her situation was welcome.

The reading would have to wait though. She looked longingly at the hammock. She had not been able to sleep properly between the cold, hard cement and the fear of the rats. She went to the hammock, arranged one of the blankets over the roping and lay on top of it, pulling the other blanket over herself. Within minutes she was fast asleep.

CHAPTER 31

1

Sean Hutchinson was in a hurry. He had promised to give Carter a ride and he was already running late. Sean had always been in awe of Carter, intimidated by him. But ever since the situation with the street bum and Danny's suicide, Carter had changed for the worse. With that change, Sean's feelings of intimidation had turned to something more akin to fear.

Carter had always been mean spirited, but recently that meanness had gained focus, like a broad-beam laser that had been adjusted to a pinpoint of light that could cut through steel.

Sean walked across the parking deck toward his car. His dad paid for a spot in this deck that was across the street from his school. His dad didn't want him on public transit, thought it wasn't safe. Pretty funny considering he was the police commissioner. Not that Sean minded. Even though driving in the city was a bitch, it sure beat waiting for cabs or being crammed on the subway with the lowlifes.

His foot hit something that skidded across the floor with a metallic sound. He looked down and saw a metal casing that looked like it was from one of those security cameras. He glanced up at the cement pillar to his right and, sure enough, there was an empty metal bracket with wires hanging out of it.

He turned toward his car. There was some guy standing next to it. He looked to be in his thirties, wavy dark hair, eyes hidden behind sunglasses. He was dressed in a black leather jacket and jeans. The jacket and jeans looked expensive; however, the guy himself looked like he had seen better days. Even with the dark sunglasses, he looked like he had been in a prize-fight and lost. One whole side of his face was purplish and swollen. He looked like he hadn't had a shave in several days either.

The guy had one hand in his coat pocket; the other was holding out a badge.

"Sean Hutchinson, I need you to come with me."

Sean looked at the badge and suppressed a smile. "Do you know who my father is, Detective? I am not going anywhere."

"He sent me to get you."

An alarm began to trip deep in the recesses of Sean's brain. "Oh yeah? If my dad sent you, what is the code word?" With such a high profile position, Sean's father had been concerned for his son's safety, afraid he may become a target for the city's seedier elements. They had a code for just such a situation so Sean could verify that whoever he was dealing with was kosher.

The man in front of him hesitated and that alarm started to get louder. Sean slid one foot back slightly, shifting his weight, preparing to make a break for it. "Code word?" Sean repeated.

The guy pulled his hand out of his coat pocket.

"The code word is Gun," Al said. "Now get in the car and let's go meet your friend Carter."

Sean stared at the muzzle of the gun, the alarm now screaming incessantly.

2

Carter stood on the sidewalk, shivering on the outside and steaming on the inside. Sean was supposed to have picked him up thirty minutes ago. Carter didn't like to be kept waiting. He pulled out his cell phone and was about to call Sean when he saw the white BMW with the tinted windows turning the corner.

The car pulled smoothly to the curb. Carter open the door and bent to get in. He hesitated halfway in, Sean's appearance causing him to pull up short.

"What the hell is wrong with you?" Carter said. Sean was deathly pale, and despite how cold the day was, a trickle of sweat rolled from under his hairline, meandering down his temple. His eyes were wide and bright. Those eyes twitched toward the rear of the car. Carter followed their motion and found himself staring down the barrel of a gun.

There was a man lying across the backseat, staying low.

"Get in the car, Mr. Stevens," said the man with the gun. Before Carter could think, the man added, "Don't do anything stupid. From this distance I can put a bullet between your eyes before you could twitch."

Carter slid the rest of the way in. "Stay calm, man, stay calm. If it is money you are looking for, you can have it."

The guy in the back let out a dry bark of a laugh. "If only it were that simple. Let's go, drive. I will tell you where."

3

Al drove through the darkened streets, his jaw set in grim determination. He had had Sean drive to the underground parking garage where Mike waited with the van. The vehicle looked like the last time it had seen the road it had been on the way to Woodstock. They had picked it up at a less than reputable establishment. That was one of the perks about being a cop—you knew of all the better places of business. Mike and Al were not concerned about the condition of the van; it only had to last them a few days and they needed something they could pay for in cash.

For the entire ride on the way to meet Mike, he had heard a whole repertoire of pleas and threats from his two captives. They offered money, threatened his life, whined like children and then threatened him some more. Al tuned it all out; he had chosen his course of action and was committed to it.

Al had been concerned that, with him in the backseat of Sean's BMW, they might both try to bolt when the car stopped at a light or slowed down due to traffic. He was fairly certain from observing these two the last few days that Carter ran the show, so he had kept the muzzle of his gun pressed firmly to the base of Carter's skull for the entire ride. He figured this would keep Carter from doing anything drastic and that Sean wouldn't have the guts to make a move unless Carter led the way.

He had Sean park the BMW next to the van. Al took the keys, stepped out of the car and ordered them to do the same. He could feel the tension rise. Both boys kept their heads down but he could sense their eyes darting about like trapped rats.

Then the back doors of the van opened and Mike stepped out, all 6' 3" of him, black ski mask pulled down over his face, the M4 resting in the crook of his arm. Those furtive rat looks were replaced by looks of fear and despair.

"Kneel, shitheads. Hands behind your back," Mike ordered.

Al didn't feel the need to wear a disguise or insult their prisoners. He figured even if he managed to stay alive over the next few hours, he was a dead man in the near future anyway. Once their precious boys had disappeared, Sean and Carter's fathers would make sure anyone who might even remotely be involved would disappear. Al figured he and Mike would be on the top of that list.

As for the insults, it was not like Al didn't share Mike's contempt for the two, but he had a feeling they would be getting what they deserved and then some. No sense piling on.

Al duct-taped their mouths and zip-tied their hands and ankles. They then loaded them like sacks of laundry into the rear of the van. Once they were safely stashed away, Al could breathe a sigh of relief. If either of the two had had the balls to resist, the whole operation could have gone south quickly.

Mike climbed into the back and Al shut the doors, went up front and climbed into the driver's seat. He found his palms slick with sweat as he grabbed the wheel. For all his determination, he was still coming to grips with what he was about to do. He was about to turn two people over to be killed or worse. It wasn't that he doubted they were guilty or deserved what was coming to them, but he knew he was crossing a line. There was something primordially wrong with what he was doing. To betray his own species, to turn those of his own kind over to be killed…if there was such a thing as eternal damnation, he figured he was punching his own ticket.

He conjured up a picture of Anne in his mind, blocking out all other thought. If she had any chance at all, he could not waver.

CHAPTER 32

1

Anne lay in the hammock reading *Tarzan of the Apes*. She had moved the desk next to the hammock and had set the lit candle upon it.

The torch overhead was also lit. There was no noise; the world beyond the tarps was quiet. Since the moment she had removed her blindfold to see the additions to her cell, her benefactor had come back to visit her several times.

She would hear the sound of a chair being pulled up just outside the tarp that enclosed her cage and then she'd hear the voice. She had gotten used to its gruffness and the brogue and was able to carry on conversations quite easily.

She had been surprised how intelligent and literate the person who belonged to that voice ended up being. He would not answer any questions about who her captors were or why she was being kept, but he would discuss any other topic with her.

He was very interested in what she did for a living and in how she lived. He asked questions about her childhood, about how she was raised. It was like he was someone from another planet who had no idea what it was like to live a normal, modern life and was very curious about it.

He was also very interested in history, in old civilizations. He taxed her memory on all things from the ancient Romans, through the Middle Ages, the World Wars, up till modern times. He seemed very well read on all these subjects but was interested in her opinion on the cause and effect of major occurrences throughout history.

During their conversations, she felt her fear start to slip away, if only for a moment. She wasn't sure whether it was the distraction these discussions offered from her current situation or the thoughtful intelligence in that gruff voice, but she almost felt normal during these times.

She began to look forward to hearing the chair being pulled up outside the tarp and experienced disappointment when there was too much time between his visits. He would come and they would talk and then he would abruptly state that he had to leave. The chair would slide back and he would be gone.

Now, as she lay in the hammock, she again heard the chair being positioned outside her cell. She carefully closed her book and set it down on the desk, thankful for the chance to have a conversation. The seconds ticked by and he didn't say anything.

"Aren't you going to speak?" Anne asked as she turned her head in the direction of the sound. She let out a gasp of surprise and abruptly stood, turning to face that direction.

The tarps were parted, and in the gap that was created she saw a small, hideous face. It was about the size of a ten-year-old's but narrower, with stretched gray skin, a pronounced ridge of a brow and yellow eyes. The tarp was being held open by two small, gnarled grey hands. The child thing was standing on the chair, so though it was child-size its face was level with Anne's.

As soon as Anne turned, it let out a surprised grunt and disappeared. Anne could hear its footsteps as it ran away.

The tarps remained parted. Anne walked slowly toward the gap that was formed, almost too frightened to look through. Finally, taking a deep breath, she peered through the opening. She stared, open mouthed, for several minutes, then she carefully reached through the bars to close the tarps. The rope that had been tied through the eyelets in the canvas to hold it together was gone. Anne did her best to overlap the edges so that the opening wouldn't be seen. If anyone knew she had looked out, she had a feeling things would not go well.

She sat back down in the hammock and began to shake uncontrollably, her mind racing, trying to make sense of what she had seen.

2

Anne had just finished a breakfast of fresh fruit when she heard the grating of the chair outside the tarp, followed by that now-familiar voice.

"Good morning, Anne. I hope you slept well. I wanted to let you know that the time may be coming soon when you will leave us."

"Have you heard from Al? Is he safe?"

"He has been seen and seems to be fulfilling his promise. I just wanted to say..." There was a pause, and Anne saw the two edges of the tarp part slightly. "Has someone been here? Have you looked out?" he asked, his voice lowering to a whisper at the last question.

Anne took a deep breath. There was no denying it and she felt, on some level, she could trust him. "One of your youngsters untied it and looked in at me, and then ran away. And yes, I did look out. Don't you think it is time you were honest with me? What is this place and what are you?"

She heard a sigh of resignation from the other side of the material. "You must understand the danger in what you have done. If any of my kind were to find out, you would be killed immediately. We guard our secrecy at all cost; our survival depends on it."

"I don't understand who and what you are. What is going on?" Anne demanded.

He did not answer. "Anne, please put the bag over your head. I am going to enter, and if anyone should be watching as I do, we must keep up appearances."

Anne found the cloth sack and pulled it over her head. "I am ready," she said.

She heard the now familiar grating sound of metal on metal. "I must warn you before you remove the sack that my appearance will shock you. You must not yell out. I will not harm you. I am the same being you have been having conversations with these past days. Are you ready?"

Anne found she was trembling with apprehension, but also unbearably curious. "Yes, I am ready."

"All right, you may remove the sack. Keep it close at hand though. If, while we talk, someone begins to open the cover of your cell, you must replace it before they see you without it."

"I understand," Anne said as she slowly raised the material from over her eyes. She almost let out a startled gasp in spite of herself—the visage before her was so alien. She thought the sight of the youth would have prepared her, that her benefactor would just be a larger version of that small misshapen face, and to some extent that was true. However, looking at an adult version just a few feet away was unsettling. It was like staring at a living, breathing Halloween mask, the powerful jaws, the V-shaped nostrils, gray skin, the Mohawk of long black hair. She found herself focusing on the incredibly blue eyes. They were the only feature that contained any humanity.

She found herself repeating breathlessly, "What are you?"

"My name is Tabon, and we are called the Eaton. Well, to be clear, the others are Eaton. I am half Eaton and half human."

"You are half human?" Anne repeated, doubting that she had heard him correctly.

"Yes, my human mother was raped by my Eaton father; I am the result of that union," he said.

The sound of his voice released Anne from the trance his unusual appearance had placed her in. She took in the rest of him. He was dressed in shabby but normal clothing: an oversized hooded sweatshirt, tattered and stained work pants and battered construction boots. Except for his strange countenance, he would have looked like he was off to work at any of the dozens of construction sites across the city.

"Where did you come from? Why has no one ever heard of you?"

"We are originally from England, though there are Eaton in other countries as well. We have been around as long as, if not longer, than humans. Eaton have warred with humans from the beginning of time. They have fought Celts, Romans, Angles, Saxons and the North people. One of our greatest victories was against the Romans; the Eaton defeated an entire Roman legion sent to destroy them. We took these from the dead Roman soldiers," he said, lifting his sweatshirt, pulling a short sword from his belt and laying it on the scarred top of Anne's desk. "Their short length make them good for carrying up above. They are easily hidden."

He returned the sword to his belt, cocking a leg he sat on the desktop, one foot still on the floor in a very human posture. Anne sat on the edge of her hammock.

"Only once in our history did we ally with humans," Tabon continued. "When the Normans invaded England, they sought out and made a pact with the Eaton to assist them in their conquest, promising the Eaton they would be rewarded land of their own where they could do as they please. However, they betrayed us and we were almost completely destroyed. My own father was killed during that betrayal."

"Wait a minute. Your father was killed by the Normans?" Anne tried to remember her history lessons; it had been a while since she had taught world history. "That's impossible. How old are you?"

"We do not track our age like humans, but I am almost one thousand years old. Unlike man, Eaton can live for thousands of years. You may not think that is possible, but I assure you it is. After the betrayal, there were few Eaton left. Those that remained hid in the deep forests. As humanity thrived and grew, we slipped into the cities, hiding among the poor and destitute, in the squalid sections of man's cities. When those cities grew, we hid in their underground places and back alleys, lurking in the shadows."

Anne studied Tabon closely as he spoke, trying to determine if he was telling the truth. Whether it was true or not, he appeared to believe what he was saying.

"This is all very hard to believe," Anne said. She knew what she was hearing was unbelievable, yet the fact that she was in a cage, underground, talking to this strange creature challenged the very parameters of what was believable and what was not.

"It is not a matter of what you believe or do not believe; it is just a matter of what was and is," said Tabon.

Anne decided to put aside the plausibility of what she was being told for the moment to see where this story led. "How did the Eaton end up in New York?"

"Slowly, our numbers began to grow again. We built a society in the London underground. Then man's World War II started. London was being bombed. Between the danger from the bombing and the risk of being discovered by the humans who were themselves seeking shelter underground, it became too dangerous for us, so we migrated to America. There were many freighters going back and forth to the United States, we stowed away on them, eventually ferrying all our number to this city. Once here, it was easy to find places to establish ourselves underground. When we go above ground, we blend in with the human homeless. No one looks too closely at a homeless person on the street. It is quite easy."

"Why would you hide? Why wouldn't you try to make contact with us, reach out?"

Tabon looked at her the way someone may look at a small innocent child, a patient yet condescending smile spread across his face. "Anne, don't be naïve. Look at me, look at my face. I have read human history; I read your newspapers daily. Humans kill their own kind if their skin is a different color, if they pray to a different god, if they lay with the wrong person. How do you think we would be treated, being an entirely different species? I will tell you how: we would be hunted down and killed like animals. Or placed in confinement so that humans can walk past and stare at us, throw us scraps of food."

Anne was angered by his demeanor, but sadly thought what he said was true. Of course what was also true was that judging by what she had experienced so far of Eaton behavior, they deserved to be hunted and destroyed. That was a debate for another day though. "If the Eaton have been around for so long as you say and have been in contact with man, waging war against man, all that time, why is there no historical record of it?"

"Over the years, as our numbers declined and as the encounters became less and less, man relegated us to the realm of

myth and legend, stories to scare young children. In those stories we are given absurd names like orcs, goblins or trolls;
man's attempt to trivialize that which he fears. Those stories
have their basis in truth but that truth has been lost over the
centuries. Evidence from our past does exist; however humans
refuse to recognize it for what it is."

"What do you mean? What type of evidence?" Anne
knew there were many legends, stories and ballads about all
sorts of creatures, but no physical evidence that any of it was
true, that any of them ever really existed.

"The place you call Stonehenge, for one, was built by
the Eaton. It is one of our holiest shrines. Your archeologists
come up with any manner of theory on how ancient humans
could have moved those huge stones without modern equipment." Tabon laughed. "The answer is quite simple: they
couldn't. Eaton strength is far superior to humans. Eaton
strength built Stonehenge. The Eaton built several holy sites
similar to Stonehenge around England. Even when we were
pushed out of those sites by man and our numbers had been
decimated, we would meet in open fields of grain to recreate
the holy markings and perform the holy ceremonies. Man saw
those places and thought the holy markings were made by beings from the sky."

Now Anne was convinced he was making all this up.
Why he would start out so angry at the fact she had learned
their true nature but then would spin such frivolous lies in response to her questions didn't make sense.

"I just had my class study Stonehenge; it was supposedly
built by Druids. They say it was a burial site. They even found
graves with the cremated remains of men there; they did not
find any non-human remains."

Tabon began to laugh again. "Graves with cremated remains; that is humorous. Those remains are buried refuse. The
humans used to present their own kind as sacrifices to the

Eaton in payment to ward off attack. The Eaton would roast and devour these humans and bury the charred remains from the meal. Those aren't graves, they are garbage pits." He laughed again as if this was one of the funniest jokes ever told.

The comment was like an injection of reality to Anne. She had to be very careful; she had no idea what she was involved with. As intelligent as Tabon may sound and as human as those blue eyes may appear, she was dealing with what amounted to a wild animal. As she had witnessed firsthand, if only through sound and smell, these creatures were capable of extreme cruelty and worse, if there was any truth to what Tabon had just told her.

Seeing the look of disgust on Anne's face, Tabon got control of himself. "I am sorry this offends you but it is as it is. To an Eaton, man is no different than any other animal on the Earth. Meat is meat. Before you judge the Eaton too harshly, know this: men themselves have treated the Eaton no better. Men used to take captured Eaton and the Eaton dead and chop them up to be fed to their dogs."

"That may have happened in the past when man was less civilized, but that wouldn't happen today. What about the Eaton? Do the Eaton today, the ones that live down here, are they killing and eating people?" Anne asked, not sure she wanted to know or could handle the answer.

"Not normally. Our king has forbidden it. He has not forbidden it because he thinks it is wrong—remember, they are a different species; they do not see it as cannibalism—he has forbidden it for the safety of the Eaton. We would not be able to maintain our secrecy and our safety if humans kept disappearing. Besides, this city provides plenty of food without resorting to eating humans."

"What do you mean, not normally?"

"Those that captured you and killed the other woman have committed acts in response to the human's murder of one of our own," Tabon said. He then told Anne of the events that led to her abduction.

Anne had trouble accepting what he was saying; the whole idea of it was so horrible, so brutal, so foreign to anything she could comprehend as to make it almost unfathomable. It was like trying to understand the mysteries of space and time or the origin of dark matter. She could not wrap her head around it, on some level rejecting that it could even be possible.

However, the conviction with which he relayed the information and the sincerity she saw in that wreck of a face left little doubt that what he was saying was true.

Anne felt the tears begin as wave after wave of sorrow and anguish washed over her, eroding the foundation of her self control. "How could they? Those poor innocent children and a young woman who had done no wrong, how could they kill them that way over the actions of a few thugs? What type of evil is this?"

"Get yourself under control and lower your voice," Tabon commanded. "You will understand the murder those thugs, as you call them, committed brought great shame upon the Eaton. This was not just any Eaton, it was the druid Kustaa, our eldest and most revered cleric. He had lived for thousands of years, had witnessed the rise and fall of civilizations, and his life was ended by three insignificant humans barely on this earth a minute. There is only one way we can regain our honor, and that is to perform the Cleansing. For that, we need the murderers."

"Fine," Anne said, "then go after the murderers. Why innocent people? How does it justify killing innocent people?"

"It is complicated. We did not know who the killers were; that was the task that Detective Russo had been given. The detective did not cooperate in the beginning and Einarr, who has ambitions of his own, used the detective's resistance to justify the other acts. Now I will admit to you that Einarr knows that to a human, what he did is unacceptable. He committed these acts for his own purposes; however, to the Eaton these acts are justifiable."

"Nothing justifies such acts."

"To you, to a human, maybe," Tabon hissed. "It is justified to the Eaton. You must look at it like an Eaton. Unlike humans, we do not put arbitrary rules around conflict and then break them in secret. When the Eaton are at war, they do whatever it takes to gain victory. If you burn a village to the ground and kill every man, woman and child, the next village will surrender without lifting a sword. This is the Eaton way. This is why your detective must not fail. If the Eaton are denied justice on their terms, this city will burn. However, before you judge us too harshly, Anne, read the truth about your own history. Read the newspapers of today. Humans are no different; they are just better at deceiving themselves.

"But enough talk. You must never look outside your cell again, and you must never reveal what you have seen. Your detective has given his word that once this is over, he will not reveal our existence. You must swear to do the same. There will be a great deal of bloodshed on both sides if we are not allowed to live in peace."

Anne thought of the irony of a creature who had committed such violence wanting to live in peace, however, she gave her word that she would say nothing. Whether she would keep her word, she wasn't sure.

CHAPTER 33

1

Tabon sat to the right of Rangvald. The old king rarely ventured to the surface anymore. Not because he was old and frail—quite the opposite. He was one of the most physically powerful of the Eaton despite his great age. However, maintaining calm among the Eaton had taken constant tending and vigilance over the past few months.

There was rebellion in the air and Rangvald knew it. The Eaton were a ferocious and warlike race; however, over the many years spent in hiding they had become lethargic, almost entering a state of stasis. They tended to their settlements, brewed their own beer from the mushrooms they cultivated underground, captured their food, ventured above ground in their disguises to lie in the sun or observe the night sky.

This had been a good thing; in the past, when the Eaton had been on equal footing with the humans they shared the planet with, any extended period of inactivity would have led to restlessness and internal squabbles. This would eventually bubble over. Generally one Eaton, more charismatic than the rest, would rise from amongst them to lead them to war. They would raid the human settlements, take what they wanted and then, their bloodlust sated, they would return to their own lands until the next time.

However, when they had first been forced into hiding, this same bloodlust would rise, and with no way to relieve the pressure, internal struggles would set Eaton upon Eaton. During that time, Rangvald had risen as the king and, through his own strength of will, had maintained the peace, keeping the Eaton in check, keeping them from fighting amongst themselves, or worse yet, venting their aggression against man, an act that could only lead to their ultimate destruction.

This forced passivity had saved them, however the lethargy and ambivalence had manifested itself almost as a natural survival mechanism. The times when Rangvald had to use violence or intimidation to maintain the peace had become less and less.

Recently that began to change, and it began to change because of Einarr. Einarr had begun to move among the Eaton, talking of days long gone, of glorious victories and battles well fought. He had started providing weapons training to some of the younger Eaton who had never known battle. His stated intent was so that the Eaton traditions would be maintained by the young, and also they would be trained in case the need ever arose for the Eaton to defend themselves.

The sound of clashing swords, blade against blade, rang through the Eaton settlements once more and one could notice the elder Eaton, those who had known war, taking notice: listening to the sounds, eyes off in the distance, nostalgic for past glories. The younger ones who did participate began to strut around with a certain swagger, a certain arrogance.

Like a flame lit under a pot of still water, Einarr's actions began to have their effect. Small bubbles of discontent began to rise. He added fuel to the fire when he came out victorious in his confrontation with four human police officers. Of course, he maintained that he did not instigate the encounter, but the story of his victory was told, embellished and retold, the words providing oxygen, like a bellows, to the dormant, smoldering embers of the Eaton warrior spirit.

Then Einarr had started to campaign openly for war against the humans, speaking of the glory of battle, discussing plans for hit and run attacks that would bring the great city above to a standstill and generate fear among the populace. When presented with the argument that these efforts would ultimately result in many Eaton deaths, he would speak eloquently of the glory of dying in battle and the rewards that awaited those who fought and died bravely in the Great Hall of the Gods.

Einarr's views were dangerous; however, he had shown his prowess in battle and was respected and revered by many of the Eaton. Rangvald could not openly move against him without inviting a civil war. He had to find a way to keep Einarr in check while appearing to treat him fairly and give him the respect many felt he had earned.

In attempting to do so, Rangvald had, in Tabon's opinion, made a grave error. He had let Einarr handle the response to the murder of the druid Kustaa. Rangvald had miscalculated Einarr's motives; he had assumed all the talk and bluster had been Einarr's desire for prestige and recognition, calculating that giving him this important mission would fulfill that desire. By doing so, he had presented Einarr the opportunity to create the perfect atmosphere for advancing his ambitions.

Rangvald still thought he could regain control. Einarr had been overly aggressive in his actions and placed the Eaton in danger. Rangvald was concerned about what may happen due to Einarr's actions; however, he felt that this would make it clear to the others how dangerous the course of action Einarr had taken was and allow Rangvald to clip his wings and still maintain the peace.

Tabon admired the king, but was convinced he had misjudged the situation. Being half human, Tabon was considerably more intelligent than the other Eaton. He had combined the best of both species. He was just as strong and agile as an Eaton and as intelligent as a man. Tabon had taught himself to read and had collected and studied all forms of human literature. Rangvald appreciated Tabon's intelligence and made him his chief advisor despite the fact he was a half breed, however he did not listen to his guidance regarding Einarr. Tabon and Einarr had had their differences in the past, and Rangvald assumed this was clouding Tabon's judgment.

They sat at the head table in the Long House. The head table ran across the far end of the hall. Two other longer tables ran down each side wall. Pews taken from an old abandoned church formed the benches behind each of the tables. The large tables were composed of a variety of smaller tables taken from the city above and placed end to end. The smaller tables were covered with large cloths that would have given the appearance of one continuous piece of furniture if it weren't for the different widths of the tables underneath.

Those handpicked by the king as his advisors, such as Tabon, sat at the head table. The two side tables were occupied by the rest of the King's council, comprised of the eldest of the clan. Torches flickered in sconces spaced around the interior of the hall. A fire pit had been hacked into the cement in the middle of the room. The smoke from the torches and fire drifted up toward the ceiling and out through a long narrow opening in the peak of the roof.

Rangvald pounded the table with his large fist and the room grew quiet. "I have called Einarr before this council to answer for his recent actions. He was tasked with finding and capturing Kustaa's murderers and in doing so has exposed the Eaton to great danger." He looked toward the two Eaton guards standing at the doors to the hall. "Bring him in."

They opened the doors, all eyes turned in that direction as Einarr walked in. He stood tall as he walked to the center of the room between the tables on either side. Now, fear was not an emotion commonly felt amongst the Eaton, however even the bravest among them would feel some anxiety being brought before the King and the council. Einarr demonstrated no such anxiety; he walked between the tables and around the fire pit, that single eye scanning the faces around the room, as if he was attending his own coronation. One side of his face formed a calm easy smile; the other was locked in that perpetual fang-displaying sneer.

"You wished me before the council, my king," he said, bowing his head slightly.

"The things I hear, they trouble me, Einarr. You are playing a very dangerous game. You broke into the war chests and took weapons. You are aware that our survival depends on secrecy, yet, in the name of finding the killers of Kustaa, you have killed humans. You have even brought one alive into our very midst. You have gotten your fellow Eaton killed. There is even suspicion that you and others have eaten human flesh, which I have forbidden. These are grave and dangerous actions. What have you to say?"

Einarr again scanned those assembled with that lone eye, his gaze lingering on Tabon. "Everything I have done, my king, has been to fulfill my task to capture the killers of Kustaa so that the Cleansing may be performed. Until that day, we are all shamed, are we not?" Many heads around the room nodded. Tabon did not like the mood of the room. While the king was describing Einarr's actions, there were some concerned looks from those assembled; there were also those who smirked, eyes glinting with a smoldering fire.

"You do not need to tell me the importance of the Cleansing," Rangvald admonished. "It is the methods and the involvement of the humans that is in question here."

"If I may, my king, I will address this. We needed the assistance of a human to discover the murderers. He would not cooperate, so certain actions were taken to make him assist us."

"You let a human see you? He knows of us?"

"Yes, but he will tell no one. We have his female. Besides, the humans, in their arrogance, would not believe the word of a single man. As for the humans we killed, we left no trace behind of our existence—only human corpses." Einarr turned slowly as he said this, favoring the room with his smiling, sneering face.

There were many grunts of approval from those assembled, accompanied by a few snorts of suppressed laughter.

"As for the captive, she has never seen us. She will believe she was abducted by other humans. The Eaton that died, they died proudly—" at this point the smile disappeared, replaced with a grim look of determination, "—with swords in their hands, with blood on their blades. Better than to die while sitting in an alley eating rat as those who are lesser than us walk past without a care."

"Watch your words, Einarr. We may not have the glory of battle, but we survive." Tabon saw Einarr's jaws clench at this. There were some in the room that nodded in approval, but there were also a few grumbles, like low thunder, a barely heard rumbling just beyond the horizon.

"What about the eating of human flesh?"

Einarr's single eye flashed. "Eaton warriors have devoured the flesh of their enemies since time began. It is their right," he hissed.

"I have forbid it," Rangvald bellowed, slamming his fist on the table. All heads snapped around at the sound and Tabon could see many looking down, cowed. The outburst, at least temporarily, had the desired effect of reasserting Rangvald's dominance. "If the humans become aware that this has occurred, they will not rest until they find out who did it. You risk much."

Einarr persisted. "They have discovered it, and it has made them bend to our will. As we speak, the human is doing my bidding. He is finding the murderers and he will bring them to me. Humans only understand strength and power. They must fear us."

"They will fear us until they find how few we are," Rangvald countered. "Then they will come with their guns and their war machines and that will be the end of us. You say this man does as you ask. He is bringing you the killers?"

"Yes, in exchange for his female. We will trade her for them."

"If this one man and the female are the only humans who may have knowledge of us, you must kill them once the trade is made. But that ends it, Einarr, I warn you. You are to take no other actions. Obtain the killers from this man and kill this man and woman, and put an end to it. There will be no other interaction with man."

Tabon was completely caught off guard by the sudden change of events. "May I speak, my king?"

"You may."

"Einarr's actions did not have the results he intended. The violence he committed did not make man do his bidding. It had the opposite effect. I found the man. He had a gun and he was following the trail that Einarr left. He was close to discovering this village when I found him. He was determined to rescue the woman."

"You lie," hissed Einarr.

"I have no reason to lie; I have nothing to gain by lying. No, your plan was not as perfect as you suspected. He was following you and he was armed. If not for me, he may have discovered our settlement and brought the word to others."

Murmurs of surprise and concern passed between those seated at the tables.

"I spoke with him and convinced him to do what needed to be done. This was made more difficult by Einarr's actions, not easier. The murder of innocents will harden man against us. I convinced him to do what we needed, but I also gave my word that he and the female would not be harmed. In return, he promised to keep our secret."

The good side of Einarr's face matched the ravaged side in a sneer. "You lie. Even if what you say were to be true, man cannot be trusted. The last time the Eaton trusted man, we were almost destroyed. Your human half is turning you against us."

Tabon remained calm. "I have lived my life with the Eaton. I have only known the ways of the Eaton. I am only trying to resolve the problem that you, in your lust for blood, created. If we kill them, we will surely end up facing the police and their guns. If he does as we have asked, he will have committed a crime in the eyes of his fellow humans. He will have turned three of their own over to be killed. He needs to keep this a secret as much as we do, or his own kind will punish him severely. Also, I have given him my word."

Einarr's anger grew. "You talk of nothing but fear and weakness. I have faced the human police before." He grabbed the necklace of ears and badges, shaking it for emphasis as he stalked toward where Tabon sat. "And they are all dead."

"What good is starting a war with man?" Tabon continued. "We cannot defeat them, there are too many. What do you hope to accomplish? What is your goal?"

"What is my goal?" Einarr mocked. "The human blood that flows through your veins has you thinking like them. We do not wish to take over land and settle down like the humans, rushing around every day playing out their short, tedious lives. We are Eaton! War is the goal. The dying screams of your enemies. The glory of battles well fought and victories won, the camaraderie of warriors who have faced death together. A life worth living. These are the goals. If you were truly Eaton, you would know these things."

Many of the elders began to pound the table in approval, voicing their support in a cacophony of snarls and growls.

"ENOUGH!" shouted Rangvald, raising his hand. "Have you all forgotten the sheer numbers of the humans, of their weapons, the machines that can kill us from the sky? All this talk of glory is not what it seems. It is talk from an era that no longer exists. This talk will only lead to death and sorrow.

"Einarr, you will finish this business with the human and that will be the end of it. Further contact is forbidden. Tabon will accompany you as my representative. Tabon, on the point of the fate of these two humans, I am in agreement with Einarr. Man cannot be trusted. Once we have the killers, the two humans are to be killed. That is the only way to ensure they will not reveal our existence. That is the last I will speak of it."

"As you wish," Einarr said, bowing slightly. Shooting a sly half grin in Tabon's direction, he turned and strode from the Hall.

2

"Anne." Tabon spoke from behind the tarp.

"Yes." After their last discussion, she had been afraid he would not return to speak with her again. As much as she was angered and disgusted by what he had revealed, she had come to count on him, and even though the things he had revealed about the Eaton were horrible, she could not believe they were true about him. Surely his human side had a civilizing influence on his character. He couldn't be half human and truly condone what the Eaton had done.

"The time of your leaving draws ever closer."

Anne could not believe the intensity of the feeling of relief that washed over her, triggered by that simple statement.

"Really?" Then, she had to know, "Is Al safe?"

There was a pause. "Yes, I believe so. He should fulfill his part of the bargain soon. First I want to tell you that despite the disagreements caused by our differences, I have enjoyed our discussions. You have provided me with great insight into a part of myself that I never really understood before, and I am grateful."

"I am grateful myself. Your visits made this ordeal bearable. I don't think I would have kept my sanity without you." Anne had to admit to herself that this was true. This strange creature had watched over her, provided for her, and his visits offered a distraction that helped her cope.

"I need you to listen carefully to me. You are not completely out of danger. The exchange has to happen with Detective Russo and if anything goes wrong, it could be bad for you. Know that if things do go badly, I will attempt to get you to safety. But to have a chance, you must do what I say without question. If you hesitate for even a moment, it could mean death for both of us."

Anne sensed he wasn't being completely honest. "You're scaring me. It sounds like you are almost certain that it will not go well."

"Not certain, but this will be a very unpredictable situation. I am not completely sure your detective can be trusted, and I know Einarr cannot be. But this is the only way to avoid even more bloodshed, so we must let things run their course. You have no true stake in any of this. If things do not go well, I will do my best to protect you."

Anne hesitated, then said, "Thank you for your help. I will be ready to do as you say should there be trouble."

She waited for a response but he was gone.

CHAPTER 34

1

Al parked the van down a narrow side street next to a construction site. The site was at the location Einarr had written on the note he had stuffed in Al's pocket after Carrie's murder. The steel skeleton of the building rose above him into the night sky. Security lights dotted the structure, giving it an almost dreamlike quality, as if it were suspended in the air.

Al turned to Mike, in the back with their two guests. "Listen, Mr. Blonde."

"Hah. *Reservoir Dogs*. I get it, Mr. Brown," Mike said, a grim smile crossing his lips, barely seen through the hole in the ski mask.

"I'm supposed to go up here and get instructions. Keep that weapon ready; this may be a trap. When I come back I will knock three times on the side of the van. If you don't hear those knocks, get ready to blow away anyone or anything that tries to get in. If I'm not back in forty-five minutes, take off. Turn these two loose and burn the van."

He looked through the window, peering into the shadows. He didn't see anything. He opened the door and slipped out, closing it quickly to cut off the dome light. He stood there for a few moments studying the darkness again, trying to detect any movement. Seeing nothing, he walked slowly toward the construction site.

Al walked the perimeter fence looking for an opening, a way to get in. He could see into the site: the steel girders stretched up into the darkness, the concrete floors had been poured and the metal stairways were in place. Everywhere was building equipment, generators, cement mixers, pallets of building materials; the torn plastic wrappers flapped in the cold wind.

He continued along the fence. Then on the sidewalk he noticed the symbol that he had become all too familiar with painted in orange day-glow spray paint: concentric circles bisected on one side by parallel lines. Next to the symbol was an opening where the chain link of the fence had been cut. Al spread the opening, being careful not to snag his clothing as he passed through.

Deep ruts had been formed by the construction vehicles, and Al stumbled along the uneven ground. Several times he stepped into water that had collected in tire ruts, soaking his feet. He finally got to the concrete slab that formed the ground floor, and weaving his way between machinery and building materials, he made his way to the stairs.

The stairs had steel risers and poured cement treads; the soles of his shoes made a scuffing noise as he climbed. The stairway was completely open and the higher Al got, the more the wind whipped around him. Between the wind and his wet feet, he was shivering by the time he made it to the tenth floor.

He walked around the floor, assuming he would see another symbol, something to direct him. Then, as if on cue, he saw a metal drum with the same symbol he had seen on the sidewalk, in the same day-glo paint. He walked over to it but noticed nothing unusual, just a drum filled with garbage.

Al turned, looking around, not sure how to proceed. Then, out in the dark, he saw a flame bobbing in the air, coming his way.

A hunched figure came into view. It was wearing a filthy blanket or tarp draped over its head and shoulders like a cowl, a torch held aloft in one gnarled gray hand. It looked like a leper in one of those Cecil B. Demille Bible epics. Al could make out the yellow eyes glowing dully under the tarp. The strange shuffling, jerking gate was unmistakable. Hop Frog.

"Ah, Detective, you have them?"

"Yes," Al replied. "What's next?"

"It is a pity. I was hoping you would fail. Your female looks very tender, just like the last one, mmmmm. I was looking forward to cracking her bones for the juice." This was followed by a wet sucking sound. "Well, we are not done, maybe I get my chance yet, eh?"

Al resisted the urge to pull his gun and empty the clip between those two glowing orbs. He promised himself once this was over, once Anne was safe and if he survived, he was going to personally hunt down this disgusting piece of filth and kill it. "What's next?" he repeated.

Hop Frog didn't say a word; he pushed past Al, so close that Al could pick up his rancid smell. He obviously felt Al did not pose a threat. He tossed the torch into the drum with the symbol painted on it. The garbage in the drum must have been soaked in something flammable. There was a *whoomp* and flames sprang from the top of the barrel.

Hop Frog stepped back, raising his arm, the tarp riding up and exposing the twisted, corded muscles. He pointed up the street. "Look."

Al eyes followed the crooked pointed finger. Up the street, on the roof of a building several blocks away, he saw another fire spring to life.

"Follow the flames, Detective. Tie this to the machine you are riding in. You will be directed to the meeting place." He produced a long, garish, orange- and green-striped scarf from beneath his shroud.

Al took the scarf and without another word, Hop Frog turned and scuttled off into the dark, moving remarkably quickly in that strange hitched gait. Al noticed his cloak was not a blanket or tarp at all, but a faded tapestry with a large letter M on the back in fancy script.

2

It had begun to rain in cold, icy drops as Al slowed the van to a roll. He gazed through the rivulets of water running down the van window. He was at the mouth of an abandoned pier. Off in the distance, at the end of the pier, he could see the flames dancing in another of the oil drums, the light from the flames forming orange starbursts in the droplets on the window.

After his meeting with Hop Frog, Al had gone back to the van. It was just as he left it. He pounded on the side three times to let Mike know it was him, then tied the scarf to the side view mirror. Climbing into the driver's seat, he turned back toward Mike. "Everything good?"

"Yeah, no problems, and our guests have been behaving themselves."

Al had given him the lowdown on his conversation with Hop Frog. They had driven toward the flame and as they got close, saw a hooded figure silhouetted against the light from the fire. The figure stretched out an arm, pointing up the block, and they had kept driving. When they had gone two blocks farther, another dark hooded figure had stepped out under a streetlight, pointing up a street to the left. Al had taken the turn and that was how it had gone: dark hooded figures stepping from the shadows, pointing, beckoning, like silent living signposts pointing the way to hell.

They had finally found themselves down at the waterfront and this abandoned pier. Al turned toward Mike. "Looks like this is the spot, down at the end there."

Mike looked out. "I don't like the looks of this. We go down that pier and we are trapped, only one way in or out."

"You're right, but what choice do we have?" Al turned onto the pier, rolling slowly. "Listen, Mike, when they come, you stay in the van. They are only expecting me and I don't want you to be seen. You keep the M4. If all goes well, you won't need to do a thing. Keep an eye out though, if things are going south I am going to try to get to Anne and you need to cover me. It takes a lot to bring one of these things down, but if you keep pouring it on, you may be able to keep them suppressed until I can get Anne out of there."

"You know, that doesn't sound like much of a plan. If I'm in the van and you and Anne are out there, they could kill you before I have a chance to do anything."

"Yeah, I know. I'm hoping they live up to their end of the bargain. If not, Anne and I don't really have much of a chance, but with you as an ace in the hole and a little luck, we may make it. Listen, if they do kill us, don't be a hero. Get behind the wheel and get out of here."

Al scanned the area as he talked. Not much cover. The pier was a wide open expanse. There was an abandoned building to the left. Half of the structure was on the pier itself; the other half jutted out over the water, supported by pilings. That could provide some cover if things went bad. Al knew he was grasping at straws; out here they were going to be completely at the mercy of the Eaton.

When Al got down to the end, he turned the van around so the nose was pointing the way he had come. If the need arose, Mike could just gun it for the mouth of the pier. The fire in the drum had died down by the time they had reached it. Al stared through the beating wipers at the expanse of pier before him; the building was now about twenty yards away to his right.

The rain looked like drops of quicksilver, falling through the beams of light from the streetlights that lined both sides of the pier. The pier was empty.

The minutes ticked by. All was quiet inside the van except for their breathing. Al was glad he wasn't in the back with their captives. Looking at them, duct tape over their mouths, wide scared eyes staring, pleading, would have made him feel ashamed. He was afraid if he looked at them too long he may not be able to go through with what had to be done. He may try to save them all. Get Anne and then try to shoot their way out. That kind of thinking would get everyone killed. He had to stay focused. Saving Anne was the goal. Everyone else, including himself, was expendable.

Al fully expected not to make it through the night. But if he did, the deaths of these two would haunt him forever, whether they deserved what was coming to them or not.

Up ahead, five shadows detached themselves from the blackness of the night and walked slowly toward the van. There was no deception this time. As they passed through each pool of light formed by the streetlights, Al could see the glint of the metal of exposed weapons.

Al looked back over his shoulder. "Well, this is it. Sit tight, Mike. I'm going out there. I don't want them to get too close until I am sure they have Anne with them. I'll come back for our two friends if everything looks good." He pulled his gun, slipped it into his coat pocket and climbed out of the van.

The rain, icy cold, stung Al's face as soon as he opened the door. He flipped up the collar of his coat, keeping his right hand on the gun in his pocket. He started to walk toward the group up ahead.

They were strung out across the width of the pier, advancing slowly, like gunfighters at the O.K. Corral. Three of them were naked except for kilts, broadswords held in their hands. They seemed impervious to the cold, the icy rain running down the channels formed by muscle fiber and sinew.

The two remaining were walking side by side. One was in a long coat and did not appear to have a weapon. The other was Anne.

Al felt his breath catch in his throat. She looked so vulnerable, hands tied in front of her, cloth bag over her head. The one in the coat held her elbow, guiding her.

They got to within ten yards of him when Al held up his left hand. "That's far enough for now." Al could see Einarr was the one in the middle of the three with the weapons. That one eye flashed in the light. The other two may have been from Al's previous encounter, but he couldn't be sure.

Then he looked to the one in the coat. It was Tabon. The sight of him took Al by surprise. He wasn't sure if this was a good or bad development. Was he here to help, or was Al being double-crossed?

"Do you have the three men?" Einarr said.

Al ignored him. "Anne, can you hear me? Are you okay?"

He saw the bag nod. Her knees buckled slightly and Tabon grabbed her elbow more tightly to steady her.

"I have them," Al said. "Well, I have two of them. The third is dead."

There was a sigh. "Again you are trying to play games with us, Detective?"

282

"No, no I'm not. He killed himself before I could get to him. I have proof."

"This is not what we agreed to. You have not kept your word," Einarr said.

"What proof do you have?" Tabon interrupted.

Einarr turned toward him, flashing his fangs in a snarl before saying, "Leave this to me, half breed. This is not your affair."

"It is my affair," Tabon said, ignoring the hissing sound Einarr uttered in response. He turned toward Al. "What proof do you have, Detective?"

"I have the newspaper article that tells about the suicide and has a picture of the boy. I also have an article of his clothing. You said that your kind can identify someone through scent. This item would contain his scent."

"Do you have these items with you? If so, give them to me."

Al walked toward Tabon, reaching in his coat at the same time. He took the folded newspaper article and the baseball cap from the inside pocket he had stuffed them in. Tabon steadied Anne and then stepped forward, meeting Al halfway.

As he handed over the items, Al looked into those remarkably human blue eyes and felt calmer. He didn't detect deceit there. Tabon calmly returned his gaze.

Tabon turned toward the other three Eaton. "Asger, take this to Cwen. If this is the truth, bring her back with you. If not, come alone."

The Eaton to Einarr's left came forward and took the items from Tabon. As he came forward, he studied Al with dull yellow eyes, eyes filled more with curiosity than hate.

Al heard a snarl and snapping of jaws from his left and turned to see Einarr's monstrosity of a face contorted in rage. "You have no authority here. You are here to observe."

Tabon showed no emotion as he answered calmly, "Rangvald instructed me to ensure the deal was completed without problems. I have not, as yet, seen deceit from this man, and yet you show anger. In your own words, this is a simple bargain: one life for three. If he is speaking the truth, why the anger?"

The calm in Tabon's voice seemed to anger Einarr even more.

"He has already broken the bargain," snapped Einarr. "The bargain was for three. By his own admission, he only has two. Maybe not even the two. We have not seen them as yet."

"If one is dead, what was he to do? Not even the great Einarr can overcome death," Tabon responded.

Einarr's one eye flashed and he raised the tip of his sword. "Do not mock me, half breed. I'll have your head before you could unsheathe a weapon."

"You claim to want only justice for the Eaton," Tabon said, looking around, addressing the others as much as he was Einarr. "If the one is truly dead and he has the other two, is that not all that matters? Is not getting the two that remain what is most important?"

Al could see Einarr shoot quick glances at the other two Eaton, carefully weighing their reaction. They in turn stared at him, awaiting instructions, but also questioning.

"Fine, Asger. Go. But if this proves a lie, I will gut you, human, and you and I will meet in the trial ring, half-breed."

As if relieved at the chance to get away, the one called Asger sprinted toward the building to the side of the pier. Al again marveled at the speed and fluidity of the Eaton. Asger ran bent at the waist, those long muscular legs covering the ground easily in graceful strides.

"While we wait, can you remove the bag, please, so that I can see she is all right?" Al said, nodding toward Anne.

Before Einarr could protest, Tabon responded, "Certainly." He lifted the bag off of Anne's head. She was still blindfolded and her teeth were clenched around a gag. "She has not seen us, Detective, and it will remain that way."

Al was about to ask them to remove the gag when Tabon spoke again, nodding in the direction of the building. "He appears to have told the truth, Einarr."

Asger was returning. Walking next to him was another, about the size of a ten-year-old child, dressed in a pale blue coat with a hood that completely hid its features in shadow. If Al didn't know better, he would have thought it was a human child dressed for the snow.

3

Mike's face was pressed between the front seats of the van, watching the proceedings between the side-to-side strokes of the wipers. The rain made it hard to see. With each beat of the wiper, it went from blurry to clear to blurry again. Even through the rain he could see that Al had not been crazy. There was no chance these creatures were human. The arms and legs of these beings were too long in proportion to the torsos, the skulls strangely shaped. However, Mike could not make out many other details through the rain.

At one point there seemed to be some type of disagreement, and one of them had raised the sword it was carrying. Mike was getting ready to intervene when things seemed to calm down. Now the one that had left for the building on the right was returning with a child.

Mike looked down at Stevens and Hutchinson and was greeted by two sets of eyes wide with terror. Mike knew how they felt. He had a feeling no one was making it out of here tonight. They weren't the only ones trapped by this situation.

He pulled out his cell phone and stared at it. Neither of these two had seen his face. He could call in backup for Al and then just slip out the back of the van and escape into the dark. No one would even know he had been here, except for Al, and if things went badly Al wouldn't be doing any talking.

I mean, look at these things, think about what they did to that SWAT team. Could he and Al expect to get out of this alive? It didn't make any sense for him to throw his life away on a hopeless situation.

There was still the issue of the tape. The commissioner would still have his goons out looking for him. He wouldn't be able to show his face around the city again. He would have to get out of town. He wouldn't be able to explain where he had been, and if he thought the commissioner had him marked before, imagine once his little boy disappeared, or worse yet, was found murdered.

Mike could sneak out of the city, go underground. It would mean never seeing Joan and the girls again, but if he got himself killed, he wouldn't see them anyway. Better alive and lonely than dead and dead.

He looked out through the windshield again and saw Al walking toward the van.

CHAPTER 35

1

So far, so good. Their witness, Cwen, a young female Eaton, had recognized Danny Edwards from the newspaper photo and had picked up his scent on the hat. Einarr was not happy, but so far Tabon's read on the situation had proved accurate. Einarr was reluctant to do anything that would make the others think that he wasn't truly interested in the exchange happening.

Al opened the van's rear doors. Carter and Sean were seated facing each other, their backs leaning against opposite sides of the van. Mike was up near the front, behind the seats.

"How's it going? Is Anne there? Is she okay?"

"She appears to be scared and shaken, but other than that, okay. Slide this way, gentlemen. Hang your legs out the back."

They didn't move. Mike put the muzzle of the M4 against Carter's temple and gave his legs a kick. He reluctantly swung them out the back. "Keep them covered," Al said as he pulled a razor knife out of his pocket and cut the zip tie around Carter's ankles. They went through the same procedure with Sean.

Al grabbed them each in turn by an elbow and helped them slide out. Once they were both standing behind the van,

Al pulled out his gun and motioned them forward. "Sit tight, Mike. If this goes well, you won't even have to show yourself. I'll bring Anne back and we'll get the fuck outta here."

"Sure thing, Al," Mike said, his voice shaking slightly, but that was to be expected.

2

Al marched the two toward the Eaton, who had closed protectively around the young female. Al again stopped about ten yards away, though seeing how fast they moved, it was more philosophical than practical. When they stopped, the two boys got a good look at the Eaton for the first time.

Sean started to shake visibly, tremors running through his body like electricity through a bare wire. It was Carter who broke first, falling to his knees, sobbing loudly. This was the moment Al dreaded. Every fiber in his body wanted to tell Anne to run for it while he backed toward the van with the boys, firing away, holding off the Eaton. That may work in the movies that Mike was always quoting, but here, in real life, it would just get everyone killed.

"All right, you can check them out so that you are satisfied, but only the female and the one in the coat can come forward." Al did not want them to know he and Tabon had met before, not knowing that that cat was already out of the bag.

"You do not dictate the terms here, Detective," Einarr predictably responded.

"I think that is fine, Einarr. I am certainly capable of seeing to Cwen's safety from the likes of these," Tabon said.

He put his hand gently on the shoulder of the youngster. "Come, little one. Do not be concerned," Tabon said with surprising gentleness. The pair walked slowly forward. Al noticed Einarr give a subtle signal and the other two Eaton spread out to each side of him. Al decided right then and there that if they rushed him, he was going to pump every slug he had into Einarr's snarling, ugly face; the hell with the other two. Al might die, but he would take that piece of shit down with him for what he had done to Carrie.

The young one walked up to Sean first. Tabon stayed right behind her, ready to intervene should the need arise. The hood tilted as she lifted her face to look at Sean. The light fell on her features. Al wasn't sure what he had expected, and he had certainly gotten a good look at the other Eaton. Maybe it was her small size and youthful movements that had lulled him into complacency, but he was not ready for the wizened, skull-like face gazing with mustard eyes from the recesses of that pale blue hood.

In direct contrast to her looks, she spoke and her voice was soft and girlish. "Your hand, please, sir."

Sean, as if in a trance, slowly lifted his hands, fingers shaking. Cwen reached up and grasped them in grey, bony, skeleton-like fingers. She gently brought one to her face and sniffed. She dropped his hand and turned to Tabon. "He is one."

"That is good. Well done. Now the other."

She stepped in front of Carter. He was on his knees, head bowed, sobbing. Slowly he lifted his head. They were face to face. He let out a little cry and sank back on his haunches, turning his face away. Cwen seemed unperturbed by his reaction. Once again, she looked back at Tabon.

"He is one as well, my elder."

"All right, go back to Asger now. Asger, take her away."

3

Mike didn't like what he was seeing. The creature with the coat and the little one had come forward, right up to Al and the two teens. The other three had stayed back, swords drawn. One now moved to the left and another moved to the right so that they bracketed Al and the boys. The one in the middle began to make figure eights with the tip of his sword, as if warming up.

Mike looked down at his phone again. If he didn't call for backup, he would probably die here. However, if he did, he and Al would, in the best case scenario, go to jail for what they had done. More likely, they would both be dead before they ever got to trial. Those were the choices: hacked to pieces or taking a bullet behind the ear. In both cases, he would be dead, and his family, not knowing the circumstances, would be disgraced.

Unless he could slip away. He didn't have many options here at the end of the pier. He could slip out the back, keeping the van between himself and the others. He could go over the side, into the water. He wondered how strong the current was here. Between the current and the cold water, he wasn't sure he could make it.

Still, at least there was a chance. Al and Anne were dead anyway; no need to add himself to the list. He pictured it now: he made the call and soon squad cars would block off the entrance to the pier. The creatures—what did Al call them? The Eaton—would be trapped, and in the confrontation that was sure to follow, he could get to the edge of the pier and go over the side. If the cops came quickly enough, who knew? Al and Anne may be saved as well. Al would have no idea what Mike had done. He wouldn't give him up, and the teenagers hadn't seen Mike's face.

These thoughts filled his mind, loud voices reverberating through his brain, trying to drown out the feeble whispers of his conscience. But try as they might, that whisper wouldn't go away. Like music bleeding into a radio broadcast from a too-close station on the dial, that whisper of conscience kept seeping in.

He couldn't see himself abandoning Al. He had given his word, promised to help. Things may actually be going okay; he couldn't be sure. If that were the case, if things were going okay, then the cops coming in sirens blaring would probably fuck things up, seal Al and Anne's fate, get them killed.

He looked through the windshield again. One of the creatures, one of the ones with a sword, was walking with the little one back toward the building to the right. The one with the coat was still standing in front of Al and the two teens. The other two hadn't moved.

Whether he was going to run for it or he was going to stick and help Al, Mike couldn't do either from inside the van. If they moved on Al now, he would be dead before Mike could get out of the vehicle.

Mike reached up and removed the plastic cover from the van's dome light. He then took out the bulb. He didn't want it coming on and giving him away when he opened the back door.

He had to hunch over to stand in the van and not hit his head. His hand trembled slightly as he reached for the door handle. He took a deep breath and turned the handle. The internal struggle continued. He wasn't sure, when he stepped out the back, whether he would move round to the back corner of the van so that he had a good vantage point to cover Al or whether he would break and run.

Unfortunately, he would never find out the answer to that question.

4

As Asger walked toward the building with the young female, Cwen, Al turned to Tabon. "You can move back now."

Tabon backed away from Al and the two teenagers.

Al turned his attention to Einarr. "I have kept my end of the bargain. Let Anne walk to me and then you can take these two."

To Al's surprise, the right side of Einarr's mouth turned up in what should have been a smile. However, the permanent sneer on the left side distorted the final result into a grotesque jester's mask.

"You are correct, Detective. You have delivered those we seek." He turned to the other Eaton, ignoring Tabon. "You see, we can bend the humans to our will."

Asger came back from his trip to the building on the side of the pier. Instead of walking up next to Einarr, however, he stayed split out to the right.

To say that Al didn't trust them would have been an understatement. The palm of the hand grasping the butt of his gun was slick with sweat. His mind was racing, weighing the possibilities, calculating the angles, sequencing his shots.

He didn't think Tabon would do anything. If the others charged, there was a slim chance that he could break toward the building, put a few slugs in Asger, grab Anne's hand and get to the building. A very slim chance. If Mike started to fire from the van, his chances would go from "very slim" to "slim to none".

"You won't need the gun, Detective," Einarr said as the other Eaton made grating sounds in their throats that Al assumed was laughter. "Tabon, since you are so fond of these humans, could you please walk the female to the detective and escort our two prisoners to me?"

Al could tell Einarr was enjoying this. He had lost a little face in front of the others during his previous confrontation with Tabon. Now that the deal had been made and, from their end, was successful, he was trying to regain some of the authority he had lost.

For his part, Tabon did not protest. He took Anne by the elbow and guided her toward Al. Al put his arm around her shoulders and she leaned into him, sobbing quietly.

"Shh," Al whispered. "It's not over yet."

Tabon grabbed Sean's shoulder in one hand. With the other, he reached down and grabbed Carter by the scruff of the neck, easily lifting him to his feet. Carter's legs seemed to have lost their ability to stand. It didn't matter as Tabon moved him along easily with the one hand, Carter's feet dangling and bouncing on the ground like a marionette's. Al could hear both boys sobbing in fear. He would be hearing that sound in his nightmares if he lived long enough to have any.

Asger and the other Eaton stepped forward at a signal from Einarr and took custody of the two youths.

As the others turned and began to walk away, Einarr stood there facing Al, his one eye regarding him. "This is justice, Detective. Any pain or loss you suffered is due to your own unwillingness to do the right thing from the beginning. I hope you remember the rest of our bargain. You are not to speak of our true nature to anyone. Our transaction is complete." With that, he turned and followed the others.

CHAPTER 36

1

Mike twisted the handle on the back door of the van and swung it open. He found himself staring into the snarling face of a hunched and twisted creature.

Before Mike could react, Hop Frog launched himself into the van. His shoulder caught Mike squarely in the chest, sending all 6'3" of him sprawling flat on the van floor. One large gray hand grabbed Mike by the throat, pinning him to the floor and choking off his shout of surprise.

Hop Frog moved quickly, straddling Mike's chest, his knees pinning Mike's arms, that malformed face inches from Mike's own. Saliva dripped from the exposed fangs and pattered onto Mike's cheeks.

Mike heaved mightily, trying to buck his assailant off, but Hop Frog hung on like a rodeo cowboy, still able to keep Mike pinned easily. The whole time he was laughing, a spine-chilling, grating noise.

"You surprised me, large man, I thought the machine was empty. Not a worry." He raised his right hand. It held one of those short swords, the type Mike and Al had found near the traffic accident what felt like ten years ago. He quickly flipped it around in his hand, holding it like a dagger and pressed the point in the hollow of Mike's shoulder.

"Farewell, large man," he said as he drove the blade down through the shoulder and under Mike's ribs. Mike shuddered and was still.

2

Al could hardly believe it as he watched them just walk away. The rain had stopped and he and Anne stood alone on the pier, the wind from off the water coming in fits and starts to whip around them and then dash away.

Al felt exhaustion wash over him. He had not realized how tightly he had been wound through the whole encounter. The release of that tension made him lightheaded, sapped his strength.

He turned to Anne and untied the gag, easing it from between her jaws. He then lifted the blindfold. Her eyes were red from crying and tired. Taking out the razor knife he freed her wrists.

"Oh my god, Al," she said, and threw her arms around his neck. They stood like that for several moments, supporting each other, each drawing strength from the other.

"Someday," she whispered, "maybe years from now, maybe you can fill in the blanks about all this. I don't think I can handle it now."

"I don't think I have the energy to go through it all," Al responded. "Come on, my partner Mike is in the van. Let's get far away from this place. There is still a lot we have to work through."

He put his arm around her waist, guiding her toward the van. He found it hard to think. He had been so scared he would lose her, that he would fail her the way he had failed Carrie. There was a great deal he had seen and done over the last several days that was going to be tough, if not impossible, to live with, but if in the bargain Anne had also been killed, he felt sure he would have broken. He would not have been able to recover.

As they walked up to the van, Al pounded three times on the side. "Hey Mike, we're coming in." They walked around to the back doors and Al grabbed the handle, popping it.

He pulled the door open and saw a flash of steel. Jumping back, he pulled Anne with him, almost knocking her off her feet. A sword blade sliced down through the opening between the doors, missing Al's face by inches.

Al stumbled backwards, pushing Anne behind him with one hand and pulling his gun out of his coat pocket with the other.

The doors to the back of the van flew open and Hop Frog leapt out, landing in a crouch on the ground. He was like a twisted knot of hate, lips drawn back in a snarl, eyes flashing. Like the other Eaton, he was naked except for a kilt. He presented a perverted figure: one leg emaciated and turned inward, the other muscular and powerful looking. His spine bent like a question mark, the hips turned so they weren't properly aligned with the shoulders. Those shoulders were broad and powerful looking; the muscular arms almost reached the ground due to the hunched curvature of the spine.

Hop Frog held one of the short swords in his gnarled gray fist. He swung it expertly, making cuts in the air as he circled Al and Anne.

"Run!" Al yelled as he backed away, firing a shot at the creature before him.

Hop Frog sprung sideways, and then leaped toward Al. The bullet whizzed harmlessly past him. Al got off two more shots in quick succession. They slammed into the leathery grey chest of his attacker. The flat of the sword came down on Al's gun hand; the weapon discharged as it was knocked from his grasp. He watched it go spinning away along the ground.

Al grabbed his wrist in pain. He glanced around for Anne and was dismayed to see her standing just a few feet away. "Run!" he screamed.

"Oh no, you won't be runnin' now," Hop Frog snarled as he covered the distance to Anne in two ungainly hops. He grabbed her arm and, with a quick twist of his wrist, sent her sprawling to the ground. He then turned his attention back to Al.

Al stood next to the van, holding his wrist, calculating the distances between himself, Anne, the gun and Hop Frog.

Hop Frog looked down at the two holes in his chest, oozing black ichor, and laughed that rusty, metal gear laugh.

"Now that you don't have your toy, I will be taking my time. First I will kill you, Detective, one small cut at a time. But before you die, I want you to know it is your female I will be having for my supper." With that he lunged forward, flicking out his sword.

Al felt like he had been branded and looked down to see a slit in the thigh of his jeans, the material slowly turning red. Al glanced toward Anne and saw her on all fours, moving slowly toward his gun. She had to pass behind Hop Frog to get there. If Al could just keep his attention, she may have a chance.

He got in a crouch and circled to one side so that as Hop Frog turned with Al, it placed his back to Anne. The sword flicked out again and Al was just barely able to dodge the tip of the blade. The fiend was incredibly fast. Al didn't know how long he would be able to avoid further cuts.

The blade flicked again, and again Al just managed to dance away. Looking past Hop Frog, he could see Anne had the gun and was slowly rising to her feet. She raised the weapon, pointing it at the creature's back. Al did a little back and forth shuffle, keeping Hop Frog's attention and praying that Anne didn't miss and shoot him instead.

She steadied the weapon with both hands and squeezed the trigger. There was a loud click. The gun had jammed.

Hop Frog spun around at the sound and snarled, "Sure but you're a sneaky bitch," as he lunged toward her, raising the sword above his head.

Al charged, lowering his shoulder. He hit Hop Frog in the small of his misshapen back, wrapping his arms around his waist. He heard a satisfying woofing sound as they both crashed to the ground.

As soon as they hit the ground, Al felt like he had his arms wrapped around a jungle cat. Hop Frog thrashed violently, twisting, turning, spinning. In one motion, he threw Al off him, twisted around and lunged with gaping jaws toward Al's throat. His fangs snapped shut on thin air, inches from Al's jugular.

Al fell backwards and skittered along the ground in a crab walk. Hop Frog was on his feet again and advanced toward him, sword raised. "Enough games."

Al heard the rapid staccato of gunfire so close his ears rang. Standing above him, Hop Frog was doing a twitchy little dance as bullet holes stitched a seam up his side.

Al looked in the direction of the gunfire and was stunned by what he saw. Mike stood there, swaying on unsteady legs. The front of his clothing was soaked with blood. The handle of a short sword protruded from the top of his shoulder like the misshapen head of an absorbed twin. The M4 was on his hip, belching smoke and flame as it pumped bullets into Al's attacker.

It didn't last; whatever magical power had been holding Mike up ran out. His eyes, glassy and trancelike the whole time, shut and he fell sideways, twisting as he went. He landed on his back, the barrel of the M4 pointed at the sky, tendrils of smoke from the muzzle drifting off on the breeze.

The impact of the bullets had caused Hop Frog to drop his sword. He stood there, eyes vacant, each beat of his heart forcing a gout of black blood between the fangs of his gaping mouth, where it ran down his chin, spattering his already bloodied and bullet-riddled chest.

Amazingly, Hop Frog shook his head, droplets of blood flying to the left and right, and awareness returned to those mustard yellow eyes. He staggered toward Al, who had reached the side of the van and was using it to help pull himself to his feet.

Hop Frog reached for Al's throat with both hands. Al grabbed his wrists, trying to pry the hands from his throat. It was no use. Al felt like he was holding onto a pair of iron bars. Hop Frog pulled Al forward and then back, slamming his skull into the side of the van.

Al fought to remain conscious. Through the waves of gray that clouded his vision, he made out the gaping jaws of the monster coming toward his face. He just managed to move his head to the side in time, hearing a loud snapping sound near his right ear.

Again he was slammed into the van and then suddenly released. He slid, boneless, down the side of the van. Through his blurred vision, he barely made out the figure of Hop Frog standing before him, twisting and writhing, reaching around and clutching at his own back. Then everything went black.

CHAPTER 37

1

The Eaton walked in a group up the street between two warehouses. This section of the waterfront was abandoned, had been earmarked for redevelopment, so they had little fear of being discovered.

There were eight of them altogether. Einarr, Tabon and the three that had been on the pier, plus three others that had been posted as lookouts and had now joined the group. The two captives were being carried, one each over the shoulder of an Eaton, as easily as if they were carrying a sack of laundry. Carter Stevens was whimpering quietly. Sean Hutchinson had fainted.

Einarr was quiet as well. He did not appear to be pleased. Considering the human detective had supposedly did as he asked and turned over the murderers, he should have been reveling in his accomplishment. But he wasn't. He walked along silently, deep in his own thoughts.

None of them seemed to notice except for Tabon. Einarr's reaction supported what Tabon had believed all along. He was hoping to draw the Eaton into a war with the humans and now his plan had unraveled. Tabon was not naïve enough to believe this would be the end of it. The more he thought about it, the more he admitted to himself that Detective Russo had been right: there would always be the threat of war as long as Einarr was alive.

Suddenly Tabon heard gunshots coming from the direction of the pier. He looked over at Einarr and saw a smile play over the side of his face that still worked properly.

"What is that?"

"Did you forget that Rangvald said the humans must die?" Einarr answered.

"But he kept his word. He did what you asked."

Einarr turned toward him, the smile disappearing. "I do what is necessary to protect the Eaton. Everyone here would do the same. There is no confusion as to where my duty lies, half human," he spat. "I am here to serve my king." The smile returned.

Tabon did not bother to reply; he turned and began running back toward the sound of the gunfire.

"Asger, Ulf, Geir, stop him," Einarr commanded. The three hesitated. "He has shown his true allegiance. Go."

All three broke into a run, covering the ground at cheetah speed in the long strides of the Eaton.

2

Anne stood there, stunned by the results of her actions. She had lifted the dropped sword off the ground, and holding it above her head with both hands, she had plunged it into the back of the monster attacking Al.

The thing had convulsed so violently that the handle of the sword had been ripped from Anne's grasp and the weapon had remained imbedded in his back.

The creature twisted and turned, its apelike arms reaching back as it tried in vain to grab the sword. The head twisted around, neck craning, as it snapped at the sword handle with its jaws.

Anne stepped back to avoid the thrashing creature. He was convulsing so violently she couldn't get by him to see if Al were alive.

Finally Hop Frog's body seemed to shudder; he turned and gave her one last questioning stare as if to ask "How could you?" before he collapsed in a heap on the ground.

Anne heard splashing in the puddles left by the rain. She took her eyes away from the twisted, bullet-riddled body before her, and looked around to see Tabon running toward her at full speed. Crossing the street at the mouth of the pier and coming on fast were three of the Eaton.

Tabon shrugged out of his coat as he ran. Never slowing, he scooped her up at full speed, sprinted for the edge of the pier and dove, head first, into the icy cold water.

The shock of the cold knocked the wind out of Anne, left her gasping for air, her mouth and nose filling with frigid water.

3

Asger held up his hand, stopping the other two in their tracks. He took in the scene: one human he had not seen before lay in a heap, obviously dead. The other human, Russo, slumped against the machine, covered in human and Eaton blood, dead as well.

He walked over to the third body, Hop Frog. Asger bent to one knee and examined the corpse. Judging by the severity of the wounds and the number of them, Hop Frog had fought bravely and well.

He turned to the other two. "Go find Tabon and the female. I will tend to Hop Frog's body. We cannot leave him here to be discovered by the humans. I will bring him below, where he can be honored properly for his bravery."

The two went to the edge of the pier, scanning the surface of the water.

"Go along the bank. Humans are too weak for him to have her in the water for long. They will have to come on shore soon."

He bent to pick up Hop Frog's corpse as the others went back to the mouth of the pier and started along the water's edge.

CHAPTER 38

1

Al regained consciousness. He gingerly felt the back of his head. He could feel a large knot through his hair. Despite the dizziness caused by any movement of his head, he quickly scanned the area. Al's heart sank. Anne was gone. She would not have left him here and run off, which meant she was in the hands of the Eaton once again.

Al pulled himself slowly to his feet. He looked for the body of Hop Frog, but it wasn't there. Either it had been carried off by the Eaton or Hop Frog had somehow managed to survive. He was alone on the pier with Mike.

Al took inventory. He had a nasty cut on his thigh that, for the moment, had stopped bleeding. His clothing was covered in black Eaton blood as well as his own. Except for that and the bump on his head, he was in remarkably good shape considering what he had just been through.

Al walked over toward his partner. On the way, he picked his handgun off the ground. He popped the clip and cleared the chamber, then reinserted the clip and chambered a round. It must have been the hit it took from the flat of Hop Frog's blade that had caused it to jam on Anne. He stuffed the gun in his belt and continued over to Mike.

He looked down on Mike's body. He was greeted with a dead, glassy stare. Those eyes were fixed on the night sky as if it held all the answers. Mike's jaw was frozen in grim determination. Al couldn't imagine the willpower it took for Mike to get himself moving with that horrific wound. He had managed to hold off death just long enough to save Al's life.

Al heard sirens off in the distance; he was going to have to move fast. He couldn't afford to be picked up now. He had to find Anne, if she was still alive.

He grabbed the barrel of the M4—it was still hot to the touch—and twisted it out of Mike's death grip. He went over to the van as fast as he could, stopping once as his head started spinning, threatening to pitch him onto the pavement.

He reached the back of the van and climbed in. He found the zip ties, the duct tape and clips for the M4. He looked for one other item and found it.

Climbing back out, he went over to Mike's body and, with some effort, rolled it over on its side, pulling the arms behind its back. He zip tied the wrists together and ripped off a piece of duct tape and put it over Mike's dead lips.

If he could make it appear Mike was a victim instead of a perpetrator, maybe Mike's family would still get his pension. It was the least he could do.

Al returned to the van. He pulled his shirt tail out of his pants and ripped off a piece of the material. He looked down and noticed his leg had started to bleed again. He tore off a second strip.

The sirens were getting closer; he had to move fast. He opened the gas cap and stuffed one of the strips of material in to form a fuse. He tied the other strip around the cut on his leg. He then took the lighter he had retrieved from the van, the lighter he had purchased when they got the zip ties just for this purpose, and lit the fuse. He hobbled away across the pier as quick as he could.

He could see the flashing lights of the police cars through the gaps between the buildings to either side of the pier as they came up the street from both the left and the right.

Al was afraid he may be trapped out here. His mind raced. Then he had an idea and headed for the building on the side of the pier. The Eaton had brought the young female to the building, but he had not seen her or the others who he assumed were there to escort her leave the building. Maybe there was another way out.

He got to the side of the structure just as the police cars screeched to a halt out on the street. Behind him there was a loud crack and then a *whoomp* as the back end of the van exploded and the vehicle was engulfed in flames. Hot pieces of metal whizzed all around Al as he half ran, half hopped around the side of the building. Al made it to the back and saw a small platform on the side of the pier and stairs heading down toward the water.

He took the stairs. Below the pier, there was scaffolding that ran underneath, back toward the shore. Al stood on the platform for a minute, looking out at the water. He saw the red and blue lights reflecting on the surface as the squad cars drove slowly and, he assumed with the recent explosion and fire, cautiously, up the pier. Al didn't wait for the cops to get out of the cars and start searching the place; he headed out along the scaffolding passing beneath the pier unseen.

2

They stood facing each other in the narrow confines of the tunnel. Tabon had a perplexed look on his simian face. This was his first exposure to the wrath of the human female. Anne stood before him, shivering in her wet clothing but defiant nonetheless.

"We have to go back right now," she demanded. "Al was still alive; we can't let them take him."

"I could not save both of you. He looked to be dead anyway."

"He wasn't, I tell you, we have to go back."

They had been going back and forth like this ever since they emerged from the water and Anne had caught her breath. After they had hit the water, Tabon had immediately made for shore, knowing that Anne would not last long in the cold water. He swam easily, even with her under one arm.

They had come to the seawall and Tabon had paddled along the slimy, moss-covered concrete until they had come to a drainage tunnel. There was a heavy iron grate covering the mouth of the tunnel. Water from the recent rain poured through the grate. Tabon shifted Anne behind him.

"Grab me around the neck," he ordered. She had regained some of her composure but her limbs felt too numb to swim. She wrapped her arms around his neck, letting her legs float out behind her so the water supported her weight; she was floating behind him like a human superman cape.

For a split second the thought crossed Anne's mind to just let go. Let the current take her, try to escape. The thought was rejected as soon as it occurred. The current was strong and the water cold; she was already losing feeling in her limbs. Her chances of survival, trying to swim for it, were slim at best.

Tabon grabbed the bars of the grate with both hands and braced his feet against the concrete wall for leverage. The water coming from the tunnel washed over him. Anne had to turn her head to the side to breathe and still found herself choking and gulping air between mouthfuls of water. She felt the muscles in Tabon's back bulge as he strained against the grate. For a moment nothing happened, then the bars began to bend. The concrete where the ends of the bars were imbedded began to crack and crumble. Tabon relaxed and then gave one

307

final heave. One bar bent outward; another burst free in a shower of chunks of cement. The gap left was just barely big enough for them to slip through.

Tabon turned sideways to squeeze through and Anne lost her grip. He was just able to grab her arm before the current took her away. He made it into the tunnel and hauled her in after him. Once inside, they had to bend at the waist to fit, the rushing water up to their knees. They made their way along the steadily rising incline of the tunnel, their faces inches above the streaming torrent.

Finally they reached an intersection where a larger tunnel formed a T with the one they were in. Once they entered this larger tunnel, they still had to stoop over somewhat; the water was now just above their ankles. That is when Anne had started in.

"We cannot go back. You saw the three following me; we would fall right into their hands. If your detective was still alive, I am sorry to say he probably isn't any longer."

"Don't say that," Anne said. "There is always a chance. We can't just go."

Just then an eerie hollow howling sound echoed down the tunnel.

"They've found the opening," Tabon said, looking back the way they had come. "We must go now. At least all this water should keep them from picking up our scent. Once we have lost them, we can discuss what to do about your detective." He grabbed her hand in his calloused claw and they ran together up the tunnel away from the sound of the howls.

3

Al found himself back underground. The scaffolding had ended at the shore with a ladder heading up to the deck of the pier. That would have put him right in the arms of the cops, so instead he had dropped down to a spit of gravel and refuse that was piled up where the pier met the sea wall. He found a drainage tunnel that at one time must have been closed off with a grate, however several of the bars had rusted through and others had been bent, leaving an opening Al could easily step through. He didn't have to think too hard to imagine who had the strength to bend those bars.

He had traveled about fifty yards underground, stooped over in complete darkness, water rushing by up to his knees. He resisted the urge to switch on the light on the M4's barrel. He figured after his last adventure underground, those batteries didn't have much juice left, and he wanted to conserve what little there was until it was absolutely necessary.

He had to stop several times along the way to vomit. He probably had a concussion, but that didn't concern him at this point. At this point he was motivated by one thing: revenge. He had played by their rules, he had sacrificed his own sense of morality to save Anne, and he had been double crossed.

He hated to face the truth, but the Eaton had no use for Anne now. Al doubted she was still alive, or if she was, that he would ever see her again. He would deal with the grief of that later. Right now he had the M4, several clips of ammunition and only one thought: he was going to kill as many of them as he could find.

He reached a larger tunnel that formed a T-shaped intersection with the first one. He could almost stand in this tunnel, only had to bend his neck slightly. At some point the sun must have come up. Al could see twin rays of light up ahead filtering through the holes in a manhole cover. There was also faint light coming from side tunnels that must have ended in sewer grates in the street above. There wasn't much light, but it was something.

He stood there at the T junction looking like some post-apocalyptic scarecrow, battered and bruised, clothes in tatters and covered with blood, M4 locked and loaded, trying to decide which way to go. Then he noticed something move through the twin beams of light coming down from the manhole to his right.

Al slowly, quietly, turned to face that direction, pointing the M4 down the tunnel. He listened. It was hard to hear anything with the water streaming by but he thought he heard a slight snorting noise.

Al flipped on the light under the gun's barrel. There, about twenty yards away, bathed in the light, looking like a silver statue, was an Eaton. The creature had been standing there, head tilted up as if sniffing the air. It was one of the ones from the pier, clad in only a kilt, sword in its hand. As soon as the light hit it, it spun toward Al and went into a crouch, lips pulled back in a snarl, fangs exposed, mustard-colored eyes glowing like caution lights. It let out a hiss and charged.

Al stood his ground. After being a part of several encounters with these creatures and seeing how hard they were to bring down, he had decided quality of fire was better than quantity. He aimed right for the center of its gray, hairless chest and fired in several short, controlled bursts, limiting recoil and grouping his shots.

He was aided by the narrowness of the tunnel. The creature could not spring from side to side as the others had, making them hard to hit. He was rewarded by three holes appearing like magic in the center of its chest, then three more. It stumbled and hitched slightly as each burst hit home, but kept coming. It was within five yards of Al when another burst hit home and it pitched forward onto the tunnel floor, sliding on the wet brick, and ended up lying at Al's feet, those mustard-colored eyes glassy and dead.

4

Tabon grabbed Anne around the waist and hoisted her to his hip. "What the hell are you doing?" she demanded.

"You are too slow; they will be on us in no time. We have to move faster." Despite her additional weight, he raced easily up the tunnel, her holding on like a side-mounted jockey. "We have to get to street level, then maybe we can lose them." As if to emphasize his point, the howling came again, closer now.

Tabon stopped. They were under a manhole. Light from the street above filtered through the holes in the manhole cover. Anne could just make out one of the smaller tunnels like the one they had just come out of to their right. Tabon headed down it. The water was not as deep as before.

"What are you doing? This heads back down toward the harbor."

"I know. Be quiet." He stopped and turned around, facing back the way they had come. He pushed her down lower. They both waited, their heads just above the rushing water. Then Anne thought she heard splashing, and a shadow flitted through the faint beams of light above.

"Wait a moment," Tabon said. "That was one of them; let's wait to make sure the other one isn't following."

Just then they heard the sound of gunfire echoing through the tunnels, the enclosed space amplifying the sound.

"That could be Al," Anne offered, the excitement and hope in her voice palatable.

"I doubt it is the detective. It could be other police," Tabon replied.

They heard splashing up above. The shadow flitted through the light beams again, this time going from right to left in the direction of the gunfire.

"Wait here," Tabon commanded. "Do not move until I return." With that, he splashed his way to the mouth of their tunnel and sprinted off to the left, leaving Anne alone in the dark.

5

Al was on one knee, leaning on the butt of the M4. He had unclipped the light from the bottom of the barrel and was using it to examine the dead Eaton. Black blood oozed from the holes in the chest, mingled with the water flowing along the floor of the tunnel, creating what looked like an oil slick that trailed off in the distance. The snarl was frozen on the cold, dead face. Al looked in amazement at the size of the fangs, the foreign structure of the skull, the reptilian structure of the ears. He ran a finger along the raised, stippled scarring of the symbols carved in the skin of the creature. He puzzled again at how they could have survived undetected for all these years.

Al's thoughts were interrupted by the sound of splashing coming from up the tunnel. He cursed himself for the momentary lack of focus. He pointed the light in the direction of the sound and saw another creature barreling up the tunnel toward him. He fumbled with the light, attempting to clamp it back on the gun barrel, realized he wouldn't have time. He held the barrel in the crook of his left elbow, holding the light in his left hand. He squeezed the trigger; the recoil caused the barrel to jump, spoiling his aim. The creature instinctively squeezed to his left as he came, the bullets hit the tunnel wall and ceiling harmlessly to his right, spraying chips of old brick.

Al backed up, fumbling to attach the light. He heard a loud splash. Finally, he had the light reattached and pointed the beam back up the tunnel. There were two Eaton wrestling on the floor of the tunnel—though wrestling wasn't quite an apt word; it was like watching two large jungle cats fight. All thrashing limbs, snapping jaws and flashing fangs, they spun, feinted, attacked in a fury of motion and spraying water. Despite the confusion of the struggle and the splashing water, Al could make out a mane of black hair and knew one of the two was Tabon.

CHAPTER 39

1

Anne stood in the darkness, shivering. Her clothes, completely soaked through, provided no warmth. She was in complete darkness. The water had slowed and the level had dropped; it eddied lazily around her ankles. She stared up at the tunnel that intersected the one she was hiding in. Her eyes fixed on the two narrow beams of light coming through the holes in the manhole cover up there, looking for any movement, any disturbance of those beams.

After Tabon had unceremoniously dashed off, there had been a few moments of silence except for the gurgle of the water. Then she had heard more gunfire. That had been about ten or fifteen minutes ago, and since then, nothing. She wondered what she would do if Tabon didn't return. She would not be able to lift the manhole cover to get out. She would have to wander in complete darkness, hoping to come to a sewer grate or some other opening to the world above where she could get someone's attention.

She was not confident in the results of such an endeavor and determined to wait a little longer. How much longer, she wasn't sure. Every time she thought about moving, the dread would rise inside her. What if she went off just as Tabon was returning and missed him?

She stood there hugging her elbows and shivering. She finally went up to the intersection with the other tunnel. She had been reluctant to do this with Eaton roaming about, but she had heard nothing for some time now.

At the intersection, she looked left and right and saw nothing—nothing except the beams of sunlight through another manhole farther up to the right. Then she caught something to the left: a glow, a light coming slowly in her direction.

It had to be a human; Eaton had no need for light. Still, she wasn't taking any chances; she ducked back into the mouth of the side tunnel and peeked carefully around the corner.

Two figures came into view. The taller one carried a gun with a light on it; he shuffled slowly, his feet causing small waves in the water. The other figure was Eaton, the unnatural proportions a dead giveaway. The Eaton was Tabon; that would make the human…?

"Al?" she said, barely able to believe there was a possibility it could be true. "Al," she repeated.

"Anne?" he replied, his voice cracking. "Oh my God, thank God, Anne?" He stumbled through the water, practically falling into her arms. They stood there, hugging. The emotions washed over them: disbelief, relief, gratitude, caring and affection. The tears flowed freely. "I thought I'd never see you again," Al managed, his voice cracking.

"I hate to break up your reunion," Tabon said, still breathing hard from his struggle with the other Eaton. "But we have to get moving. I only beat Geir senseless. We must be out of here before he regains consciousness. I do not wish to be responsible for the death of a fellow Eaton."

315

2

Traveling through a convoluted route composed of tunnels, alleys, abandoned buildings and empty lots—the Eaton travelogue of New York City—they made it back to Tabon's personal lair without further encounters. Tabon was seated in his desk chair; he had popped a Cream tape into the 8-track. Anne and Al were on the couch. They had both changed out of their wet clothing into clothes that Tabon had provided them. They could have passed for any of the homeless, or Eaton, in the city.

They were all exhausted. Al had his arm around Anne's shoulders. Her head rested on his chest. Tabon was sprawled in the desk chair, head back, eyes closed, in a very human posture.

Anne lifted her head. "Al, your leg is bleeding. You better let me have a look at that." Without waiting for a response, she sat up, undid the button and pulled down the zipper on Al's pants, working the waistband down Al's hips. He lifted his butt and she worked the pants down to his ankles. The rag he had tied around his thigh had completely soaked through. She untied it and carefully peeled it away, exposing the wound. "Oh my. Al, you need to get this stitched up. It's pretty deep."

"Well, it's not like I can walk into the nearest emergency room. I show my face and I'm as good as dead."

"What do you mean?" she asked as she pressed the wound with the soaked cloth, attempting to slow the flow of blood.

"Anne, you didn't see what went on because of the blindfold, and I want you to hear me out before you pass judgment. I traded two teenage boys for you tonight. Boys who had killed one of theirs." Al nodded toward Tabon.

"I know about the boys and what they did; Tabon told me," Anne said.

"Do you know who those two teens were? Do you know what I've done?" He went on to explain the background of his two former captives, going slowly, watching Anne's widening eyes, wording it carefully. The last thing he wanted was for her to be disgusted by him, though he didn't know how she couldn't be.

"If I show myself, if I am lucky, I will be arrested and have a few days before they get to me. If I'm unlucky, I won't even get the few days. I'll be killed on sight."

This brought a grating laugh from Tabon. "We are in the same situation, my man friend. I call you a friend because it appears we are all we have. To save you, it was my king I defied. I also will be killed by my own kind if found."

Anne didn't seem to hear Tabon; she was still staring wide-eyed at Al. "I understand you thought you had no choice, but I wish you hadn't done that for me, Al. Whatever they did, it's not right for them to be handed over for who knows what kind of torture, and it's not fair to you, Al, not fair for you to have to do such a thing." A solitary tear rolled down her cheek, making a path through the grime.

Tabon said, "You must understand, it was not just for you that the detective did this. With this one act, he saved untold thousands of lives. It was the only way."

Anne was silent for a moment and then, as if pushing it away with great effort, she said, "We can talk about that later. Right now, Al, you need attention. Tabon…" Anne looked around at the piles of articles cramming every space in the tunnel. "Do you have anything, a first aid kit, sewing supplies, even clean cloth, anything?"

"I will look," Tabon answered and he got up and began rummaging through an overflowing dresser next to the desk. Anne didn't like the look of Al; he was pale and despite the cold of the tunnel there was a film of sweat on his brow.

Tabon had disappeared among the stacks. She heard his voice from amidst the clutter.

"I believe this may suit your needs."

3

Tabon had found a tackle box containing fish hooks, lures and a spool of fishing line. Anne had sterilized one of the hooks using the lighter Al had from the van. Then, threading the hook with the fishing line, she had stitched Al's wound closed.

Tabon had also found an old, battered first-aid kit that contained some bandages and antiseptic cream. Anne applied the cream liberally to the cut and bandaged it as best she could.

Despite her best efforts, Al developed a fever and spent the next two days slipping in and out of consciousness. Finally, on the second full day, the fever broke and he began to get some of his color back.

During the time Al was recovering, Tabon would periodically slip out of their hideout and come back with food and water. More of the type of fare that Anne had received while in captivity: bottled water and Styrofoam containers full of leftovers.

While she was stitching Al's wound, and several times over the subsequent days when she was tending to him—wiping his brow with a wet cloth, coaxing liquid between his lips—she had looked up and caught Tabon staring at them with those incredibly human blue eyes.

The depth of the loneliness in that stare was so pronounced as to almost be a physical thing. Each time, she looked away feeling uncomfortable. It was more personal than seeing someone naked; it was like seeing his soul exposed.

How must it be to be the only one of your kind? Not fully human, but not fully Eaton either?

Anne was not familiar with Eaton society, but whatever exposure she had to the creatures did not lead her to believe it was the most caring and nurturing. Didn't the human side of Tabon crave what all humans craved? Caring, compassion, love? To live your whole life without basic human needs, with no hope of ever meeting those needs... No hope of true companionship... Alone in the world, alone forever.

CHAPTER 40

1

Al cursed the delay his illness had caused. When it came down to it, you could only push the human body so far before it took matters into its own hands. This realization made him even more in awe of Anne. She had been through a grueling ordeal herself, but though appearing tired and haggard, she showed no sign of impending collapse.

Even now, she was dividing food that Tabon had brought from above onto paper plates as naturally as if she were at a buffet or backyard barbecue. All the while, she was engaging Tabon in conversation.

Al was also amazed at her easy relationship with this creature. Anne had told him of how Tabon had cared for her when she had been in captivity and about the long conversations they had had, and how those conversations helped her cope. The casual way they interacted now showed that they had developed a bond, a friendship, in spite of his appearance and their differences.

Unfortunately, now was not the time to rest or marvel at cross species détente. They had only temporarily spoiled Einarr's plans; they had not stopped him.

"We have to try to determine Einarr's next move," Al said. "He isn't going to let this drop."

"You are right," Tabon replied, looking up from his plate of food. "He will want to leverage the esteem he has garnered with the capture of Kustaa's killers. He will have more support now than he has ever had before. I don't think he will do anything until after the Cleansing. His popularity will be at its peak after the ceremony."

"When is that supposed to take place?"

"From what I have observed down below," Tabon replied, pointing down the tunnel past the piles of his collection to where he and Al had observed the Eaton before, "the ceremony will occur tonight. The heavens are properly aligned."

"All the Eaton will be down there tonight? Including Einarr and all his followers?" Al asked.

"Yes, but I hope you are not thinking this is an opportunity, Detective. You must remember our agreement. It was for Einarr and his followers, and that is all. The fact that I am no longer welcome amongst the Eaton changes nothing; our agreement was that the Eaton as a species must survive. We must isolate Einarr and those that follow him before we take any action."

"What is your plan for doing that? How do we get them together?" Al asked.

"Einarr and those closest to him do not stay in the settlement below. No one is sure where they stay, but they are only here on occasion."

"We have to find out where they are holed up and we have to find out soon." Al cautioned, "He isn't going to wait. He is going to try again to provoke something, and this time he is going to want to go bigger to ensure it works. Is there any way you can follow them after the ceremony tonight? I can't— if they travel through the underground, I am going to need light and will be spotted. You can see down there."

"I can try. It isn't going to be easy. If they catch sight of me, I stand as much of a chance as you do of surviving the encounter. However, you're right in that this is something that only I can attempt."

"You have to discover where they are holed up. Then I can see if I can bring the police in. In the meantime, Anne and I have to get topside. We can't stay down here in this climate, eating this food forever. We'll pick up a couple of burner phones so we can stay in touch."

"You're getting me my own working phone device?" Tabon asked, his face lighting up like a teenager's.

Despite the situation they were in, Al couldn't help but laugh at the expression on his face. "Yeah, do you know how to use one?"

"No, you will have to show me." Tabon held out his hands with their thick fingers. "I will need one with large buttons."

"I'll set it up so you won't have to hit a lot of buttons. A couple of touches and the call will go through. We'll wait till dark, then Anne and I will head out."

"You should leave during the Cleansing," Tabon suggested. "All the Eaton will be at the ceremony. It will be safer. And when you travel, stay out of the subways—they are watched. Also, don't walk, take cabs. They can't follow your scent if you take cabs, it breaks the trail."

"Where are we going to go, Al?" Anne chimed in. "The police will be all over your place and mine. If you're seen, you'll be picked up."

"Yeah, I know. We'll have to get a room in some out-of-the-way hotel. We'll have to get cash. We have to be careful using ATMs and credit cards; they'll be tracking our numbers. We'll have to keep our faces covered when we hit the ATMs, and we'll pay for the room with cash." Then Al turned to Tabon. "Do you have some overcoats we can use? We'll never get a cab dressed like we are."

"Yes I do, I have several."

"All right, good. You need to get me to the surface now so I can get those burners. Anne, I hate to leave you but it would be safer if you stay here until we get back. Then we'll head out after dark."

"All right, Al, but you better make it back."

"You can count on it. Okay, Tabon, let's go." Al turned and saw Tabon holding a trench coat and a long piece of cloth. "What's the cloth for?"

"A blindfold, Detective. I know we are now the best of friends, but I can't take the chance of you being able to find the settlement on your own."

"You can call me Al, and I think we are a little past that, don't you? I gave my word the Eaton would not be harmed— just Einarr and his bunch."

"Still, I would prefer we use the blindfold. Then you won't have to put your word to the test."

Al shrugged in resignation and allowed himself to be blindfolded.

2

Al told Tabon where he wanted to go to get the phones. They had walked, staying underground, taking rights and lefts until Al had lost count and was totally disoriented. His leg began to throb from all the walking and he was afraid he may pop the stitches and start it bleeding again.

When Tabon removed the blindfold, they were under a grate in the pavement. Al had no idea whether he was ten feet or ten miles from Tabon's underground lair. Tabon reached up and lifted the grate with ease, sliding it to one side.

"You will come up in an alley behind a building on the street you wanted. I will wait here. Once you have finished your transaction, return here and I will take you back."

Al was a little nervous he would draw too much attention. He was dressed in a battered trench coat over stained khakis and a tattered sweatshirt. A knit cap pulled low over his eyes and worn-out sneakers completed his outfit. But as he stepped from behind the building and onto the sidewalk, he realized he needn't have worried. The legendary indifference of New Yorkers was in full effect. He might as well have been invisible.

3

Before they had returned to Tabon's lair, Al had programmed the number of his phone into the one he was giving to Tabon. He explained the need to test them before they went back and the issues Tabon may run into if he tried to use the phone underground. It was almost comical how he hung on to Al's every word and seemed completely enamored with his new toy. He insisted on testing the phone several times before they headed back. Each time the call went through and Al answered, Tabon seemed quite pleased with himself and would break into that rough, gravelly laugh. Al was sure that if Tabon had been human, he would have been a tech geek.

"You sound quite different through this burner phone device," he said. "Quite different. It is very strange. And my voice comes out of your burner phone device. Amazing."

"Yeah, it's a wonder of wonders," Al replied. "You can just call it a 'phone', you know, and I'll know what you're talking about. Let's get back. I don't want to leave Anne alone too long."

When they got back, they found Anne safe and sound, if a little anxious. "You took much longer than I expected."

"Yeah, between our friend here having me walk around in circles to confuse me and having to keep playing with his new phone, I'm surprised it didn't take longer."

At that moment they heard a rhythmic, deep, thrumming beat followed by a deep trumpeting sound. Not like the sound of an elephant, but deeper, more melodic. The sound echoed through the underground.

"The drums and the god's horn," Tabon said. "The Cleansing. It is starting. You should both leave now; the Eaton will all be at the ceremony."

"What is going to happen?" Anne asked. "What are they going to do with those two boys?"

Tabon hesitated, something he would not have done several days ago when he had only the sensibilities of the Eaton to draw upon. "They will be sacrificed. Their blood will be used to cleanse away the shame of the Eaton."

"Oh my God, can't we do something? Can't we stop it? There must be another way. Al?" She turned toward him, eyes pleading.

Tabon answered, "This is the only way. They attacked and murdered one of us. The Eaton must have their justice; they deserve their justice. These men deserve to be punished. You should not waste your pity on them."

"Al?" she repeated.

Al turned from her, his expression unreadable. "Anne, there is nothing that can be done. This has to happen. You stay here. I am going to watch the ceremony."

"You're what?" Anne asked.

"I am going to watch the ceremony," Al repeated, his jaw set, eyes grim.

"If you wish to watch the ceremony, we can go down to the end like we did before, Detective. You will be able to see from there," Tabon said. "But you should leave now. It would be safer."

"Please, Al, let's leave. You don't need to see this," Anne pleaded. "Why would you want to witness such a thing?"

"Because I don't deserve not to see it. I shouldn't be let off the hook. This is my doing. I need to face the consequences of my actions." He turned back and took Anne by the shoulders. As she looked into his eyes, she thought she had never seen someone look more haunted. "I'll not take the easy way, Anne. These boys are going to die, there is no way around that, and I made the call. I won't be able to live with myself if I don't face this. A man should be able to face what he has done."

He released her, turned. Hesitated for a moment. And then followed Tabon through the stacks.

CHAPTER 41

1

They were again seated slightly back from the bars that crossed the end of the tunnel. Below, all seemed much as it had the last time Al found himself at this spot. The shacks and pathways forming their circles within circles, the torches, the Long House and what had been Anne's cell.

The elevator had two occupants now. Both had their wrists bound together and to the bars of the cell. Neither was blindfolded; there was no need to be concerned if they saw the Eaton or not. They weren't going to be telling anyone.

Looking at the elevator again triggered something in Al's mind. He couldn't put his finger on it. Like an annoying tickle in the back of the throat, it wouldn't go away.

In the small, open plaza next to the Long House, a pyre had been built from broken pieces of wooden furniture. The top of the pyre was covered by a piece of canvas. Two step-ladders had been set up, one on each side of the pile of wood. A heavy plank had been laid across the top step of the ladders, forming a bridge over the pyre. The Eaton, it turned out, were masters of recycling. They found all sorts of uses for the cast-off flotsam and jetsam of human society.

Hanging down between each ladder and the pyre was a heavy chain. These chains were draped over girders high above, the ends pooled on the floor near the ladders. A circle of white painted rocks had been placed on the ground encircling the entire setup: pyre, ladders, chains. Just outside this circle, an Eaton stood between two overturned metal drums. He had a thick piece of wood; it may have been a table leg in a previous life. The end was swaddled in a thick layer of cloth. He struck first the bottom of one drum and then the other with this padded end, producing the rhythmic thrumming Al had heard. To the right of the drummer was another Eaton, who held the narrow end of a large horn to his lips. The horn was about six feet long and curved, the large open end resting on the floor. The horn was fashioned out of sheets of copper that had been beaten into a curve to form the walls of the horn, the seams hammered together. The copper had taken on a green patina. The Eaton puffed up his chest and blew into the horn. The resulting sound resonated through the tunnels. Al could feel the vibrations in the fillings of his teeth. The drums and thundering horn called the faithful to worship.

And they came. They came from several tunnel mouths in the walls that surrounded the village. They walked in single file, each fourth or fifth carrying a lit torch, the flame guttering in the damp, stagnant air. They were in various forms of dress. Some wore nothing but the kilt-like garments Al had seen on the warriors. Others wore all forms of human clothing: old, ragged coats, pants, sweatshirts. Some were emblazoned with the logos of the sane world above—Nike, Reebok, Abercrombie & Fitch. They looked like a mismatched collection of medieval warriors, frat boys, construction workers and the homeless.

It may have been comical under different circumstances. The weapons visible in belts and scabbards in this surreal procession, combined with the serious, businesslike expressions on those horrific countenances, removed all thought of mirth.

Something horrible was going to happen here; of that there was no doubt.

The processions entered the perimeter of dwellings and followed the pathways that formed the circles. They proceeded along the paths, winding around and around. The ones in the lead filled the central circle. Once that was full, the next circle began to fill with Eaton, and then the next. As the circles filled from the center out, the light from the torches gave the impression of molten metal being poured into the center of a mold and working its way to the perimeter.

All the while, the drumming continued, setting the pace of those filing in, and the horn sounded.

Al saw that Tabon had not been lying about the number of Eaton. It appeared they were all here.

Finally the procession stopped. The drumbeat stopped; the horn went silent. The Eaton stood silently, torches flickering, grim faces impassive. Then, starting quietly and building in volume as more and more joined, the sound of feet stamping in unison. The drummer joined in. The sound was like the heartbeat of the under-city. A chant went up in time to the beat: Rang – vald, Rang – vald, Rang – vald.

Tabon leaned toward Al and whispered, "They summon Rangvald, our king."

As if to validate Tabon's statement, a small group of ten came into view from around the end of the Long House. This group was led by an Eaton that, by his very demeanor, projected authority. He walked with a long staff; on the top of the staff was the figure of an eagle cast in gold.

Tabon, following Al's gaze, said, "That is the Golden Eagle of the Ninth Legion of Rome, defeated by the Eaton in a great battle. It has become the symbol of power for our clan."

Al could see walking to the right of the king was Einarr. Even from here, Al could see the black hole where his left eye had been.

"That is not good," Tabon added. "Einarr walks in a place of honor. Our king is making a mistake to recognize Einarr this way for all to see. It gives him too much power."

Rangvald walked once around the inner circle of chanting Eaton and then came to a stop in front of the drummer. Those with him took up positions standing in the inner circle. Rangvald raised his hands above his head, palms out. The chanting, the drumbeat, the stomping abruptly stopped.

"A great shame has befallen the Eaton. The most worthy among us was struck down. At the moment that this happened, the doors of the Great Hall were closed. They can only be opened again by the cleansing of this shame.

"Many despaired that the current plight of the Eaton, living in the shadow of the humans, would doom us to eternal shame and despair. One Eaton stepped forward as my champion to right this wrong. That Eaton was Einarr."

Rangvald dropped one hand and extended the other toward Einarr. Einarr stepped forward next to the king. Rangvald placed his hand on Einarr's shoulder. "To honor him for his service, Einarr shall conduct the Cleansing."

The stomping began its rhythm again. The drummer joined in and the thousands of voices were raised once more. *"Ei-narr, Ei-narr, Ei-narr!"*

"Bring the prisoners forward," commanded Rangvald.

Caught up in observing the spectacle before him, Al had almost forgotten about the two teenagers—the ones he himself had doomed to this fate. He looked toward the elevator cage and saw one side had been opened and the boys were being led toward the pyre. They walked silently, their heads down. Al could tell by the hitch of their shoulders that they were sobbing. Al's gaze lingered on the now-empty elevator for a moment. That tickle again…something was fighting through the random circuitry of his mind, trying to make a connection. It would flicker, he thought he had it, then it would go out.

Each boy was escorted by an Eaton guard and marched to where one of the chains pooled on the ground. They were stopped there. The guards knelt and fumbled at the feet of their prisoners. Two other Eaton went over and grabbed the opposite ends of the chain. They began to pull on the chain, hand over hand. The pools of chain at the boys' feet began to unwind, the links rising in the air like a snake rising out of a charmer's basket.

As the chain tightened, each guard supported a boy by the shoulders. Soon their feet were being lifted off the ground. The Eaton continued to reel in chain. The boys' feet rose slowly, their bodies parallel to the ground, then higher, until they were suspended upside down. They continued to rise into the air, their guards released their shoulders and they began to sway slightly like human pendulums.

Those manning the chains stopped and stood holding their end of the chain as easily as if it were a kite string.

A procession of five figures in brown, hooded robes came from around the side of the Long House. Three carried torches; the other two carried incense burners hanging from thin chains. The group proceeded over to Sean and began to circle around his suspended body, chanting and swinging the burners, the smoke drifting up and curling around him like the tentacles of some ghostly octopus.

"The Holy Men of the Eaton: the druids," Tabon offered.

Once they had circled Sean three times, they went over to where Carter hung and performed the same ritual. They then walked to the front of the pyre where Einarr stood.

Einarr drew two short swords from a belt around his waist and held them with the blades pointed upward.

The clerics with the incense burners stepped forward, each toward a sword blade. They each slowly circled an up-turned blade with a burner. The smoke played across the metal and drifted into the air. Three circles and then they stepped back.

Einarr held the swords up above his head, arms in a V as the stomping and chanting started again. *Ei-narr, Ei-narr, Ei-narr.*

Two of the clerics stepped forward and pulled the canvas from the top of the pyre. Al felt he should have realized it all along, but as the canvas fell away, a body was revealed. Or at least, what was left of a body—it was horribly mangled and twisted. The long-lost corpse from the morgue.

The boys began to rise again as the chain attendants began to once again pull, hand over hand, on their end. They rose until their heads were six feet higher than the plank suspended over the pyre between the two ladders.

The Eaton working the chains stopped pulling and, holding the chain taut, began to jerk it sideways, causing the chains to slide on the girders high above. The boys began to sway even more. This action brought them directly over the pyre. The Eaton stopped moving the chain and the boys' swaying slowed to imperceptible little circles.

Einarr went to the right, climbed the ladder and walked out across the plank. Stopping in the center, he raised his arms above his head in a V again. The boys hung just above him on either side, the mangled body and the pyre directly below. Al felt like he was watching the setup of some elaborate magician's trick. The stomping stopped. The chanting stopped. Silence drew out in a long beat.

Einarr spread his arms further, pressing the tip of each sword blade to a teenager's throat. "I, Einarr, by the blood of our enemies, cleanse the shame of the Eaton and provide transport to the Great Hall for our brother."

With that, Einarr slashed backward with the blades simultaneously, opening up the throats of both his victims. Blood spurted in great gouts from their severed jugulars, spraying Einarr and the corpse beneath him. The blood ran down the sword blades, ran in rivulets down his arms, highlighting the muscle and sinew. Blood streamed down his face, his one malevolent eye glowing like a hot yellow coal in a sea of red.

The clerics with the torches stepped forward as Einarr leaped effortlessly from the suspended plank to the ground, arms still raised in a V. They lit the pyre behind him and it went up with a whoosh. The flame licked at the wood, climbed quickly. When the flames reached the corpse, they seemed to like what they found in the tattered clothing and dried rotted flesh as they sprang higher.

Einarr stood, arms raised, the glare of the flames making the blood that covered him appear black. The chant started again, louder and more enthusiastic than before. *"Ei-narr, Ei-narr, Ei-narr!"*

The good half of Einarr's mouth drew back in a leering grin, revealing fangs to match the perpetual snarl on the other side of his face.

"This is not good. He has more support than ever. Rangvald has made a mistake by trying to appease him with this honor," Tabon said, looking over at Al. A single tear was running down Al's cheek. "Why shed a tear for them? They got what they deserved."

"I am not shedding a tear for them; I am shedding a tear for myself. For some things there is no forgiveness," Al replied as the flames now reached the two suspended bodies, eagerly climbing them.

"Surely your god will forgive you for punishing the guilty."

"I am not talking about the forgiveness of my god; I am talking about my forgiveness of myself. For the immoral man, punishment begins with God's final judgment. For the moral man, punishment begins as soon as he commits an act he can't reconcile with his own conscience. I will be haunted by what I have done," he said. He turned his gaze from the conflagration before him and back to the now empty elevator. He paused for a moment, and then, in that same far-off voice, said, "I think I know where Einarr and his followers are hiding out."

CHAPTER 42

1

They had returned to their usual places: Al and Anne on the old couch, Tabon seated at the desk.

"Where do you think he is?" Tabon asked.

Al answered the question with one of his own. "The elevator that was used as a jail, where did it come from?"

"Einarr and his followers brought it and set it up right before they captured your woman that was killed."

Al glanced at Anne and saw her wince at the comment.

"I thought so. On that elevator is an emblem, a large scrollwork W. When I met Hop Frog to get instructions the other night, he was wrapped in an old faded tapestry. I thought it had a large M on it, but it was upside down. It was the same W that is on the elevator."

"So what does it mean?" Anne asked.

"I think they're in the old Windsor Hotel," Al answered. "It's perfect for them. It has been abandoned for years, it's all boarded up, you can't see in from the street. I'll bet anything that is where they are. They are probably gaining access from tunnels underneath."

"So what do we do?" Tabon asked.

"Well, we have to make sure they are really there. Then I'll contact the captain. I'll have to convince him that this is legit and get him to set up a raid of the place."

"What if he doesn't listen to you?"

"I'll have to make him listen to me. If not, then at the very least I will go in and see if I can take out Einarr myself."

"Al, leave it up to the police," Anne said, grabbing his arm. "You've done enough. Just call it in and leave it up to them. You've seen what these things are capable of. What could you possibly accomplish by yourself except maybe getting yourself killed?"

Al glanced over at Tabon. "Tabon, can you leave us for a moment?" he asked.

Tabon looked first at Al, then at Anne. Shrugging his shoulders, he got up and walked back between the stacks.

Al turned toward Anne, taking her two hands in his. "Anne, cops or no cops, I have to make sure he is destroyed. Einarr was responsible for those children being murdered. He threatened your life, he butchered Carrie right in front of me, and believe me, he is capable of much more. I have to make sure he's stopped."

Anne paused, looking down at their clasped hands. "I feel small and petty for asking this, Al, especially after all that has happened, but did you love her?"

Al raised her hands to his lips and kissed them, then looked up into her eyes. "No, Anne, I didn't love her. I cared for her a great deal, I'll admit, but I didn't love her. Somehow, though, that makes it worse. I caused her death. She died a horrible death just for being associated with me. The least I could have done in return was love her. But I didn't. I was and am in love with you. It is almost obscene that this can happen to her and if we get through this we get to continue on with our lives as if it never happened, as if she never existed. Oh, there will be some guilt, some sleepless nights, but in the end we will survive. We get to go on. It doesn't seem fair. It feels like somehow we've forfeited our right to ever be happy. Don't you see the least I can do is stop this thing, make sure he doesn't kill anyone else?"

Anne sighed in resignation. "Al, you can't beat yourself up over this. You couldn't have stopped it and you didn't cause it. But I also understand you will never get past it if you don't do what you can."

"There is one more thing," Al said, still holding her gaze. "I want to put you in a cab and I want you to go home."

"Al, I couldn't possibly leave now," Anne protested.

"You must. I can't bring you along; I would get myself killed worrying something may happen to you. Since Einarr got the two boys, he has no more use for me, so he has no more use for you. You will be safe at home. Just stay there until this is all over. They won't be coming for you again."

"What if the cops come by looking for you? What do I say? Even if they don't come to me about you, I have been missing for a long time. I'm sure somebody reported it. How do I explain it?"

"Tell them you haven't seen me. Tell them what happened to you just as it happened, but say that you were being held by Einarr and a group of ten or so, and you didn't know where you were. Do not mention the Eaton village. I promised Tabon that the existence of the other Eaton would remain a secret. I wasn't going to keep that promise, but now it is the least we can do for him, considering all he's done for us. He says they have been living here peacefully for decades and they will again now that their holy man has been avenged. We should give him the chance to prove it."

"I'll go, Al, only because I can't see how I can help you, but I don't like it. I don't like it, but I'll do what you say."

Al leaned in and kissed her. She returned the kiss, her hands at the back of his neck, cradling his head. He had been waiting to do that again for what seemed like an eternity. He held her tightly to him. He could feel the humanity slowly seeping back in. He felt if any good had come from what he had done, this was it, saving Anne. It was as if his salvation resided with her. Through some strange osmosis, she would be able to restore him.

When they finally parted, the dread came back. Like black ink dripping into clear water, it spread. It was much easier to be brave when you had nothing to lose. To think, here he was holding Anne again, and in a few short hours, if things went badly, he would most likely be gone. He hadn't told her, but he didn't see this ending well. It didn't matter; if he was ever going to look in a mirror again he had to see it through. And if it didn't end well, he had this moment. He had Anne back.

2

Tabon had escorted them to the surface and waited below street level while Al said goodbye and put Anne in a cab headed for home. Then Al had returned and Tabon had lead the way underground to the address Al had given for the Windsor Hotel.

They spent some anxious moments looking for a way into the building from below, but could find none. At every corner or twist in a tunnel they ran the risk of running into one of Einarr's followers. Al was only armed with his Glock sidearm, having run out of ammo for the M4.

Al had gone to street level and scouted the perimeter of the building. The large windows on the first several floors had been sealed with brick; the next several floors had plywood over the windows. Higher than that, the windows weren't covered. The front and side main doors were encased in plywood and all the service doors were padlocked shut.

Al found a service door facing an alley behind the hotel not visible from the street. He went and got Tabon. Tabon grabbed the lock on the door and, with a quick twist, snapped it as easily as pulling the sales tag off of a new shirt.

They entered the hotel and proceeded up a short hallway past doors leading to service and utility rooms. At the end of the hall was a windowless door. Al drew his gun as Tabon turned the knob and eased the door open.

It opened onto the lobby for the hotel. This being an older hotel, the lobby was a cavernous, columned, two-story affair. Scattered about in various groupings were large overstuffed couches and chairs. These had been covered at one time, however the covers lay in puddles on the floor. The original material, faded and threadbare and covered with dust, was exposed.

To their left were the large front doors of the hotel, dark due to their plywood shroud. In the ceiling two stories above was a domed, stained-glass skylight. To the right across the large space and opposite the front doors was the front desk.

The desk ran the length of the back wall. Straight across from where they stood was a grand staircase that ran up to an open balcony on the second floor that extended along the back wall over the front desk. Al realized the service door they had entered through was under a similar staircase on their side of the room. The sets of stairs and balcony formed a U shape around the back half of the lobby.

To the right of the front desk were an empty shaft and some cables that dangled through a square hole in the balcony above: the former home of the Eaton's jail cell.

They had explored the space and found that it was, or at least had been, the lair of Einarr and his followers. The tile floor of the lobby was blackened and buckled from the heat of camp fires built right on the floor in several places. The couches and chairs had been arranged haphazardly around these fire pits. The bones of small animals were strewn about the floor. Al was relieved to see there were no human bones amongst the refuse. Tabon pointed out there were no weapons either.

"Einarr had broken into one of the war chests we brought from England with us. They used those weapons when they attacked your police officers. Those weapons are not here. I fear they are doing exactly what you suspected: committing an act that will demand a response from your people."

"We have no way of knowing where they have gone. All we can do is wait for them to return and have a surprise waiting when they get here."

Al then sat on one of the couches, pulled out the burner phone and placed a call to the captain. The captain was surprised to hear from Al, but more in the "I didn't expect you to call me" way than the "I thought you were dead" way. When Al gave the shorthand version of his story, the captain was also more ready to accept the fact that the perpetrators he had been searching for were not human than Al would have expected.

It turned out that the forensic team had collected Eaton blood from the site of the SWAT team massacre. At first they weren't sure what the black substance was; however, after running tests, they determined it was blood—just not any type of blood anyone had ever seen before.

Al also found out what had become of Schrager and Tasker of the commissioner's special unit. The tactical unit's truck that they had been using as a command center had been found several blocks from the warehouse where the massacre took place. The back doors were open and riddled with bullet holes. The bodies of Schrager, Tasker, and the others had been found inside, hacked to pieces. Schrager's head had been placed out on the hood like a macabre hood ornament, his mouth frozen open in a death scream, eyes wide with terror.

Al couldn't say the news surprised him; they had all underestimated the situation, not that anyone could have fully comprehended what they were up against. He felt the least sorrow for Schrager. If the man hadn't been pushing so hard for a quick resolution, maybe they would have been more thorough and cautious in their planning and execution. Al realized immediately this was a copout. They had all misjudged the situation. To blame Schrager, despite how unlikable the guy was, wasn't fair.

He explained his current location and the situation. They determined that Al should stake out the place and contact the captain when the Eaton returned. In the meantime, the captain would get assets moved into position to conduct a raid.

Al passed on all he had observed regarding the Eaton's amazing strength, speed and resilience. He stressed that the teams should use focused fire at the chest area—spray and pray was not going to get the job done.

"There is another matter we need to discuss, Al," the captain said.

"What is that?" Al asked, knowing all too well what was coming.

"The police commissioner's son and Charles Stevens's son have disappeared. We found Mike out on the pier next to a burning van. There are an awful lot of unanswered questions, Al, and they all revolve around you, Mike, that security tape and that accident. Al, do you know what happened to those boys?"

Al was silent, trying to think of how much he should tell the captain.

"If you had anything to do with their disappearance, you'll never make it to trial, Al. You know that."

"I know, Captain. Just get me the backup. Once this is all over, I will fill you and you alone in on what has been going on, hopefully to give you peace of mind that you backed the right side. But I have no illusions about how this is going to end for me."

"I hope you were right in all of this, Al. Give me the call. You'll have your backup."

Al disconnected the call, looking over at Tabon's alien face. Once you got used to it, it wasn't too bad. "You need to leave."

"What? Why?"

"I am staying here until they return, and then I'm calling in the cops. They will send in several heavily armed teams. Those teams will take out anything in here that is not human, even those that are half human. You will be killed if you stay. I won't be able to protect you."

"I understand. You will keep your word, Detective? Once Einarr and his kind are killed, you will not be speaking of the other Eaton? I know they will continue to search, but if you tell them everything you saw, they will never stop searching. We won't have any chance at all."

"Listen, I want to thank you for protecting Anne and getting her out of this alive and for saving my life. I am truly sorry for the troubles that that caused you. You have my word, I will not mention the other Eaton," Al said, holding out his hand.

Tabon took it in his own large, leathery hand, his blue eyes staring into Al's. "May you have success, Detective Russo. Al."

CHAPTER 43

1

Ben Carson was tired and more than a little buzzed. He had just barely made it onto this train before the doors had closed. His head felt like it was floating just slightly above his body, as if it were a balloon attached to his neck by a short, slender thread. The train lurched as it pulled away from the platform, adding to that floating feeling.

It was late and there were only two other people in the train car with Ben. He took this train into the city from New Jersey every day, and during rush hour it was usually packed, but late at night most of the commuters were already home with their families. At this time, unless there was a game or concert at the Garden, the trains were pretty empty.

Ben hadn't been at the Garden. He had gone out for drinks with a group from the office and had stayed out later than he had intended. He had had a few too many and gotten into a long, flirty conversation with Laura from Legal. That sounded funny, Laura from Legal.

Ben was proud of himself. Not because of the long, flirty conversation; he was married after all. He was proud because he had gotten out of there before the situation had progressed beyond the conversation stage. Ben had never cheated on his marriage and was very much in love with his wife. But he did tread the line once in a while, pulling back just before he crossed over. It was nice to know he was still attractive to the opposite sex, that if he wanted to, he could.

The train was rolling slowly, had just entered the tunnel that would take them under the Hudson River. Ben stole a glance at the other two passengers in the car. There was a guy slumped down in his seat at the far end. He looked like he was in worse shape than Ben. In the middle of the car sat another businessman, like himself. This guy was staring intently at his phone, his thumbs doing the digital dance of the texter.

Ben had just settled back in his seat to try to get some sleep when the train lurched to a stop, the brakes hissing. The door at the far end of the car opened and the conductor stepped through, approaching the guy slumped down in his seat. "Ticket, please."

The PA system crackled. "Folks, it looks like there is some debris on the track up ahead. We are going to have to wait for a work crew to come out and clear the track. Sorry for the inconvenience, folks. We will get moving again as soon as possible."

A groan went up from the phone guy. "Ticket, please," repeated the conductor.

Suddenly something from outside slammed into the window next to Ben. He jumped at the sound of the impact. The window was covered with a spider web of fine cracks. He noticed another object flying toward the window and just had time to fling himself onto the floor in the aisle before a cinderblock crashed through the window and landed on the seat he had just vacated.

From his spot on the floor, he looked up between the rows of seats, hardly believing his eyes. The man who Ben had assumed was drunk was standing in the aisle and, with one hand, was holding the conductor by the throat. With the other hand, he was punching the conductor in the stomach over and over again. Or, Ben had assumed he was punching him, until the blood began to flow, staining the conductor's uniform and spattering on to his shoes. Then Ben noticed the blood-streaked blade.

The conductor's attacker released the man's throat and the conductor slipped to the floor in a lifeless heap. He then turned toward Ben, throwing off his coat as he did so. He was naked to the waist, his legs covered by baggy khaki pants, battered work boots on his feet. Muscles flexed under tight gray skin, yellow eyes flashed, fangs bared in a grimace of rage.

Ben tried to gain his feet and, slipping on the hard flooring of the train aisle, failed. He ended up scrambling on all fours down the aisle away from the horror behind him. He heard a derisive howl of laughter mixed with a snarl. He chanced a glance back over his shoulder and saw that the other passenger had also stumbled into the aisle between Ben and the creature and was headed in Ben's direction.

He looked like he would keep coming, would trample over Ben in his panic to get away. At that moment, the point of a blade burst through the man's throat from behind. Blood arced out from the wound, spraying Ben as he continued to scramble for the door.

He got to the door, reached up and hit the panel marked "push". He managed to claw his way up the door to a kneeling position just before it hissed open.

Ben tumbled to the platform outside the door, pulling in his legs so the door hissed shut behind him. As he got to his feet, the creature, having finished his butchery of the other passenger, slammed into the closed door. Ben could see his fanged jaws snapping in frustration at the glass in the door as if trying to chew through it.

Ben looked for the manual override on the outer door of the train car as the creature beat on the inner door in frustration. He found a red lever under a plastic cover. Breaking the plastic, he yanked the lever down.

The glass panel in the inner door shattered in a shower of jeweled granules. A large, powerful hand reached through and grabbed Ben's shoulder. He managed to push the outer door open, twisted from the clutching grasp and tumbled head first onto the gravel ballast next to the track, skinning his palms and tearing the knees of his suit.

Eyes wide with fear, Ben looked to the left and right. The light from the windows of the train highlighted a surreal scene. Several other passengers could be seen climbing out doors and windows. A woman one car down was stumbling away from the train, wailing in fright. Out of the dark of the tunnel a creature lunged, swinging a large sword in a wide arc. The woman's head leapt from her shoulders as if it were spring-loaded. Her headless body toppled to the ground, blood spurting from the stump of a neck and soaking the gravel.

Ben looked back and saw his attacker was trying to climb through the broken window of the inner door. Ben decided he had to get out of the light from the train, had to find a place to hide.

Staying low, he scrambled away from the train toward the darkness, his feet kicking up sprays of gravel in their attempt to gain traction. He came to a stack of railroad ties and hunkered down behind them, peering around one side to see if he was being followed. The creature that had been pursuing him had gotten through the window and leapt down onto the track bed. He looked around and Ben pressed himself against the ground, praying softly.

Another man was hurrying along, looking back over his shoulder toward the front of the train. Ben's would-be attacker let out a yelp and sprinted toward this new quarry. The thing moved so fast the poor guy didn't stand a chance. He had turned at the sound of the yelp just in time to have the creature drive its blade into his stomach. He let out a liquid grunt as blood burbled from his mouth, soaking the front of his shirt.

The creature seemed to have forgotten about Ben. He withdrew his blade and continued up the track.

From the opposite direction, an overweight man in a business suit came walking stiff-legged along the tracks. He was moving slowly, in a zombie-like daze. It was fitting, since he was already dead. His lower abdomen had a long, horizontal wound like the mouth on a giant jack-o'-lantern. His hands were in front of him, cradling the bloody purplish ropes of his intestines as they spilled from the wound, as if he were trying to hold them in place.

Out of the dark, one of the creatures came up behind him and with the bark of a laugh, kicked him and he sprawled on the ground. The monster then raised his sword and brought it down, completing what had been a foregone conclusion.

As scared as he was, Ben took out his phone, careful to shut off the flash. He snapped a picture. Nobody was going to believe this.

The creature continued farther down the train as well. From all around, Ben could hear screams and cries interspersed with howls of triumph. He moved farther back behind the stack of railroad ties, deeper into the shadows.

"You are missing the fun."

Ben spun around and looked up into a hideous, snarling, disfigured face with one yellow eye.

"Run," it whispered.

Ben could manage only an anemic squeak as he bolted to his feet and started to run. Death came cleanly. Ben heard a swish; it felt like the back of his neck had been branded with a hot iron, then everything went black. His phone flew from his hand, skipped across the gravel and wedged under the rail of an adjacent track.

2

After scouting out the hotel lobby, Al ended up on the balcony over the reception desk. Off the balcony were the remains of what had been a couple of restaurants, a gift shop and a barber shop, back in the hotel's glory days. Now the windows, floors and furniture were covered in dust. Al could tell by the dust on the floor that the Eaton did not make a habit of climbing the stairs up to the balcony, so he decided it was a pretty good place to wait for their return.

During his search of the lobby he had come upon more piles of trash left by the Eaton. In one of them something caught his eye, half buried in garbage and ash. He had knelt down and carefully brushed the ash away. Lifting it, he stared at a charred and cracked human skull.

Emotion hit Al in the solar plexus like a sledgehammer. If he hadn't already been on his knees, he would have fallen to them. He couldn't be sure, but on some level he knew that this was what remained of Carrie.

The build-up of pressure from the physical beatings, the sleepless nights, the raw emotion and the deep crippling sorrow of the last few days became too much. The dam of Al's self-control didn't just crack; it burst in a flood of emotion. He cradled the burnt skull to his chest and there, on the floor, on his knees, he wept.

In his entire life he had never experienced such deep anguish and despair. When it came to the job, he had always been one of the best. He had been in dangerous situations in the past but had always been able to control the outcome. But this had been different; he had been slow to recognize the danger, had been a beat behind the entire time. The innocent lives—those children, Mike and poor Carrie. How had he not been able to prevent any of it?

With great effort, Al had pulled himself to his feet and, taking a deep breath, fought to regain control. He had this one chance to prevent further bloodshed, one chance at redemption. Einarr's power was building. What had started as a few violent and sadistic acts could spread across the entire city if Al failed now.

He took another deep breath, cursed himself for his moment of weakness, of self-pity and doubt. He shook his head to clear it, carefully placed the skull back and headed for the stairs to the balcony.

There were several large, rectangular planters against the ornate balcony railing. The plants that had once grown there had long since withered and died. Al sat on the floor behind one of these. From this vantage point, he could see the lobby below while staying out of sight. He checked his phone to make sure he had a signal; he did. Then he did what cops do best: he waited.

CHAPTER 44

1

He had actually started to doze when he heard a commotion coming from the bowels of the hotel. There was shouting, brays of harsh laughter and whoops of triumph. It sounded like a sports locker room after a big win.

From directly below him, the Eaton began to file into the lobby, Einarr at the front. The lobby was bathed in silvery moonlight coming through the skylight above. Al took out his phone; the captain picked up on the first ring.

"Captain, they're here," Al whispered.

"Yeah, they just hit a train in the tunnels outside Penn Station, every passenger dead, one hundred fifty-six of them and the crew. Our guys on the scene found the victim's heads on the tracks in front of the train, lit up by the train's headlamp. They were arranged in a pattern, circles, like the bones at the warehouse. Hang tight, Al, we are on the way."

"Make it fast," Al said and hung up.

He chanced a look around the planter. They were milling around below, slapping each other on the back, laughing. They were covered in blood. Not black Eaton blood, but human blood drying to a reddish brown, highlighting the contours of their muscles and the strange patterns of scarring on their skin like a wash or stain brings out the grain in wood.

They had various types of weapons. Some had long swords that would take a human two hands to wield. Others had the short swords that Al had seen before. One of the Eaton, larger than the rest, carried a large battle axe.

Einarr circulated through them, slapping backs and shaking hands, obviously enjoying himself. Tabon had originally said that Einarr had ten diehards that would follow him anywhere. Well, that number had grown. There were sixteen Eaton below. Not many yet, but after witnessing the Cleansing and seeing the reactions of those gathered, Al thought it would only take a few demonstrations like the train attack before thousands sought his leadership. He had to be stopped before that happened.

Einarr stepped up onto one of the couches, raising his hands over his head. He was armed, as he had been at the Cleansing, with two short swords that were now shoved into a belt around his waist.

"Hear me, Eaton, hear me."

They gradually stopped their talking and milling about, one by one turning and giving Einarr their attention.

"Today we have reintroduced ourselves to mankind. Today the war has begun. They will respond; they must respond. Once they begin to hunt for us, those Eaton who are now meek, who are not with us, will see our wisdom and will flock to us for guidance. At first when they come they will be unsure. Years of living under Rangvald's rule has made them cautious and weak. They will come to us because Rangvald will not be able to protect them. We will show them the way. We will waken within them the true warrior spirit of the Eaton. Then, once we have all the Eaton behind us, we will be able to wage true war against man. Think of it: with just a handful we have caused chaos. Over a hundred humans dead, their great trains stopped.

"Imagine what we can do with three thousand. We will hide underground and strike at will. We will destroy their bridges and trains, burn their buildings, slaughter them by the thousands. The Eaton will be feared once again. No longer will an Eaton die quietly, in the shadows, forgotten. If an Eaton is to die, he will die fighting his enemies with a sword in his hand. The doors of the Great Hall will be flung open to receive him in his glory."

A cheer arose from those gathered, followed by the chant of *"Ei-narr, Ei-narr, Ei-narr"*.

Einarr stood there letting the sound wash over him. The good half of his face drew back in a smile.

After several more moments, he raised his hands again, signaling silence. "Now return to your dwellings. We must make things appear normal until the humans act, turning the others against Rangvald and toward us."

Al stiffened in his hiding place. He couldn't let them leave. He had to keep them here until the cavalry showed up. This was the only chance to put a stop to this before the others joined them. Once that happened, the chance to prevent widespread bloodshed would be lost. He had to think of something.

Al took a deep breath and drew his weapon. He stood and walked toward the railing, raising his sidearm as he went, and fired two shots toward the ceiling.

"Einarr," he yelled.

The noise below stopped. All faces turned toward the balcony in stunned silence. Einarr cast his one eye in Al's direction. "Detective," he said, the surprise in his voice apparent. "You amaze me, by the gods, you do. How did you find us?"

"That's not important. This stops here," Al said, pointing his weapon at Einarr.

Einarr waved his hand and several of the Eaton headed for the stairs on either side of the balcony. "Oh, but you are wrong. Here is where it starts. How do you intend to stop it by yourself? Even if you manage to shoot me, I will survive and you will be dead. Before the bullet hits home, you will be dead, and things, they will continue."

Two of them started up the stairs on either side, weapons drawn.

"No, you won't kill me. However, though this is truly a surprise, I am happy to see you. I was very fond of Hop Frog. Poor Hop Frog. For his death you must pay." He raised his voice. "I want him alive," Einarr commanded as the Eaton rushed up the stairs.

Al knew it was hopeless, but it would buy time, he had to make it look good. Einarr was too far away. Even if Al managed to hit him, the shots would have little effect. He spun to his left and pumped several shots into the closest Eaton, concentrating on the center of its chest. He felt a wave of satisfaction as it stopped mid-stride and pitched sideways. He took aim at the second one, too late. A weight hit him right between the shoulder blades as he was pounced on from behind.

They wrested the gun from his hand and threw it over the railing. Then, grabbing his arms and legs, they carried him down the stairs. He twisted and turned but it didn't do any good; they held him easily. He was dismayed to see the one he had shot getting to its feet. It moved slowly and stumbled, almost falling over again, but it was alive. Al wondered, not for the first time, what it took to kill one of these things.

They carried him over to a large coffee table and stretched him out on the top of it. Al saw Einarr's face hovering above his.

"For a human, you are persistent, Detective." Al heard a commotion to his right. Einarr turned in that direction. "What is it?"

"It's Egil. He has died. The man killed him."

Al smiled; at least he had taken one down with him. Einarr's large, leathery hand struck Al across the face, rocking his head back. Sparks flashed inside Al's skull and his mouth instantly filled with blood. He thought for a second he was going to black out but managed to hold on.

"You are proving a problem, Detective. I think you need a lesson. You need to pay for those you've killed, especially poor Hop Frog."

Al figured he was a dead man. The SWAT teams were not going to get here in time. Still, he had to keep Einarr talking, delay the inevitable, give them time to get here before the Eaton got away.

"I thought the Eaton were warriors. Each time, I was attacked first and I fought back like a warrior, with honor. These were not unarmed children like the Eaton cowards kill. These were your warriors. They were armed and they died in a fair fight."

"Silence," Einarr said. "Man doesn't fight fair; you hide behind your guns, you don't have the courage to fight with steel. You don't deserve a warrior's death. You deserve to die like the chattel you are."

He stood, turning to those surrounding the table upon which Al was stretched. "Who is hungry?" he said, raising his voice. A cheer went up from those assembled.

"Usually we kill and cook what we eat, Detective. But for you, we will make an exception. You will get to watch as each of your limbs is consumed."

Al twisted and kicked to no avail. The Eaton holding each limb just pulled harder until he thought his arms and legs would be pulled from their sockets.

"Let us start with a leg, shall we?" Einarr said.

An Eaton stepped forward, wrapped a piece of rope high on Al's left thigh and tied it, pulling it tight. Al could feel his leg starting to get numb.

"Can't have you bleed to death, can we? You'll miss the fun. Ulf, bring your axe here. Let's have a clean cut." Einarr started to laugh that gravelly laugh. "After we take the leg, sit him up in that chair over there so he has a clear view."

The large Eaton Al saw previously stood over him, a dull look of anticipation and hunger on his face.

"You may make the cut, Ulf. You fought well today. The honor is yours."

The creature raised the large, double-bladed battle axe over his head. Al turned his face away, not wanting to see what was about to happen.

"Hold," said Einarr. Ulf lowered the axe. "Make sure he can see."

Two rough hands grabbed the sides of Al's face in a vice-like grip and ratcheted his neck forward so he was looking down at his own leg. Twist as he might, his head was locked in place. "Nooooooooooooo." He heard a far off voice screaming. That voice was his own.

"Proceed," Einarr said. Again the axe rose.

There was a bright flash followed by a loud explosion, then another and another. Al went blind from the flash of light, his ears ringing from the shockwave of the explosions. Flashbang grenades, he thought.

He waited, sure the blade would descend; however, his limbs were abruptly released. Even though he was blind, deaf and disoriented, Al didn't hesitate. He rolled off the table and then, reversing direction, under it.

As he lay there trying to get his bearings, he heard the rapid staccato of gunfire. This was interspersed with howls of pain.

He lay there blinking, rubbing his eyes, feeling disoriented and helpless, ears ringing. As he worked the knot loose on the rope around his thigh he began to choke on acrid smoke, too much smoke just to have been from the flashbangs. Something must have caught fire.

Then he heard Einarr's voice rallying his troops. "Eaton, stay low, seek shelter, what you feel will pass." There was no panic in that voice, no fear, just a kind of exhilaration.

After a few moments, Al's vision began to return and he slid out from under the table into a crouch, looking around to take stock of the situation. To his right, one of the couches was on fire, belching grey smoke. Combined with the smoke from the flashbangs and the silvery moonlight from above, the whole scene had a ghostly, translucent quality.

There were several dead Eaton stretched out on the floor. The initial attack had been effective but far from decisive. Al could see Eaton crouching behind furniture and hiding behind columns. Some of them were wounded but far from incapacitated. To his left was the reception counter. SWAT officers—there appeared to be ten or twelve of them—had taken up position behind the counter. From this location, they had the counter to protect them should the Eaton attempt to rush them, while maintaining clear firing lanes across the entire lobby. It was like shooting ducks in a barrel.

Einarr, again with amazing calm, said, "Hold till your vision clears. This will pass. Hold."

The smoke swirled in the breeze from the service doors the SWAT teams had breached. Al could make out another team of four officers directly ahead, backs against the wall, weapons covering left, right and center. Next to them was a hallway off the lobby. With the lower windows bricked over and the front doors boarded up, that hallway was the only way out other than getting past the cops behind the reception counter. There were no calls from any of the police for surrender; they were strictly on a hunting mission.

An Eaton draped over a chair to Al's left, one he had assumed was dead, groaned and began to heave himself up. No sooner had his head lifted then weapons fire erupted. The creature did a twitchy little marionette dance, black blood flying, and slid to the floor.

Before the body hit the tile, Al heard Einarr yell, "Now, take those to the rear!" Then he saw him. He had been behind a planter to Al's left. Einarr dashed toward the four officers guarding the side hallway. On Einarr's command, the other Eaton broke from cover and charged the reception counter.

Gunfire erupted; Al stayed low, Eaton dashing past him toward the back of the room. He stayed focused on Einarr. No matter what else happened this night, he had to ensure Einarr died or all this was for nothing.

Einarr grabbed the back of one of the cushioned chairs as he sprinted through the smoke and, spinning like an Olympian competing in the hammer throw, flung it toward the SWAT team by the side hallway. He never broke stride, tailing the chair as it flew through the air and drawing his twin short swords.

The officers dodged the chair and it smashed harmlessly into the wall behind them. However, before they could recover, Einarr was amongst them.

He drove his swords into the bellies of two of the officers. Tearing the blades upward, he opened both men from navel to sternum. The contents of their torsos spilled out onto the floor in a hot flood. Before the blood and entrails had struck the tile, Einarr had spun. With one sword he parried the barrel of a third officer's gun upward, bullets flying harmlessly toward the ceiling, and drove his second sword into the man's throat.

He spun again, holding up the dead policeman in front of him. Bullets fired by the fourth officer slammed into the back of the corpse. Holding the body like a shield, Einarr rushed the last officer, flung the body at him and then followed, sliding past him on the cold marble floor, like a ball player trying to beat the throw, slashing the tendons behind the man's knee as he went by. The man's leg buckled and he collapsed to the ground. Without rising, Einarr twisted around and slammed the point of his blade through the back of the man's neck.

Al could not believe his eyes. It had taken only seconds of spinning, dizzying motion and four cops were dead, lying in pools of their own blood and intestines.

Momentarily stunned into inaction, Al roused himself. He began looking around for a weapon, anything. He couldn't let Einarr escape. The smoke was getting thicker; fire had spread along an old, dusty oriental rug, and another couch had gone up.

Al looked again toward the reception counter. The floor in front of the counter and the counter itself was covered with dead and dying Eaton. They had crashed against it in a tidal wave of fury, however the concentration of automatic weapon fire had been too much even for them. He did notice there were a few dead cops draped over the counter as well and a few less standing behind it. It looked like about half of the officers had gone down before the assault was stopped.

"Eaton, to me, to me," he heard Einarr shout. Einarr was standing in the mouth of the now unguarded hallway, bloody sword in each hand, beckoning to the others.

Those Eaton that were wounded rose and began to stumble and crawl toward the sound of Einarr's voice. Einarr broke toward them from the hallway. Gunfire immediately erupted from the police. Several Eaton fell. Ignoring the weapons fire, Einarr dashed out and grabbed a wounded Eaton under each arm, half carrying, half dragging them toward the hallway.

As much as Al despised the creature, he had to concede he was no coward. Einarr made it to the safety of the hallway, stopped and looked back toward the lobby. None of the others had made it; they were lying on the floor in spreading puddles of black Eaton blood.

Einarr, his wounded comrades in tow, turned and headed up the hall. Al broke from cover. Realizing in the smoke and confusion he may get shot, he kept low, weaving through the furniture, holding up his badge and screaming "Police Officer" as loud as he could. He made it to the four dead cops, slipping in the blood on the floor. Behind him, the flames had engulfed the furniture and were headed up the age-old drapes and tapestries. The whole building was going up.

Al grabbed a sidearm from the holster of one of the dead cops and headed up the hall after Einarr.

CHAPTER 45

1

Undulating patterns of shadow and orange light created by the fire in the lobby turned the hallway into the macabre entrance to a Halloween funhouse. Al was in time to see an open door on the left just before it closed completely. He bolted for the door and burst into the room beyond. He knew, even with the burden of the wounded he was carrying, Al was going to have to move quickly to keep up with Einarr.

The room beyond was a large ballroom. Thankfully, in the center of the ceiling was a large skylight similar to the one in the lobby. Al did not relish chasing Einarr through pitch black rooms.

Bright moonlight shone through the skylight. Smoke had begun to filter through the ductwork from the lobby, turning the moonlight into translucent curtains of silver. Across the room, Al could see Einarr, still carrying the two wounded, nearing a fire exit in the far wall. A voice in Al's head told him to let him go. The outside of the building would be surrounded by cops; Al should leave it up to them.

But after seeing what Einarr had done to the four officers inside the lobby, Al couldn't be positive he wouldn't find a way to escape. Al might be able to kill him, and he might not. Al might die in the process, but if he could get a few slugs into him, he may slow him down enough to ensure he would be finished off if he made it to the outside.

"EIIIINNAAARRRR," Al yelled, holding the handgun in front of him with both hands, keeping it fixed on his quarry.

Einarr stopped running and turned slowly around to face Al. "Ah, Detective, here you are again. Look how you rush to your death."

Einarr bent and carefully laid the two wounded Eaton on the floor. Al was struck by the care he used and the compassionate way his hands slid up each of their backs, lowering them gently to the floor; the way he cradled each head in a large hand before resting it down.

Einarr stood. "You wish to die. I believe I have time to be granting this wish before I must be gone." He was about forty yards away; even with his speed Al should be able to get several slugs into him before he could close the gap.

Al took a deep breath to steady himself, took aim and waited.

Einarr pulled the two swords from his belt. "I promised you that you would not die like a warrior. That you would die like the meat that you are. That you would be devoured alive." Einarr held his arms out, opened his hands and dropped both swords to the floor with a clatter. "That is a promise I intend to fulfill." He broke into a run, head down, full speed toward Al.

Al didn't hesitate; he stood his ground and squeezed off several shots. To his dismay, the bullets hit Einarr square in the forehead. Al saw them slough through the flesh, gouging out ragged, black-blooded furrows, but they did not penetrate the bone underneath. The beast kept coming; he closed the remaining distance in a final leap. Al fell backwards, managing to put a bullet in the monster's chest before his arms were swept to the side with one massive stroke and Einarr was upon him.

The gaping jaws were coming toward him. The jawbone itself seemed to unhinge, opening impossibly wide, the powerful fangs dripping with saliva. As he hit the floor, Al was able to twist his upper body. Those jaws missed his throat by inches, the fangs sinking into his left shoulder. Al heard his collarbone snap like a breadstick as his shoulder felt like it had been filled with liquid fire.

Al gritted his teeth against the pain and wrapped his left arm around the creature's head, holding it tight to him. If he let Einarr pull back, he would tear his shoulder wide open. Einarr stood, lifting Al easily off the floor, and shook his head violently from side to side like a great white shark in a feeding frenzy. Al wrapped his legs around the creature's waist and hung tight.

Einarr then dropped, slamming Al to the ground. Al's head snapped back, hitting the hard ballroom floor. His head spun; he fought to keep from blacking out and hung on. If he lost consciousness or lost his grip, he was a dead man.

Al had one chance, and he had to act now before Einarr lifted him again. He didn't know if he would survive another body slam.

The gun was still in his right hand. He jammed the muzzle between Einarr's ribs, pulling the trigger several times. The report of the gun, so close, was deafening. Al felt the weapon buck in his fist as it pumped slug after slug into that rough, leathery skin. Al felt Einarr's jaws loosen as he opened his mouth to scream from the pain. The creature rose up on his knees. At that instant, Al let go with his left arm, his legs still wrapped around the beast's waist, his shoulders hitting the floor as those fangs came free.

Einarr leaned back, howling in pain. Then he lunged forward again, jaws agape. Al, his ruined shoulder shrieking in protest, reached up with his left hand, grabbing Einarr's throat, arm stiff, able to hold him away for a brief second.

In that second, Al brought his right hand up and jammed the muzzle of his weapon into Einarr's empty eye socket. For a brief moment he saw realization and awareness dawn in that single hateful yellow orb in the face above him.

He pulled the trigger repeatedly. Einarr twitched violently as Al saw a shower of blood, skull fragments and brain tissue fountain into the air.

Einarr gave one last shudder. Al's shoulder gave out and his arm crumpled. The dead Eaton collapsed on top of him. Al was pinned, blood pouring from his shredded shoulder. The pain seemed to drift away on the tendrils of smoke that were now snaking across the floor around him.

He didn't think he had ever felt this tired in his entire life. He was floating. The moon, centered in the skylight above him, was slowly spinning. With great effort, he lifted his left hand from where it lay in the pooling blood on the floor and dragged it up over his thigh to the front pocket of his jeans. There he dug into the pocket, his fingers feeling limp, boneless, and tried to get to his phone. He couldn't maintain his concentration, his mind drifting toward that moon.

He finally managed to ease the phone out between two fingers and tried to work it into the palm of his hand. It slipped, sliding through his fingers. The moon was so close. He was so tired. A black hole seemed to open up around him and he began to slip gratefully into it. He was so tired, so tired, he just needed to sleep. As he faded, a whisper of thought trailed through the fading vapor of his consciousness.

She was safe; Anne was safe. It had been worth all this and more.

EPILOGUE

The doctor entered the room, medical chart in hand. "How are you feeling today?"

"I guess I'm okay, Doc. Still very sore."

"Sore. You're lucky to be alive. If an ambulance driver hadn't spotted you when he did, you wouldn't be with us. You were found behind the hospital, stuffed in a shopping cart. You had lost a lot of blood. Still can't remember your name?"

"No, Doc, sorry. Everything is still kinda fuzzy."

"That is unusual. If you were experiencing some kind of shock brought on by what you went through, I would have thought it would have passed by now. You don't recall anything? How you came by your injuries? Who brought you here? Who sewed your leg together with fishing line? Nothing?"

"No. Like I said, it's all a blank."

"Okay, well, if you're up to it there is someone from the police department that wants to ask you some questions. He has been coming by for days but you weren't up for visitors. Maybe he has some information that can help you."

"I guess I'm ready to talk to him, Doc. Sure, send him in, it can't hurt, right?"

"No, it can't hurt. I'll leave you with him, then. Buzz if you need anything." The doctor turned and opened the door to the room. "You can come in now."

As the doctor left, a sour-faced black man entered the room.

"Hey, Captain. How did you know to come looking for me? I would have thought you would assume I was dead."

"Hey, Al. You seem to have a way of getting lucky. I wasn't sure your body wasn't amongst the ashes of the Windsor hotel; they are still sifting through them, you know. I figured if you got out of there alive you would try to lay low. This little John Doe routine of yours isn't going to keep you safe forever."

"I know, Cap, just trying to buy myself some time until I can figure something out. I bet the commissioner and Stevens want my head."

"What did you expect, Al, their sons have disappeared. The commissioner has his dogs out. They found his son's BMW in a parking garage and they found some human hair in the backseat. They sent it out for DNA analysis along with hair they got from a brush in your apartment. Why they thought to compare it to your hair, I don't know. What do you think they are going to find, Al? What is this all about?"

Al figured he owed the captain an explanation. He told him the whole story—well, almost the whole story. He left out the underground settlement of the Eaton and Tabon and told it as if Anne had been held at the Windsor the whole time. He figured that gave the captain what he needed and still kept his word to Tabon. He owed the captain an explanation, but he owed Tabon his and Anne's lives. He ended with, "I don't expect you to accept what I did, Captain, or condone it, but those young men were as guilty as hell and it was the only way I could see to get Anne out alive."

"I would like to think that if you had come to me, we could have come up with a way to extract Anne and eliminate the threat without sacrificing lives," the captain said.

"You mean like the operation at the warehouse? Come on, Captain, it would have been taken out of our hands and they would have sent men in guns blazing. Anne would have been the first casualty."

"There is also the consideration of the greater good. We may have lost Anne, maybe not, but if we had moved sooner we could have prevented the attack on the commuter train."

"Yeah," Al admitted, "I had thought I could find them before they had a chance to act again." Al left out the fact that his way had prevented three thousand homicidal creatures from rampaging across the city killing untold thousands. Though it would help explain things to the captain, to do so would be breaking his word to Tabon. He would let the captain think it was all about Anne and let the chips fall where they may.

"You're right, Al. I can't condone what you did, but with the people involved I can see how you may feel a successful operation that would have spared Anne wouldn't be possible. I do want to thank you for keeping my name out of this. If the commissioner had any idea that I saw that tape as well, I don't think I would be standing here."

"Well, that was Mike's doing, but thanks anyway."

"Yeah, poor Mike."

"Yeah, poor Mike."

"Where did these things come from, Al? They didn't just drop out of the sky."

"I know as much as you do, Captain. I don't have any idea where they came from," Al lied.

The captain stared at Al for a moment. Al was sure he was going to grill him further, but instead he sighed and continued, "Anyway, I'm working on a few things. I want you to stay put and keep up the John Doe routine."

"Sure, Captain, I'm not going anywhere. Do what you need to do. I understand."

As the captain left the room, Al wondered what he could be working on. Maybe he was looking to bring the Feds in to make the arrest, figuring that Al may have a chance to make it to trial alive if he was in federal custody.

Al didn't see what good it would do. With the power and money that Stevens and Hutchinson had, they would have no trouble getting to him eventually. Did it make much difference whether he caught a bullet now or, a year from now, took a shive between the ribs in some prison? If Al had his choice, he would rather have it end quickly than spend months looking over his shoulder just to bleed out lying in the dirt of a prison yard.

It was bound to end one way or the other. Even if Al was in good enough shape to slip out of the hospital, which would take at least another couple of days, where would he go? How far would he get before he was picked up? No, the ride was coming to an end; the roller coaster was reaching the end of the line, everybody out, watch your heads as you leave. Not that the thought caused him much anxiety at this point. Anne was safe, and considering how many times Al had cheated death over the last week or so, he had been pretty lucky. At some point, though, your luck had to run out. Keep rolling the dice long enough and sooner or later they came up snake eyes.

****

Al woke shivering. The window to his room was open, the curtains moving in the breeze. There was a shadow sitting in the open window. Al shifted up in his hospital bed, the busted shoulder complaining.

The shadow detached itself from the nighttime darkness behind it and entered the room, standing next to Al's bed.

"You are alive, Detective."

"Yes, Tabon, thanks to you. I appreciate what you did. You could have been killed, you know, coming back for me. How did you even know I needed help?"

"I got your message on my burner cell phone device." He looked at Al sheepishly. "I mean my phone. The strange thing was I did not hear your voice as you said I would. There were letters on the phone; they spelled RUSSO. I assumed you were in trouble and could not speak."

"I remember reaching for the phone, but that is about it." Al had programmed the numbers in each of the phones; this was a very fortunate butt dial. "Anyway, I am grateful you came when you did."

"I was just keeping my end of the bargain. I am glad to see you also are keeping your word. There is nothing in the newspapers about the Eaton at all. They are blaming the deaths on the train and the fire at the hotel on terrorists."

"That makes sense," said Al. "Give people a threat they are familiar with, that they can understand, they can wrap their heads around. Not the perfect solution, but it will lead to less fear and panic than the true story would."

"I had my doubts that you would keep your word, Detective," Tabon said. "Tell me the truth. Did you originally plan on betraying us?"

"Yes, I did. When I saw what the Eaton were capable of, I felt it was too dangerous to spare them. That it would only be a matter of time before they were again a threat to the city. But after all you did for us, and seeing how you believe peace can be maintained, I felt I owed it to you to give them a chance."

"You have to realize, Detective, the Eaton have been living peacefully and secretly amongst man for hundreds of years. This is the first real threat to that peace in all that time."

"That may be true, but there may be others like Einarr, who resent taking a backseat to mankind.

Tabon started to laugh. "We all resent it, Detective, but remember, our life span is thousands of years. With man constantly warring and inventing new ways to destroy themselves…well, it is like the Rolling Stones song. *'Time is on my side, yes it is.'* When humans finally do destroy themselves, the Eaton will be waiting. However you humans choose to do it, the Eaton will survive. Germ warfare? We are immune to disease. Nuclear weapons? I am fairly certain we will be able to survive radiation. Now I ask you, Detective, if man has a global war and there are only the Eaton and a few humans remaining, who do you think will inherit this Earth?"

Al started to laugh. "So they are going to sit around waiting for us to kill ourselves, huh? I wish I could say it was a ridiculous plan, but I'm not so sure."

Tabon smiled, "Whatever the future brings, Detective, I will always fondly remember the bravery of two humans I once knew."

"You risked as much as us and more," Al said. "Have the Eaton taken you back then, even though you went against Rangvald's orders?"

"No. I managed to meet secretly with Rangvald and explain to him how things came to be. He had been concerned with the threat that Einarr posed but could not deal with it directly without risking a split in the clan. He was grateful that I found a way to eliminate Einarr without the blame falling on him. He is keeping the Eaton off the streets for now; they have gone deeper into the tunnels to avoid detection until things are calmer. However, since I openly disobeyed him, he cannot risk allowing me to return. To do so would make him appear weak and invite further challenges to his rule."

"I'm sorry to hear that. So you are completely alone. What are you going to do now?"

"I have decided to return to England. There is a ship leaving tomorrow night; I intend to be on it. One of the reasons I am here is to say goodbye. There are other Eaton clans still in England; there may even be others like me, half breeds. Maybe even a female half breed. Forgive me for saying this, but after coming to know Anne, I long for female companionship. That is not possible with the Eaton or the humans, but if I can find one such as myself, it just may be."

"I hope it works out for you and you find someone."

"I must be going, Detective—I mean, Al."

Al took a moment studying the creature before him, wondering why he had ever seen him as ugly, and then extended his hand. "I can't thank you enough for what you did for Anne and me. You risked everything to help us. Human or Eaton, you are the bravest, most honorable being I have ever met. Certainly better than any man I have ever known."

Tabon took Al's hand in his leathery grasp and shook it. "Thank you, my friend. If you are ever in England, look me up," he said with a gravelly chuckle. Then he was at the window and gone.

****

The captain was in his room, pulling clothes out of the small closet. "Hurry up, get these on. Oh, I forgot your arm's in a sling. I'll help you."

"What's going on, Captain?"

"I'm getting you outta here. I checked the place out. There is a stairway at the end of the hall here; we won't even have to pass the nurse's station. We can get to ground level that way, won't be able to get out though. The door at the bottom is alarmed. We'll have to cross through the pediatric floor, but I figure they will be looking out for escaping kids, not escaping adults."

Twenty minutes later, they were out on the street and the captain was hustling him up the sidewalk toward an old, battered SUV with a small trailer hooked to the back.

"What's this?" None of this made sense. "Where am I going, Captain? What's going on?"

"Al, just shut up," the captain commanded. "It's all taken care of."

The driver side door of the SUV opened and Anne stepped into the street, that crooked smile beaming. "Come on, Al, hurry up."

Al stopped dead in his tracks, stunned. He felt the captain's hand between his shoulder blades, giving him a push. He stumbled forward as Anne came to meet him. She threw her arms around Al's neck, kissing him.

"He's all yours," the captain said, for once a broad smile crossing his face. Al still looked puzzled.

"We're going off the grid," Anne said, smiling. "The captain got us IDs and Social Security numbers. We're going underground, Al. I don't know, out to the midwest somewhere maybe. We'll figure it out."

"Anne, you sure you want to do this? I mean, there is nobody after you. You can return to a normal life."

"After what we've been through, that sounds kind of boring, Al, don't you think?"

"I guess it does at that," Al said, smiling. "I guess it does at that."

THE END

ACKNOWLEDGEMENTS

I am very fortunate to have the support of so many in bringing this book to life.

First there was my spirited team of beta readers who graciously devoted the time to plow through the first unedited draft. These included my sisters, Fran Bostick and Linda Turczak, as well as my dear friend Cindy Tomarchio. I want to thank them for their valuable feedback and even more valuable encouragement.

I would also like to thank the editor, Melissa Frain, who through her copyediting skills did her best to make me look good. Melissa took that original manuscript and polished and buffed, until she had bestowed upon it the luster of professionalism.

Much gratitude to the gifted artist Angela Jones, who employed her incredible talent in the creation of the artwork for the front cover.

Last, but certainly not least, I would like to thank you, the reader. There are many things in your life competing for time and the fact that you chose to spend some of those precious hours on these pages is an honor. I hope I held up my end and you found that time enjoyable.

Printed in Great Britain
by Amazon

84190014R00215